A Study in Sparkling

Jodi McAlister

ATRIA BOOKS

New York · Amsterdam/Antwerp · London · Toronto · Sydney/Melbourne · New Delhi

A STUDY IN SPARKLING
First published in Australia in 2026 by
Atria Books Australia, an imprint of Simon & Schuster (Australia) Pty Limited
Level 4, 32 York St, Sydney NSW 2000

10 9 8 7 6 5 4 3 2 1

New York Amsterdam/Antwerp London Toronto Sydney/Melbourne New Delhi

Visit our website at www.simonandschuster.com.au

A catalogue record for this book is available from the National Library of Australia

ISBN: 9781761635205

Cover design: Sarah Horgan
Edges design: Daniel Valenzuela

Printed and bound in China by RR Donnelley

The paper this book is printed on is certified against the Forest Stewardship Council® Standards. FSC® promotes environmentally responsible, socially beneficial and economically viable management of the world's forests.

'Jodi McAlister has once again written a book that's clever, sexy and full of heart. *A Study in Sparkling* is a rom-com of a fine vintage – a full-bodied, complex and delightful story about second chances and passion. Fiona and Satoshi's steamy and heartwarming romance is a heady delight from the beginning to end – I couldn't put it down.'

Steph Vizard, author of *The Love Contract*

'A beautiful champagne pop of a novel, this is romance at its finest.'

Nina Kenwood, author of *The Wedding Forecast*

'Jodi is a master of addictive, smart romances. Pour yourself a glass of wine and settle in – *A Study in Sparkling* is a steamy, inclusive romance, rich with heart, brimming with chemistry and full of green flags.'

Karina May, author of *Duck à l'Orange for Breakfast*

'*A Study In Sparkling* is an effervescent, intoxicating romance. If you're into competency porn, secure, sexy, softboy sommeliers and delicious wine, look no further. Romance mastermind Jodi McAlister builds out the background characters we fell for in *An Academic Affair*, with newly single mum Fiona living a friends-with-benefits fantasy with Satoshi, the younger babe behind her favourite local wine bar. Delicious to the last drop, this is a book to savour with a glass of something special.'

Clare Fletcher, author of *Love Match*

OCTOBER

Prologue
Satoshi

Tasting today: 2022 Sancerre, Loire Valley, France.
You might think you know sauvignon blanc backwards and forwards, but a good Sancerre will make it feel like a revelation.

I fell in love with Fiona Fisher-Sinclair at about 7 pm on a Tuesday. It was inconvenient for several reasons, like it happening while I was short-staffed during a busy service, and her being married with three children.

It wasn't the first time I'd met her, or the second, or the hundredth. Fiona had been one of my regulars for two years now, ever since I'd first opened my wine bar Tsundoku. I'd thought nothing of it when she and her husband had walked in that particular Tuesday, except that I was happy to see her, because I was always happy to see her.

It wasn't the first time I'd been in love either. I'd loved my ex-boyfriend Kieran very deeply, until I hadn't. In both directions – falling in love, and out of it again – it had been a slow thing, sparkling wine made méthode traditionnelle, a love maturing slowly through first and second fermentations into something beautiful and effervescent, until it was left in the glass too long and went flat.

This time, though, it was a simple pop of the cork from the bottle: a sudden explosion – a release of pressure – and a deep, profound sense of relief.

Of course, I thought dazedly, as I looked at the woman who had suddenly become the centre of my universe. *Of course it's her.*

The first time I didn't fall in love with Fiona

Two years ago, I stood leaning against the beautiful Huon pine of the bar, taking in the space I'd spent so much time and effort and money creating: the warm wood of the tables, the rich jewel tones of the velvet chairs, the shelves overstuffed with second-hand books.

I'd put my whole heart and soul into Tsundoku, overriding all my older brother Isamu's objections that surely this wasn't what I wanted to do with my share of the money we'd inherited from our father; that yes, I technically *was* a part-owner of his winery Bibliophile, and was well within my rights to set up an urban cellar door for it, but didn't I – who had been working as a sommelier in some of the finest restaurants in the world since I was barely of legal drinking age – have anything better to do than that; that fine, he'd partner with me if I was so set on it, but what did I *mean* it was also going to be a bookstore? I'd lovingly chosen every wine on the list, painstakingly collaborated with the chef on the menu, meticulously selected all the fixtures and glassware and books to create the venue of my dreams.

Everything was perfect for today, the opening day of my beautiful bar – except no one was here.

My phone buzzed in my pocket. I normally didn't look at it during service – the head somms I'd worked under in Geneva and Paris and Tokyo would have fired me on the spot – but I was in charge now, and there was no one around to see.

It was Isamu. *How are things going?*

I exhaled. At least figuring out how to answer without technically lying would give me a distraction from—

The door opened, and a woman poked her head in. 'Hi,' she said brightly. 'Are you open?'

'Yes!' I said, dropping my phone in my enthusiasm. 'We are!'

She laughed. It was the first thing I noticed about her, that laugh, bubbling out of her like shaken-up champagne. 'Sorry,' she said, coming inside and perching on a barstool. She was a petite woman, somewhere in her thirties, with dark brown hair tied back in a ponytail that wisps were starting to escape from. 'I didn't mean to scare you. Only I've been stickybeaking for *weeks* watching this place take shape, and I'm so excited you're finally open.'

'You don't need to apologise. I'm so excited you're here. You're my first customer.'

'I won't be the last. This place is beautiful.'

'You think so?'

It was the kind of needy, anxious thing I almost never let slip out of my mouth – as a young Japanese man, I'd already had to work harder than most to prove myself in the largely old, white world of wine – but she didn't pounce on the vulnerability. 'It's stunning,' she told me, lines crinkling at the corners of her eyes. 'The perfect combination of refined and relaxed.'

'Do you want to do my marketing?' Something in me started to unknot, my shoulders coming down from around my ears. 'That was exactly what I was going for, only the words I was using weren't half as good.'

She grinned. 'Hazards of the profession. I'm a copywriter. What words were you using?'

'I wasn't, really. I just knew that I wanted it to feel like . . . home.'

I gestured at the bookshelves. 'I never really had one growing up. My father was a contract winemaker, and he did one- or two-year stints in various wineries all around the world. We moved here when I was thirteen, and it was the sixth country I'd lived in.'

'Sixth?!'

'New Zealand, France, South Africa, the US, France again, Japan, then here.' I ticked them off on my fingers, accidentally counting France on two fingers instead of one and having to readjust. 'Anyway, for obvious reasons, we travelled light. But he died when I was fifteen and the rest of my family settled in Tasmania permanently – and my brother Isamu and his wife Noriko started accumulating books. I've been working overseas for several years, but when I moved back to open up this place, I crashed in their spare room for a while. When I saw their library, it all just sort of clicked, the vibe I wanted.'

'Well, you've achieved it.' She had a lovely smile, a truly warm one. 'My family's bookish too, and this *does* feel like home.'

'Thank you.' I took a glass down from the overhead rack. 'Can I offer you Tsundoku's inaugural glass of wine? On the house?'

'You don't have to do that!'

'I want to.' I took a bottle of Bibliophile pinot gris out of the fridge and poured her a glass. 'You've made my day. And it's also a naked ploy to tempt you back for another one.'

She laughed again. There were five freckles on the left side of her nose, a perfect constellation. 'No temptation necessary, trust me. My husband and I are a bit pretentious about wine, and I've been dying for a good bar to open up in Bellerive.'

'Then we're going to get along great, because I'm *extremely* pretentious about wine.' I offered her my hand. 'Satoshi.'

She took it. 'Fiona.'

I didn't fall in love with her that day. But when she left – after that first glass of pinot gris, and a second of chardonnay that she'd insisted on paying for – I'd breathed a long sigh of relief. My beloved dream bar might actually make it.

The thirty-fourth time I didn't fall in love with Fiona

'Can I ask you a question?'

'Of course.' I gestured at Fiona's empty glass – I'd just poured her a splash of the new release Bibliophile rosé to try – and filled it when she nodded. 'Is it why Isamu made a rosé out of blaufränkisch when everyone else in Tasmania uses pinot noir? Because I have questions about that too.'

'Ha! No. I like this a lot, actually. It's got personality. It brought a gun to a knife fight.'

I hated to admit it – Isamu and I had argued a lot about this particular wine – but Fiona was right. The past nine months had proved that she had astonishingly good wine opinions for someone with no formal training, as well as a knack for articulating them. We'd come to an arrangement where, if I poached some of her phrasing for my tasting notes on Tsundoku's website, I'd give her a glass for free. I'd definitely be including *brings a gun to a knife fight* on this one.

'I wanted to ask you about those.' Fiona gestured to the pins I habitually wore, dotted on my dove-grey work waistcoat.

'Which ones?' There were a lot of them: wine qual pins, flags, books, wineglasses. Kieran had told me once that I looked like a cross between an army veteran and a Christmas tree whenever I got dressed for work.

'These ones.' She reached across the bar and touched her finger to my progress pride pin, and then the pansexual flag. 'Where did you get them?'

She looked down into her glass. 'Lex finally told us they're non-binary. And Matt . . . well, let's just say I wish he'd reacted a bit more sensitively.'

Lex was the eldest of Fiona's three kids. They were a real bookworm, and Fiona regularly brought them into Tsundoku during our afternoon cafe hours to browse the shelves. (*Bless you for giving me all three things I need within walking distance of my house,* she'd told me once, *a bar, a bookshop* and *somewhere to get coffee that's open at school pick-up time.*) It had been clear to me fairly quickly that Lex was in a questioning period, and while Fiona and I hadn't discussed it explicitly, she'd been quietly passing me request lists of queer middle-grade books to plant in my otherwise adult-centric bookshelves for months.

Fiona sighed. 'I know Matt doesn't want Lex's life to be harder, but I can't seem to get across to him that he's *making* it harder every time he says something like, "I love you, kiddo, but you never know, you might grow out of this once you hit puberty."'

I had to restrain myself from making a face. As much as I liked Fiona, I'd never particularly warmed to her husband.

'I don't want to make Lex's life harder either by being too performatively supportive, but it feels like I have to do *something*,' she said. 'So, I thought . . . they've always liked your pins. What if I got them some of their – Oh, no, Satoshi, you don't need to do that.'

I'd already unpinned the pride flag from my waistcoat. 'I've got a million of these. I can spare one for Lex. I don't have a non-binary flag, but I can get one.'

'Thank you. I'll pay, obviously – just let me know how much.'

I shook my head. 'They're cheap as chips. And I feel like it's my duty to pay it forward, you know? Coming out is exhausting. You have to do it over and over again. These—' I tapped the pin '—have been a very handy short cut for me. It's the least I can do.'

There was a look in Fiona's eyes which told me she'd find a way to pay me anyway – I was probably going to end up with an extravagant tip – but she nodded. 'Is there any advice you can give me? On supporting them? I don't want to pry or make you go over painful ground, but . . .'

'It's not that painful.' I shrugged. 'I came out to my family when I was fourteen. Not as pan – I didn't have the language for that yet – but I told them that I was attracted to everyone, not just girls. Nobody was surprised – I was in a bit of a femme fashion era, I was really into jewellery and dramatic eyeliner, and I was completely heartbroken over one of the boys at school, it must have been *very* obvious – but it wasn't a big deal. Isamu patted me on the shoulder and said, "All right, Sato." My mother hugged me. So did Noriko. My father grunted and went back to what he was doing.'

'So the opposite of performatively supportive, then.'

'I didn't expect anything else. I was braced for worse, honestly – I'd heard some horror stories – so I appreciated them being pretty low-key about it.' I shrugged. 'Anyway, we're not a very demonstrative family, so having them make some big declaration of support would have been weird. Our love language has always been acts of service – doing, not saying.'

'That's my love language too.' Fiona wrinkled her nose fondly at me.

'I worked that out the first time you handed me one of those book lists for Lex.' I wrinkled my nose back at her. 'But while they did all the right things, it still would have been nice to have some words of affirmation too – or something like this.' I tapped the pin on the bar again. 'Not just *okay, makes no difference to me,* but *I see you.*'

She nodded contemplatively. 'Thank you. That's very helpful.'

'You're very welcome.'

'And for what it's worth,' she said, 'I see you.'

I blinked.

'I sure as hell saw you yesterday morning making out with hot day spa Kieran like your lives depended on it.' Mischief sparkled in her eyes. 'There I was, minding my own business, innocently heading down to the bakery, thinking, *Oh, I'll just cut through that alleyway next to Tsundoku,* and—'

'Stop,' I groaned.

'I'm assuming you're either the black sheep of the Tsukamoto family or you don't know what *demonstrative* means.' Fiona poked me playfully in the arm. 'Because you, my friend, are clearly very demonstrative.'

I didn't fall in love with her that day either. But later that night, lying beside my beautiful boyfriend, aware that no matter how much I tried to demonstrate my love to him, it was fading away, those three words echoed in my mind: *I see you*.

The eighty-second time I didn't fall in love with Fiona

'Isamu, will you just listen to me?' I said. 'I understand what you're saying. But—'

'But you want to do it anyway.' Isamu folded his arms over his chest. I was several inches taller than him, but he was twice as wide across the shoulders, and he always managed to look down at me somehow, in a way that made me feel every second of our twelve-year age difference. 'Even though it makes no financial sense. Even though you categorically do not need to be an MS to run this place. Even though it'll mean working yourself to the bone – you want to do it *anyway*?'

'Yes.'

Isamu pinched the bridge of his nose. 'Sato, this is ridiculous. Why would you—'

The door opened. 'Sorry, Satoshi, I know it's not quite two yet, but—' Fiona paused, looking between us. 'Am I interrupting?'

'No.' I beckoned her inside. 'I'm about to open, and Isamu was just leaving.'

My brother glared at me. 'We're not finished talking about this.'

'You can talk as much as you want. I'm not going to change my mind. Take a seat, Fiona – I have some new things I want your opinion on.'

I poured her a splash of a Slovenian orange field blend as Isamu, with one last grunt of displeasure, left. 'Do you want to talk about whatever that was?' Fiona asked. 'I was only popping in to see if any of those books I ordered for Lex had arrived, but they're on camp, Matt's in Melbourne for work, and the girls are going straight from school to a sleepover. I've got time.'

'There's not that much to tell.' I took another glass down and poured a splash of the orange wine for myself. 'I told Isamu I'm going to sit the MS.'

'The MS?'

'The Master Sommelier exam. The highest qualification you can get in wine. It'll be a lot of work – it's the hardest exam in the world, it's got a pass rate of about five per cent – but I've wanted to do it for as long as I can remember. It's the whole reason I went back overseas to work. I didn't *want* to leave home, not when I finally had one, but I knew I had to if I wanted to get enough serious experience. I've basically been preparing for this my whole life.' I swirled the wine in my glass. 'But Isamu doesn't think I should do it. Doesn't think I *can*.'

'Did he say that?'

'Not in so many words, but . . .' I paused. 'I was more . . . fragile, when I was younger. Anxious. All the moving around did a number on me, and even after my father died and we settled here for good, I used to have panic attacks. I don't anymore – I did a lot of therapy, and I've got strategies to manage it now – but in Isamu's mind, I'm still a delicate little flower.'

'Is that why you want to do the exam? To show him you're not?'

'No. Wine isn't just the family business to me. It's genuinely my passion.'

'I know,' she murmured, an unreadable expression crossing her face for a moment. 'I know how passionate you are.'

'But if I'm being honest – proving myself is starting to become a bigger part of the reason.' I exhaled. 'Isamu's not wrong. I don't *need* to be an MS to run Tsundoku. But I want to be one. I want to prove – to him, and to everyone – that I can do it.'

Fiona tapped her fingers against the foot of her glass for a few moments before she spoke again. 'Is it weird to say that I completely get it and also don't get it at all?'

'A bit, yes,' I said. 'Explain.'

'Have I told you much about my family? Not Matt and the kids, I mean – my parents? My brothers?'

'A little. They're in Sydney, right? Where you grew up?'

'Mostly. My dad is a big-time professor at Eastern Sydney University. My mum dropped out of her PhD to marry him. Both my brothers have PhDs – Elias is a historian, Jonah did English like my dad – and I was expected to do one too.'

'Bookish,' I said, remembering that first time we'd met.

'Very.' Fiona leaned her chin against her hand. 'But one of the first things I ever remember knowing – like, *knowing* in my bones – was that academia wasn't for me. They were furious when I told them I was dropping out of my undergrad, but I knew I didn't have the passion for it. Not like they did.'

'That seems pretty unfair. Did they want you to be miserable?'

'In their defence, they thought I was dropping out to get married. The one person whose footsteps I *wasn't* supposed to follow in was my mother.' She offered me a grin. 'For all their giant brains, none of my family could get their heads around the fact that correlation wasn't the same as causation, that I was dropping out *and* getting married. And it put this fire in my belly to prove that I could live just as good a life as any of them – better, even – even though they thought I was making a completely idiotic choice.'

She inhaled the bouquet of her wine. 'So I don't know what it's like to have that all-consuming hunger to do something – especially when that something is an extremely difficult qualification in the family business. But I really do understand wanting to prove a point, even if the people around you think it's a terrible idea.'

'It sounds to me,' I said, 'like you're the wisest one in your entire family, Fiona Fisher-Sinclair.'

She laughed, that champagne laugh of hers that had endeared her to me from the start. 'I'll drink to that.'

I clinked my glass against hers. 'Cheers.'

'Wait, wait, wait.'

I paused, glass to my lips.

'I can't believe you're planning to sit for the ultimate wine exam and you don't know that you have to look me in the eye when we toast!' she said. 'Otherwise it's seven years of bad sex.'

I chuckled, pulling the turquoise frames of my glasses down my nose so I could exaggeratedly look her in the eye. 'The whole Kieran breakup is still so fresh that I'm not in a place to worry about that for myself—' I clinked my glass against hers again '—but I wouldn't want to doom you to a fate like that.'

'Thank you.' Fiona winked at me as she drank. 'Mama's got needs.'

It was another day on which I did not fall in love with her – but as I closed up that night, mopping the floor and cleaning down, I did idly wonder what needs Fiona had, and whether her husband could possibly be satisfying them.

The time I did

The night it happened, falling in love was the furthest thing from my mind.

Mostly, I was busy worrying about my junior sommelier Birdie. Isamu had insisted on me hiring another qualified somm so I didn't have to run every single shift myself, freeing up time for me to study. Realistically, though, Birdie was taking up more of my time than she was saving. I didn't want to fire her – she was a lovely person, and she was supporting a sick mother – but she'd worked for me for three months now and I still couldn't trust her to run the floor alone, because her service skills had a nasty tendency to fall off a cliff when things got busy.

Tuesdays were usually quiet, though, and we didn't have many bookings – Fiona and Matt were one of the few – so when the other staff member rostered on had called in sick, I'd been confident that Birdie and I would be fine on our own. However, a string of walk-ins had taken us to capacity, and we were run off our feet.

Birdie had been looking increasingly stressed as the bar filled up, so I'd told her to focus on waiting tables while I looked after beverage service. I was trying to keep an eye on her at the same time, but for all my years of hospitality experience, I was, alas, still only human.

'Mate, come here a second.' Matt beckoned me over to their table with one finger.

I gave myself a quarter of a second to exhale and adjust the cuffs of my crisp white dress shirt before pasting on my best customer service smile. This was not the first – or the second, or the tenth – time Matt had summoned me like this, the crook of his finger tracing a line between entitlement and condescension. He'd looked me up and down the first time he'd ever come into Tsundoku, eyes passing over my pin-dotted waistcoat and hot pink glasses frames before getting stuck on my hair. *Aren't you a bit old to be bleaching your hair like a surfie teen?* he'd asked.

He dropped a ton of money whenever he was here, though, so I had long since resolved to take it on the chin. Forty-something white finance bros were an occupational hazard when you ran a wine bar. Plus, this particular finance bro came as part of a package deal.

Fiona smiled at me as I approached their table, eyes crinkling at the corners, and I couldn't resist smiling back before I turned my gaze to her husband. 'What can I do for you, Mr Sinclair?'

'I appreciate you're busy,' Matt said, 'but we've been waiting nearly half an hour for our food, and I'm not convinced your girl has even taken our order to the kitchen.'

'Let me check on that for you. I'll pour you another glass of wine in the meantime, on the house. The same again?'

'That would be lovely,' Fiona said. 'Thank you, Satoshi.'

I ducked back behind the bar. Matt had bought them both a glass of the Bibliophile Noriko reserve pinot noir, the most expensive wine Isamu made. They'd finished my open bottle, so I grabbed a fresh one and took my wine knife out of my pocket.

I was just about to open it when there was an incredible crash, a scream, and Birdie burst into tears.

Everyone froze. Including me.

Afterwards, I would remember that so clearly. Everyone froze – except Fiona.

'Oh, honey,' she said.

She hadn't run, but she'd moved swiftly nonetheless, helping Birdie out of the mess of smashed glassware. 'You're having a night, aren't you?'

'I'm sorry,' Birdie sobbed. 'I'm so sorry.'

'It's all right.' There was Fiona's laugh, that champagne laugh, bubbling up under the words. 'We all have one of those nights sometimes.'

She put her hands on Birdie's shoulders. 'Here's what we're going to do, okay? We're going to go out the back. You're going to sit down and take some deep breaths, cry it out, whatever you need to do. I only need you to do one thing for me – show me where the cleaning stuff is. I'll take care of this.'

'Fiona!' Matt barked.

But she didn't look at him. Instead, she looked at me, eyebrows raised inquiringly.

Still frozen – wine knife in one hand, bottle in the other – I nodded, and fell in love with her.

I did not let anyone work on the floor of my bar without training. *Anyone.* Even Isamu, who'd spent his entire life working in wine and had several somm qualifications to go with his winemaking ones, had to consent to doing things my way.

That night, though, I was so utterly undone I barely remembered to check Fiona had Responsible Service of Alcohol training. 'Yes, don't worry, your liquor license is safe,' she replied, busily pouring glasses of Margaret River cabernet sauvignon, making herself as at home behind my bar as if she'd helped me build it. 'I worked in a pub when I was at uni, and then I re-upped a few years ago so we could have a cash bar at the Parents and Friends Association Christmas party. How about you run some of those plates from the kitchen to the tables? People look hungry.'

Then she winked at me.

I stared.

It felt like I'd been kicked in the head and something in my brain had fundamentally shifted, or like I'd woken from a coma after many years to see a world that was exactly the same and yet entirely different all at once. She was still Fiona – my friend Fiona – but – but . . .

'Go!' she laughed, shooing me away.

No one except Isamu had ever tried to give me an order in my bar before. It was *mine.* I exerted tight control over every single aspect of it.

I went.

Service is like a dance. I'd designed Tsundoku to have as service-friendly a layout as possible, but when we were having a bad night, it felt too small, like no matter what you were doing, you were in the way. When things went right, though, it was elegant, graceful, fluid, all the different parts of the machine working together in harmony.

That night should have been a disaster, but it wasn't, because Fiona was the perfect partner. She let me lead, a few murmured instructions all she needed. When I was behind the bar, she was on the floor; when I was on the floor, she was behind the bar; the transitions seamless, effortless. It was the kind of service chemistry that took years to develop, if it ever did at all – Isamu and I had never managed it – and I knew, in a way that I had never known anything before, that I would think about this night on my deathbed.

'I'd better take this one.' Fiona laid a hand on my shoulder in warning as I emerged from the kitchen, before taking a plate off my forearm. 'He's about to blow his top.'

I glanced over at Matt. A muscle in his jaw was twitching.

'Tell him it's on the house.' The place where she'd put her hand felt hot, like if I stripped my shirt and waistcoat off, there would be a perfect impression of it, burned into my skin. 'Obviously. Along with another glass of the Noriko.'

'Will do.' I was treated to another glimpse of her luminous smile. 'Would you mind pouring it, though?'

'Of course.' I was amazed I'd managed to get the words out. I was fluent in three languages and conversant in several more, but I'd forgotten every word in every one of them that wasn't her name.

She was still standing at Matt's table when I came over, a stutter in our perfect service rhythm. '. . . to Melbourne tomorrow,' he was saying. 'We agreed—'

'—that we'd sit down and connect tonight, I know, but—'

'—you decided playing waitress was more important?'

'So sorry for the delay, Mr Sinclair.'

I set the glass of pinot down in front of him. Matt glared up at me. 'I don't want your wine, mate.'

'Honey, I won't be much longer,' Fiona said. 'Once things get a bit quieter—'

'Forget it.' He stood. 'I guess the babysitter can go home early.'

'Matt—'

'I'll see you at home – if you can fit that into your busy schedule.'

The door of the bar slammed shut behind him. Fiona sighed. 'Sorry about that, Satoshi.'

'There's no need to apologise.' Married, she was so *unbelievably* married, and yet she was fizzing through my blood like sparkling shiraz anyway. 'If you need to, please go. I'll be fine.'

'No.' She picked up Matt's abandoned glass and took a long swallow. Her eyes fluttered closed for a second with pleasure, and I fell even deeper in love with her. 'There's no point talking to him while he's like this. Besides, I—' she took another sip before grinning at me over the rim of the glass '—have work to do.'

It was incredible, really, how the loveliest person in the world could completely ruin your life in a single evening.

🍷

Later, when dinner service had passed, the chef had gone home, and only a few quiet drinkers remained, I made Fiona sit down. 'Not only do you not have to do this,' I said firmly, taking the cloth she was using to wipe down tables out of her hands, 'I'm not going to let you.'

'But you sent Birdie home already. And it's no trouble.'

I put my hand between her shoulder blades and steered her towards the bar, the world tilting briefly on its axis as the ends of her hair brushed my knuckles. 'This is my bar. I'm the boss. And the boss says sit down.'

The chef always left post-service plates for the floor staff. We never ate in front of customers, but I broke my own rule and brought the plates earmarked for Birdie and me out to the bar. 'You ordered this, about, oh, two hours ago?' I set one in front of Fiona. 'Sorry it's late.'

She laughed. 'I should have known you'd never forget my order.'

The seasonal special that evening was a spring vegetable and goat's cheese risotto. It had suffered a little from being left under the heat lamps, some of the cheese going gluey, but it was still fresh and flavourful, full of sugar snap peas and asparagus. 'Can I pour you something?' I asked, desperate to find my way back to more well-trodden neural pathways. 'I've got a new Sancerre and I could use some pithy phrasing for the tasting notes.'

'Oh no, my arm, you're twisting it so hard.' Did she have to keep smiling at me? I only had so much strength.

I busied myself with the familiar ritual of pouring wine – taking down glasses, opening the bottle, smelling the cork, tasting to check for faults – so I didn't do anything ridiculous, like falling at her feet and telling her I would die for her. 'What do you think of this?'

Fiona closed her eyes, inhaled the bouquet – oh fuck, *oh fuck,* I'd always thought she was pretty but how had I not realised she was exquisite? – then sipped. 'Oh, that's lovely. Like a summertime salad – charred peaches and basil and sunshine.'

'That's much better than what I've written so far.' I leaned into the bar, trying to make it take some of my weight. 'Although *silex soil influences, aged in old oak, bottled à la chèvre* has a certain poetry to it, I guess.'

'We can pretty it up, don't worry. What's bottling à la chèvre?'

'Hand-bottling direct from barrel using gravity. It's not very common outside Sancerre, but Isamu learnt how to do it one of the times we lived in France, and he's made a few vintages of sauvignon blanc that way. I'll dig one out of his cellar next time I'm at the winery so I can show it to you.'

'Won't he mind?'

Isamu would definitely mind me raiding his museum stock, but I shrugged. 'Wine is about pleasure, not preservation. It's meant to be drunk.'

'Speaking of Isamu—' she took another mouthful of risotto '—is he still annoying the shit out of you?'

'Oh my *god,* Fiona, I can't even tell you how much he's annoying the shit out of me.'

This, at least, was safer territory. We'd both scraped our dishes clean and were nearing the bottom of our wineglasses by the time I'd finished telling her the latest instalment in the ongoing saga of Isamu channelling all his repressed emotion, about the fact he and Noriko had gone no-contact after their recent divorce and she'd elected to do all her business with us solely through me, into trying to micromanage my half of the Bibliophile/Tsundoku dual enterprise even more intensely than usual.

'He's been talking about moving out to the vineyard full time,' I said. 'Which would make my life easier, to be honest. It's bad enough that he won't shut up about me taking the MS. If he'd stuck his head in here tonight and caught me letting a customer help run service, he'd insist on being a god-like overseer of everything I do until the end of time.'

'I'll never tell him, I swear.' She drew a cross over her heart. 'Although surely I'm not just another customer, Satoshi.'

'Of course you're not,' I replied hoarsely, the simple sound of my name on her lips sending blood rushing to my head. 'Do you think I complain about him to anyone who walks through the door? He's my business partner as well as my brother. We have an image to maintain.'

Fiona chuckled. 'In that spirit, then – can I complain about Matt for a minute?'

It was the worst thing she could have said.

There was nothing crueller than hope. That was one of the first lessons you learnt when you grew up the way I had, constantly uprooted the second you managed to settle somewhere. If you allowed yourself to hope things might be different this time, you were only setting yourself up for pain. Better to accept the things you could not control and focus on the ones you could.

Maybe if she hadn't said it, there would have been a way out of this for me. I could have drunk a lot of black coffee, taken a lot of cold showers, given myself a lot of sobering reminders about how extremely married she was. Then, once I had exposed this impossible infatuation to enough time and air, it would oxidise, and I could tip it down the sink and get rid of it.

But she had said it, and now here it was: that awful flicker of hope.

'Complain away,' I said.

'Don't get me wrong, I love him, but sometimes I feel like I'm drowning in him.' Fiona leaned one elbow on the bar, resting her chin in her hand. 'He made a big production of wanting to come here tonight so we could have a serious conversation, and I'm pretty sure it's because he wants to have another baby—'

My soul left my body.

'—but just the thought of it,' she finished, thankfully unaware that my spirit was somewhere in the Milky Way, 'makes me feel so, *so* fucking exhausted.'

'Three kids are enough?' I managed to force out.

'More than. We'd originally agreed on two, but then – twins.' She flashed me an almost apologetic smile. 'It's not even that, though. Do you remember when you told me about deciding to take the MS? How badly you wanted to do it?'

I nodded.

'It made me think – what do *I* want?'

Fiona traced her fingers up and down the stem of her glass. 'It's not like I'm secretly yearning for some big career like Matt or my brothers have,' she said. 'I like my life. I'm incredibly privileged to have it – to be able to focus on the kids and write a bit on the side. But there's been this . . . thing that's been niggling at me. Matt will take me to one of his work functions, and the place card will say

Matt Sinclair plus one, and no one will call me by name the whole night. Or – I love my kids more than anything, but it's so easy just to be their mum and not a person in my own right. The thought of doing it all over again . . . I'm not . . . hungry for it, the way you should be for a child. I'm hungry for something else now – to *be* something else now, not just a wife, not just a mum – but I have no idea what.'

She sighed. 'I'm so jealous of you sometimes, Satoshi. You're barely twenty-seven, and you know exactly who you are and what you're doing with your life. I'm thirty-five and I still don't know what I want to be when I grow up.'

'If you ever go into wine, there's a job for you here.' Icy adrenaline was pulsing through my veins, a primal desire to keep her here, safe, with me. 'You just excelled in your trial shift. Get your Certified Somm qual, and I'll hire you as my second-in-command tomorrow.'

Fiona looked at me, our eyes meeting for just a little too long. 'Don't tempt me,' she said softly.

Something in me started to ache, and then it started to burn.

I wanted to say so many things. I wanted to do so many things. I wanted to reach out and caress a lock of her hair between my fingers and tell her that if she was ever in the market for something else – some*one* else – I would be right here waiting.

'So, alas, I'll have to politely decline,' Fiona said. 'It's Birdie's job anyway. I was just filling in.'

I was starting to feel light-headed, in the way that had, in the past, often preceded a panic attack. How was I supposed to let Fiona walk out the door tonight? How was I supposed to simply wave her goodbye and send her home to get potentially impregnated without offering her an alternative?

'Speaking of Birdie – you're not going to fire her, are you?' she asked. 'When I took her out the back to calm her down, she was worried that you were.'

And there it was. The reason I had fallen in love with her – and the reason I would never, ever have her.

Fiona Fisher-Sinclair was a fundamentally good person. All the way down to her bones, she was kind and considerate and loving, the kind of person who, when everyone else was frozen, was already on her feet to help.

There was no version of her that would ever say yes if I propositioned her. Even on the infinitesimally small chance she wanted to – Fiona had a *family*, and she would never put her wants above their needs.

So all I could do was smile at her; affectionately, but platonically. This across-the-bar friendship of ours was all I was ever going to have of her, and it was going to have to be enough.

'Of course I won't fire her,' I said, as I resigned myself to a lifetime of unrequited yearning. 'Everyone deserves a second chance.'

🍷

The last customers left Tsundoku at about 10.30 pm. I locked the door behind them, poured myself another splash of the Sancerre as a nightcap, then unbuttoned my cuffs and rolled up my shirtsleeves so I could clean down.

It was a familiar routine. I did it six times a week, and it was usually somewhere between mindless and meditative. Rituals like these usually made me feel calmer: when I felt myself spiralling out of control, I sank into something familiar to regain my equilibrium.

Not tonight, though. Fiona had left about an hour ago, but she was still, somehow, everywhere.

She'd forgotten her jacket, I noticed, mopping around the foot of the coat rack. It wasn't a particularly cold night by Hobart standards, but it wasn't warm either.

Perhaps I should take it to her. Perhaps if I did, I could somehow stop her from giving in to Matt's desire for another child, and—

No.

I exhaled sharply through my teeth. Every atom in my body felt magnetised, like there would now just always be this inexorable pull towards her, but I couldn't function like this. How was I supposed to go on living my life with this doomed longing hanging over me?

I shoved the mop into the bucket. This had to be some kind of temporary insanity. Service could have been a disaster this evening, but Fiona had ensured that it wasn't. Maybe this was just some kind of extreme form of relief, or gratitude, or something. I'd been working very long hours for the past couple of years to get Tsundoku off the ground, along with the intense MS study schedule I'd recently started. It was bound to catch up with me. Wasn't that what Isamu kept telling me?

Whatever it took, I had to get myself under control, or I was going to lose my entire mind.

The front door rattled. 'We're—' I called on autopilot.

The word *closed* died on my lips. There, on the other side of the door, was Fiona.

My heart stopped beating.

This wasn't real. This was a fantasy, one where I would open the door and she would fall into my arms.

I opened the door. She fell into my arms.

'Fiona!' I staggered for a moment under her sudden dead weight. 'What's wrong?'

'I'm sorry,' she sobbed. 'I – I – I didn't know where else to go.'

Even in the warm lighting, her face was pale, so drained of blood she looked almost green. Her hair was a mess, as if she'd clutched her fists in it. She was still in the little black dress she'd worn to dinner, but her feet were jammed into two different sneakers.

When she looked up at me, her eyes were wide and wild, whites visible all the way around the iris, and she was shaking, teeth chattering, fingers icy as they clutched at my shoulders.

I grabbed her jacket off the rack and wrapped it around her. 'What happened?'

'Matt,' she choked. 'He – he—'

'He what?' My hands fisted into the lapels. 'Did he hurt you?'

'N-n-n-no.' She was on the borderline of hyperventilating. 'Yes, but – not like you're thinking. He – he – fuck, Satoshi, what am I going to tell the kids?'

Her knees gave way beneath her. It was so sudden that I only just managed to catch her before she crumpled completely to the ground.

'Come on.' I bent down so I could loop her arm around my shoulder. 'Come with me.'

I half-led, half-carried Fiona out to my office, sitting her down in my desk chair. She was still shivering, so I took my winter coat off the hook on the back of the door and draped it around her shoulders like a cloak. 'Here.' I grabbed a bottle of wine from an open case, uncorked it quickly and poured her a splash. 'Let's slow everything down, all right? Take a few breaths. Take a few sips. You're safe. I've got you.'

Fiona wrapped her hands around the bowl of the glass and did what I said, inhaling and exhaling shakily. 'I can't taste anything.' Her voice was small. 'There's nothing.'

'Don't worry. It's not important.' I knelt in front of her. 'Can you tell me what happened?'

She squeezed her eyes shut, entire face screwing up with the force of it, but she couldn't stop the tears falling down her cheeks. 'I'm so stupid, Satoshi.'

'No, you're not.' I took the glass from her and put it on the desk so I could try and warm her icy hands in mine.

The sound that escaped her could only be described as a laugh, but there was no joy in it. It was the kind of laugh that someone who wasn't in love with her might call hysterical – humourless and half-crazed.

'Yes, I am,' she said. 'Matt doesn't want another baby. He has a whole other family in Melbourne – and he's leaving us for them.'

OCTOBER
ONE YEAR LATER

Chapter One
Fiona

Tasting today: $6 supermarket NV prosecco, indeterminate region. If you want to get depressed or drunk, this will get you there. If you want literally anything else, you know you've headed down the wrong path, right?

'All right, girly-pops.' I squatted down to Rosie and Georgia's level so I could hug them goodbye, careful not to let the hem of my grey court dress touch the muddy ground. 'You have a good day at school, okay?'

'Yes, Mummy,' my eight-year-old daughters chorused.

I kissed them each on the cheek. 'Remember, it's Thursday, so Uncle Jonah and Auntie Sadie will pick you up so you can stay the night with them.'

'Yay!' Georgia said. 'Thursdays are my favourite!'

'Uncle Jonah makes the best dinners in the whole world,' Rosie said.

My offended face was not entirely faked. Intellectually, I understood the novelty for them of spending one night a week with my brother and his wife. The regular presence of Jonah in their lives at all was still a novelty, really – he and Sadie had only moved to Hobart eight months ago. Emotionally, though, it was still difficult to hear that the twins preferred their Thursdays with them to every other night of the week with me. 'And what am I, chopped liver?'

They both giggled. It was one of my favourite sounds in the world, that identical laugh of theirs, and I couldn't resist hugging them again. 'Be good, okay? I'll see you tomorrow. I love you.'

'Look, Georgia, there's Madison!' Rosie said.

The twins scrambled free of my embrace and ran after their friend, the backpacks they still hadn't quite grown into bouncing around on their backs.

Just like they had too often over the past year, tears pricked at the corners of my eyes. Watching them run away from me always made me conscious of the fact that my heart lived outside my body.

'Mum?'

I blinked the tears back. 'Yes, sweetheart?'

'Do you want me to come with you today?'

Lex had a serious expression on their face. They were twelve now and approaching the end of Year 6, so they were usually out of the car at school drop-off the second I turned off the engine, too cool to be seen with their mother or little sisters. Today, though, they'd lingered, shifting awkwardly from foot to foot. 'I didn't want to say anything in front of the twins, but I heard you on the phone to Uncle Elias the other night. I know you're seeing Dad today. I thought maybe it would be good – maybe it would be helpful – if I went with you.'

'Oh, Lex.'

I pressed my tongue hard to the roof of my mouth. I was not going to burst into tears at school drop-off. *I was not.* There were several other mums and dads watching us curiously, and I was already the laughing-stock of the Parents and Friends Association. If I started crying now, I would never hear the end of it.

'That's so lovely of you to offer,' I said, 'but you don't need to worry. Your dad and I are going to figure things out like grown-ups. It's going to be fine.'

'You don't have to lie to me.'

'Sweetheart, I'm—'

'You don't,' Lex insisted. 'You don't have to say it's fine. I know it's not. I know Dad hasn't paid you any child support. I know you had to ask Grandpa for money.'

I scribbled *patricide* on my mental to-do list. I'd tried to keep the worst of the brutal realities of the split from Lex and the girls, but when my parents had come to Hobart a few months ago to visit Jonah and me, my father had bellowed, *So when exactly is that chump going to pay up so you can stop bleeding me for money?* at the top of his lungs over the dinner table. The girls hadn't understood, but Lex had, and the ugliness of that realisation written all over their face had made me want to vomit up all my internal organs.

'That's true,' I said, tasting bile in the back of my throat, 'but that's what today's meeting is about. We're going to get that sorted. And your dad—'

'Don't say he loves me.'

Of course he loves you, I wanted to say, but I didn't like lying to my children. I had to press my tongue to the roof of my mouth again.

'I just thought it might be helpful to have me there,' Lex said stubbornly. 'So if Dad really doesn't want to have anything to do with us anymore, he has to say it to my face – and everyone has to hear him do it.'

'Sweetheart, can I give you a hug?'

Lex paused for a moment – they weren't much of a hugger, preferring fist-bumps to most other forms of physical contact – then nodded. I wrapped my arms around them, jaw aching from how tight I was clenching it, my eyes feeling like someone was inside my skull scrubbing them from behind with steel wool.

'You,' I said into their shoulder, keeping my voice low so no one around us would hear, 'are the best, bravest kid in the entire world, okay? And I love you so much.'

They tolerated the hug for a few moments before they drew back, the flag pins on their collar catching briefly on my hair. 'So can I come?'

I shook my head. 'It's going to be very long, very boring, and very, very sensible. And I'll have my lawyer and Auntie Chess with me, making sure everything goes smoothly.'

Lex studied me. I had to resist the urge to hold my breath.

'Okay,' they said at last. 'But Mum . . . don't be nice to him.'

'Sweetheart—'

'I mean it. You're so nice to people, all the time. Don't be nice to him. He doesn't deserve it.'

They were completely right, but it wasn't the kind of thing I could say aloud, not with the prying eyes of a thousand school parents nearby. 'Tell you what,' I said instead. 'How about next Tuesday, when the girls have indoor soccer training, you and I go and have a hot chocolate at Tsundoku? I bet Satoshi has some new books for you.'

Lex gave me a withering look. 'Cool bribe, Mum.'

'Is that a no, or . . . ?'

They sighed, exasperated in the way only a pre-teen could be. 'Obviously not.'

I grinned, then pecked them on the cheek. 'Have a good day, okay? And don't let the girls terrorise Uncle Jonah and Auntie Sadie too badly.'

'I'll try,' Lex said long-sufferingly, 'but I don't have magic powers.'

I pressed my tongue to the roof of my mouth again as I watched them walk through the school gates. I'd fucked up so many things in my life, but somehow, in the midst of it, I'd produced three perfect children.

And Matt had walked away from them.

I dug my keys into the meaty part of my palm as I headed back towards the car. I had to face him today – in person for the first time in a year, instead of over Zoom – and I was going to have to find a way to keep calm and behave like an adult and not just scream *how could you?!* and leap across the table to scratch his eyes out.

'Fiona!'

Fuck.

'Michelle!' I pasted a smile onto my face. 'How are you?'

Once upon a time, Michelle had been – if not a friend, then a friendly acquaintance. Her son Henry was in the same year as Lex, and we'd volunteered together in the school library every second Friday. We were in the same parent WhatsApp groups and we'd bonded over our shared dislike of some of the sleazier dads.

But then Matt had left.

I couldn't volunteer anymore, needing every spare second of every day to either work or look after the kids. I'd tried to keep the more salacious details of Matt leaving out of circulation, but Hobart was small. Once it was out, it was *out* – and the humiliation began.

'I'm doing well,' Michelle said. 'How are you, honey? That dress looks great on you.'

I submitted to her hug, which came complete with a patronising rub of her hand up and down my back. I'd learnt the hard way that the quickest way out of these interactions was through. The trick was to be as boring as possible.

So instead of *Thanks, I'm wearing it because I'm about to go to mediation with my almost-ex-husband,* I just hugged her back and said, 'I'm fine, thanks.'

Michelle pulled back, both hands on my shoulders. 'You don't need to put on a brave face for me. How are you really?'

I thought about saying *late* and making a dash for it, but then *Oh no, poor Fiona's run off her feet, she might be about to completely lose it* would go circulating through the WhatsApp groups. The last time that happened, a group of parents had organised a fundraiser for me, and it had been the single most excruciating experience of my life.

'Oh, you know,' I said, mentally crossing my fingers and praying she hadn't overheard any of my conversation with Lex. 'It's not easy, but I'm managing. My brother and his wife moved down in February for work, and they've been a huge help.'

'You're so brave.'

I resisted the urge to grit my teeth. 'Just doing my best.'

Michelle leaned in closer, and I braced myself. 'So, have you met her yet?'

I didn't need to ask who she meant. 'No,' I replied, keeping my voice breezy and businesslike. 'I don't want to, to be honest.'

'Oh god, Fiona, you're a better person than me!' Michelle rubbed my arm. I dug my keys harder into my palm. 'If I were in your shoes, I'd be hunting her down like a stalker. So I could try and understand, you know?'

I might be the only one of my siblings without a PhD, but it didn't take a genius to read the subtext. *Tell me why Matt picked her and not you. What does she have that you don't?*

The moment that news of what Matt had done had started to spread, people had been hungry for the gory details. At one point, the questions – so polite, but so pointed – had been coming so thick and fast I'd considered just holding an Ask Me Anything in one of the WhatsApp chats. *Her name is Laura. She's eight years older than me. They've technically been together longer, but I'm the one he's legally married to (which was surprisingly difficult to work out, save your follow-up questions until the end). They have two kids: Micah is twelve, and Nikki is five. I don't know much about her otherwise, but considering I had no idea that whenever Matt went to Melbourne for work he was actually going to see them, I'm confident she's probably smarter than me. What else do you want to know, you fucking ghouls?*

If the only person that would have blown back on was me, I might have actually done it. But parents' gossip always spreads to the playground, and Lex and Rosie and Georgia were already the kids of The Man With The Secret Second Family. Better they also be the kids of The Woman Who Is Keeping Her Chin Up (Although Seriously, How Could She Not Have Known?) than The Woman On The Verge Of A Nervous Breakdown.

'I don't think I'll ever be able to understand it,' I said to Michelle. 'So why bother trying?'

'Oh, come here.'

I submitted to another hug. 'You're so brave,' Michelle whispered.

What I wouldn't give for her to say something – anything – else to me. For the things she whispered to be the petty bullshit we used to gossip about while working in the library. For her to ask me if I thought the new kindy teacher was hot. To bitch about the ways they kept jacking up the prices of school uniforms. To talk about the fucking *weather.*

But this was the only conversation I was allowed to have now. When Matt had left, he'd ensured that my entire life revolved around him, more than it ever had when we were together.

'Thanks, Michelle,' I lied. 'That means a lot.'

🍷

I was twenty-one when I met Matt. I'd been in the middle of my undergrad degree, and I had an essay on *Paradise Lost* I should have been writing, especially if I didn't want to be the recipient of yet another stern lecture about my grades and all the things that were expected of me as a scion of Professor Christian Fisher.

But when my best friend Kaitlyn texted me, inviting me to go out with a group of our friends, I'd said *fuck it,* and gone.

We'd gone to the divey suburban Sydney pub we both worked in, because we got a staff discount. I'd been at the bar getting the next round when a handsome man in a well-cut suit had come up to me. *That's a lot of drinks you're trying to carry*, he'd said. *Can I give you a hand?*

I'd said yes. He'd helped me deliver the drinks to the table, then left. *Hello, Daddy*, Kaitlyn whispered.

Ew, shut up, I whispered back.

The glass of sparkling had arrived five minutes later. *From that guy*, my manager said, nodding over at the bar. *He wants to know if you'll drink it with him.*

I'd paused, looking over at him. He'd raised his eyebrows at me, then his glass, and a shiver had gone through me, like someone had walked over my grave.

I'd taken the glass, hissed *shut up* again at Kaitlyn when she wolf-whistled at me, then walked over to him. *Just so we're clear*, I'd said, sliding onto the barstool beside him, *this doesn't mean I owe you anything.*

His smile had been wolfish, sending that shiver rushing through me again. *Oh, I think it does*, he replied. *Your name, pretty girl.*

I'd crossed my legs tight against the fluttery feeling building between them. *Fiona.*

He probably knew I was a done deal by the time he took my hand. *Fiona,* he'd repeated, pressing a kiss to my knuckles. *I'm Matt.*

I'd gone home with him, back to an apartment that made it clear this was a man, not a boy. He'd laid me down in his thousand-thread-count sheets, and as he kissed his way down my body, I was already thinking about how I'd tell the story of my first ever one-night stand to Kaitlyn the next day.

But it wasn't a one-night stand. I'd tried to sneak out at 2 am, and Matt's hand had fastened around my wrist like a manacle. *You*, he'd growled, *are not going anywhere.*

We'd got married about eighteen months later, despite the strenuous objections of my family. I'd fallen pregnant with Lex soon afterwards, and Matt moved us to Hobart. *Big cities are no place to raise a family*, he'd said, stroking a stray strand of hair behind my ear when I'd asked why we weren't moving to Melbourne instead, where he already worked several days a week. *I always loved visiting Tasmania as a kid. I'll commute when I need to: it's a quick flight to Melbourne, just a hop across the strait. Tassie will be my oasis with my baby* – he'd kissed me – *and our baby.*

Naïve, twenty-three, knocked up and in love, I'd agreed, completely failing to see the red flags that were even then waving in my face.

Matt didn't want me in Sydney because that was where my family was: my family, who were united in firm agreement that I was throwing my future away on him – my family of professional argument-havers, who just might convince me they were right if I spent too much time with them.

And Matt didn't want me in Melbourne because that was where Laura was. No, he wanted me on a whole different island to her: Laura, his childhood sweetheart, who he'd also been laying down in his expensive sheets; Laura, who was also pregnant with his child; Laura, who I never, ever, *ever* wanted to meet.

Laura, who was standing on the other side of the mediator's office, Matt's arm around her shoulder, very obviously pregnant again.

'Fiona, stay calm, okay?' my lawyer Kavita murmured in my ear. 'It's important you keep your composure.'

'Matt's lawyers will have advised him to bring her along so you'll have an emotional response and come off looking crazy.' Chess angled her body so I couldn't see them anymore. 'And we're not going to give him that satisfaction.'

I nodded. My mouth was dry.

Chess took my hands in hers and squeezed tight. 'Remember, he doesn't know what we know,' she whispered. 'We're about to take him to the fucking cleaners.'

I squeezed my eyes shut and took a deep breath in through my nose. 'Okay.'

'It's all going to be over soon,' Kavita said comfortingly.

'And he's going to pay,' Chess said, much more menacingly. 'Big time.'

I exhaled slowly, opening my eyes again. *This could be worse*, I tried to make myself believe. *This could all be so much worse.*

At least I had Chess and Kavita. Chess, a high-powered corporate lawyer who had flown in that morning from Sydney, was Sadie's sister. They'd had some kind of falling out after Sadie and Jonah had got married that I didn't really understand, but they'd mended fences a few months ago, and she'd been a massive help ever since. She'd taken one look at the family lawyer representing me in the divorce, said a flat *no*, found me Kavita (*She seems like a marshmallow on the surface, but she's a shark*, she'd assured me over a glass of wine at Tsundoku) and talked her into taking my case pro bono. Then, when Chess found out I was married to *that* Matt Sinclair, who was apparently notorious in some of the circles she ran in, she'd taken on digging into his finances personally. *He's a rich arsehole business bro*, she'd told me bluntly when I protested that she was doing too much. *I deal with them all the time and I know all their tricks for hiding money. Let me use my powers for good for once.*

I wished I could have enjoyed the way the colour drained from Matt's face in the mediation meeting as Chess outlined everything he'd tried to conceal, ticking various offshore accounts and shell companies off on her fingers in response to his lawyers' argument that he didn't have the assets to pay me more than the bare minimum in child support. I wished I could have enjoyed the muscle that started to twitch in his jaw as he realised that despite all his money, my legal team was better than his; the way his nose started to turn red as he figured out he wasn't going to get away with leaving as cleanly as he thought.

But I still had the memory of all those years in my veins. Every time I'd let him touch me. Every time I'd let him kiss me. *I love you,* he'd told me time and time again, this pathetic, venal, red-nosed man – and blithely, without a doubt, I'd believed him.

'Fiona, you need to be reasonable here.' It was the first sentence Matt had said directly to my face in months, ever since that cold, grey morning last year when Satoshi had walked me home. 'I've got four other children to support.'

'Four?' escaped me before I could bite it back.

Matt caressed Laura's belly. 'Twins.'

Cold sweat began to bead in my hairline.

I was barely half-aware of what was happening as Kavita and Chess hammered out a child support agreement with Matt's lawyers. I only really understood that we'd got what we'd wanted – the house, the car, and a generous monthly sum which would mean I could stop taking money from my parents and wouldn't have to take every single copywriting gig I could find just to keep us afloat – when Chess squeezed my fingers under the table. I could hear my own blood, rushing in my ears.

'All right,' the mediator said. 'Let's move on to custody and visitation.'

'My client agrees that Ms Fisher should have primary custody of Alexan—'

'Lex,' Chess, Kavita and I all snapped at the same time.

'Yes, of course, my apologies – of Lex, Rosemary and Georgia,' Matt's lawyer said. 'We would, however, like to discuss visitation.'

'No.'

Both Chess and Kavita's hands landed on my knees under the table, but I ignored them. 'Absolutely not.'

'Fiona,' Matt said, his voice infuriatingly even, 'they're my children too.'

'You don't deserve them.'

'I know the circumstances aren't ideal, but—'

'The circumstances aren't ideal?! You abandoned them!'

'How about we take a quick five-minute break?' Kavita suggested.

'I thought it would be easier for you,' Matt said. 'Not to have to see me. And for them not to see me either for a bit, so they didn't get confused.'

'*Confused*?'

'Fiona—'

'They know what you fucking did, Matt! They know you chose *her*—'

'Her name is Laura.'

'—and your other kids over them, and they're going to have to carry that for the rest of their lives! Do you know how long it took for Rosie to stop crying herself to sleep? How Georgia keeps having nightmares about waking up all alone? How angry Lex is? Do you really think I'm going to let you see them again, after what you fucking *did to them*?'

'That's not your choice to make, Fiona,' Matt said. 'That's what we're all here to decide. And if you could calm down and stop swearing at me, maybe we could figure it out like adults.'

'Don't tell her to calm down,' Chess said sharply.

'Don't address my client, Ms Shaw,' Matt's lawyer shot back.

'I just want my kids to meet their siblings!'

The words erupted suddenly from Laura, the first thing she'd said the whole meeting. 'I just want Micah and Nikki to meet their siblings,' she repeated, flushing bright red as one hand came to rest on top of her belly. 'I know this whole situation is a mess. I'm so sorry, Fiona, I really am. I can't imagine how tough this is for you.

But we need to think about what's best for the kids – and surely what's best is for us all to try and be a family?'

Her eyes were wide and earnest and well-meaning, and it made me want to scream until my throat was bloody.

Matt put his arm around her, thumb tracing protective circles on her shoulder the same way he used to do to me. 'Exactly,' he said. 'We have to put the kids first.'

Dots started swimming in front of my eyes. 'Kavita,' I said, 'did you say something about a five-minute break?'

I only just made it to the bathroom before I threw up the entire contents of my stomach – everything except the humiliation, which no matter how hard I retched, would not come out.

Afterwards, Kavita and Chess tried to reassure me that everything was going to be all right. 'I know it might not feel like it, but this is a good result,' Kavita said. 'We could take him to court, of course, but given there was no abuse of the children, it's not likely we'd get a ruling for no visitation whatsoever. At least this way most of the contact they have with Matt will be by phone or video call, and none of it will be without you being present.'

'He doesn't deserve to even look at them,' I sniffed. I'd managed not to cry in the meeting, but back in Kavita's office, the water-works had started.

'No, he doesn't,' Chess agreed. 'But if we went to court and pushed for an extremely hardline custody agreement, that might reopen the discussions around child support – *why should he pay for kids he's not allowed to see?* would be the line his lawyers would run – and we could end up with a much worse outcome.'

'Exactly,' Kavita said. 'Settling this now in mediation is much better for everyone involved, Fiona. I promise.'

I ached, suddenly, for my children. I wanted to put my arms around the three of them and hug them as tight as I could, holding them to me even once the girls started wriggling and Lex told me that they'd reached their quota of hugs for the month, thank you very much; to tell them I loved them and that I would protect them and that I would never, ever leave them.

Kavita opened her desk drawer and took out a bottle of prosecco. 'We won today,' she said, handing it to me. 'And you should celebrate, okay?'

Chess's phone started vibrating. 'I have to go,' she said. 'But I've got a couple more days before I have to go back to Sydney. How about I take you and the kids and Sadie and Jonah out to dinner tomorrow, somewhere nice? My treat.'

I nodded. I didn't have the energy to do anything else.

The house was quiet when I got home, my footsteps echoing on the floorboards as I dropped my handbag on the kitchen bench, put Kavita's prosecco in the fridge, and stooped to pick up Georgia's discarded stuffed elephant. I pressed it to my face for a moment, inhaling her smell before putting it on her bed.

Maybe she'd take her elephant with her when she and Rosie and Lex met Micah and Nikki. Lex, who was reserved at the best of times, was almost certainly going to refuse to speak to them, but the girls had never met another kid they couldn't bulldoze into being friends. *Here*, Georgia might say, marching up to Nikki and thrusting her elephant into her hands. *Come and play with us.*

We'd get through the visit. I'd lull myself into thinking the worst was over. But then we'd all be sitting around the dinner table, and *When can we see Daddy again?* Rosie would say. *I miss him.*

I like having a little sister, Georgia would add. *Can we go and live with them?*

I clutched the back of the couch as the world started to swim in front of my eyes again. 'Stop catastrophising,' I ordered myself.

It was something I'd been working on with my therapist, although I wasn't sure I'd made much progress. I'd always had a tendency to get ahead of myself, but when Matt left, it had got a million times worse. The smallest thing could send me spiralling, unable to breathe because of the endless torrent of worst-case scenarios. An unfamiliar car parked on the street might belong to a banker here to foreclose on me. My dad's name flashing up on my phone might be because he was about to tell me that money doesn't grow on trees, Fiona, it's time for you to stand on your own two feet. The smallest sideways glance from another parent might snowball into a future where the kids got taken away from me because I was too much of a mess to be a mother.

Once I'd taken several deep breaths and was reasonably sure I wasn't going to throw up again, I sat down at the kitchen table to make some calls. The first was to the kids' therapist, to make appointments for them as soon as possible. Matt effectively ghosting us had already traumatised them enough. I shuddered to think what seeing him again – not to mention meeting their half-siblings – might do.

The second was to my own therapist, which was going to put a strain on our monthly budget but definitely wasn't optional, given the circumstances.

Then I called Jonah. 'How did it go?' he asked the instant he answered the phone. 'Did you win?'

I resisted the urge to sigh. *Did you win?* was such a quintessentially Fisher thing to ask.

I gave him a brief outline of the child support and visitation agreement. 'While I'd much rather pretend Matt and his other family don't exist, I suppose that isn't realistic,' I said, trying to force some brightness into my voice. 'At least he has to fork out a bunch of money. You should have seen the way Chess steamrolled his lawyers in there, Jonah, she was amazing.'

Jonah made a sound in the back of his throat. He'd never quite forgiven Chess for the falling out she'd had with Sadie earlier in the year, even though she'd gone to exorbitant lengths to make it up since.

'Seriously.' I shifted the phone to my other ear. 'Kavita too – they were both so great. Without them, I would have completely embarrassed myself. Poured a jug of water over Matt and Laura.'

'He brought her with him?'

'Oh. Um. Yes.'

Jonah was silent for several moments after I explained. 'He brought his *mistress* to your divorce mediation?' he said at last. 'And she's *pregnant*?'

My scalp started to prickle. *How the fuck did you marry this man?* he didn't say, but I heard anyway.

I loved my brother. I really did. The relationship between Jonah, me and our older brother Elias had been distant for a long time, but when Matt had left, they'd both come through for me in ways I never would have anticipated. Elias had taken a leave of absence from his research fellowship in Germany so he could stay with me for a while and help with the kids. Jonah had gone even further. It had been coincidence that brought him to Hobart – his then-girlfriend Sadie had got a job at a university here, which led to them getting married so she could bring him with her on a partner hire – but since he'd been here, both he and Sadie had helped me so much.

So yes, I loved him. I was more grateful to him than I would ever be able to express. But I could never forget that he – just like the rest of my family – had *told* me not to marry Matt, that I would be making a massive, life-ruining mistake if I did; and so sometimes, even though he didn't mean to, he made me feel so fucking stupid.

'—can't believe he'd do that to you,' Jonah was saying. 'And what's he going to do now? Make a long weekend of it? Parade her around Hobart?'

My prickling scalp turned into another full-blown cold sweat. I hadn't even thought of that.

Matt, taking Laura out to dinner. Matt, showing her the sights of the city. Matt, with his arm around her, inevitably running into Michelle or another one of the parents from school.

Their eyes drifting to Laura's pregnant belly.

The way all the WhatsApp groups would fucking *light up*.

'I'm so sorry he did that to you, Fi,' Jonah said. 'What a piece of shit.'

I made myself laugh. If I didn't laugh, I would cry. Again. 'Yeah. He is.'

🍷

The last call I had to make was to my parents. Theoretically, it was a good news call – *Guess what, Dad, that chump is finally going to pay up, so I can stop bleeding you for money!* – but I couldn't make myself do it. Instead, I just leaned my elbow against the dining room table and rested my chin in my hand, staring into space.

I'd made a mistake, letting the kids go to Jonah and Sadie's for the night. I hadn't wanted to disrupt their routine – if I did, I'd have to explain to them why, and the twins had only *just* stopped asking whether Daddy might ever come home – but I should have done it anyway. Without them, the house felt achingly, excruciatingly empty.

I couldn't stop seeing it. Matt's arm around Laura. That look on her face – that fucking wide-eyed, innocent, look-what-a-good-wife-and-mother-I-am look – when she told me that we had to put the kids first.

I gritted my teeth against it, but the thought slipped through anyway. *No wonder he picked her.*

I did not want Matt back. I was very clear about that. Almost every Thursday night while the kids were with Jonah and Sadie,

I toyed with the idea of downloading an app and finding a hookup, just so the last hands to touch me weren't his.

But just because I was done with him didn't make the sting of the humiliation any less. He'd had both of us – and he hadn't chosen me.

I groaned, letting my head fall forward against the table. My therapist and I had had many, many discussions about this. *Given everything you've told me about the competitive environment in which you grew up, it's completely natural that part of you views this as a competition she won and you lost,* she'd said. *And given you like to express your love through actions, it's also natural that you feel that you didn't do enough. But let's try and reframe this thought pattern, shall we? I think we can agree Matt isn't a prize you wish you'd won, so can we think about it as you being free of him instead?*

I'd tried. But it was difficult to revel in being free of him when everything was just so fucking *difficult*, all the time. Losing Matt might have helped me regain my relationship with my brothers, but I'd lost so much else in the process.

I sighed. This wasn't helping. I should do what Kavita and Chess had said and try and focus on the positives.

I texted my parents a brief summary of what had happened, with a promise to call and explain more later. Then I got up, reached up on tiptoe to get myself down a wineglass, and poured myself some of the prosecco Kavita had given me.

'You won today, Fiona,' I told myself, as firmly as I could manage. 'Cheers.'

I took a sip, then spat it back out again. The prosecco was so sweet that it tasted almost like soft drink, the bubbles so aggressive they nearly went up my nose.

I glanced at the label. It was a cheap supermarket brand. If I showed this to Satoshi, he would probably faint – and then, when he came to, he would ban me from Tsundoku for even thinking about drinking something so terrible. *Wine is supposed to be about pleasure, Fiona,* he'd say firmly, steering me to the door. *Come back when you remember that.*

Then I blinked, remembering something that had happened back in February, when Sadie and Jonah had just moved to Hobart and I'd left Jonah with the kids so I could take Sadie out for a drink.

It was the first time I'd been to Tsundoku in the four months since the night Matt had told me about Laura. I'd been petrified that I'd walk through the door and the sight of Satoshi would send embarrassment screaming through my veins so powerfully that I'd run right back out again. *So you know that wine mum who comes into my bar?* I'd spent a lot of time imagining Satoshi texting his (young, beautiful, unspeakably cool) friends. *Turns out her husband's been cheating on her for years – and somehow *I'm* the first person she wanted to tell?????*

But it hadn't. Instead, an enormous grin had spread over his face and he'd practically leapt over the bar to hug me, and as he lifted me clean off my feet, just for a moment – the barest moment, the space between breaths – I'd felt like myself again.

Matt didn't ruin it for me, I'd told Sadie, gesturing at the bar around us, with its artfully mismatched velvet chairs and overstuffed bookshelves. *He might have taken just about everything else, but Tsundoku is still mine.*

It was true practically as well as emotionally. Matt had been in Hobart for work in July (a fact he hadn't bothered to tell me), and he'd tried to go to Tsundoku. I hadn't been there, but Jonah and Sadie had, and according to them, both Satoshi and his brother Isamu had told Matt in no uncertain terms that he was never welcome there again.

I tipped my glass of terrible prosecco down the sink.

There were any number of places in Hobart Matt could take Laura tonight. Any number of places, full of any number of people

I knew, any number of ways he could humiliate me even worse than he already had.

But he couldn't take her to Tsundoku.

And if I really was going to celebrate today as a victory, then I could do much worse than having a glass of nice wine in the one place Matt had never managed to take.

Chapter Two

Satoshi

Tasting today: 2023 arneis, Piedmont, Italy.
Excellent expressions of this mischievous grape are elusive – but if you manage to get your hands on one, don't, under any circumstances, let it slip through your fingers.

'Sorry, Birdie, I know I'm late,' I said, doing up the last two buttons on my work waistcoat as I half-ran into the bar. 'Study group ran over and traffic back across the bridge was a nightmare. Give me five minutes to run upstairs and feed Yquem, and then you can—Isamu?'

'Okaeri.' Isamu glanced over his shoulder at me, elbow-deep in one of my fridges.

'What are you doing here? Please tell me you're not reorganising that.'

'Of course I'm not. I know how you feel about your systems. I'm just checking—' he pulled out a bottle of Bibliophile fumé blanc '—your stock levels.'

He eyeballed the level in the bottle, then put it back in the fridge. 'And I'm here because Birdie had a family emergency. She couldn't get a hold of you, so she called me – in a panic, I might add. I was in town anyway, so . . .' He shrugged.

'Why were you in town? We didn't have a meeting scheduled.'

'Dinner plans.' He took out a bottle of grüner veltliner. 'Not everything I do revolves around you, Sato.'

I gritted my teeth. I really thought I'd fixed the issue of Isamu interfering in my half of the business when, earlier in the year, he'd rented out the Hobart apartment he used to share with Noriko and moved to the vineyard full-time. And for a while, things had been fine. I'd even begun to hope that maybe – finally – I'd proven myself enough that he considered me capable of doing my job without crumbling into dust.

But once again, hope had kicked me in the teeth. As soon as vintage – Isamu's busy period – ended for the year and he no longer had to spend all his time in the winery, these unannounced, occasional pop-ins had started back up. *I've got a few things to do in town, just thought I'd stick my head in and see how things are going,* he'd say, as if there were an endless amount of tasks a winemaker had to do in the city.

I knew he missed Noriko. I knew he was probably lonely out at the vineyard, with only our mother, the occasional guests in her B&B and his books for company. And if he wanted to sit down and talk about it, that would be fine.

He didn't, though. My brother had never talked about his feelings in his entire life. Instead, he threw himself into other things so he could pretend he didn't have them.

I, unlike him, had been to therapy, and so I understood that our nomadic upbringing had instilled in us both a strong need for control. But just because I understood that need for control didn't mean I didn't loathe him trying to exert it over me.

Isamu closed the fridge. 'We need to have a conversation about Birdie.'

'She's really come along. Her service skills are excellent now.'

'Her skills aren't the problem. The fact that this is apparently the fifth time she's called out in a month is. It doesn't matter how good she is if she never turns up.'

'Her mother's sick.' I folded my arms. 'If Okāsan got sick, we'd both drop everything to look after her. I'm not about to fire someone for doing exactly what I would do.'

'You can't keep picking up her slack, Sato.' Isamu switched to Japanese, presumably so the customers in the corner wouldn't hear him lecturing me like a child. 'I assume you've been the one working her shifts?'

I didn't say anything. He knew the answer.

One of the core promises of Tsundoku was that there was always a qualified somm on the floor. That meant me, Birdie or – in a pinch – Isamu. I'd also used to have Noriko on call, but since the divorce, she was no longer an option. If Birdie couldn't work, I had to.

'I know you can't afford to hire another junior somm,' Isamu said. 'But something has to change. You can't study for the MS and run your half of the business and work every single shift at the same time – especially not if you're still set on sitting all three parts of the exam in August.'

I clenched my jaw. He wasn't wrong, but it didn't mean I was going to give up ground.

I'd set myself this ridiculous goal soon after the night I'd fallen in love with Fiona and she'd promptly vanished from my life for several months. Birdie hadn't been ready to run a shift by herself then, so I'd been working constantly, but it still wasn't enough. I'd needed something to hurl myself into the way that Isamu hurled himself into micro-managing me; something to distract me from the gnarled, twisted-up ball of emotions in my stomach – the longing, the yearning, the agony, and worst of all, the hope – and the MS was the thing I'd chosen.

The exam had three components: theory, tasting and service. I was hoping to pass all three – something few people rarely managed, especially not on their first attempt – at an exam date in Paris in less than a year's time. Isamu had been livid when I told him – *Are you trying to kill yourself?* he'd demanded – but I'd held firm.

'It's all right for now,' he went on. 'I've got the time to pinch-hit. But what about when vintage hits in the new year? I won't be able to leave the winery, and then—'

'This is my side of the business, Isamu.'

'I know, but—'

'I'll think about it, all right?' I said. 'I'll work something out. Just give me a minute.'

Isamu regarded me for a long moment, but eventually, he nodded. 'How was study group?' he asked in English.

'Fine,' I lied, taking a microfibre cloth out of my pocket so I could polish my glasses. Birdie's absence meant I had to ask him a favour, and I really, *really* didn't want to. 'Carlton's boss invited me to work a shift tomorrow night. He works at Abode, over on Brooke St Pier. It's fine dining, so staging there will be useful for practicing all the fiddly bits for the service exam I haven't had a chance to do properly since Geneva. But I'm rostered on here, and . . .'

'. . . you need me to fill in. Because you don't have anyone else who can run the floor.'

I gritted my teeth. 'I can say no, if you can't come up from the vineyard.'

'I have to be in Hobart tomorrow anyway.'

Sure he did.

'But you can't keep going like this, Sato,' Isamu said. 'You're going to burn out.'

'I'm fine,' I said tightly. 'Everything's under control. Now if you'll excuse me for a minute, I have a cat to feed.'

I took the stairs up to my apartment two at a time. Yquem mewed from her spot in a sunbeam on the couch as I refilled her food and water bowls, but she didn't move. Some days, when I came in, she was all over me, pouncing on me the second I walked in the door. Other days, though, like today, she ignored me completely.

I sighed. I adored her unreservedly, but she – like the notoriously expensive and temperamental wine I'd named her after when I'd adopted her late last year, trying to find somewhere else to put all the frustrated love in my heart – was so all-or-nothing. On days like today, when I could really use a hug, it was hard not to take her disinterest personally.

I took my glasses off – red frames today – so I could splash cold water on my face in the bathroom. Much as I resented Isamu's lack of faith in me, I was going to have to figure something out. Unless I at least gave the appearance of changing something, he wasn't going to stop trying to boss me around.

I really couldn't afford to hire another qualified somm, but maybe I could mentor one of my more experienced bar staff through some certifications. Admittedly, it'd be a significant investment of time and energy, but perhaps it could be a stopgap until Birdie's circumstances stabilised.

And maybe Yquem would be in a snugglier mood once I closed up this evening. I was going to have to put in some serious study time, but it would definitely be easier if I had the little warm lump of her in my lap.

I sighed again, sliding my glasses back on. Study group this afternoon had been an unmitigated disaster.

We'd been focusing on tasting: specifically, old world white wines. Maxi and Carlton, the other two somms in the group, had each nailed at least the grape or appellation of a respectable four of the six we'd blinded, but I hadn't been close to a single one.

It's okay, Satoshi, Maxi had told me afterwards as we washed up our spittoons. *We all have bad days. You just need to practise.*

She was completely correct, but that just made it even more frustrating. *In whose time?* I'd wanted to yell.

But there was no point. Complaining wouldn't make my chances of passing the MS any higher, and it would just take up more time that I didn't have.

I adjusted my shirt collar, straightened my cuffs, combed my fingers through my hair (the bleach had dried it out, I should do a hair mask tonight while I studied), and put on my customer service smile. One thing at a time. I would get through service, I would sacrifice a few hours' sleep so I could study, and tomorrow would be a new day.

I should rip the bandaid off and give dating apps a try, I thought, taking two steps at a time as I headed back downstairs to the bar. It had been nine months since I'd been with anyone – a deeply unhealthy and unsatisfying backslide with Kieran, aggressively reinforcing that I wasn't remotely in love with him anymore. Going to bed with someone wouldn't solve anything – the Kieran incident had proven conclusively that I couldn't fuck Fiona out of my system – and casual hookups really weren't my style, but everything was just so *frustrating*, and I could use—

'Hello, stranger,' Fiona said, beaming at me.

Every single thought left my head.

'Hello!' I replied, as she twisted sideways on her barstool and put her arms around my neck.

It was an awkward position for a hug. Fiona was contorted in a way that had to be uncomfortable, and the barstool beside hers dug painfully into my ribs. But she was warm against me, like sunlight was caught beneath her skin, and when she turned her head to brush her lips against my cheek, I had the exact same feeling as when Birdie had dropped all those glasses and everyone had frozen except her: a sudden pop, followed by an overwhelming sense of relief.

'I'm so glad you're here.' Fiona drew back. She was wearing a grey dress with a cowl neck: pretty, but unusually corporate for her. 'I thought maybe you had the night off.'

I'd forgotten Isamu was there until he made a disapproving noise in the back of his throat. I opened my mouth to respond, but Fiona got in first. 'Oh, I'm sorry, Isamu! I didn't mean to imply that I wasn't happy to see you. But—'

One corner of my eternally unsmiling brother's mouth twitched upwards. 'It's fine, Fiona. No offence taken.'

She put a hand on her heart. 'Good. Because if you ever decide to ban me from drinking Bibliophile, I don't know what I'd do.'

'I would never,' Isamu replied, at the same time as I said, 'I wouldn't let him.'

Fiona chuckled. Isamu gave me a long, inscrutable look before rapping his knuckles on the bar. 'I'm heading out, Sato. I haven't decided whether to go back to the vineyard tonight after dinner. If I don't, I might crash on your couch.'

Fuck. That would put a cramp in my study plans. 'No problem. Yquem will be delighted to spend some time with her uncle.'

He grunted. 'Nice to see you, Fiona.'

'You too, Isamu.'

Once he'd gone, Fiona turned to me. 'Can I ask an impertinent question?'

'Is it "Why is your brother always so rude about your precious angel of a cat, Satoshi?" Because I'd like to know that too.'

She laughed. 'No.'

She slid her mostly full glass of wine across the bar. 'Will you pour me something else? I don't want to waste wine, but this one isn't for me. Isamu doesn't get my palate like you do.'

Had I just spent a year thinking I was in love with her? I was wrong. *Now* I was in love with her. 'I think I can manage that.'

I sniffed the wine that Isamu had poured for her. It was an off-dry riesling – a sweeter style of wine that had its devotees, but Fiona was not among them. 'Is there a particular vibe you're feeling today?'

She twined a lock of hair around her finger, an image that was definitely going to replay like a GIF in my mind later. 'Something fun. Light-hearted. It's been a fucking *day*, and I just want something that will cheer me up.'

'Fun and light-hearted. I can work with that.'

I regarded my wine fridges for a moment before I selected a bottle. 'Let me introduce you,' I said, taking two glasses down from the overhead rack, 'to my good friend arneis.'

I took my wine knife out of my pocket, opened the bottle, smelled the cork, poured a splash into one glass, tasted it quickly to make sure it wasn't faulty, then poured a tasting measure into the other glass and set it in front of her. 'Tell me if you like this, or if you'd prefer something else.'

Fiona inhaled the bouquet. 'Oh yes, this is much more my vibe. There's pear, apple . . . maybe a bit of hazelnut? It's nowhere near as sweet as the other one, but it reminds me of a fruit crumble.'

'Exactly.' She was so on the nose she might as well have been reading out of one of my textbooks.

She tasted it. 'Oh, *yes*.'

One of the thoughts I usually prohibited myself from thinking slipped through the barricade. Fiona's ankles locked at the small of my back, her arms wound around my neck, her voice breathy in my ear. *Oh, yes.*

I forced it away as I filled her glass. 'Arneis is a difficult grape to work with. It's a mischievous grape. A trickster grape. The name literally means *little rascal*. If you leave it on the vine even a day or two too long, it'll lose all its acidity and you'll have the most boring wine in the world. But if you get it right, then it's magical.'

Fiona closed her eyes, but she didn't pick up her glass again. Instead, she took a long breath, in and out, shoulders relaxing on the exhale.

'Today's been a lot, Satoshi,' she said. 'Like, *a lot*. And this is the first thing that has made me feel even a little bit better.'

'Wine will do that.'

'Oh, come on.' She opened her eyes. 'You know I'm not just talking about the wine.'

I didn't know whether I wanted to thank or murder the customer who chose that moment to come through the door, just like I didn't know whether Fiona's words had delighted or tortured me. 'Excuse me.'

'Go, go.' She saluted me with her glass, still smiling. 'For once, I've got time.'

🍷

One year ago, I'd walked Fiona home at four-thirty in the morning. The pre-dawn air was cold and the streets were quiet, the only sound the fall of our feet against the pavement. She had her arms wrapped around herself, fingers clutching at her elbows, shivering, although I'd insisted she wear both her coat and mine.

This is me, she said.

There were some big, expensive houses in Bellerive, and given Matt's finance bro money, I'd assumed they lived in one of them. Fiona's home, though, was a modest brick number, a little table and two chairs on the porch, an abandoned hose snaking through a slightly overgrown front garden.

Fingers shaking, she unbuttoned my coat. *Thank you, Satoshi*, she said, handing it back to me. *I'm so sorry to have dumped all this on you.*

You don't need to apologise. I clenched my fingers tight in the coat's malbec-red fabric, resisting the urge to wrap it back around her, throw her over my shoulder, and carry her away. *Anything you need – anything at all – I'm here. Always.*

She nodded.

I'll see you soon, okay? It probably wasn't a good idea, but I couldn't resist taking her hand and squeezing her fingers.

She squeezed back. *Soon.*

Then she let go, and I didn't see her for four months.

When she'd finally come back to Tsundoku again in February, she'd had a pretty red-headed woman – her new sister-in-law Sadie, I would find out – in tow. *I'm sorry it's been so long,* Fiona had said, voice muffled in my shirt as I hugged her, lifting her off her feet. *It's just been impossible to get away, with the kids and everything.*

Not to worry. I'd allowed myself to stroke her hair just once before I set her back down. *You're here now.*

In the months since I'd seen her, I'd tried so hard to talk myself into believing that what I'd felt that night last October had been an anomaly. But the second Fiona walked through my door again, all the lies I'd been telling myself had gone out the window, because I felt it again: the pop of the cork, the hard knot of pressure released, the swift spread of relief.

After that, she didn't come into Tsundoku as frequently as she used to, but she was in and out often enough to still be considered a regular. Mostly, she came in with Lex during cafe hours so they could pick out some books. Sometimes it was with Sadie or Jonah (also now regulars), while the other watched the kids. Once, before she'd fired him and replaced him with a better one, she'd come in with her divorce lawyer, a conversation that had left her so despondent I'd made her take home an entire case of free wine.

This was the first time, though, since Matt had left, that Fiona had come into Tsundoku by herself.

The bar was starting to fill up for dinner service, so I could only watch her out of the corner of my eye as I worked. She was sipping her glass of arneis slowly, one elbow leaning on the bar, hand wrapped around the nape of her neck, the cowl neckline of her dress pulled slightly to one side. The expression on her face was weary, but not in a bad way, not like the pure exhaustion that was written all over it far too frequently. Rather, she looked like someone who'd run a marathon and was finally getting to sit down: not quite relaxed, and not quite rejuvenated, but reprieved.

'You're really nursing that,' I said, gesturing at her half-full glass once things started to quiet down. 'I can pour you something else, if you're not vibing the rascal anymore.'

'Don't you dare.' Fiona pulled the glass towards her. 'I love the rascal. I'm savouring it, that's all.'

'Can I top you up, then? Or do you need to get home to the kids?'

'No kids tonight.' She nudged her glass towards me so I could refill it. 'They stay with Jonah and Sadie on Thursdays. Look.'

She showed me a photo on her phone. Her daughters were snuggled up on either side of Jonah on the couch, listening to him rapturously. They were wearing fairy wings, while he was wearing a unicorn headband. 'Sadie says he's trying to get them started on *A Midsummer Night's Dream* early, and that was the closest thing they could rustle up to a donkey's head.'

'I see Lex is super engaged.' Lex was curled up in an armchair on the edge of frame, absorbed in a book, ignoring everyone.

Fiona chuckled. 'I bribed them this morning with the promise of coming in next week to browse the bookshelves, so . . .'

'I'll lay out some Lex-bait. What's the bribe for?'

'There was a mediation meeting today. Me. Matt. The lawyers. Lex wanted to come.'

She traced circles on the bar. 'I said no, obviously. But then Matt turned up with Laura – who's pregnant, by the way, with twins, because my girls just aren't good enough, I guess, and . . .'

She stopped, swallowing convulsively. Tears were starting to slip down her face.

'Oh, Fiona,' I said softly. 'I'm sorry.'

'No, I'm sorry.' She sniffed. 'I didn't mean to come in here and ruin the vibe by crying. It's just . . . today was so fucking *much*.'

She scrubbed at her eyes with a serviette. 'Oh god, all my makeup's coming off. What kind of idiot doesn't wear waterproof mascara on a day like today?'

'Satoshi, why don't you take Fiona out the back?' Charlotte, one of my bar staff, materialised at my side. 'It's quiet now. The dinner rush has passed. I can handle everything out here.'

'Oh, you don't need to do that!' Fiona was off her barstool in an instant. 'I didn't come in here to distract you – you've got a job to do! – and—'

'Don't even worry about it,' Charlotte said. 'You did the same for Birdie last year, right? We owe you one.'

Just for a second, Fiona wavered.

I used that second to survey the bar quickly. Under normal circumstances, I'd never dream of leaving the floor without a qualified somm in charge, but Charlotte was right. There was hardly anyone here, and she was one of my most experienced staff – and I'd only be ten steps away if she needed me.

So even though it went against my most hard-wired, professional instincts, there I was, coming around the bar and taking Fiona by the elbow. 'I actually have something you can help me with. Come out to the office with me, finish your glass of wine, and give me a hand, all right?'

'I, um—'

'Charlotte, come and get me if you need me,' I said over my shoulder, steering Fiona towards the back. Charlotte gave me a thumbs up in response.

Fiona scrubbed her wrist across her eyes as I closed my office door behind us. 'So what is this thing I can allegedly help you with?' she asked. 'I don't have many useful skills.'

'Firstly, that's nonsense, Ms Copywriter. You *know* how often I plagiarise from you in my tasting notes. Secondly, if you can follow instructions, you can help me.'

I pulled my glasses down my nose so I could look at her over the top of them like a stern schoolmaster. 'You can follow instructions, can't you?'

That made her laugh, just a little. 'Yes, Satoshi, I can follow instructions.'

My anxiety at leaving the floor started to recede, overshadowed by a different set of feelings. If I lingered too long on the idea of her following my instructions . . .

'What do you need me to do?' she asked.

'I had a disaster of a blind tasting today.' *She's still half-crying, Satoshi, get your mind out of the gutter.* 'Stunningly bad. Songs will be written about what an incredible failure it was. Forget becoming an MS, if this gets back to the powers that be, they'll kick me out of the Court of Sommeliers entirely.'

She laughed again. My heart swelled so much it was almost painful.

'So, I need someone to help me study old world white wines – which, coincidentally, is what you're drinking, that arneis is from Piedmont in Italy. How would you feel about being my study buddy for the evening?'

'I can do that.' Fiona thumbed the last of her tears away. 'What do I have to do?'

I took some blind tasting sleeves from the shelf. 'Can you grab a tasting sheet from the second drawer of the desk? It's laminated with six circles on it, with numbers underneath.'

She did. I lined up six wineglasses on it, aligning them precisely with the outlines, and set a spittoon beside them. 'Now I'm going to turn my back. See those three cases of wine in the corner, next to the fridge?'

'Yep.'

'Choose six bottles from them – any six – and put them into these sleeves, so I can't see what they are.'

I faced the wall. There was some rattling and rustling as she did what I'd asked her. 'Done.'

I turned back around. 'If you look in the same drawer as before, there's a stack of deductive tasting grids. We need six.'

I started opening the wines she'd put in the sleeves, eyes cast up to the ceiling so I didn't get any hints from the foils or the corks, while Fiona scrabbled around in my desk. 'Okay,' she said, 'here we are – oh my *god*, Satoshi.'

'What?'

She gestured. 'How can you do that so fast? Without looking?'

'It's just practise.' I discarded the sixth cork and put my wine knife back in my pocket. 'And maybe a dash of genetics. Strong fingers.' I waggled them at her.

'That must make you popular.'

It took me a moment to process what she'd said, by which time she'd covered her mouth with her hands. 'Oh my god, I'm so sorry!'

She was so mortified I couldn't help but laugh, despite the flood of extremely vivid images rushing through my brain. 'Come on, Fiona,' I said, starting to pour tasting measures from the open bottles into the glasses. 'We've talked about sex before. You can't scandalise me that easily.'

'That doesn't mean you want to be sexually harassed by a woman old enough to be your mother!'

'You're only eight years older than me. If you think you're old enough to be my mother, there might be some significant gaps in your sex education.'

She buried her face in her hands and groaned.

'Tsukamoto-sensei can run through some basics for you, if you like,' I said, unable to stop even though this was an *extremely* dangerous conversation. 'The human reproductive system—'

'Don't you dare, Satoshi.' She looked at me from between her fingers, and there it was, that mischievous sparkle in her eye, the one that had gone so dim since Matt left. 'Don't you fucking dare.'

I wrinkled my nose at her. She wrinkled hers back.

Then she dropped her hands. 'Anyway, I believe I'm supposed to be the one assessing your knowledge right now, young man, not the other way around,' she said, putting on a mock-businesslike tone. 'Tell me what to do.'

I gestured for her to sit down in my desk chair, then took a seat across from her. 'The way the MS tasting exam works is that you have twenty-five minutes to taste six wines blind and figure out what they are: the grape, where they're from, the vintage, any quality markers,' I explained. 'It's like maths – you get points for showing your working, in the categories you can see there on the grid. So if you come to the wrong conclusion but you get things right along the way—'

'—then you still get some points.' Fiona was studying the deductive tasting grid, squinting slightly, and my fingers itched with the desire to reach over and smooth the furrow between her brows. 'I get it. So I just mark down what you say, and then at the end we work out how many points you get?'

'Exactly. Think you can do it?'

'I can give it a try.' She reached into her handbag and took out her phone. 'I'll put a timer on. Are you ready?'

I wasn't, really. My brain was stuck on her saying *tell me what to do*, busy producing images so graphic they could probably get me sent to some kind of horny jail.

'I'm ready.' I scooted my chair as close to the desk as possible. 'Are you? Got enough wine? Twenty-five minutes is a long time.'

'I'm still working on the rascal.' Fiona raised her glass of arneis to me, an innocuous gesture that was somehow the sexiest thing anyone had ever done. 'And if I run out, there are six open bottles for me to try.'

She grinned at me, eyes crinkling in the corners. 'Now show me what you've got, Satoshi. Your time starts . . . now.'

I picked up the first glass, taking a deep breath as I tilted it so I could look at the wine's colour against the white of the tasting sheet. 'Wine number one is a clear white wine,' I began. 'No sediment. It's deep gold, with some brownish hues, which could indicate either age, oxidation, or the presence of botrytis.'

I smelled it, doing my best to sink into the familiar ritual of blind tasting. 'On the nose there's ripe pear, peach and baked apple, as well as—' I swirled it a couple of times, then smelled it again '—honey and chamomile, with notes of saffron, toasted almond and burnt sugar. It's spent some time in oak, almost certainly old oak.'

I tasted the wine, sucking in air at the same time to oxygenate it, and let it sit on my palate for a few seconds – there was jasmine there too, along with all the honeyed ripe fruits on the nose – before reaching for the spittoon and rattling off structural characteristics: sweetness, tannin, acid, alcohol, body, age, complexity. 'My initial conclusion is that this is a cool climate old world wine, probably French. It could be sweeter-style riesling from Alsace; but my final conclusion is that this is chenin blanc from the Loire Valley, Vouvray appellation, vintage 2015.'

I dared a glance at Fiona. Her pen had been scratching busily against the grid, but she'd stopped, and she was looking back at me, cheeks flushed, mouth slightly open.

Well, I'd clearly got that one right.

I smiled at her, buoyed, filed her facial expression away to think more about later at extremely great length, then picked up the second glass.

🍷

'That was *amazing*,' Fiona said once we were finished. 'Should I get you some water?'

'Please.'

She pulled a water bottle out of a half-open case I had in the corner and handed it to me. I drank most of it in two gulps. Exam condition blind tastings always made me feel like I'd run a marathon.

'I could watch you do that for hours,' she enthused. 'And you got all of them right! You were perfect!'

'Perfect is going a bit far,' I said, although I was very pleased with myself. I'd never managed six from six accurate conclusions before. 'This was much easier than a proper blind tasting would be. It's not like I didn't already know what was in the cases you picked the bottles from.'

'Will you just let me compliment you?'

I rolled my eyes to the ceiling dramatically. 'Ugh, if you *insist*.'

She laughed that champagne laugh of hers, and I wanted to bottle it and keep it with me, always.

'Seriously, though,' Fiona said. 'I feel . . . privileged to have seen you do that, Satoshi. To see an expert at the top of their game. To see you *think* like that. I've never been good at anything the way you're good at that.'

'Don't sell yourself short.' I lobbed my empty water bottle into the bin. 'You're good at thinking about wine too. Do you think I'm always using the things you say in my tasting notes just because I like you?'

She didn't shrug exactly, but there was the smallest rise and fall of her shoulders. 'I'm decent at snappy wording. That's not hard.'

'You know how to paint a picture.' I gestured at the glasses in front of me. 'Talking about wine like this is scientific. Technical. But the way you talk about it – that's different. That's art.'

I nudged glass number four toward her, an albariño from Rías Baixas. 'You heard me break down this wine. Now you do it. Your way.'

Fiona looked at me almost suspiciously before she accepted the glass. 'You said it had notes of lemon and green olive brine.' She smelled it. 'I definitely get that – the citrus and the saltiness. And—' she tasted it '—there's something almost like tonic water.'

'Exactly. That slight bitterness. It's like quinine.'

'It reminds me of this day last January.' She took another sip, letting the wine sit on her palate for a moment. 'My brother Elias was here, and it was hot, so we took the kids down to Bellerive Beach. The girls were playing in the water, and Lex was lying next to me on a towel, nose buried in a book like usual, and Elias pulled out this little container of olives and these cheap canned gin and tonics, and we sat there eating and drinking together. The drinks weren't very good – I mean, they were G&Ts in a can, you would probably rather die – but it was the first time in ages I didn't feel completely miserable.'

'See?'

Her smile was sheepish. 'That's a bit too specific for your tasting notes.'

'Forget my tasting notes. That's not the point. The point is that you're *good* at this.' I tapped the foot of one of the wineglasses. 'I can give wine specs until the cows come home, but you know how to make a glass tell a story. And that's how to make wine into what it should be about. Enjoyment. Appreciation. Pleasure.'

'I don't think I really understood that,' she said, 'before I met you.'

Those words stole the breath from my lungs.

'One of the first things you ever told me about wine was that it was the opposite of shots.' She looked into her glass, contemplative. 'That instead of being a means to an end – something you drank to get drunk, that was gone in a flash – it was something to drink slowly. To stop. Sit. Sip. Savour.'

Those words were part of my standard spiel – I'd said them thousands of times – but coming out of her mouth, they felt brand new.

'I've always remembered that,' she said. 'Especially this past year. Sometimes it feels like the world is spinning so fast I'm going to get flung off. But whenever I get to sit down with a glass of wine, then just for a moment, everything slows down. It's . . . mindful, almost.'

She smiled at me. 'Then I get to talk about it with you. And that's pleasure, isn't it? A lovely experience you can share with a friend?'

I defied anyone in the world not to melt when Fiona Fisher smiled at them like that.

'Of course it is,' I said softly.

She held up her glass. 'To pleasure?'

I picked up one of the half-full tasting glasses and clinked it against hers. 'To pleasure.'

She held my gaze as we drank. 'This is obviously redundant for me,' she said, gesturing with two fingers first at her eyes and then at mine, 'given I'm probably never going to have sex ever again, good or bad, but it would be unfair for me to drag you down with me for the next seven years.'

I blinked.

She winked at me.

And something in me – a carefully erected barricade, constructed deep within my mind – cracked.

'Fiona,' I said, setting my glass down, 'do you really think that?'

'That I'll never have sex again?'

I nodded. It felt like someone was slowly turning up the thermostat on my entire body, like there was heat in my bones and it was slowly spreading.

'I'd like not to think it.' She looked into her glass again. 'But let's be realistic. Men don't usually come beating down the doors of single mothers on the verge of middle age.'

The flush, which had receded from her cheeks, started to reappear. 'I've thought about getting on a dating app. But I haven't been single since I was twenty-one – I don't know shit about dating apps. And where would I find the time? I get one night a week to myself while the kids are with Jonah and Sadie, and I'm usually so tired I just fall into a boneless heap on the couch. The thought of trying to date is exhausting. The thought of trying to trust someone is *unthinkable*. And that's—'

'Fiona.'

'—before you take into account that only, like, fifteen people live in Hobart, so I'd constantly be swiping past people I know. Probably dads from the kids' school – married dads – and then I'd *know* they were out there trying to cheat on their wives, and they'd *know* that the woman so stupid she didn't realise her husband had an entire second family was out there trying to get fooled again and—'

'Fiona.'

'—I suppose the obvious answer is just to leave men out of the equation altogether and buy a vibrator. But the second I do, one of the twins will find it. And it's not like I'm opposed to giving them comprehensive sex education or teaching them about pleasure and their own bodies, but I wasn't planning to do it at the age of eight, and – oh my god, I can't believe I'm talking to you about this!' She buried her face in her hands. 'Why am I like this?'

'Fiona, look at me.'

'No,' she moaned. 'I'm just going to sink into the floor and sneak out later when you're not looking. Don't mind me.'

'Come on. Look at me. Please.'

She dropped her hands slightly, fingers digging into her cheekbones just beneath her eyes.

'You're beautiful.' I felt like I was standing on the lip of a volcano. Everything was burning, and I was on the edge, about to fall in. 'And you're lovely. Anyone would be lucky to be with you. Especially men, but also vibrators. They'd be so lucky.'

That drew a laugh from her, muffled in her palms. 'Thank you,' she said. 'For not throwing me out all the times my mouth gets ahead of my brain.'

My mouth did not get ahead of my brain. I thought about it before I said it. I was on the very edge of the volcano's crater, and the ground was shaky beneath me, but I probably had just enough strength left to step back from the brink.

But then she dropped her hands, and she smiled at me, and it was like sparkling wine in my veins, and I lost control of my footing.

'We're friends, right?' I asked.

'Of course we are.'

'You deserve pleasure, Fiona,' I said. 'And if you need someone to give it to you, I'm here.'

Chapter Three

Fiona

Tasting today: 2021 albariño, Rías Baixas, Spain.
A day at the beach in a glass: bright sun and sea-spray,
until the inevitable bitterness of getting burned.

I had a problem with getting ahead of myself.

It had been worse since Matt left, fantasising turning to catastrophising, but I'd been this way my entire life, forever skipping to the end of the story while everyone else was still at the beginning. Age five, I'd spotted another girl with the same colour ribbons in her pigtails as me, and I'd decided we were going to be best friends before she'd even told me her name was Kaitlyn. Age thirteen, I'd failed one history test and immediately concluded that I was eternally destined to be the black sheep of my academic family. Age twenty-two, a man I'd been sleeping with for nine months asked me to marry him, and I'd jumped straight to happily ever after without asking a single question.

Age thirty-four, I had a graphic sex dream about the nice boy from the bar a few days after seeing him passionately making out his boyfriend in the alley, and my mind had skipped forward like a rock over water to a future where I got all in my head about it and made things between us *extremely* weird.

That was the last thing I wanted. I had come to truly value our friendship, and he'd been so, so wonderfully supportive helping Lex navigate coming out. So in the interests of preventing that future from coming to pass, I'd boxed the dream up and put it away. It wasn't that deep, I told myself, burying it in the dark recesses of my mind: just a combination of misfiring synapses and Matt being gone for work more than usual. It wasn't the first random sex dream I'd ever had about someone inappropriate, and it wouldn't be the last. It didn't *mean* anything.

But then the words, *You deserve pleasure, Fiona, and if you need someone to give it to you, I'm here* came out of Satoshi's mouth, and that box I'd hidden exploded open.

It felt like I'd been hit with a computer virus that had suddenly flooded my system with pornography, all the thoughts I hadn't let myself think happening to me all at once. Satoshi's lips on mine. Satoshi's body against mine. Satoshi's hands on me, those deft, capable, strong fingers currently curled around the stem of his wineglass caressing me gently before gripping me tight, and—

Wine. Wine was supposed to be about pleasure. He was talking about giving me wine, not an orgasm.

'You already give me plenty of pleasure.' I raised my glass to him, trying my best not to let my face turn tell-tale red.

'I'm not talking about the wine.'

. . . oh.

'I don't want to make you uncomfortable,' Satoshi said. 'Tell me no, and I'll never raise this subject again. But I mean it, Fiona. You deserve to feel good. Let me give that to you.'

I seemed to have forgotten how to breathe.

For a long moment, we sat there, looking at each other across his desk. My heart was racing so fast that I wouldn't be surprised if he could hear it. My scalp was tingling, but not in the icy way it had earlier, sitting across from Matt in the mediation meeting. It felt charged, like all my hair might stand on end. Electric.

I couldn't speak. I'd forgotten how to do that too.

But Satoshi was looking at me, nothing but kindness and a question in his eyes, and I – sad, lonely, touch-starved Fiona, who maybe hadn't buried that dream quite as deep as she should have – was nodding.

The corners of his mouth curved upwards, cheeks dimpling. 'All right, then.'

He stood. Reflexively, I stood too, then immediately felt awkward as he started clearing the glasses and open bottles from his desk. I didn't know what to do with my hands, so I twined my suddenly sweaty fingers together in front of me.

Fuck. This was a terrible idea, wasn't it? It would be nice to have the last person to touch me not be Matt – but what was I *doing*? I was about to make a complete laughing-stock of—

'Come here,' Satoshi extended a hand to me.

I had to work hard to unclench my fingers. 'I'm sorry.'

'What are you sorry for?'

'My hands. They're all clammy – *oh*.'

He'd grabbed me by the waist, picking me up and sitting me on the edge of the desk in one swift movement. My knees fell apart and he stepped between them, body not quite touching mine but so close I could feel the warmth of him, radiating outwards.

I swallowed. 'Are you sure? You – we – don't have to.'

One of Satoshi's hands came up to frame the side of my face. 'I know.' His thumb stroked along my cheekbone. 'I want to.'

'Why, though?' His fingertips were nestling into my hair, drawing soft little circles, and the feeling was mesmerising. 'Why would you . . .?'

He paused. The tip of his tongue was pink as he licked his lips, and time seemed to slow down, stretching, expanding.

'Because I like you,' he said at last.

He leaned in closer, his forehead coming to rest against mine, and I barely repressed the shiver that ran through me as his glasses pressed lightly into my eyebrows. 'I'm going to kiss you now, okay?'

'Okay,' I only just managed to whisper.

The first brush of his lips against mine was featherlight, fleeting, the gentlest possible question, but it made me shiver again, irrepressibly this time, an almost-panicked high-pitched needy sound erupting from my throat. 'I'm sorry,' I said. 'I don't know where that came from. I'm just – it's just—'

'A lot?'

I nodded.

Satoshi stroked his thumb along my cheekbone again. 'We can stop whenever you want.' He folded the fingers of his other hand through mine. 'But it's just me, Fiona. You're safe. I've got you.'

I know, I wanted to say, but it felt too weighty, too fraught, too dangerous somehow, so I just squeezed his fingers.

That drew a smile from him. I touched the pad of my index finger lightly to the dimple in his right cheek, then the left one, then beneath his chin, drawing his face to mine again.

I had never been kissed like this before – so softly, so tenderly, so respectfully. The barest touch of my finger beneath his chin was enough to hold him to me. His hand against my cheek was a request, not a demand, his fingertips in my hair making me feel like I was turning to liquid.

The first nudge of his tongue against my lower lip drew another sound from me – less a squeak this time, more a sigh. 'Okay?' he asked, letting go of my hand and tracing his fingers up the length of my spine to curl around the nape of my neck.

'Yes.' My free hand came up to rest against his clavicle, fingers under his collar, thumb resting in the divot at the base of his throat. 'Okay.'

It might have been a minute that Satoshi kissed me like that, tongue sliding gently against mine, or an hour. He was so leisurely and unhurried that I completely lost my sense of time.

With Matt, sex had always been about milestones. It had got more pronounced over time, but even in the early days, there had been a routine. We'd kiss for a while, more as a signal to the other that we wanted to have sex than something to be enjoyed in its own right. He'd work on me for a bit (*real men make sure their partners are enjoying it as much as they are,* he'd said to a much younger Fiona, head between her thighs, and she'd been foolish enough to find that romantic instead of smug), I'd work on him for a bit, relishing the sounds I could get him to make, and then he'd slip inside me. He'd always come, I usually would, and I'd thought that overall, I was pretty lucky. I'd heard how some of the other school mums talked about their sex lives. Mine might not be rip-your-clothes-off passionate, but it certainly wasn't terrible.

. . . God, the things those mums would say if they could see me now.

Satoshi used the hand he had on the nape of my neck to tilt my head back so he could kiss his way down my throat. This time it wasn't a squeak or a sigh but a moan he drew from me, and his laughter was a soft hum of approval against my skin, especially when he pressed his lips behind my ear and I jerked like I'd been electrocuted. 'There?' He licked the same spot. 'That's good?'

'Yes,' I breathed, curling my fist into his shirt, trying to pull him tighter to me. 'That's so good.'

He kissed me there again, laughing when it elicited the same shudder. 'I'm going to have to hold you still if you keep doing that,' he murmured, tracing the shell of my ear with his tongue and then gently teasing the lobe between his teeth.

'I'm sorry.'

'Don't apologise.' He nipped at the spot behind my ear this time, and I would have fallen off the desk if not for his body holding me there. 'I like it.'

He caressed my cheekbone one more time before he trailed his knuckles gently down my body. 'Can I figure out where else makes you jump like that, I wonder?'

My breath was coming shallowly as he traced the curve of my breast through the grey wool of my dress. 'What about here?'

I'd never had particularly sensitive breasts – Matt was more of an arse man, and once he'd figured out that I didn't get much out of having my tits touched, he mostly left them alone – but Satoshi's thumb against my nipple made me reflexively swallow and clutch at his waistcoat. 'Oh, that's – that's—'

'Not your favourite?'

'I like it, though.'

'I definitely like it.' He cupped my breast in his hand, kissing that spot behind my ear again in a way that made my head fall back. 'You feel so good.'

He drew back so he could kiss me again. I sighed into his mouth as he dropped his hand from my breast to my hip, caressing my hip bone. His other hand was firmer now against the nape of my neck, his tongue more insistent in my mouth, and I looped my arms around him, digging my nails into his shoulder blades, inviting him deeper.

Satoshi's fingers fell again, tracing the line of my left thigh until they brushed the inside of my knee. He pulled it tighter around his hip, and I gasped at the sensation against the ticklish crease of the joint.

'I'm going to touch you,' he told me, fingertips teasing the skin just beneath my hemline. Even through my pantyhose, it felt electric. 'Okay?'

'Please,' was all I could reply.

He didn't make me wait. His fingers traced a quick, scorching line up my inner thigh before his hand settled firmly between my legs.

He ground the heel of his hand against my clit, and my body jack-knifed, the sound erupting from me somewhere between a sob and a wail. He kissed his way back to the spot behind my ear, and when he ground his hand into me again I nearly burst into tears. 'I think we've found another spot you like.'

My hips started rocking involuntarily against him. 'Please don't stop,' I begged. 'Don't stop – *oh*.'

The world narrowed to the pressure of his hand between my legs and the feeling of his lips behind my ear, and then it went white. The orgasm hit me like a train, sudden and violent, his fingers around the back of my neck the only things holding me up as it ran me over, leaving me a shaking, quivering mess. 'Oh my god,' I moaned.

Satoshi drew my head to the curve of his throat. 'Are you okay?'

'Oh my god,' I panted into his collar. 'Oh my god.'

He chuckled. '"Oh no, Satoshi, sex is over for me forever, orgasms are simply something that happen to other people."' He kissed the top of my head. 'That took, what, seven seconds?'

'Please don't—' I gulped down some air '—don't tease me.'

'Don't worry. I have no intention of teasing you.'

He pinched a section of my pantyhose and let it snap back against my skin. It made me jump, and he chuckled again. 'Can I take these off?'

My brain was struggling to catch up. 'What?'

'You're so wet, Fiona.' Satoshi's voice dropped almost an octave. 'I can feel it through your stockings. Let me touch you properly.'

He stroked a line up the gusset of my pantyhose, and the world went from white to pink, a rosé haze. 'Yes,' I breathed.

He slid his nose against mine as he smoothed his hand up my side, under my dress. 'Just how high up do these go?' he asked, laughing.

'Oh, shit, sorry.' Things started to come back into sharper focus. 'They're control-top. With the mediation meeting today – it wasn't that I wanted to look *good*, but I didn't want to look bad either, and . . . oh god, they're so ugly, please don't look at them.'

Satoshi had peeled the pantyhose off me as deftly as he'd opened those bottles of wine, taking my underwear (sensible, practical, motherly) with them and tossing them behind him. 'I don't care what you're wearing.' He kissed me gently, lips just brushing against mine. 'I care that you're not wearing them anymore.'

His fingers were back between my legs half a second before I remembered that, like orgasms, bikini waxes were also something only happening to other people. 'Oh, wow,' he said, tracing a line up and down the slippery centre of me, circling my clit with his fingertip until I started trembling, and then stroking back down again to dip ever so slightly inside me. 'My goodness, Fiona.'

I could only whimper.

Two of his fingers slipped inside me, and he made a noise of satisfaction as I gasped and clenched around him. 'Fuck.' He bit my earlobe. 'You really needed this, didn't you?'

'Yes,' was all I could manage. 'Please.'

He curled his fingers against my G-spot and stroked. I shrieked as his thumb found my clit, a sound he swallowed with a kiss. 'Like this?'

'Yes.' It was more a mess of sounds than a word, yanked out of my throat as he found a rhythm. 'Yes, yes, oh – oh – yes – yes—'

'Satoshi?'

The knock at the door was like someone had emptied liquid nitrogen over our heads. We both froze, stiff and still as statues.

'Satoshi?' Charlotte called again. 'Sorry to interrupt, but Mr Richardson's here and—'

'No worries,' Satoshi called back. 'I'll be right there. Just a second.'

His fingers made a sound that could only be described as a squelch as he took them out of me. 'I'm so sorry,' he said, leaning his forehead against mine. 'I'm doing a cellar appraisal for this guy. He's got thousands of bottles – a big spender. I need to—'

'It's fine,' I managed to say. 'Go, go.'

He kissed me quickly, tugging his shirt hurriedly straight with his left hand. 'Stay here. Wait for me. I'm not finished with you yet.'

He was out the door before I could reply. I heard water running in the bathroom across the hall as he washed his hands, then the sound of his footsteps echoing as he stepped onto the bar floor.

I took a long, shaking breath.

A second.

A third.

For a few moments, my mind was perfectly, entirely clear, empty of everything except the words *I'm not finished with you yet.*

And then suddenly, like I was a cartoon character standing under a piano, the world crashed back down on my head.

What the *actual fuck* had I just let happen?

This was Satoshi. *Satoshi.* I had let sweet, kind, *young* Satoshi Tsukamoto, who could probably sleep with anyone he wanted – who I'd once seen practically crush his boyfriend against an alley wall with the force of his passion – methodically, meticulously catalogue my body to work out what got me off. I'd let him take pity on the poor, sad sex-deprived single mother he'd befriended – no, adopted, like a stray cat – and selflessly slide his hand up her skirt in a gallant act of service so he could give her one second of pleasure in her otherwise miserable existence.

Dots started swimming in front of my eyes, the same way they had in the mediation meeting. I had to get out of here before I died of embarrassment.

I managed to put my underwear back on, but my pantyhose laddered almost instantly. I stuffed them into my handbag with shaking hands.

They weren't the only thing that was shaking. My whole body was trembling violently, worse than it had been when he'd traced circles around my clit. I could barely stand, but I had to go, *I had to go*, I had to hold it together long enough to get out of here before he came back and smiled at me with eyes full of well-meaning kindly compassion and said something like, *Now, where were we?*

'Got to run!' I announced as I almost sprinted past the tables, Satoshi and Charlotte's faces a blur behind the bar (oh fuck, *Charlotte,* what had she heard?). 'Thanks so much for tonight – I really appreciate it!'

'Fiona—' Satoshi began.

But I was already out the door – and I didn't know how I could ever go back inside again.

Chapter Four
Satoshi

Tasting today: 2019 Etna rosso, Mount Etna, Italy. Made from nerello grapes grown in volcanic soil, this light red wine can be explosive on the palate. Drinking well now, but its peak is still to come.

'This isn't what I ordered,' the woman said as I set the Aperol spritz down in front of her. 'I wanted green tea.'

I blinked. Of course. The spritz was for the women at the table near the classics shelf – and there should have been three of them, not just one. 'My apologies. I'll sort this out for you right away.'

She didn't seem particularly offended, but of course, Isamu chose that moment to walk in. 'Problem?' he asked, joining me behind the bar.

'No.' I kept my tone casual as I started making two more spritzes. 'Just a mix-up. I assume you went back to the vineyard last night? My couch was un-slept-upon. Yquem was despairing.'

He ignored the bait. 'I can finish this up for you, if you want to go and take a breather.'

'No need.' Given this was the third order I'd confused in as many hours, I really should take him up on it, but 1) there was no way I was opening the door to another 'you can't do *everything,*

Sato' lecture, and 2) the idea of stopping even for a second made me feel nauseous. If I stopped, I'd start to think, and then mixing up orders would be the least of my worries. 'It's under control.'

I delivered the spritzes, then made the green tea. 'Sorry for the delay,' I said, setting it down in front of the customer. 'I've given you some extra wagashi to make up for it.'

My mind started to wander as she asked me questions about the wagashi, my mouth automatically supplying the answers. Fiona's daughters loved the traditional sweets we served with green tea, and I'd sent her home with boxes of what I'd told her were leftovers many times. Could I use that as an excuse to turn up on her doorstep so I could apologise to her?

The customer was looking at me expectantly. 'What was that, sorry?'

'Do you have your sweetmaker's card? If these taste as good as they look, I'd love to get my hands on more.'

'Of course. I'll just grab it for you.'

Isamu was opening a bottle of Bibliophile syrah behind the bar. 'Go upstairs, Sato.'

'I'm fine.'

He fixed me with a penetrating stare, the kind that was impossible to respond to without sounding petulant. 'There's no point staging if you're not in the right headspace. Go upstairs, go over your supplies, and take some deep breaths.'

I gritted my teeth. Much as I was loath to give him ammunition, he wasn't wrong. I'd get nothing useful out of the shift I was working tonight at Abode, the fine-dining restaurant my study buddy Carlton worked at, if my head wasn't in the game.

'The woman at Table Four wants Noriko's card,' I said. 'Do you need me to give it to her?'

'I can do it.' Their divorce might still be an actively bleeding wound for him, but there still wasn't a flicker on Isamu's face at the mention of his ex-wife. He nodded his head towards the back. 'Go.'

Much as I truly, *truly* hated being ordered around by my brother, I went.

Yquem was in an affectionate mood today, leaping at me the second I walked in the door. 'I love you too,' I told her, as she nuzzled her golden head under my chin.

I'd nearly slipped and said that to Fiona last night. I'd found that tiny sliver of an opportunity, that window just cracked in a house that had hitherto been locked, and I'd tried to jimmy it open. *Because I like you,* I'd only barely managed to say when she'd asked me why I wanted to sleep with her, a pale shadow of what I really meant.

Not that me biting back *I love you* had mattered. I'd clearly come on way too strong anyway. The second she'd had a chance to think about what she was letting me do to her, she'd fled as fast as her feet would carry her.

I groaned. Yquem mewed in response.

It wasn't that Fiona hadn't been into it. She clearly had. But just because she'd been into it didn't mean she was *ready* for it, and yet I'd let things escalate so fast from kissing to her riding my fingers, and—

I groaned again. The only part of that my cock had listened to was the bit about her riding my fingers.

I let myself think about it in the shower, wrapping my fist around my erection and stroking. What might have happened next, if Charlotte hadn't knocked at the door?

Fiona would have come again, clenching tight around my fingers. I would have licked them clean. She would have turned pink, squeezed her eyes shut, but, *Look at me,* I would have told her, and I would have made her watch.

Or maybe I would have held out my fingers to her, made her take them into her mouth instead. *See how good you taste,* I would have told her, and she would have turned even pinker.

But then she would have grinned, that spark of mischief catching in her eyes. I would have let her unbutton my waistcoat – my shirt – my pants – and I would barely be able to control myself when she finally took me in her hand. She would laugh as she stroked me, that champagne laugh bubbling over at the hungry sounds I couldn't stop myself from making, and then she'd wrap her legs around my hips, and I would slide against her for a moment before I slid into her, and . . .

I didn't come as quickly as she had the night before, but I wasn't far behind.

Yquem was still demanding affection when I came out of the bathroom, but I had to deny her, lest I get cat hair all over me. 'I'm sorry, princess,' I told her, doing up my tie, shrugging on the jacket of the charcoal three-piece suit I only wore to formal trade events, and attaching just one pin – my Advanced Sommelier pin, the highest qual I currently held – to the lapel. 'I'd much rather stay here and snuggle with you.'

I selected a pair of black-framed glasses, the most conservative pair I owned, combed product through my hair, then checked my carrying case of somm supplies. The restaurant would supply most of the things I needed, like decanters and service cloths, but I liked to make sure I had my own stock of the small things, like my favourite wine knife and ah-so, as well as pens, candles and matches.

It was calming, going through my supplies and making sure everything was in order. I let out a long breath and did not let myself think about Fiona, my hand around the nape of her neck holding her upright, the sounds she'd made when my fingers were between her legs.

Later. I would think about it later, at great length, and I would agonise over all the things I had done wrong. For tonight, though, I had to put it out of my mind. If I was going to have any chance of becoming an MS, then surely the first thing I had to demonstrate was my capacity to be a fucking professional.

Fiona wasn't the first person I saw when I walked onto the floor at Abode for service. It was her daughter Rosie who shrieked 'Satoshi!' at a pitch so high it was amazing it didn't shatter half the glasses as she came cannonballing into my legs.

She wasn't the second person either. That was her other daughter Georgia, who did the same thing half a second later.

She was, however, the third. Her cheeks were flushed red – a sight I'd relished the night before – but her face was a mask of horror, an expression that made me want to turn on my heel, walk into the kitchen, and stab the largest knife I could find directly into my heart.

'Well, hello, ladies.' I crouched down to the twins' level. If I was looking at them, then I didn't have to see the way Fiona was looking at me. 'What brings you here tonight?'

'Auntie Chess is taking us out for an *elegant* dinner party!' Georgia announced.

'These are our prettiest dresses.' Rosie gestured to their matching purple Peter Pan-collar dresses, speckled with a white daisy pattern. 'Do you think they're *elegant*?'

I pretended to consider it. 'Hmmm . . . yes, it's official. You're the most elegant ladies in the whole restaurant.'

'Girls!' Fiona called. 'Leave Satoshi alone.'

I dared another glance at her. The red had drained from her cheeks, and it had taken every other colour along with it. I was reminded immediately of how she'd looked when she'd stumbled into the bar the night Matt had left, and had to swallow down a wave of nausea.

I followed the girls back to their table, because fleeing wasn't an option. 'Lovely to see you all.' I reached deep to find my customer service smile. 'Welcome to Abode. I'll be your sommelier this evening.'

They were a table of seven: Fiona, her kids, Jonah and Sadie, and Sadie's sister Chess. 'Lovely to see you too, Satoshi,' Sadie said. 'But what are you doing here? Surely you've got enough to do at Tsundoku without moonlighting.'

I made myself chuckle. 'You're not wrong. But one of the components of the Master Sommelier exam is service. Tsundoku is more casual than this environment, so the owner was kind enough to let me make a one-night-only guest appearance so I can practise some more formal elements.' I presented the wine list to Chess, making sure I was standing on her right side as per Court of Master Sommeliers protocol. If she was paying, she was the host. 'Feel free to ask me as many questions as you want. I'm happy to make recommendations.'

'Thanks.' Chess studied the list. 'The adults are going to do the tasting menu. Can we do matched wines?'

'Chessie, that's so expensive,' Sadie protested. 'You don't have to.'

'I want to. Besides, we're celebrating. Would the first course work with a sparkling?'

I let my eyes flicker to Fiona again. She was staring determinedly at her silverware, tension radiating from every line of her body.

'Yes, a sparkling would be a wonderful pairing,' I said. 'There's nothing more celebratory than champagne. They have an excellent 2018 Grand Cru one here from a small Épernay grower that I'd highly recommend: an elegant expression of a classic style.'

'Like us!' Rosie exclaimed. 'Elegant!'

'Very elegant, just like you, Miss Rosie. But it's also a bit pricey, so if you'd prefer I suggest something else—'

'No need,' Chess said. 'We'll take the champagne.'

Fiona hadn't looked at me once. It felt like someone had uncoiled my intestines, tied several knots in them, and then stuffed them back into my body. 'Champagne it is.' My cheeks ached from smiling. 'I'll be back with that momentarily.'

It was a struggle to keep my breathing even as I found a bottle of the champagne in the cellar. I hadn't had a full-blown panic attack in years, but I had to lean heavily against the wall and stand still for a few moments until my head stopped spinning and my heart stopped feeling like it was about to explode out of my chest.

There was nothing I could do to fix what I'd fucked up with Fiona. Not here, not tonight, not until I could get her on her own and talk to her. For now, I just had to get through this evening, one excruciating step at a time.

I took another deep breath and started loading up my guéridon, the little cart somms used for at-table wine presentation. The champagne. An ice bucket, to keep it at the right service temperature. Glassware – I served sparkling in pinot noir glasses at Tsundoku because I thought it showed the fruit better, but for a restaurant this formal, tulips were more appropriate. Service cloths. An underliner for the cork.

I thought for a moment, took down another bottle and added a second ice bucket, took a final deep breath, and pushed my guéridon back out to the table. '2018 Grand Cru champagne,' I said, presenting the bottle to Chess.

'Wonderful,' she replied.

I did not let my eyes wander to Fiona as I placed the glasses on the table. I did not let myself think of her as I went through the familiar ritual of opening sparkling wine: two swipes of my wine knife to cut the foil, six twists to loosen the wire cage, thumb over the top of the cork as I held the bottle at a forty-five degree angle, opening it silently. I placed the cork on the underliner and set it on the table before I poured a splash into Chess's glass. 'For you to try.'

She tasted it. 'Oh yes, that's excellent. Thank you.'

'You're very welcome.' Court rules of service dictated that ladies be served first, gentlemen second, and the host last, so I began by filling Sadie's glass. 'Every region has its bad wines, of course, but it's difficult to go wrong with champagne.'

I had to move to Fiona's right shoulder so I could fill her glass. It gave me a view of her lap, where she had her fingers twined so tightly together her knuckles had gone white. I had a very steady hand, but that was almost enough to make it waver.

'I've poured a few champagnes for you before, Fiona,' I said casually, because if I didn't say something – anything – to break this tension, I might die. 'Any stand out in your memory?'

'Oh. Um . . .'

I had to move around the table to fill Jonah's glass. I could no longer see Fiona's hands, but I could see her pale, drawn face, which was worse.

'You – um – maybe this is a bit of a basic opinion, but you poured a pink champagne for me a couple of years ago that I still think about sometimes,' she said. 'It was lovely.'

I remembered that day. It had been late afternoon, the sun sinking behind the mountain, and she'd brought Lex in to browse the bookshelves. Lex had asked me if I could answer a question for them about their French homework, and we'd ended up chatting for about half an hour as I explained a few grammatical points and helped them find a pronoun they'd be comfortable with. About ten minutes in, when it had become clear that Lex and I would be there for a while, I'd poured Fiona a glass of a rosé champagne I'd just got in and told her it was my payment for the very interesting conversation her firstborn and I were having.

'That is a lovely one,' I agreed, filling Chess's glass. 'Unfortunately, everyone else thought the same, because the price rocketed up. If I can ever afford to stock it again, it'll be going straight back on my list.'

I put the champagne bottle in the ice bucket, tucking a service cloth around the neck. 'Speaking of pink,' I said, 'elegant ladies, does this meet your approval?'

I took a bottle of pink lemonade from the second ice bucket and presented it to the twins. 'Yes!' Georgia exclaimed, clapping her hands.

'Fantastic.' I set glasses down in front of the three kids. 'Lex, I'm pretty confident your sisters will like this, but if it's not to your taste, let me know, and I'll get you something else. My job tonight is making sure you have the best beverage experience of your life, so don't be afraid to tell me if you want something different.'

Lex tried the splash I'd poured for them. 'This is nice. Thanks, Satoshi.'

'You're very welcome.'

One of the waiters came to the table with the first course as I nestled the bottle of pink lemonade back into the ice bucket. I took the opportunity to disappear, even though some deep, animal instinct in me screamed that I should stay – smile, chat, show Fiona that nothing had changed, that everything was fine, that we could completely forget it had ever happened if she wanted to, although if she wanted to do it again, then—

No. Not now. Not here.

I did my best to focus on service, making myself pay close attention to what each table was asking and what their ideal wine pairing would be, but it was impossible not to let my eyes wander sometimes. Sadie and Chess were having a spirited conversation, both laughing, and Jonah was doing the same with the kids, but on Fiona's face was a faint, forced smile.

She was sipping her champagne slowly. I watched her covertly from the corner during a pause, unable to tear my eyes away from the movement of her throat as she swallowed. She was wearing a dark green dress tonight – one I'd seen her wear before and always thought she looked nice in – but now I knew what her breasts felt like in my hands, it was difficult not to look at the hint of cleavage rising out of her neckline, to imagine tracing a line across it with the pad of my finger, and . . .

'Satoshi, I think Table Twenty-Two is trying to catch your attention,' one of the waiters said as they passed me on their way to the kitchen.

I made myself smile and nod.

By the time I'd served Table Twenty-Two (and had to work hard to come up with a pairing for them, given they wanted a structured white wine with notes of vanilla but were insistent they hated anything that had even glimpsed oak), Fiona's table was done with their first course. 'How did you enjoy that?' I asked the girls, topping up their glasses.

'It was delicious!' Georgia replied.

'Ah, but was it elegant?'

They both giggled. 'Satoshi, you should use two hands when you're pouring,' Rosie told me seriously. 'Otherwise, you'll spill it all over the floor. That's what Mummy says.'

'Mummy's completely correct.' I wrapped the fingers of my left hand exaggeratedly around the neck of the lemonade bottle as I topped up Lex's glass. 'I should be much more careful. Thank you for reminding me.'

I allowed myself a brief glance at Fiona. Her face was still pale, but she met my gaze. *Thank you*, she mouthed.

I winked back. She immediately looked down at her lap.

'Would you like a recommendation for the next course?' I asked Chess as I moved around the table refilling the champagne glasses, trying my best not to show how much that reaction had stung.

'Actually, Chessie, before you order another bottle,' Sadie said, 'can we make an announcement?'

'I'll come back when you're ready.' I put the empty bottle back in the ice bucket.

'No, no, stay. We'd like you to hear this too, Satoshi. We have a favour to ask, if you don't mind.' Sadie glanced at Jonah. 'Do you want to tell them or should I?'

Jonah looked back at her. He had his arm around her, thumb lightly stroking the bare skin of her upper arm, the adoration in his eyes obvious. 'We're getting married,' he said.

'I thought you were already married,' Georgia said. 'Mummy showed us pictures.'

'We are.' Jonah tore his gaze away from his wife. 'But we had to get married very fast, and that meant hardly any of our favourite people got to be there. Auntie Chess wasn't there. Mummy wasn't there. Lex wasn't there. And you know what we didn't have any of?'

Rosie gasped. 'Flower girls?'

'Absolutely zero flower girls,' Sadie said. 'And is it even really a wedding if there are no flower girls?'

The high-pitched shriek both twins emitted was so loud that several other tables looked over. 'Shhh, girly-pops,' Fiona said. 'I know you're excited, but remember – elegant.'

She looked up at me. *Sorry*, she mouthed.

I shook my head. *It's fine.*

She didn't look away this time. Neither did I. I could feel the pulse of my heart in my ears. Pink roses started to bloom in her cheeks.

'. . . our anniversary in February,' Jonah was saying.

'We were thinking maybe we could have the ceremony out at your vineyard, Satoshi,' Sadie added. 'If that's okay with you and Isamu?'

'I'll have to check – the vineyard is his territory – but I'm sure that'll be fine.' Dragging my attention away from Fiona felt like dragging a ten-tonne plough. 'Perhaps you could come into

Tsundoku this week and we can sort out the details?'

'I think we can manage that,' Sadie said, but she wasn't looking at me. She and Jonah were gazing at each other again, two human versions of the heart-eyes emoji.

Chess, leaning back in her chair, had an inscrutably neutral expression, but Fiona swallowed reflexively, then – in a move I recognised all too well – pasted a smile onto her face. 'I'm so happy for you.'

'Thanks, Fi.' Jonah turned to hug her. 'I want you to be my best man, by the way. Elias had his turn last time.'

Fiona's laughter was forced. 'I'll do my best.'

'And obviously I want you to be my maid of honour,' Sadie said to Chess.

'But we're the flower girls?' Rosie asked anxiously.

'Yes, you're the flower girls,' Jonah reassured her. 'Lex, how would you feel about being the ringbearer?'

Lex thought about it. 'Okay,' they said, and Jonah reached across the table so they could bump knuckles.

'I think we'll need another bottle of wine,' Chess said to me, 'so we can toast. Run me through your recommendations?'

'Excuse me for a second,' Fiona said quietly, getting up from the table. 'I'll be right back.'

Everything in me was screaming to sprint after her. I curled my toes inside my dress shoes, trying to keep myself rooted to the ground. 'There are a few ways you could go. The next dish is roast chicken, so I'd suggest a medium-bodied white that'll stand up to it without overpowering it. There's a lovely 2021 Rhône Valley marsanne that would work well; or a 2022 Yarra Valley skin-contact pinot gris if you're feeling a bit more adventurous; or you could even try—' I tried to swallow the dryness in my throat down '—an arneis.'

Of course Chess picked the arneis.

Fiona still hadn't returned to the table as I wheeled my guéridon away. The twins were chaotically excited about the prospect of being flower girls, and the happy couple weren't helping matters much by enthusiastically discussing it with them, so I reordered the mental drinks map I'd created for the kids in my mind. I'd been planning a series of different coloured lemonades, but maybe I'd switch to a flavoured mineral water for the next course. The family had come out to the vineyard in June for Sadie's birthday, and I'd seen what the twins were like on a sugar high.

Abode's wine cellar was around a corner at the end of a long corridor, past the doors to the bathrooms. I was halfway along it, trying to decide whether a citrus mineral water was the best bet or whether I should go for something with more tropical fruit flavours, when the door to the women's bathroom swung open and I almost ran over Fiona's toes.

'I'm so sorry!' she exclaimed. 'Shit, shit, shit!'

'Hey, hey, it's fine.' The ice buckets had wobbled, but the only damage was a few drops of water. 'You're fine. Everything's fine – have you been crying?'

'No.' She sniffed.

'Fiona.'

'Not much.' She sniffled again. 'Is it that obvious?'

'Your eyes are a bit pink. The lighting out there is dimmer, though, no one will be able to tell. What's wrong?'

She shook her head.

'Is it—' I hesitated. 'Is it me?'

'No!' Her face flooded with colour – the way she could go from pale to red in the blink of an eye was astonishing – but her voice was firm. 'I promise, it's not you. I'm . . . god, I'm so embarrassed, but I'm not crying about you.'

'Why are you embarrassed?'

She gave me a look that wasn't quite a glare but was definitely on its way.

'Let's try an easier question. Why are you crying?'

'That answer might be even more embarrassing.'

'Try me.'

Fiona let out a long breath. 'Jonah and Sadie,' she said. 'I'm so happy for them, and I love them so much – but god, I'm so fucking jealous.'

She tipped her head back, sniffing again. 'I thought I had that. For so long, I was such a smug married lady – but what I actually was, was stupid. And it's so *obvious*. When I see the way Jonah and Sadie look at each other – Matt never looked at me like that, not once, and . . .'

'Fiona, come here.'

I held out my hand to her. She hesitated for a moment, before letting me tug her into my embrace.

Something unknotted in me as I put my arms around her, hers snaking around my waist. Her forehead came to rest in the crook of my neck, and I turned my head so I could rest my cheek against her hair. I didn't dare let my hands travel the way I wanted to, but I rubbed slow circles on her back, just above her shoulder blades.

'You're not stupid,' I murmured. 'Matt's stupid. He's the stupidest motherfucker on the planet. But not you. Never you.'

She made a strangled sound, one that might be her choking back a laugh or trying not to cry. 'Thank you for saying that.'

'I'm not just saying it.' I drew back, putting my hands on her shoulders so I could look her in the eye. 'It's the truth. There's nothing stupid about believing someone when they tell you they love you. There is, however, something very stupid about having a wonderful wife and cheating on her repeatedly.'

This sound was strangled too, but it was recognisably a laugh this time. 'You always make me feel better, Satoshi.' She offered me a smile – shy, but genuine, a proper Fiona smile, not a pale facsimile. 'Thank you.'

'My pleasure.'

'Of course, you don't need to go to the lengths you went to yesterday – that was asking way too much of you! – but I appreciate it so much. You always do so much for me, and you never complain, and—'

'Hold on.'

She stopped.

'Back up,' I told her. 'Say that again.'

Her cheeks were starting to colour again. 'Which part?'

'The part about how you asked too much of me.'

Pink blossomed into red as she looked at the floor. 'You know what I'm talking about. I make one sexually frustrated comment too many, and then you have your hand up my skirt like – like a – like a mechanic, trying to sort me out.'

'Mechanic?!'

'You know what I mean.' She made a frustrated gesture. 'You – you're always so kind, Satoshi, so generous, even when there's nothing in it for you, and – *oh*.'

Her body collided with the wall as I backed her swiftly against it. I twined the fingers of my left hand through her right and drew it up, up, up, until it was pressed above her head.

'You think I got nothing out of it?' I asked.

'I thought . . . I thought you might just feel sorry for me.'

I wrapped my other hand around her waist and pulled her into me, letting her feel my hardening cock against her belly. Her intake of breath was sharp and swift, and when I tightened my hand again, it turned into one of those hungry, needy whimpers that had set my heart pounding when I'd had her on my desk yesterday. 'Does this feel like I feel sorry for you, Fiona?'

Her head fell back against the wall as I grazed my teeth against the spot behind her ear, the one that had made her leap about twelve feet into the air when I'd discovered it. 'Oh,' she sighed, fingers clenching tight around mine. 'Oh, Satoshi, oh my god, oh – *oh my god stop stop stop.*'

I released her immediately. Sadie was standing at the other end of the corridor, expression somewhere between agape and a grin. 'I was coming to see if you were all right,' she said to Fiona. 'You – well, you seem to be just fine.'

I turned swiftly so Sadie wouldn't see my extremely unprofessional erection. 'We'll talk later, all right?'

Fiona nodded, the movement so short and sharp it looked like her teeth were chattering.

I couldn't resist reaching out and squeezing her fingers in mine, just once. 'You're not asking anything of me,' I told her quietly, 'that I don't want to give you.'

I had to stand in the cellar for a long time until I was composed enough to go back onto the restaurant floor. When I finally emerged with the arneis, I didn't allow myself even a single glance at Fiona. I was teetering on the edge of something, and she'd only have to use one finger to push me over.

A while later, though, when I came out with their red wine, an Etna rosso, our eyes met.

I'd lit a candle on my guéridon so I could decant the wine over it and see when the sediment began to flow. You were never supposed to look away from the bottle while you were decanting, but Fiona was directly in my line of sight, just beyond the flickering light of the flame, and I only had so much strength.

She smiled at me. Just a little, just the gentlest curve of the corners of her mouth, but she smiled, and relief washed over me.

And for the first time in many years, despite having decanted more bottles of wine than most people would ever lay eyes on, I spilled a few drops.

Chapter Five

Fiona

Tasting today: pink lemonade, served to your children in beautiful glasses.
A drink that will melt your teeth, but maybe also your heart.

'Rosie, please slow down,' I said, phone jammed between my ear and my shoulder as I slid a piece of toast onto her plate. 'You're going to make yourself—'

'—sick if I eat too fast, I know!' Rosie kept shovelling scrambled eggs into her mouth as I put the other piece of toast on Georgia's plate and craned my head to look down the corridor for her.

'—sue for back payment!' Dad was saying on the other end of the phone.

'Kavita said we can explore that option. But we need to get the divorce finalised first, or – Georgia, don't run, please! – it could lead to a renegotiation of – Georgia! – Sorry, Dad.'

'I'm not looking for my money back here.' If my dad had one superpower, it was being able to carry on a conversation by himself. 'No grandchild of mine will ever go without. But it's the principle of the thing, Fiona.'

'I'm doing my best,' I said tightly.

He grunted. I flicked the kettle on. He was clearly about to launch into a monologue about my inadequacies, and I needed the fortification of a cup of tea.

But, 'Your mother wants to talk to you,' was all he said. 'Here she is.'

My mum already knew all the details, but I had to relive them for her anyway, taking my tea out into the backyard so I could watch the girls through the kitchen window without them overhearing all about how their father was a scumbag. 'What an awful, awful man,' Mum said. 'Rubbing that woman in your face like that – sickening.'

'Yeah, it was.' I shifted the phone to my other ear. 'But it was bound to happen sometime. At least it wasn't in front of the kids.'

'Still.' She made a tutting sound. 'I hope you're doing something for yourself, Fiona.'

'What?'

'Something for yourself,' she repeated. 'You've been so laser-focused on holding things together for the kids. You need to make sure you're doing things for yourself too.'

For a moment, I was back in the restaurant corridor, Satoshi grinding his hips into me. My face heated.

'I'm going to send you a gift voucher,' Mum said. 'For a night in a nice hotel. Jonah can take the kids and you can have a self-care evening.'

'You don't need to do that.'

'I want to.' My mother was by far the least assertive member of the Fisher family, but her tone made it clear that this was the end of the discussion. 'I know it's just a little thing, but sometimes little things can go a long way.'

She wasn't wrong. I was already a long, *long* way ahead, in a world where Satoshi was in that hotel room with me, throwing me onto the bed and making me forget everything, and . . .

'Thanks, Mum.' I rubbed my hand against the fluttery feeling in my abdomen. 'That's nice of you.'

'Mummy, you're all red,' Rosie said, when I re-entered the house. 'Did you get sunburned in the backyard?'

'I'm just a bit hot.' I fanned myself.

'But it's not hot,' Georgia said.

'I was walking up and down while I talked to Grandma.' I thought there were no new depths of embarrassment for me to plumb, but if my eight-year-old daughters somehow managed to intuit that I was having explicit sexual fantasies about the nice young man who ran the bar . . .

It had just been so *sexy*, though. The feeling of his fingers against my waist – the other ones twined tight through mine as he pushed my hand over my head – the press of him against me – it had just been so – so – so—

So much. It had been so fucking *much*, making me feel like the tightly-wound cords holding me together might come swiftly unravelling, and I might shatter into a million little pieces.

My phone buzzed with a text. It was Jonah. *Heading to the farmers' market. Do the girls want to come on a little adventure?*

The girls were indeed keen on a little adventure, and I'd just finished braiding Georgia's hair when Jonah arrived on my doorstep. 'Do you want to – Rosie, no, your jumper's fine, it's just the farmers' market, you don't need to be elegant – take my car?' I asked. 'That'll be easier than trying to manage the girls on the bus – Oh, hi, Sadie.'

'Hi, Fiona.' Sadie leaned in to hug me, a twinkle in her eye. 'I brought you a coffee and some croissants. Chess went back to Sydney this morning, so I thought you and I could have breakfast while Jonah and the girls are at the market.'

Fuck. 'Sure,' I said, so brightly it must sound completely fake. 'That sounds lovely. Girly-pops, be good for Uncle Jonah, okay?'

'We're always good for Uncle Jonah.' Rosie took his hand. 'And we know the rules. No running where he can't see us, and—'

'—definitely no running into the road,' Georgia finished.

'Good. Don't get so excited you forget, all right?' I bent down to hug them. 'I love you.'

'Lex, do you want to come too?' Jonah took my proffered keys. 'There's room in the car.'

They shook their head. 'Can I have a croissant?'

'Sure,' Sadie replied. 'There's plenty.'

Like a coward, I hoped Lex's presence would get me out of having this conversation, but no such luck. The instant they had a croissant in hand, they disappeared into their room, leaving me alone with my very lovely, very clever, very much grinning-at-me-knowingly sister-in-law.

'How about we sit outside?' I suggested. If we had to have this conversation, I didn't want Lex to overhear. I wasn't at all sure how they'd react to the idea of their queer hero hooking up with their mother.

The memory of it made my face heat up again as Sadie and I made our way out onto my front porch. The firm, slippery pressure of Satoshi's fingers inside me as he crooked them, stroking. The way I would have come again so fast and so violently if Charlotte hadn't knocked at the door. How I would have slid off the desk and onto my knees the second I recovered the capacity for thought and motion, how once I got my mouth on him any question of him doing this solely out of a misplaced sense of charity would be completely obliterated, and—

Sadie started laughing. 'Your *face*, Fiona.'

I covered it with my hands. 'Stop.'

'You and Jonah are exactly the same. You both go red so fast when you're embarrassed.'

'I'm not embarrassed.'

I was, obviously, but not the way she meant. Nice suburban mothers were not supposed to have vivid sexual fantasies about younger men while having nice suburban conversations with their sisters-in-law. My face was so hot against my fingers it felt like I might burn myself.

'Good, because you shouldn't be.' Sadie took one of the coffees out of the cardboard holder and set it down in front of me. 'If anyone in the world deserves some fun, it's you.'

Fun wasn't the right word to describe it. It had felt very, very serious when Satoshi had backed me into the wall, intense in a way that I hadn't felt since . . .

I swallowed. Nothing had felt even remotely like that since Matt Sinclair had taken twenty-one-year-old Fiona Fisher home with him, fastened his hand around her wrist, and told her she wasn't going anywhere.

'We don't have to talk about it.' Sadie tore off a corner of her croissant. 'Not if you don't want to. But we're friends, right?'

'Of course.'

'So you can talk to me. And I won't tell Jonah. Not that I think he'd be particularly keen on hearing about his sister's sex life, but if that's something you're worried about, I can keep my mouth shut.'

'There's not much to talk about.' I tore a corner off my own croissant, the words *sex life* sitting awkwardly in my stomach in a way I couldn't quite identify. 'It's . . . I don't know what it is, to be honest. It's . . . new.'

'Have you had sex?'

I started to shake my head, then stopped. 'Depends how you define it, I guess.'

Sadie raised her eyebrows.

After a moment, I sighed. 'Fingers.'

Her grin deepened. I had to bury my face in my hands again.

'Come on, Fiona, there's no need to be embarrassed,' she said. 'Was it good?'

'I think I saw the face of God,' I moaned.

'Even less reason to be embarrassed! I love this for you.'

I looked at her from between my fingers.

'Seriously,' Sadie said. 'After all the shit you've been through, you deserve to see the face of God. And Satoshi's such a sweetheart. If there's one person in the world you could trust to look after you, it's him.'

'I thought that about Matt.'

The words were out of my mouth before I was even conscious of saying them. Slowly, Sadie's grin melted away.

'Not that the situations are even remotely the same.' I picked up the piece of croissant I'd dropped, tearing it into even smaller pieces. 'Satoshi and me could never be anything . . . you know, serious. And it's not like I think he'd ever set out to hurt me – not on purpose, anyway – but . . .'

My voice trailed off. I wasn't even sure of what I was trying to say.

'Trust is hard,' Sadie said. 'Especially when you've been burned.'

I nodded.

'But I think you're underselling it,' she said. 'What the two of you could be.'

I snorted. 'You know I'm eight years older than him, right?'

'So?' She popped a piece of croissant into her mouth. 'You're both adults.'

'Adults who are at completely different stages of their lives, though. I have three kids. He works about eight hundred and forty-seven hours a week. And he's – Satoshi.'

'Exactly. He's Satoshi. You know him. Your kids love him. And sure, he works a lot, but wasn't Matt always at work?'

I bit back my immediate thought – that at least I could trust Satoshi to actually *be* at work when he said he was – and picked up my phone instead. 'Let me show you something.'

I opened up Tsundoku's Instagram and scrolled back through a few years' worth of beautifully curated photos. 'Here.'

'What am I looking at?' Sadie took my phone. 'Who's this? Satoshi, obviously, but who's the other guy?'

'Kieran. His ex. That's the kind of person he usually goes for.'

'Men?'

'No! I mean, yes, sometimes, he's pansexual, but – look at how hot he is!'

I'd only encountered Kieran a few times, but even setting aside the time I'd seen him going at it with Satoshi in the alley, he was hard to forget. He worked at the day spa across the street from Tsundoku, and he was one of the most ethereally good-looking people I'd ever laid eyes on. He and Satoshi together had reminded me of elves from *Lord of the Rings*: tall, blond, willowy, effortlessly charming.

'And you, famously,' Sadie said dryly, putting my phone down, 'are a troll who lives under a bridge?'

'No. But that doesn't mean I can compete.'

'You don't need to. They're exes. Competition concluded.'

'Yes, but . . .' I'd reduced my piece of croissant to crumbs, so I tore off another one. 'It's less about the specific person, and more about the genre. You don't go from a ripped young massage therapist to a thirty-something single mother who isn't even properly divorced yet.'

'Sounds like he did, though.'

I looked at her. Sadie waggled her fingers at me. I squeezed my eyes shut and made a noise of pained protest.

She chuckled. 'Seriously, though,' she said. 'You like Satoshi – and no matter how hot his ex is, Satoshi obviously likes you. I know your marriage left you with a ton of shit to deal with and I don't want to minimise that, but you're never going to have a softer landing place than with him. What have you got to lose?'

A million different images went racing through my head.

Satoshi against me, behind me, below me, above me, pressing *me* up against the wall in the alley this time. Satoshi moving inside me, his breath hot and hungry behind my ear, fingers laced tight through mine. Satoshi holding me close after, laughing at the ridiculous things that came out of my mouth as he stroked my hair, pouring me a post-coital drink.

Me loving it.

Me trusting it.

Me starting to believe I could keep it.

Someone from school spotting us. The WhatsApp groups catching alight. *Did you hear Fiona's fucking a bartender who's barely out of high school? She really is having a nervous breakdown, poor thing.*

Satoshi meeting some new beautiful person like Kieran and doing his best to let me down easy. *This has been fun, Fiona, but I think it's run its course, don't you?*

Me losing everything I had left, all at once: the only place Matt hadn't taken from me; Lex's hero; and the person who had somehow become my best, truest friend.

And everyone seeing it happen all over again – Fiona Fisher smashed to pieces. *Poor Fi,* Jonah would murmur to Sadie in the dead of night, two true, equal partners, curled up in bed together. *I love her, obviously, but god, she makes some fucking terrible choices.*

'I can see you overthinking it,' Sadie said. 'What if you simply didn't do that?'

My laugh was so short and sharp it sounded almost like a bark. 'Too late.'

'Look.' She sipped her coffee. 'Let's come at it from another angle. You've already – let me find the right metaphor . . . you've already popped the cork, right? The genie is out of the bottle. You've already seen the face of God once. So, you've got two options. You live the rest of your life knowing that he could show you the face of God again, but you deny yourself; or you say *fuck it* and get railed.' She paused. 'Not that I've ever thought of Satoshi as the railing type.'

'I think he is,' I admitted. 'He hides it well, but he can be quite, um . . . authoritative.'

Sadie grinned. 'So the nice boy with the silly glasses has a dominant streak. Well, well, well.'

For what felt like the thousandth time, I felt the blood rushing to my cheeks. 'Can we please change the subject?'

I'd managed to get her talking about the plans for the wedding – and she'd only suggested that Satoshi be my date about four hundred times – when Jonah pulled the car into the driveway. 'We can talk more about the Satoshi thing later,' Sadie said. 'Or not. It's up to you. But I'm here, Fiona. If you need me, I'm just a text or a phone call away.'

'I know,' I said. 'Thank you.'

Jonah turned off the engine, then jumped out to open the door for Rosie and Georgia. 'Fi, we need to have a chat,' he called. 'Something happened at the—'

The rest of the sentence was drowned out by the girls exploding out of the car. 'Mummy, guess who we saw at the markets?!' Georgia exclaimed.

Even if Rosie had left me a nanosecond to guess before joyfully screaming out the answer, I wouldn't have needed it. My stomach fell out of my body and plummeted into the depths of hell.

'We saw Daddy!'

🍷

'It was an accident.' Matt's voice was long-suffering on the other end of the phone. 'You think this is how I wanted to see them again?

Five minutes at the farmers' market, with your brother glaring daggers at me?'

'You shouldn't have been there at all.'

I had to hiss instead of doing what I really wanted, which was shout. Lex was reading in their room, the girls were playing in the backyard, and the only worse thing than this happening was them picking up how upset I was about it.

'You don't own the farmers' market, Fiona.'

'You know how small Hobart is! You could have gone back to Melbourne the second mediation was over. But no, you had to stay. You had to—'

'This might be the last time Laura will get to travel before the babies are born. Can you blame me for wanting to make a weekend of it?'

'Don't fucking talk to me about Laura.'

He exhaled. 'Sorry. That wasn't fair.'

Instinctively, I wanted to soften. Matt rarely admitted to being wrong. I had Pavlovian conditioning telling me to reward his concessions, if I ever wanted him to make them again.

I clenched my fist instead. 'You introduced her to them,' I snarled. 'You introduced her to them *without telling me first.*'

'It wasn't like I intended to! But she was standing right next to me. And I just said that she was my friend, nothing else.'

He was telling the truth – Jonah had given me a full rundown – but it didn't quell the fury in my belly. 'I'm sure that won't be confusing for them at all in the long term. Well done, Matt, really.'

'Can you cut me a break here?'

'Are you joking?'

'I know what I've done to you is awful.' There was a conciliatory, almost condescending note in his voice, like he was talking to a skittish horse. 'And I feel terrible about it. I really do.'

'You've showed it so well. This whole year, when I was working myself to the bone and grovelling to my parents for money so

I could keep the kids fed and clothed – I spent the whole time thinking, *Wow, Matt sure does feel terrible about fucking me over.*'

'Come on, Fi. You've got your pound of flesh now. Your lawyers saw to that.'

'*Pound of flesh*?!'

'Bad phrasing. Sorry.' There was a rustling sound, and I knew he was tugging at his collar the way he always did when he got stressed. 'But put yourself in my shoes. This hasn't been easy for me either. I've done my best to make things as clean and clear as possible, so we all know where we stand.'

'If you're waiting for me to thank you for abandoning us,' I said tightly, 'you're going to be waiting a long time.'

'I'm not asking you to. I'm just asking you to acknowledge that things are hard for me too.'

I didn't say anything. My jaw was clenched so hard my teeth were in danger of shattering.

'We need to talk about what things will look like moving forward,' he said. 'Now mediation is done, we can finalise the divorce – and I'd like to talk about seeing the kids.'

I glanced out the kitchen window to make sure Rosie and Georgia were still safely playing in the yard. If they looked back at me, they'd probably see steam coming out of my ears.

'Seeing the girls today – getting to hug them, after all this time – made me realise just how much I've missed them.' Oh *fuck off*, was he about to start crying? 'And what Laura said in the meeting was right. I do want them to meet Micah and Nikki. The babies too. Think of how excited they'll be to be big sisters.'

That ranked somewhere between 'the threat of nuclear war' and 'asking my parents for money' on the list of things I wanted to think about.

'And I want to be able to introduce them to Laura,' he added, 'as their stepmother.'

The word *stepmother* sent me into space. I felt like a dragon, like I might vomit up fire at any moment.

'You don't have to say anything right now.' He was using the skittish horse voice again. 'But you need to start thinking about this, Fi. Now the divorce is on the home stretch, we need to have a serious talk about the long-term.'

'We're not doing shit until I consult with their therapist,' I managed to force out from between my gritted teeth. 'You haven't been in their lives for an entire year. They need to be prepared.'

'Of course. I'd like to be part of that discussion, so we can make the plan together.'

If I had been holding a glass, I would have crushed it in my hand.

'I don't want to hurt them.' Matt's tone turned gentle, and I was reminded, suddenly, of the way he'd talked to me when I was pregnant, wrapping his arms around me from behind, resting his chin on my shoulder, and cooing to my belly. I'd used to cherish those memories, but now they made me want to climb out of my own skin. 'They're my kids too. I love them.'

'You haven't—'

'—done a great job at showing it, I know. I tried so hard to make things clean that I went too far. But I want to fix it.'

'When are you leaving?'

He sighed. 'Tomorrow morning.'

'Good. Stay on the west side of the river until then. We'll stay on the east. You can text me when you're back in Melbourne. I'll let you know what their therapist says.'

'Fi—'

I hung up. If I had to speak to him one second longer, I was going to burst into messy, violent, angry tears.

I didn't remember much of what Matt had said the night he'd told me about Laura – entire stretches of it had blurred into one long, endless scream – but two words had burned themselves into my brain. *Clean break*, he'd dared to say. *I know this is difficult, but I think it's best for everyone if I just leave and we make it a clean break* – as if the fact that their father was choosing his other family over them was like a broken limb that would heal perfectly if we just got the kids in plaster casts soon enough.

Then he'd made it so clean that I hadn't heard a word from him for months. No phone calls picked up, no messages responded to, no emails replied to, no answers at all to very reasonable questions like, *So are you planning to contribute any money at all towards the raising of your children?* or *Are we actually legally married or is our marriage certificate some kind of forgery?* or *How the actual fuck have you kept this going for so long?*

I hadn't been happy with Matt before he'd left. I'd been hungry for something more – a lot more – than what he was giving me. But I hadn't realised just how badly I needed him – just how much I relied on him – until he was gone.

I let out a long breath. Thank god it had been *that* night Birdie dropped all the glasses. Otherwise, Matt would have told me about Laura in the middle of Tsundoku, the way he'd clearly planned to so I couldn't make a scene. No matter how much I loved the place, and no matter how much I adored Satoshi, there would have been no way I could ever go back there then.

Satoshi.

I leaned back against the kitchen bench.

I'd wanted to sink into the ground when we'd run into him at Abode. I hadn't thought I'd ever be able to feel anything but embarrassed in his presence ever again, but something had melted in me when he'd presented that pink lemonade to the kids like it was a bottle of the finest wine.

I wasn't wrong. I was me, he was him, and we could never really *be* anything.

But Sadie wasn't wrong either. There could be no softer place to land than with this kind, generous, patient man.

And what had happened in the restaurant corridor had shown that he was offering to be that landing place not out of charity or pity or compassion, but because – somehow – he wanted to. *You're not asking anything of me,* he'd said, *that I don't want to give you.*

There were things I didn't want to ask. There were things I didn't want to need. I didn't want to rely on anyone, ever again. No one knew better than me the humiliating depths in which relying on someone could land you. I had no desire to hand anyone the hammer they could use to break me.

But as I watched my daughters play, I surrendered to the ever-present, dangerous urge to get ahead of myself, and let myself imagine Satoshi standing here with me. Not some fantasy sex dream version of him, ripping my clothes off and setting me alight, but just Satoshi, my friend Satoshi, here in my kitchen, putting his arms around me and letting me lean back against his chest.

You're safe, he would murmur, breath warm against the shell of my ear. *I've got you.*

Chapter Six
Satoshi

Tasting today: tea-based sparkling alcoholic alternative. This is not wine, nor is it like it. The key to enjoying an artisanal non-alcoholic alternative is not to dream of what you really wish you were drinking – it might be a pale substitute, but try to enjoy it on its own merits.

'Yes, Okāsan, everything's fine,' I said in Japanese, flipping the page of the massive binder of MS theory notes that I had open on the bar. 'Sorry I missed dinner yesterday. I had a cellar appraisal in the afternoon, then study group, and by the time we wrapped up, it was getting too late to come out to the vineyard.'

'You work too hard, Sato,' my mother said on the other end of the phone. 'What is all this work for, if you never take a moment to enjoy your life?'

I resisted the urge to sigh. I had no problem telling my brother to butt out – even if he never listened – but my mother was another matter. 'I'll be there next Monday, I promise. How are things with you? Any guests at the B&B this week?'

Tsundoku was still empty by the time I hung up. Although it usually picked up in the evenings, this wasn't terribly unusual for a Tuesday afternoon, and while it wasn't ideal from a business standpoint, I usually enjoyed it. There was something peaceful about being in the bar when no one else was, sipping something while I sorted out some admin or studied.

On this particular Tuesday afternoon, though, my head was anywhere but in my theory notes. I'd been trying to shovel information about Barolo soil types into my mind for the better part of two days, and none of it had stuck.

Being in love with Fiona Fisher was many things. Some were rapturous. Most were torturous. For the last few days, it had been both – and on top of them, it had been a huge fucking distraction.

You did a great job, Satoshi, Carlton's boss had told me on Friday. *Your wine knowledge is impeccable. Your service skills are top-notch. But there were a few moments, especially as the night went on, when it felt like you weren't really present.*

Thank you, I'd replied. *That's great feedback. I'll work on that.*

I'd only been half-listening. I could still feel Fiona's fingers, twined through mine, pressed above her head.

A good night's sleep hadn't helped. Frankly, a good night's sleep hadn't happened. I'd mixed up more orders over the weekend than in the entire three years Tsundoku had been open. I hadn't been lying to Okāsan about being too busy to come to our regular Monday night family dinner, but I'd left out the part about sitting down to study and getting so distracted by the memory of Fiona smiling at me in the candlelight – flickering like that little flame of hope in my heart – that I didn't realise I'd been staring into space for a full hour until Yquem jumped on me, demanding her dinner.

Outside the front window, it started to rain – a slow drift at first, but then gradually getting heavier. I glanced at the weather app on my phone. It was set to continue well into the night.

I grabbed my umbrella so I could retrieve my A-frame chalkboard from the footpath. People tended to stay home when it rained, which, tonight, was probably a good thing. The last thing

I wanted was to fuck up something so badly it impacted Tsundoku's pristine online reviews.

'Satoshi!'

I blinked. 'Hello, Lex!' I held my umbrella out to shelter them from the rain. 'Fancy seeing you here.'

'You're not closing, are you?' Anxiety was written large in their eyes.

'No, no. I'm just rescuing this—' I hefted up the A-frame with my free hand '—before the rain washes it clean. Are you here by yourself?'

Lex shook their head. 'Mum's parked over there.' They pointed down the road.

My heart had almost disintegrated at the notion that Fiona would rather sit in her car than come into Tsundoku when Lex added, 'Rosie and Georgia are at indoor soccer training, and she's calling their friend's mum to confirm they're going to their place for dinner. She said she'll be in in a minute. Do you have any new books?'

'Do I have any new books? It's like you don't know me at all.' I only just managed to find an appropriately jovial tone as my heart reformed in my chest and started racing. 'Come on in.'

I'd pointed Lex towards the queer YA books I'd planted in the shelves for them, listened to them talk for seven unbroken minutes about the latest one they'd read, and got them set up in a corner with a hot chocolate by the time Fiona finally came in, holding her jacket over her head. 'Oh my goodness, it's pouring!' she said, peeling it off and causing me to feel momentarily faint at the sight of her exposed, damp, slightly flushed collarbone. 'I'm so sorry, Satoshi, I don't mean to drip all over your floor, but I forgot my umbrella, and—'

'It's fine, don't worry!' Did I always sound like this? *Everything is fine, I'll do anything for you, I'll lie down on the ground so you can walk all over me if you'll just let me touch you again.* 'Let me hang that up for you.'

I took her jacket. 'The coat rack's all yours today,' I said with forced casualness. 'You're my only customers. The rain scared everyone else away.'

'Everyone else is clearly more sensible than me.' Fiona plucked at her damp shirt. 'But I promised Lex they could come and look at the books – god, I'm so wet.'

She heard what she'd said before I did. It was only when colour flooded her cheeks that I realised the double entendre.

'Are you?' I hooked the tip of one finger under the elbow-length sleeve of her shirt and tugged at it, just a little.

Fiona's breath caught in her throat.

It was difficult to resist the urge to grin. 'I could help you out with that, if you want.'

Her eyes widened, darting towards Lex.

'I'm sure I've got a spare shirt out the back,' I clarified, in my most professional voice. 'Do you want me to take you back there?'

If she said yes, I would have my hands on her before she could say a single word. I'd close my office door behind us and kiss her hard against it as I hiked her skirt up. Then I'd go to my knees, yank her underwear off, pull one of her legs over my shoulder, and—

'That's probably not a good idea.' Her face had gone the colour of Beaujolais. 'You have to . . . you know, look after things out here.'

She was, unfortunately, right. My evening staff weren't due in for another hour, and no matter how fast I could make Fiona come, there really was no appropriate length of time to leave a twelve-year-old as the sole person in charge of a bar, even if it was completely empty.

'Whatever you want,' I said, trying to keep my voice light. 'Drink?'

Fiona slid onto a barstool as I retreated behind the safety of the bar. 'I shouldn't. I'm driving.'

'There's always tea or coffee. Or I added a few new things to the artisanal non-alco list the other day. You could help me figure out how to talk about them.'

She eyeballed me. 'How do you always make you doing something for me sound like I'm the one doing you a favour?'

'Is that a yes?'

She held my gaze for a long moment before she nodded.

Relief, rich and potent as madeira, washed over me as I took some glasses down from the rack. 'Hey Lex, want to taste test some drinks with me and your mum?'

'Hmmm?' They looked up from their spot in the window.

I repeated the question. Lex shook their head. 'That's okay. I'm reading.' They took their noise-cancelling headphones out of their schoolbag and put them on.

'Thank you,' Fiona said.

'For what?' I took a bottle out of the fridge.

'For always being so good with them.' She nodded towards Lex. 'And for the way you were with all the kids at the restaurant the other night. You made it so special for them.'

'It was no trouble at all.' I uncapped the bottle, which hissed gently as the pressure was released. 'It was good practise.'

'You think they're going to bring a group of kids in for the Master Sommelier exam?'

'They might.' I poured a tasting measure into her glass and then mine. 'You never know. The Court pride themselves on it being the hardest exam in the world. Surprise kids would kneecap a lot of people.'

'Not you, though.' Fiona accepted the glass I set in front of her. 'The girls have started insisting that every beverage that comes out of the fridge gets presented to them. I had to do it with the milk this morning before they let me put it on their cereal.'

I had a sudden vision of it, piercing my brain in a way that was almost painful. Fiona holding the milk out, offering it to them solemnly. The girls' giggles as she poured it.

Me coming up beside her and taking it from her. *Please allow me to show you the correct technique. We have to use two hands, or we'll spill it all over the floor.*

'—never should have taught them the word *elegant,*' Fiona was saying. 'I was hoping I could trick them into keeping relatively quiet in the restaurant, but it's backfired. Now everything has to be elegant, and – Satoshi, did I lose you?'

'Sorry.' I blinked. 'My head's been all over the place for the last few days.'

There was a pause before she spoke again, her voice soft, almost shy. 'I know the feeling.'

I glanced over at Lex. They were absorbed in their book, paying no attention to us, so I inched my hand across the bar until my right index finger was just brushing Fiona's left pinky. It was the tiniest, most plausibly deniable of touches, but judging by her swift intake of breath, I wasn't the only one who could feel it everywhere.

'Cheers.' I held my glass up with my free hand.

'Cheers,' she replied.

We looked each other in the eye, the moment stretching far longer than the quick clink of our glasses. The flush that had receded from her face came back, the salmon pink of Provençal rosé.

'We need to talk about this,' she said.

I let my fingertip slide against the bed of her nail. 'I know.'

She looked over at Lex for a moment before she spoke again. 'I told Sadie. I kind of had to, after . . . you know.'

'I do know.'

'I'm sorry about that.' Her colour deepened into Italian rosato. 'Her walking in, I mean.'

'Why are you apologising? You didn't do anything wrong.' I was barely touching her, but the feeling of her finger against mine was still sending all the blood rushing away from my brain. 'If anything, I should be apologising to you. I was the one who—' I lowered my voice, even though Lex clearly wasn't listening '—shoved you up against the wall.'

'I liked it,' she admitted.

Oh god. I was going to have to take my hand away, or it was going to be a disaster.

'Just in case that wasn't clear,' she added. 'I don't know exactly where . . . whatever this is came from, but I like it. A lot. Too much, maybe.'

I let my index finger slide deeper into the space between her ring and pinky fingers. 'I know you were confused at first,' I said, 'but I hope I showed you how much I like it.'

Fiona bit her lip. 'I can't stop thinking about it,' she whispered. 'But I – I – I don't think I'm ready for it, Satoshi.'

Her words sent ice leaching through me, like I'd stepped in a puddle and water was seeping through my shoes and into my socks. 'Okay,' was all I managed to say.

'I'm such a mess.' Her eyes, when she looked at me, were somewhere between desperate and desolate. 'This last year has felt like the carpet getting yanked out from under me, again and again. Something, somewhere, is always on fire, and I'm in this endless state of panic trying to run around and put it out, and . . .'

'It's a lot?'

She nodded. 'And not the fun kind.'

Her thumb started brushing up and down the base of mine. We were basically holding hands now, her middle three fingers in the gap between my index finger and thumb. 'It feels like I'm constantly falling on my face,' she said, 'and everyone has to keep helping me up. And I . . . I think I need to find my feet again, on my own – sort my life out – before I can really . . . explore anything like that.'

She looked at me. 'Is that okay?'

There was only one thing I could say.

'Of course it's okay.' I squeezed her hand as the cold crept up from my feet into my chest, wrapping its way around my heart. 'Trust me, if there's one thing I understand, it's needing to feel like you're in control.'

'Thank you,' she said softly. 'For bearing with me.'

'Always.' I would dream of what might have been forever, but if this was what I got to have of her, it would be enough. I would *make* it be enough. 'I'm not going anywhere.'

Fiona squeezed my fingers back, and then disentangled them from mine . 'I'm working on it, though. Sorting my life out. And I have a question to ask you, if you don't mind.'

'Of course.' Below the bar, I flexed my hand. For all my resolve, her letting go had felt like getting kicked in the kidneys.

'I—' She hesitated. 'I need you to be honest with me. If I'm being stupid, you have to tell me. Please don't let me make a fool of myself.'

'I would never.'

She unlocked her phone and handed it to me. 'The Instagram algo served this up to me,' she said. 'Do you – and you have to *promise* to tell me the truth – do you think I could do this?'

I looked at it. She'd opened one of the country's best-known wine websites, on a page with the headline 'New Viniferous Voices'.

She kept talking as I scrolled through. 'It's a competition for emerging wine writers. The winner gets a column on their website for the next year – paid. It wouldn't be anywhere near enough money to live off, obviously, but . . . well, I'll have child support coming in, which means I won't have to hustle quite as hard at copywriting to make ends meet. I like copywriting, but that hustle has been getting harder and harder – AI has really fucked things up – so I need to diversify anyway, and . . . why not get into something I enjoy, you know? And you always say such nice things about the way I talk about wine, so I thought . . . obviously I won't *win* this, but if they like my writing there's a chance I could publish some pieces freelance for them, and—'

'You could absolutely win this.'

Fiona stopped, apples of her cheeks flushing pink. 'You really think so?'

'Yes. This is perfect for you.' I meant it, too. I was almost jealous of it, this innocuous little webpage with *Fiona Fisher* written all over it.

'They recommend people have some wine education, though. I've learnt a lot from you, but—'

'I'll tell you anything you need to know.' My fingers itched with the urge to reach out and take her hand again. 'But if you want a formal qual – I'm sponsoring Charlotte through the Introductory Sommelier certificate next month. Two days, with an exam on the third. I could sponsor you too.'

She regarded me suspiciously. 'Does "sponsor" mean "pay for me"?'

'Call it an early Christmas present.'

'No. You already do way too much for me. But could you send me the details?'

'Of course.'

'And maybe you could read my draft? Not in an I-like-you-this-is-great way – in an I-know-everything-about-wine-so-let-me-stop-you-from-making-terrible-mistakes way? I know you're incredibly busy, but—'

'Fiona,' I interjected, 'of course I will.'

She beamed at me, and – god, she was beautiful. She was so, so beautiful.

'I've got some books that might be helpful,' I said. 'Want to come browse my office bookshelves and see if you want to borrow anything?'

She hesitated.

I held my hands up. 'No funny business. I swear.'

She blushed again, almost to the roots of her hair this time, but nodded.

Given the rain, there was little chance any customers would come in, but I locked the front door anyway, told Lex – so absorbed in their book they barely acknowledged it – that I was taking their mum out the back for a sec, then led Fiona to my office, leaving the door open as a representation of my promise not to crush her to me and kiss her until her knees gave way. 'These ones are wine writing,' I told her, tracing my finger across half a shelf's worth of alphabetically organised books. 'They'll probably be the most useful, so you can get a feel for some different approaches. But maybe one or two of these—' I pulled out some of my more encyclopaedic reference guides '—might be handy too?'

'Don't you need them? For your studies?'

I paused for half a second too long, and she jabbed me in the shoulder. 'You *do*.'

'I'll be fine.'

'No,' she said firmly. 'I don't want to be a charity case.'

'All right,' I said, a wave of inspiration hitting me. 'How about being my study buddy, then?'

Fiona blinked. 'What do you mean?'

'Jonah and Sadie take the kids on Thursday nights, right?'

'They're not this week – it's Jonah's birthday dinner – but usually, yes.'

'You need some formal wine knowledge,' I said. 'I've got a lot of it – and a lot more I need to get my head around. How about you spend Thursdays here, helping me study? You'll be giving me a hand and picking up some knowledge for yourself at the same time.'

'Don't you work on Thursdays?'

'I'll see if Birdie can pick up an extra shift – which would also help me out. Isamu and my mother have both been telling me I'm working too much. This might get them off my back.'

Fiona twined her fingers together, sucking her bottom lip between her teeth and looking down at the ground.

'If you're worried about me pushing you into something you're not ready for,' I said gently, 'you don't need to be. I promise.'

'I'm not worried about you, Satoshi!'

Her eyes, when she looked at me, were full of fire. 'I'm worried about *me*,' she said. 'I know myself. If I spend too much time alone with you, I'm going to get carried away again and I'll end up climbing you like a tree.'

My heart skipped about fourteen beats before it started hammering.

'Because, god, I want to,' she said. 'So badly. It scares me how badly I want to. But I just – *can't*.'

'Will you . . .' I paused. I had to tread carefully here, or I might lose even the little bit of her I got to keep. 'Will you tell me why not?'

Fiona sniffed, swallowed, sniffed again. 'I don't think you realise how important you are to me,' she said at last. 'Everything in my life has changed this past year. And it's not just Matt. My brothers showing up for me the way they have has been incredible – of course it's been incredible – but it's the opposite of what I expected them to do, and . . . Satoshi, you might be the only person who's stayed the same.'

She wiped a shaking hand over her face. 'You're one of the only stable things in my life. The kids' lives too, for that matter – especially Lex. And I *need* that. If I ruin things – if I lose you—'

'Hey, hey, hey.' I gave in and let myself reach out to her, pulling her to me in a tight hug. 'No one's losing anyone, all right? I'm not going anywhere.'

Her breath was ragged against my throat. 'You say that now, but—'

'I promise, Fiona.' I drew back, framing her face in my hands. 'No matter what, I'm not going anywhere.'

She blinked, once, twice. Tears were beading on her lashes.

I thumbed them away. 'Here's an idea,' I said. 'You can say no. No pressure, all right? But – what if we go slow?'

'What do you mean?' There was a quaver in her voice.

'You're not the only one who got carried away. I should have known you weren't ready for some of the things we did.'

'Satoshi, please don't blame yourself for me freaking out. That was all my bullshit, and—'

I put my finger against her lips before she could launch into one of her spiralling monologues. 'But we don't have to jump back into the deep end,' I told her. 'We could go slow. As slow as you like, so you feel safe and in control.'

I took Fiona's hand in my free one. 'We could hold hands,' I said. 'We could cuddle. We could—' I let my fingertip gently strum her lower lip '—kiss.'

'Like – sort of like high school?' Her breath was coming shallowly. 'Like when you're young – before you're ready to have sex – those kinds of things?'

'Just like high school. You can help me with my homework, and then—' I raised her hand to my lips '—we can make out.'

She made a sound that I thought was halfway to a chuckle.

Then, though, she swallowed. 'What would you get out of it, though?' she asked. 'You're young and hot and brilliant, Satoshi. You could have sex on tap every night of the week, with anyone you wanted. I know – I've seen – I know you have this . . . other side, underneath all this.' She slid a finger under my waistcoat, sending blood somehow rushing both to and away from my head. 'Why would you want the world's most G-rated friends-with-benefits situation?'

For a moment, I thought about just saying it. About letting the secret that had been sitting heavy in my heart for the past year out in the open. *I'm in love with you, Fiona. I would agree to anything if it meant I got to be with you.*

But because I loved her, I had to listen to her. She needed to find her feet again. Me confessing the full force of my love wouldn't be helping her to them – it would be kicking them out from under her. She needed me to be exactly who she'd always thought I was.

'Because I like you,' I said instead.

There was a long silence.

'And,' I added, desperate to fill it before she did with the word *no*, 'honestly, I think foreplay's wildly underrated.'

She made a noise in the back of her throat and shook her head, and every organ in my body turned to stone. I'd taken the shot, and I'd missed.

But then Fiona Fisher put a hand on my shoulder, went up on her tiptoes, and cautiously, tentatively, brushed her lips against mine.

'Is it okay if we don't tell anyone?' she asked. 'If it's just . . . us?'

I kissed her back, feather-light, shoving the dark, hungry part of me that wanted to push her back into the bookshelves and devour her and tattoo her name on my forehead deep, deep down. 'Of course it is,' I told her. 'No pressure. Just us.'

NOVEMBER

Chapter Seven

Fiona

Tasting today: 2022 chardonnay, Tasmania, Australia. Chardonnay is the winemaker's grape. Good grapes make good chardonnay, but great chardonnay becomes great because someone has carefully, patiently, lovingly worked out what those grapes need.

From: fionafishers@mail.com.au
To: tsu_satoshi@mail.com.au
Subject: wine piece
Attached: questions.docx

Hi Satoshi,

So: I have an idea for my wine piece.

It's due on 22 Nov, so I only have a few weeks. That means I should probably write about something I know, and – I know you.

What would you think about me writing a piece about Bibliophile? You and Isamu have such an interesting story, with the way that your dad took you all around the world before you finally established yourselves in Tasmania. I've always loved that thing you told me about how Isamu started accumulating books when you settled here and that made it feel like home. I assume that's where the name Bibliophile came from (?), which would be a great segue from talking about the two of you to talking about the wine 😉

If you'd prefer I write about something else, that's obviously fine. But if you're happy for me to make my big wine writing debut talking about Bibliophile – and if you're not too busy!! – I've attached a few questions it would be handy if you would answer. (Do you think Isamu would be happy to answer them too?)

F xo

P.S. Just checking we're still on for Thursday!

From: tsu_satoshi@mail.com.au
To: fionafishers@mail.com.au
Subject: Re: wine piece
Attached: questions_TS answers.docx

Fiona, of COURSE you can write about Bibliophile. Do you think we would ever turn down free advertising? 😉

I've attached my answers to your questions – sorry if they're not amazing, you know I'm not exactly a wordsmith – and I'll send them on to Isamu. I can't imagine he'll be a terribly good interview subject either (you know what he's like) but I'm sure he can manage a few sentences.

And yes, that's exactly where the name Bibliophile came from. Tsundoku is a riff on it – it's the Japanese word for letting books pile up in your house without reading them.

Can't wait to read your draft!

Sato xx

P.S. We're definitely still on for Thursday x

From: fionafishers@mail.com.au
To: tsu_satoshi@mail.com.au
Subject: Re: wine piece

You're the best. Thank you!! These answers are brilliant – your passion for the wine really comes through x

And I already knew that re Tsundoku 😉 I looked it up after the first time I came in. Lex clearly did the same, because Jonah asked what it meant once and they answered the question before I could even open my mouth.

F xo

P.S. Do you want me to bring anything?

From: tsu_satoshi@mail.com.au
To: fionafishers@mail.com.au
Subject: Re: wine piece
Attached: questions_TI answers.docx; CMS_Intro_Hobart.pdf

You are both very welcome and very clever.

Two other things:

1) Isamu answered your questions (attached). He was surprisingly verbose by his standards – he usually never talks about our father – so this basically counts as an exclusive 😉 He put his phone number at the bottom in case you want to text him to clarify anything.

2) Also attached is the flyer for the next CMS Intro course – next Tuesday and Wednesday, exam Thursday morning. They only run these in Hobart once a year and bookings close tomorrow, so if you want to do it, I'd jump on it.

Sato xx

P.S. Just yourself is plenty x

🍷

FIONA

Jonah, any chance you could do school pickup on Tuesday and Wednesday next week and keep the kids for a couple hours?

I've got a few things I need to take care of (boring, don't ask)

JONAH

I can do Tuesday. I teach Wednesday, but Sadie says she can do it 😊

And that she needs to have a lengthy discussion with the girls about their flower girl dresses anyway

FIONA

You're both the best – thank you!!

And don't let the girls get too carried away!

🍷

SADIE

So are these 'things I need to take care of' what I think they are? 🍆🍆🍆

FIONA

...

...

...

Think it's probably best to put the other thing to bed for now

(Not literally!!!)

SADIE

For future reference: I will *always* do my best to ensure Jonah or I can cover for any 'things' you need to take care of 😉

You deserve to be taken care of xx

From: fionafishers@mail.com.au
To: courses@mastersommeliersoceania.org.au
Subject: Introductory course

To whom it may concern,

I would love to enrol in the Introductory Sommelier course you're running in Hobart next week. Are there still places available?

Many thanks,

Fiona Fisher

From: courses@mastersommeliersoceania.org.au
To: fionafishers@mail.com.au
Subject: Re: Introductory course
Attached: CMS_Intro_enrolment.pdf; invoice748687.pdf

Dear Fiona

There are still places available, and we have reserved one for you.

Please complete the attached enrolment form. Your enrolment will be confirmed upon receipt of payment for the attached invoice. Payment must be received by 5 pm Friday to secure your place.

In vino veritas,

Joseph Collins-Smith

🍷

FIONA

Mum, can I ask a favour?

You know how you were going to send me a hotel gift certificate . . . is there any chance you could just transfer me a few hundred dollars instead?

There's some professional training I'd like to do

Matt doesn't have to start paying child support until the divorce is final and I can't quite squeeze it into my monthly budget

MUM

I'll do it right now

But I'm going to send you that gift voucher too

You should do something nice for yourself, sweetheart – not just to keep your head above water

FIONA

This is for me. I promise.

🍷

SATOSHI

Happy Thursday x

I was thinking: would you like to set some ground rules for tonight?

So you can feel comfortable we won't go past a certain point?

FIONA

This is both the sweetest and the most embarrassing thing I've ever been asked 😊

SATOSHI

Don't be embarrassed!

Having clear boundaries might help you feel like you're in control

FIONA

I feel like I should be able to maintain my own boundaries without having to put them in writing ahead of time

But you're right, this is sensible

For tonight, if we're going by high school rules – how about nothing past first base?

SATOSHI

Clothes stay on, hands stay in socially acceptable places?

FIONA

Is that ok?

SATOSHI

Of course it is

I hope flashcards are ok with you, because I need to get my head around the minutiae of Spanish wine law

FIONA

I give great flashcard 😊

SATOSHI

I should warn you this will not be a particularly sexy subject

You might not even want to go as far as first base

FIONA

• • •

• • •

• • •

I can promise you that won't be a problem.

🍷

FIONA

Thank you for last night

It was perfect x

SATOSHI

You don't need to thank me

I got just as much out of it as you did x

FIONA

~~There is no way that's true~~

• • •

I can't believe it's taken me this long to meet Yquem!

SATOSHI

I should have known she'd fall in love with you

Her heart belongs to Isamu, but you've definitely bumped me down to #3 on her affection list

FIONA

Sorry 🤣

🍷

BELLERIVE PUBLIC YEAR 6 PARENTS

MICHELLE

Hi everyone, it's time to start planning for the Year 6 graduation!! It'll be held on Wed Dec 5 on the school oval. Steve, Mei-Lin and I have done most of the organising, but we need your help with the dinner, as – like always – we don't have much of a budget. Steve will be manning the barbecue. Sausages, veggie burgers etc have been covered by a kind sponsor. What we need from every Year 6 family is a side, salad or dessert.

LYNDA

I'll bring potato salad

TARA

How do samosas sound?

JESSICA P

I'll bake one of my famous apple pies!!

Maybe I'll bring two, I remember how you all demolished it at the last P&F meeting 😉

FIONA

I'll bring cupcakes

MICHELLE

Fiona, please don't worry about it

Obviously you get a pass!

FIONA

It's fine! I can manage cupcakes

MICHELLE

We insist! You just focus on looking after yourself and those beautiful kids of yours xx

JESSICA H

Fiona, I've been meaning to ask – I thought I saw The Arsehole in Salamanca a few weeks ago. Is he back in town?

TARA

I saw him too! He was at that little bakory cafe on the waterfront with a pregnant woman

I felt so bad for you, Fiona – I nearly walked up and poured a drink over his head!

MICHELLE

Pregnant?? Oh, Fiona.

Now you *really* don't need to bring anything to graduation! It's BYO, so: who's bringing Fiona a margarita?

FIONA

Can I call on your culinary expertise and trouble you for a cupcake recipe?

JONAH

Of course you can! What kind?

FIONA

Doesn't matter, as long as they're delicious and look incredible

Lex's graduation is in a few weeks, and for various reasons, I need to turn up with the most amazing cupcakes anyone has ever seen

JONAH

You have come to the right place

Do you want me to bake them for you?

FIONA

I can do it! I know my cooking isn't up to your standards, but I'm not so useless I can't manage cupcakes

Just the recipe will be perfect

JONAH

Offer's on the table, if you change your mind.

Always here to help 😊

🍷

FIONA

Wine school day 1!

Fiona sent a photo.
[Photo: Fiona in front of a Court of Master Sommeliers banner in a hotel conference room.]

SATOSHI

You're going to kill it x

FIONA

If there are any questions about Spanish wine law, I'm going to be all over them

SATOSHI

Look after Charlotte for me!

JONAH

Oh my god, Fi, I'm so sorry I sent the kids home to you in such a state!

Baking With Uncle Jonah got a bit out of control, and I didn't even think about the sugar high

(Cold comfort, but I have perfected my cupcake recipe. Year 6 graduation won't know what hit it.)

FIONA

It's fine, don't worry!

The girls ran screaming around the backyard for 45 mins then collapsed into a heap

If I can get some dinner into them, they'll have the best night's sleep of their lives

JONAH

I'm still sorry

I promise this won't happen tomorrow!

FIONA

Wine school day 2

Fiona sent a photo.
[Photo: Fiona smiling in front of a Court of Master Sommeliers banner in a hotel conference room.]

SATOSHI

I love that green dress on you x

How's it going?

FIONA

Intimidating – they cover so much ground! But so interesting

And it made me realise: I knew you were great at your job, but you are *great* at your job

SATOSHI

You're going to make me blush

I prefer making you blush 😉

FIONA

How have I never realised what an incorrigible flirt you are? 🤣

I was thinking, for tomorrow night: maybe we start sort of . . . inching towards second base?

SATOSHI

Clothes stay on, hands start wandering?

FIONA

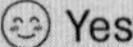 Yes

Thank you for bearing with me x

I've been sitting with Charlotte btw, and she's doing great

You're going to have another somm before you know it

DAD

What is this I hear about your mother paying for you to do professional training?

If you want to go back to university, all you have to do is ask.

I can get you a fee waiver at ESU. You can take all your classes online.

Or if you want to be in the classroom, I'm sure Jonah can do the same at Lyons.

FIONA

I'm not going back to uni, Dad

That ship has sailed

This is just some vocational training for my writing

DAD

While I'm glad to see you're not planning to just live off that chump's money – you can do better than that, Fiona.

🍷

FIONA

Exam day

Fiona sent a photo.
[Photo: A selfie of Fiona in front of a Court of Master Sommeliers banner in a hotel conference room]

It's been a long couple of days – can't wait to see you tonight xx

SATOSHI

Me neither x

I'd wish you luck, but you won't need it

🍷

FIONA

Just wanted to say thank you for not letting me get carried away last night x

I really could have

SATOSHI

The last thing I want is for you to regret anything x

Besides, you looked so good with that brand new somm pin on your collar. How could I let you take your shirt off?

FIONA

Much as I want to, I don't think I'm ready to take it off yet, but . . .

. . . perhaps next week we can commit to second base and think about going under it?

SATOSHI

I think we can manage that 😉

FIONA

xxx

Do you have a busy weekend?

Now I've crammed my head full of wine knowledge, I want to finish fleshing out the skeleton of the Bibliophile piece I've written and turn it into a proper draft

If I send it to you on Saturday or Sunday, will you have time to read it?

SATOSHI

I'll make time

FISHER SIBS

ELIAS

Fishers, a hypothetical: if I came to Tasmania for Christmas, would either of you be able to put me up?

I could pay in avuncular childcare, good company, and help with cooking Christmas dinner

FIONA

Of course!

The kids would love to have you here

Mum and Dad aren't coming for Christmas – they're doing Jonah's wedding in Feb instead – so my spare room is all yours

JONAH

You're also welcome to stay with me and Sadie, but there's more room (and more niblings) at Fi's

You're not welcome, however, to help with Christmas dinner. Back off.

FIONA

Am I allowed to help, given I assume I'll be hosting?

JONAH

No.

I have plans. It will be a masterpiece.

You can be Satoshi for a day and be in charge of the wine

ELIAS

Who's Satoshi?

JONAH

The sommelier at our favourite bar

Who is *absurdly* generous. Even if I fuck up the dinner, we'll drink well.

(I won't fuck up the dinner.)

FIONA

Chess is coming for Christmas, right?

Won't she be staying with you?

JONAH

Yes, she's coming, but she always insists on staying in a hotel

Sadie thinks she's scared she'll overhear us having sex

ELIAS

. . . so I'm *definitely* not staying with you, then. TMI, little brother

I'll kick in some $$$ for groceries etc, Fi – I know money's an issue, so don't worry about me freeloading off you

MATT

Did you talk to the kids' therapist yet about the best plan for visitation?

FIONA

Yes

MATT

What did she say?

Happy to jump on the phone if you want to talk through the specifics

I'd like to set up a video call with them on Thursday

FIONA

This coming Thursday??

MATT

Yes

Is that a problem?

FIONA

Yes

1) I'm busy on Thursday.

2) It's going to take much more time to get them ready to have you back in their lives than that.

MATT

Is that what their therapist said?

Or are you just being petty?

FIONA

I'm going to give you the opportunity to take that back

MATT

They're my kids too, Fiona

I fully admit I've made mistakes, but that doesn't give you the right to keep them from me

🍷

From: fionafishers@mail.com.au
To: kavita.prasad@smqlawyers.com.au
CC: francesca.shaw@turnerradley.com.au
Subject: Visitation

Hi Kavita (and Chess),

A quick question for you, when you have a moment. Matt can't demand visitation with the kids before the divorce is finalised, can he?

Thanks,
Fiona

From: kavita.prasad@smqlawyers.com.au
To: fionafishers@mail.com.au
CC: francesca.shaw@turnerradley.com.au
Subject: Re: Visitation

Dear Fiona,

No, you are not legally obliged to let him see the children until the divorce is final and the agreement we made in mediation comes into effect. You could, however, let him see them as a gesture of good faith, if that is something you wish to do.

Kind regards,
Kavita

CHESS

Didn't want to send this from my work email as this is DEFINITELY not legal advice, but: don't give Matt anything unless he gives you something

He wants to see the kids before you technically have to let him? He has to start paying you child support before he technically has to

You have leverage. That's the language business bros speak. Don't be afraid to use it.

FIONA

Thanks Chess

It feels wrong to use the kids as leverage, though

Even if the $$$ would be helpful

CHESS

If you ever need money, you know you can come to me, right? No questions asked

Sadie and I were broke as shit growing up. I know what it's like

Corporate law may be soulless, but I make a lot of money, and it does no one any good sitting in my bank account

FIONA

That's so kind of you, but no

I already owe you so much for all your help – I don't want to owe you money too

🍷

FIONA

I've thought about it, and I don't think it's a good idea for you to see the kids before the divorce comes into effect

MATT

Seriously?!

Don't punish them to punish me

FIONA

I'm not punishing anyone. I told you: they need time to adjust to the idea of seeing you again.

MATT

Come on, Fi. What difference will a few weeks make?

FIONA

I'll set up a call for both of us with their therapist, but you're not having a call with the kids until a) we're divorced, and b) I've had time to make sure they're ready

🍷

From: fionafishers@mail.com.au
To: tsu_satoshi@mail.com.au
Subject: Re: wine piece
Attached: Bibliophile piece_final.docx

Okay, so I *know* I said I'd get this to you to look at over the weekend and it's Wednesday (long story short: Matt's the worst), but here's the draft of my piece on Bibliophile.

The competition due date is tomorrow, so if you don't have to time to look at it before then, that's totally fine.

If you do get a few moments, though – does this read too much like a profile instead of a piece of wine writing? I'm worried it's too much about you and Isamu and not enough about the actual wine.

F xo

From: tsu_satoshi@mail.com.au
To: fionafishers@mail.com.au
Subject: Re: wine piece
Attached: Bibliophile piece_final_TS notes.docx

Fiona, this is beautiful.

I've made a few notes about some technical wine stuff, but other than that, I wouldn't change a thing.

Granted, I'm biased – you might recall that I'm quite fond of you 😉 – but in my humble opinion, you have a great shot at winning. Yes, there's quite a lot of the Tsukamoto story, and not as many wine specs as others might include, but wine *should* be a story. People will understand so much more about Bibliophile's wines and Isamu's winemaking philosophy from your article than they will from 'the entry-level chardonnay is 50% large format oak, 50% stainless steel on lees, full malolactic fermentation' (which is what I would probably write).

TL;DR – this is a stunning piece of writing. I'm so honoured that your debut article is about us, and I'm sure Isamu will be too. He might even smile!

Sato xx

P.S. Can't wait to see you tonight and tell you more about how wonderful I thought this was x

---

From: fionafishers@mail.com.au
To: tsu_satoshi@mail.com.au
Subject: Re: wine piece

Satoshi! Thank you so much – both for taking the time to look at it, and saying such nice things about it.

F xo

P.S. Can't wait to see you tonight and tell you more about how wonderful I think *you* are. Turns out I'm quite fond of you too.

From: fionafishers@mail.com.au
To: nvv-comp@casksofamontillado.com.au
Subject: Entry – New Viniferous Voices
Attached: Bibliophile piece_final_FINAL.docx

To whom it may concern,

Please find attached my entry for the New Viniferous Voices competition. It is a profile of Bibliophile Wines in the Coal River Valley, focusing on seven of their wines via the story of winemaker Isamu Tsukamoto and his sommelier brother Satoshi.

Many thanks,
Fiona

FIONA

I know I say this every week, but – thank you for last night x

It was very subtle of you, deciding you *had* to practise tasting sparkling wine on the day I submitted my article 🤣

SATOSHI

It *was* subtle. I was actually celebrating getting to touch your tits 😉

FIONA

Sorry I'm not game enough to actually take my shirt *off* yet

Having kids did a number on my body

They probably feel much better than they look

SATOSHI

Did you enjoy it, though?

I loved it (I can assure you they feel spectacular) but I know they're not your most erogenous zone

If under-the-shirt isn't for you, we don't have to do it again

FIONA

I've never really enjoyed it in the past, but if I'm being honest – it was a bit embarrassing, how much I liked it

I'm going to be dreaming of next Thursday all week

And if we're following high school rules . . . maybe it's time for third base?

SATOSHI

Below the waist?

FIONA

Yes

SATOSHI

Over or under clothes?

FIONA

Can I think about it?

SATOSHI

Of course you can

FIONA

~~I don't think I'll be able to stop~~

To: fionafishers@mail.com.au
From: noreply@feelgoodfemme.com.au
Subject: Your Order #4564649823

Hi Fiona F,

Thanks for choosing Feel Good Femme. We've received your order, and it will leave our warehouse in 2–5 business days.

YOUR ORDER
1 x Silicone rechargeable rabbit vibrator (whisper quiet)

Our chatbot is available around the clock for all your queries, and our customer service team between 9 am–5 pm AEDT.

Congratulations on prioritising your pleasure.

Fond wishes for fun times from the team at Feel Good Femme.

SMQ LAWYERS

Hi FIONA FISHER, reply Y to confirm your divorce hearing appt with KAVITA PRASAD: 2.30 PM Mon 26 Nov or call to cancel. Cancellations will incur fees.

FIONA

Y

JONAH

Fi, are you sure you don't want me to come with you to the hearing?

FIONA

Yes

It's on Zoom, and it'll be short and boring.

Kavita said it'll take fifteen minutes tops

JONAH

I just thought you might want someone there for moral support

FIONA

That's so sweet, Jonah, but I'll be fine

~~If I fall apart, I don't want you to see it~~

MUM

Good luck today, Fiona. Hope all goes well.

Transferred a few extra $$ into your account x

FIONA

Thanks Mum, really appreciate it x

DAD

Your mother reminded me that today is your divorce hearing. Don't get soft and let that man take advantage of you.

Again.

FIONA

Not planning on it

SADIE

Jonah told me you don't want anyone with you at the hearing, but if you decide you want to go for a drink afterwards and you need someone to take the kids for the afternoon, just say x

FIONA

That's so lovely, Sadie, but I'll be all right x

ELIAS

Thinking of you today, Fi – let me know if there's anything you need

FIONA

~~Any chance you could get the rest of the family to leave me alone?~~

Thanks big bro xx

From: kavita.prasad@smqlawyers.com.au
To: fionafishers@mail.com.au
CC: francesca.shaw@turnerradley.com.au
Subject: Divorce proceedings today

Hi Fiona,

Just wanted to confirm what happens next, now we've had the hearing. I know we went over this in my office, but it's always nice to have it in writing.

Basically, everything went as smoothly as we could have hoped. Admittedly, there were more questions from the registrar than there normally are, but I think it was because he couldn't believe Matt had pulled off the two-families scam for so long. Nothing to do with you.

The long and the short of it is – congratulations! The hard part is over. All that's left is for the divorce to be finalised, which will happen in one month and one day (27 December). You'll be able to download your divorce order the next day from the online portal.

Once that's done, we can have a chat about pursuing back payment for child support.

As always, feel free to give me a call if you want to talk through any of this.

Kind regards,
Kavita

CHESS

Congratulations on being almost divorced!

If Kavita sent you home with any of that prosecco, though, don't drink it – it's awful

FIONA

Trust me, I know

And thanks again – for everything x

BELLERIVE PUBLIC YEAR 6 PARENTS

MICHELLE

Hi Year 6 parents – just another reminder about the arrangements for graduation next week!
Every family is responsible for a side, a salad or a dessert (except Fiona, who gets a pass for obvious reasons!!).
Here's a link to the Google doc:
https://docs.google.com/document/1Y6GradFoodSignUpSheet2026AbCDeFgHiJkLmNo/edit
And remember, it's BYO drinks!

From: laura.blair@mail.com.au
To: fionafishers@mail.com.au
Subject: An apology and an explanation

Dear Fiona,

First of all, I'm sorry for reaching out. I'm sure you don't want to hear from me.

Secondly, I'm sorry for not reaching out sooner. I'm very aware of the role I've played in this mess, and there's no way I'll ever be able to make it up to you. You're under no obligation to accept my apology, but please know how sorry I am.

Matt doesn't know I've written to you, and he would be mortified if he found out. As I'm sure you're well aware, he's a very proud man. But I wanted to reach out to you, mother to mother, to see if there's any chance you'd be willing to let him have a call with your kids sometime soon.

I understand how angry you must be with him. I'm probably one of the only people who knows what it feels like. He told me about you a few years ago, and I was so furious I thought my head was going to explode. He promised me he was going to leave you, but then he didn't, and didn't, and didn't, and . . . you get the picture. We split up for a while, but – and I'm not proud of this – in the end, I couldn't live without him. For better or worse, he's my person.

I don't want to make excuses for him or pretend like he's perfect, but he really, REALLY loves your kids. He doesn't talk about it much, but I know he misses them every single day. It's killing him, not being able to speak to them – I've never seen his eyes light up like they did when we ran into your beautiful girls last month.

You obviously don't owe us anything, but if you could find it in your heart to let him have a call with them, it would be a huge step forward in the healing journey: for you, me, him, and especially for the kids.

Best wishes,
Laura

From: fionafishers@mail.com.au
To: laura.blair@mail.com.au
Subject: Re: An apology and an explanation

Draft saved.

Draft saved.

Draft saved.

Draft saved.

Draft saved.

🍷

FIONA

Satoshi, I'm so sorry, but can we rain check tonight?

My divorce hearing was on Monday, and I can't stop thinking about how I'm going to have to let Matt see the kids again once it's all final, and . . .

. . . sigh. Maybe it sounds silly, but I just need to keep my babies close to me.

SATOSHI

Of course we can

And it doesn't sound silly at all x

FIONA

Sorry

SATOSHI

Fiona Fisher, we have *talked* about apologising

You never need to. Not with me x

Although admittedly, Yquem is not as useful a study buddy as you are

Satoshi sent a photo.
[Photo: A ginger cat fast asleep on top of three binders of notes.]

🍷

SATOSHI

Check your front porch

FIONA

What?

SATOSHI

Just do it 😉

FIONA

Satoshi Tsukamoto, you did not!!

Fiona sent a photo.
[Photo: An open care package sitting on Fiona's front porch with bottles of Bibliophile blanc de blancs and chardonnay featuring prominently.]

SATOSHI

I can't take all the credit

Chess Shaw bought the sparkling for you over the phone

But there's a few other bits and pieces in there for you – some wagashi for the girls, a book for Lex, some cheese and wine for you

FIONA

You shouldn't have

SATOSHI

What kind of business would I be running if someone called in an emergency sparkling order and I didn't fulfil it ASAP? I have an image to maintain, Fiona 😉

Besides, I had to drop off a case for Kieran at the spa anyway. It was no trouble x

FIONA

You should have knocked at the door!

SATOSHI

I didn't want to intrude on your time with the kids x

FIONA

You are so lovely, Satoshi x

I don't deserve you

~~You might be the only thing holding me together right now~~

Thank you so much for this xoxo

Fiona sent a photo.
[Photo: A glass of chardonnay.]

It's been a big week, and this is the only thing holding me together right now

DECEMBER

Chapter Eight

Satoshi

Tasting today: Bruny Island lager, Tasmania, Australia. Wine is wonderful, but sometimes you find a beer so good you get carried away – like this hazy lager, which is brilliant (at least until you drink too much, too fast).

'Let me guess,' I said to Isamu, as he walked through the door of Tsundoku at about five pm on a Wednesday in early December. '*Another* meeting in town?'

There was no way he could have misread my meaning, but, 'Yes,' was all he said, tone mild as he joined me behind the bar. 'I might crash on your couch tonight, if it goes late or gets boozy.'

I slotted some clean burgundy glasses into the overhead rack. 'It's interesting to me, your business partner, that I'm not invited to any of these meetings.'

Isamu started slotting clean glasses into the rack too. 'Not every part of the business involves you, Sato.'

'Not every part of the business involves you either. Yet here you are. Again.'

I held out my hand to him. He looked at me for a long moment before he relinquished the glass he was holding.

I slotted it into the overhead rack. 'I'm taking an extra night off a week to study. I sponsored Charlotte through CMS Intro, and if she passes Certified in April, we'll have another person who can run the floor. I've got everything under control.'

It was true, too. Work and study were both running like clockwork. And there was no way a person could have Fiona Fisher sitting on their lap, face flushed from kissing, and say, *No, stop, this is further than you wanted to go*, when she tried to take her shirt off, unless they had things deeply, profoundly, *aggressively* under control.

. . . even if they'd had to jerk off twice in quick succession after she left and the fantasy of what might have happened if they'd let their control slip hadn't stopped playing in their head for weeks.

Isamu pinched the bridge of his nose. 'Sato . . .'

I was saved from another lecture by the Shaw sisters coming through the door. 'Hi, Sadie,' I said, practically elbowing Isamu out of the way. 'Hi, Chess. Welcome back. I know you live in Sydney, but you're here so often we're going to have to start calling you a regular.'

'Thanks,' Chess said, pale cheeks flushed from the December heat.

'What brings you down this time?'

'She's helping me look for a wedding dress.' Sadie sat in the chair I'd pulled out for her. 'I need another pair of eyes, and it felt insensitive to ask Fiona.'

I pulled out Chess's chair and made a sound of vague agreement, ignoring the glint – halfway between suspicion and glee – in Sadie's eyes. It wasn't the first time she'd looked at me this way since she'd caught us in the corridor at Abode, but if Fiona wasn't ready to talk about our Thursday night arrangement, I wasn't about to jump the gun. 'What can I get for you?'

I got them settled with a bottle of Bibliophile kyoho akai, then went back behind the bar. 'See? Under control.'

'I believe you.' Isamu held up his hands. 'But I'm here now. My meeting isn't till half-past seven. I can spell you.'

Chess was looking at us curiously, so I switched to Japanese. 'If you're so insistent on working, you can take the next customer. But I don't walk into the winery and say, "No, you're working too much, Isamu, I'll be monitoring the ferment today." You can't just barge in here and banish me from my own bar.'

'I'm not banishing you. But I've got a couple of free hours, and you've got an exam to study for.'

I folded my arms.

He sighed. 'Fine, Sato. Have it your way.'

We worked mostly in silence for the next little while. I let him serve every second customer. He didn't protest when I insisted on serving the others. The reason we'd never had particularly good service chemistry was that we both always tried to lead, but tonight, it was surprisingly seamless.

'How's wedding planning going?' I asked Sadie as she came up to pay, watching Isamu out of the corner of my eye as he talked Chess through my cocktail page.

'Fine.' Sadie tapped her card against the reader. 'Although I never would have guessed it would be so much *work*. Our first wedding took about three hours to plan, tops. This wedding feels like it's taking three hours a day.'

I handed her the receipt. 'How many of those are devoted to Rosie and Georgia's demands?'

Sadie grinned. 'At least two and a half. Are you coming, Chessie?'

'I'll stay for another drink,' Chess replied. 'I've got some work emails to answer. Can I get a negroni, please?'

'Let me make that,' I told Isamu, as the sisters hugged and Sadie left.

'I've got it,' he replied, taking down bottles of gin, vermouth and Campari.

'Yes, but—'

I was interrupted by my phone buzzing in my pocket, tearing my attention away from Isamu grotesquely over-stirring Chess's drink. It was astonishing that I ever let him behind the bar at all, if he was going to dilute my beautifully crafted cocktails like—

Every single thought left my head when I saw the name on the screen. 'Fiona?'

'Satoshi.' There was something breathy and desperate in her voice on the other end of the phone. 'I need you.'

I abandoned the bar and strode towards my office. 'What's wrong?' I kicked the door closed behind me. 'Are you all right?'

'I'm fine, don't worry!' She laughed. 'Sorry – *need* is too strong a word. But I'm in a bit of situation, and you are uniquely positioned to help me look like a huge fucking hero.'

I pressed the heel of my hand to my chest, willing my heart to stop racing. Those whispered words – *I need you* – had sent me into two different kinds of cardiac arrest. 'Of course. What do you need?'

'I'm at Lex's graduation barbecue,' Fiona said, 'and they've run out of booze.'

Her voice dropped. 'All the other parents think I'm useless. Ever since Matt, they treat me like a joke. I turned up with seventy-two cupcakes tonight, and they acted like I was a dog dropping a tennis ball at their feet. But if I can save them from the horrors of their own poor planning . . .'

I was already moving. 'Easy. What do you need? Wine? Beer?'

'Both. The cheapest you have. I'll pay for it, obviously, but I can't quite extend to serving sixty parents Dom Perignon, you know? Plus, they're already buzzed, they won't appreciate the good shit.'

'Everything I stock is—'

'—the good shit, I know.' There was a laugh in her voice, that champagne laugh, and my chest hummed. 'But I believe in you, Satoshi. Bring me the very worst of your good shit.'

She paused. 'Or, you know, send Charlotte or whoever. You have a business to run, and—'

'Fiona,' I said. 'Drop me a pin of where you are. I'll be there soon.'

She paused again. 'Thank you,' was all she said, but it turned my blood to mulled wine. It had been almost two weeks since I'd seen her, and I'd been *aching* for her.

My imagination automatically kicked into gear, but I forced all the delicious pictures it was conjuring away and headed back out onto the bar floor. 'Isamu, I have to run out for a bit. Do you mind covering?'

'*Now* you want cover?' At some point while I'd been in my office, my brother had morphed back into his usual taciturn self. 'I told you, Sato, I've got a meeting in half an hour.'

My mind, which was full of the breathy gasps Fiona made when I touched her, stuttered to a halt. 'Wait, really?'

'Yes. And I can't miss it.'

I couldn't – wouldn't – leave my bar without a somm on the floor. That wasn't something I was physically or mentally capable of doing.

But I had to go to Fiona. I *had* to. How could I let her say *I need you* and not be there?

'Please, Onīsan.' My lips felt numb. '*Please.*'

Isamu closed his eyes. He knew as well as I did that I wouldn't use the formal form of 'older brother' unless I was extremely serious, extremely desperate, or both.

Then, to my surprise, Chess spoke. 'That was Fiona, right? If she needs you, you should go.'

Isamu looked at her for a moment, then exhaled. 'Fine.'

The relief hit me so strongly I almost sagged with it. 'Thank you,' I told him. 'Thank you, thank you, thank you.'

🍷

Fiona was waiting for me in the school carpark. 'Thank you!' she exclaimed as I got out of the car. 'Oh my goodness, Satoshi, I owe you big time for this.'

She was in a dark blue blouse, half-tucked into jeans, with sensible shoes. She was wearing minimal makeup, had her hair pulled back in a ponytail, and was the loveliest thing I had ever seen.

'No problem at all.' I bent down to peck her on the cheek, the faintest shadow of what I actually wanted to do, which was shove her up against the side of my car, wrap her ponytail around my fist, and kiss her hard. 'If there's a problem that can be solved with booze, I'm your man.'

I rolled my sleeves up to my elbows, folding each cuff three times over. 'I might need some help carrying things, though.' I took the trolley out of my back seat and hefted the keg of beer I'd taken from my cool room onto it.

'Okay.' Fiona's voice was faint. I glanced at her as I hauled a case of wine out of the boot, and found her gaze fixed on my forearms.

I winked at her. She flushed pink. 'Let me, um, go find some dads.'

The barbecue was on the school oval. I spotted Lex on the fringes of a gaggle of pre-teens, looking uncomfortably dressed up. I raised a hand to them as I wheeled the keg over the grass, and they visibly brightened as they waved back.

'Everyone, this is my friend Satoshi from Tsundoku down on the Bellerive high street,' Fiona announced, as I set the keg down next to the hastily-set-up trestle table on which the dads she'd recruited had put the cases of wine, 'and he comes bearing booze!'

A cheer went up, and people began to converge on us, slowly but surely, like a horde of zombies. 'So parents can drink, hey?' I said, wiping my wrist over my forehead before starting to take wine bottles out of the cases. It was a warm night, and I'd started to sweat.

'They sure can.' Fiona's tone was wry as she helped me. 'You should have seen the despair when they realised they'd drunk themselves dry.'

'Good, because I need them to drain this thing.' I tapped the keg with my foot as I attached a bike pump to the coupler, something I would never even dream of doing for anyone but her. 'I don't have a portable CO2 system to hand, so I'm about to commit a horrible crime and pump oxygen instead, which means the beer will oxidise in about twelve hours.'

'You're not going to have a problem, trust me – Hi, Mei-Lin, what can I get you? We've got a great selection here.'

We slipped into that same effortless service rhythm we'd found on that awful, perfect night last year. Fiona poured wine, laughing with some of the other parents. I tapped the keg and, between the consistent tempo of pouring and pumping, got accosted by some dads who wanted to have a discussion about craft beer.

I felt Fiona's eyes on me again as they finally left and there was a brief lull. 'I've missed you,' I commented, pumping air into the jury-rigged keg.

'I've missed you too. I'm sorry about last week, but the divorce hearing hit me harder than I expected, and then there was this *email*, and . . .'

Her voice trailed off. I looked over at her. Her gaze was fixed on my hands, following the up-and-down stroke of the pump.

'I – um – I was going to say that I'm still a bit shaky and that maybe we should stick to second base tomorrow,' she said, 'but – um . . .'

It was probably a blessing that Lex chose that moment to come bounding up, because otherwise, I had no idea how I would have maintained my grip on my control. 'Hi Satoshi!'

'Hi Lex.' I bumped my knuckles against theirs. 'Congratulations on graduating primary school!'

'Thanks.' They beamed, flag pins winking on their collar in the bright overhead lights of the oval. 'Did Mum tell you I won an award?'

'She didn't! Tell me about this award.'

'It's the Quiet Achiever award. Do you want to see?'

'Of course I do.'

Lex showed me their certificate, and I was midway through congratulating them when another gaggle of dads approached. 'Duty calls,' I said. 'But that's amazing, yeah? Hot chocolate is on me next time your mum brings you in.'

'Cool,' they said. 'Thanks, Satoshi.'

'You're very welcome.'

They drifted back towards the other kids. 'Mate, what's this beer?' one of the dads asked, draining half the plastic cup I'd poured them in a single swallow. 'It's fucking awesome.'

I opened my mouth to answer, but Fiona got in first. 'It's a lager from Bruny Island. Satoshi has it on tap.'

'I do,' I said. 'Tsundoku is a wine bar, but we're serious about good beer too. Come in sometime for a pint.'

'I will, mate. Cheers.'

They left. 'Thanks for the plug,' I said, nudging Fiona. 'You just can't help giving me free advertising, can you?'

'You don't need it.' She nudged me back. 'You're a good enough advertisement all on your own.'

Night had almost completely fallen, the pinks and reds of the summer sunset giving way to dark blues and greys. A few stars were visible in the sky, almost perfectly mirroring the little constellation of freckles beside Fiona's nose, their light winking off the few strands of silver hair at her temples.

'Thank you,' she said. 'For coming when I needed you.'

No one seemed to be looking in our direction, so I dared to reach out and take her hand, tracing my fingers down her wrist and along her palm before clasping it. 'Any time.'

She smiled at me and squeezed my fingers, and for a few heartbeats, we were the only two people in the world.

But then more thirsty parents approached us and we slipped back into service mode, transitioning gradually, as the evening wore on, from pouring drinks to packing down. I watched her in my peripheral vision as we worked, her eyes sparkling like the summer stars were caught in them, the most beautiful person I had ever seen.

We were doing the right thing, going slow. She'd been hurt so badly, and if there was even the slightest chance she might one day trust me with her heart as well as her body, I had to show her she could trust me to keep it safe.

None of that changed the fact that right here, right now – this minute – this second – I wanted her so fucking badly.

'Lex, can you wait here and make sure no one runs off with Satoshi's keg?' Fiona called, putting a few last empty wine bottles back into the cases. 'We're just going to take these to the bin.'

Lex nodded. I picked up one of the cases. 'I'm not sure why anyone would want to steal an empty keg, but thanks for protecting it.'

'Are you kidding? You heard those craft beer dads.' Fiona picked up the other case. 'I wouldn't put it past them to steal it for a homebrew set up or something.'

I followed her across the oval and around the corner of the school hall to the bins. 'I know I've said it already,' she said, as we started putting bottles into the dumpster, 'but I can't thank you enough for tonight. Truly. The last week or so has been pretty rocky, and I really needed a win.'

'It was no trouble at all.'

She gave me a look. 'I don't know how you define *trouble*, but magically turning up with half a bar's worth of booze five seconds after I flashed the Satoshi signal into the sky for sure required some.'

'Seriously, it's fine.' I flattened a cardboard box. 'Isamu was at the bar anyway, so I had cover. Besides, this wine probably would have gone to waste otherwise – it's all leftover open bottles from study group yesterday.'

'Satoshi,' she said, 'are you telling me that so you can try and give it to me for free?'

'No.' It was mostly true. 'They all would have oxidised sooner rather than later. Plus, some of them were complete garbage. Taking money for them would be a crime.'

She chuckled. 'Fine, fine. I'm paying for the beer, though. How much for the keg?'

I named a price that was about a third of market value. She nodded, a furrow forming between her brows. 'I can make that work.'

Shit. I should have gone lower.

'Can I pay you tomorrow?' A few more bottles clanked as she threw them into the dumpster. 'When I come in for our study session?'

'Of course.' I flattened the other cardboard box. 'And I heard you before, by the way. No further than second base.'

She exhaled. 'Sorry. The second I think I've got my shit together, something else will happen that sends me into panic mode, and—'

'Hey.' I caught her wrist. 'You don't need to apologise, remember? There's no hurry. It's not a race. We can take as much time as you need.'

'It's not fair to you, though,' she said. 'I, um . . . it's okay if you want to sleep with other people.'

Some key neural pathways in my brain iced over. 'What?'

'It's – like the seven years of bad sex thing.' Fiona used two fingers to point to her eyes and then to mine. 'I don't want to drag you down with me. I need to go slow, but you have needs too, and you shouldn't have to limit yourself to high school-style making out. And I know you always say foreplay is underrated, but you . . . you don't have to say no to other things – other people – you might want because of me.'

'Fiona,' I said, 'I don't want anyone else.'

She swallowed.

So did I. She was a deer poised to flee. I had to tread lightly, or she was going to slip through my fingers.

No sweeping declarations of love. No falling to my knees and kissing her feet and swearing there would never be anyone but her. Nothing too fast, nothing too hard, nothing that would scare her away. Slow. *Slow.*

'Just because I could technically want anyone,' I said, 'doesn't mean I want everyone.'

I let go of her wrist, trailing my hand up to her shoulder. 'You know my wine philosophy?'

'Which one?' she asked. 'You have lots.'

I flicked her gently under the chin. 'Quality, not quantity.'

That made her smile.

'For me, sex is only worth having if it's with someone I know. Someone I trust. Someone I *like*.' The word felt hollow and shallow coming out of my mouth, a betrayal of the enormity of what I felt for her, but slow, slow, I had to go slow. 'You're not the only one who needs to feel comfortable.'

Her head fell forward in surrender, resting against my clavicle, and I kissed her temple. 'You don't need to worry that I'm suffering, all right?' I murmured. 'Why would I want shots when I could savour?'

'I don't deserve you, Satoshi.'

Her voice was muffled in my chest, so I succumbed to the urge to tangle my fingers in her ponytail, tugging her face up to mine. 'You deserve the world,' I told her.

Our lips had just brushed together when her phone buzzed. 'Sorry, it's probably Jonah,' she said, fishing it out of her pocket. 'He must be wondering where I am. I told him I'd pick the girls up half an hour ago, and it's past their – oh my god.'

'What?'

Fiona's eyes were wide in the glowing light of her phone. 'I've got an email from the wine writing comp.'

'And? What does it say?'

'I don't know. I'm too scared to open it.'

'Do you want me to hold your hand?'

She nodded. I laced my fingers through hers and she squeezed tight, so tight it almost hurt. 'Okay, okay,' she muttered, more to herself than to me. 'It's fine. Everything's fine.'

It took about a second, maybe a second and a half, before the widest, brightest smile I'd ever seen spread across her face. 'I won,' she said. 'Satoshi, I *won*!'

'Fiona!'

I wasn't sure if I moved first or she did, but between one breath and the next we were hugging, my arms tight around her as I lifted her off her feet. 'I can't believe this!' she exclaimed.

'I can.' I pressed my lips to her cheek. 'I'm so proud of you.'

She buried her face in my throat. 'I couldn't have done it without you.'

Teardrops were shining on her cheeks when I finally put her back down. 'I tried so hard not to get my hopes up,' she said. 'I've never won anything in my entire life. I've always been surrounded by all these brilliant people, but I've never been good at anything, not really, and—'

'You are fucking *great* at this, Fiona. I'm not even a little bit surprised you won.'

A stray piece of hair was falling in her face. I stroked it back. My fingers brushed the sensitive spot behind her ear, the one I'd studiously avoided in our month of slow, and I felt a shiver go through her. 'Sorry,' I said. 'That was an accident.'

'Don't apologise,' she whispered.

We looked into each other's eyes for one moment, two, the length of a promise made as two glasses clinked together.

And then Fiona Fisher kissed me.

It was an impossible mix of tentative and urgent, one of her hands fisting hard in my hair and the other in my shirt, even as her lips asked a question. I answered it, kissing her back harder, opening my mouth to her, sucking her bottom lip between mine and nipping it with my teeth. She made a desperate noise of pleasure and—

—the fraying thread of my control snapped.

I pinned her against the wall of the school hall, hiking my hands under her thighs and hauling her up against me. Her legs wrapped around my waist, and she moaned as I ground against her. 'I love how strong you are, Satoshi. It's—' our lips met again, hot, wet, messy '—so fucking sexy. When you were manhandling that keg around—' and again 'I thought I was going to lose my mind.'

One of her hands snuck under the open collar of my shirt, and she pressed her lips to my pulse point. 'I can't stop thinking about you,' she breathed. 'This whole last month – I have so many things I have to think about, but I can't stop thinking about you.'

'I can't stop thinking about you either.' I ground myself against her again and the hungry sound it drew from her made my blood fizz. 'All the things you let me to do to you. All the things you might let me do to you. I spend my week living for Thursdays, wondering what you might let me do next.'

'I bought a vibrator,' she gasped.

The sudden admission made me laugh. 'God, I adore you.'

'Why?'

'Why?!' I bit her earlobe. 'Why do you think? You're—'

'Oh my goodness, Fiona, is that you?'

Fiona slid swiftly back down my body, her feet hitting the ground with a thud. It felt like my heart fell out of my body and landed there with her.

The woman laughed. 'Well, this is the last thing I expected to find back here!' She waggled a finger playfully, but disapprovingly. 'Isn't making out beside the bins a bit high school?'

'Michelle—' Even in the semi-dark, I could see that Fiona's face was crimson, the colour of a full-bodied shiraz. 'I can explain.'

'Oh, you don't need to explain!' The woman's laugh was a supercilious trill. 'If anyone's entitled to be messy, it's you, Fiona.'

'Excuse me?' I interjected.

But Fiona was already speaking. 'I'd appreciate if you'd keep this quiet.' She positioned herself in front of me, trying to hide me behind her, even though she was nearly a head shorter. 'I've had enough of my personal business being public gossip.'

'Oh, babe, *of course*.' Michelle put her hand over her heart. 'I'll take it to the grave.'

I had known this woman for approximately thirty seconds, but I was confident that she would not, in fact, be taking this to her grave.

'And between you and me – get it, girlfriend.' She winked conspiratorially. 'A hot little toyboy is exactly what you deserve. But you might want to make sure you don't get carried away.' Her tone shifted to something more patronising. 'Poor Lex is standing there on the oval, all alone!'

'They're twelve,' Fiona said. 'They can—'

'Don't worry, I made sure Steve waited with them.' Michelle laughed again, and I could practically feel the hairs on the back of

Fiona's neck stand on end. 'I'd never leave them unsupervised – that'd be very bad P&F chair behaviour! But you might want to get back to them, yes?'

'I'll be right there. Thanks for looking out for them.'

'Any time, babe.' Michelle turned to go, but then turned back, pointing at me and gesturing up and down. '*Love* this for you.'

She left. 'Oh god,' Fiona moaned.

'What an awful woman.'

'She's not, she's just . . . oh *god*.'

Fiona took a step away from me, hurriedly tucking the front of her blouse back into her jeans. 'I'm so sorry, Satoshi – about all of this – but – Lex – I have to—'

'Go,' I said, even though there was a dark, yawning chasm in the pit of my stomach. 'It's all right.'

She went. Unlike Michelle, she did not look back, and I stood there beside the bins, in the still of the night, for a long time.

I was – or, at least, should be – smart enough not to take phrases like *hot little toyboy* seriously. Who would take one single thing this condescending woman had said seriously?

But I couldn't stop seeing Fiona's face: at first scarlet, and then milk-pale with mortification.

I didn't give a shit that she was older than me. But for her, age was clearly not just a number. Was *I can explain* something she would have said if she'd been caught with someone her own age?

I took off my glasses – my stupid, childish, lime-green glasses – and put my palm over my eyes, as if it could block out the awful, inexorable truth of what had just happened. Of what had already happened when Sadie caught us at the restaurant, even though I'd shoved it deep down and refused to acknowledge it.

Is it okay if we don't tell anyone? she'd asked me that day we'd decided to go slow, and I'd blithely agreed, because I would have agreed to anything if it meant I got to have her.

Fiona might like me. She might value me. She might enjoy our Thursday nights together, and she might even trust me.

But the idea that people might think we were actually *together* was something she found deeply, profoundly embarrassing.

Chapter Nine
Fiona

Tasting today: 2024 riesling, Tasmania, Australia.
This wine is dangerous. With intense fruit flavours and thrillingly racy acidity, it's difficult to stop yourself having another glass, and another, and another . . .

Satoshi, I'm so sorry about what happened at the barbecue, I typed into my phone, sitting on the sidelines on Saturday morning at the girls' indoor soccer game. *I'm sorry I ran away and left you standing there. I'm sorry Michelle spoke about you like that. I'm sorry I rainchecked Thursday night instead of apologising to you in person, it's just . . .*

I let out a long breath and deleted the message. *So I have a long list of things I need to apologise for,* I tried again.

A cheer went up as the ball thudded into the back of the net. 'Mummy, did you see my goal?' Rosie yelled.

'Yes, Rosie-girl!' I called back. 'Well done!'

I could feel, rather than see, some of the other parents looking knowingly at each other. *The worst mother in the world strikes again. Look at her, lying to her own daughter.*

I put my phone away, wrapped my hands around my keep cup of coffee and tried to focus my attention on the game. The kids blurred before my eyes, though, a mess of neon orange and green and white.

I wasn't a bad mother. I *wasn't*. My kids were safe. My kids were loved. Lex was definitely mature enough to stand alone for ten minutes in the middle of a well-lit space with dozens of adults around, and I was allowed to have a – a – to move on from Matt. I should be smarter than to let Michelle's bitchy little comments get into my head.

Maybe, in another world, when I didn't have that email from Laura sitting in my inbox oh-so-innocently implying that a better mother would simply set all her own feelings aside for the sake of the children, I would have been smarter. But I lived in this one, and – as I was so often reminded – I'd never exactly been renowned for my intelligence anyway.

After the game, I took the girls shopping for art supplies so they could make a welcome sign for Elias, who was due to arrive next week. They were both exhausted and hangry – I'd foolishly decided we could run this errand before I fed them lunch – and so, of course, we ran into one of the other Year 6 mums. 'You really saved the day at the barbecue, Fiona,' she said, effortlessly juggling her toddler and several pieces of cardboard. 'Thank goodness you have an in with that lovely barman!'

I didn't need a PhD to be able to read the subtext. *So Michelle told everyone you're fucking that hot young bartender you dragged along? I hope you don't have a drinking problem along with that midlife crisis you're having, sweetie.*

'Thank goodness,' I echoed.

'No!' Georgia howled. 'Green isn't elegant, Rosie! Silver is elegant! You don't know *anything*!'

The other mother gave me a knowing smile, and I could feel my face start to turn red as I did my best to de-escalate. *Just ran into Fiona,* was going to end up in some WhatsApp chat I wasn't in within the next five minutes. *She can barely control those twins of hers, poor thing.*

Honestly, I'm worried about her kids, someone – probably Michelle – would say. *Fiona's obviously a mess at the moment. I hate to say this, but maybe things would be better if she didn't have sole custody.*

I was dimly aware, as I finally managed to get the girls out of the shop, that my imagination was getting the better of me, but knowing it didn't make it stop. My therapist was going to be so mad at me.

'Mum,' Lex asked me, when I picked them up from Jonah and Sadie's, 'can we go to Tsundoku later? Satoshi told me he'd give me a free hot chocolate for winning the Quiet Achiever award.'

'Not today, sweetheart. Your sisters are going to have a meltdown if I drag them anywhere else.'

'Oh.' It was one syllable, but disappointment was written large all over it. 'Okay.'

Guilt swept through me. 'Soon, though. I promise.'

Lex nodded, but they started fiddling with their non-binary flag pin, and the guilt intensified into nausea. Satoshi was so, so important to them. Would a good mother really be as reckless as I had? Risk what I was risking, just for the sake of – what? My own selfish feelings?

Would Michelle? Would *Laura*?

Later that night, sitting in bed, I finally forced myself to text him. *Satoshi, I owe you a huge apology for what happened at the barbecue. I'm so sorry.*

He didn't reply.

Which I was *not* going to take personally. Apart from the panicked *Let's raincheck Thursday* text I'd sent him straight after the Michelle incident, it had taken me days to reach out. I hardly deserved an immediate reply. Besides, it was before close, so he'd still be working – and it was Saturday night, so the bar was probably packed.

. . . oh no. I'd announced to everyone at the barbecue where he worked. What if he'd been inundated with a flood of gawking school parents? What if they were there right now, laughing and making suggestive little comments about how he was helping me get my groove back?

A HUGE apology, I texted. *I know it was absolutely mortifying.*

No response.

Shit. What if he'd blocked me? What if this had been a tipping point and he'd finally decided *enough*? What would I tell Lex? What would I—

My phone buzzed. I snatched at it so violently I nearly fell out of bed.

You don't owe me anything, Fiona, Satoshi had sent.

I pressed my tongue to the roof of my mouth, head falling to my knees as I tried my best not to literally cry with relief.

How did he always react like this? Every time I dumped my bullshit on him and ran away, how, how, *how* did he always just make everything fine again?

I at least owe you for the keg! I sent back. *I'll pay for it. I promise.*

He didn't reply, and I could practically see him, glancing at his phone, raising his eyebrows, and putting it back into his pocket. *Oh no you won't,* he might as well have said, an assertion that was also a prophecy.

The relief started to ebb away, and I hugged my knees tight to my chest as a new kind of guilt started to take its place.

The thing that had always drawn me to Satoshi, even before Matt had left, was his unfailing kindness. It was so reliable you could set your watch by it: the sky was blue, the grass was green, Satoshi was kind. He was the type of person who would give Lex the pin off his own waistcoat, who would make sure the girls felt like princesses in a fancy restaurant, who would flatter my ego by saying he needed my help with his tasting notes even when he clearly didn't. *Oh, you don't owe me anything!* he'd say, *I'm getting as much out of this as you are,* as he gave and gave and gave, and I took, took, took.

He was a rock. He was a lighthouse. I broke over him like the sea, again and again, and he was still there anyway.

Maybe this time it really was okay. But how much more could I ask of him before he said *enough*? There had to be a limit – everyone had a limit – and what kind of person would I be if I pushed him to it?

Tears pricked at the corner of my eyes again. I owed Satoshi far more – and far better – than just the price of a keg.

🍷

Elias's flight was getting in on Thursday evening – which was convenient, because I was a coward. *I'm so sorry, but I have to raincheck again,* I texted Satoshi. *My brother's arriving from Germany. Sorry for being such a terrible study buddy x*

No problem, he texted back. *I have to raincheck too anyway – covering for Birdie tonight.*

Hope you're not working too hard!! I'll promise I'll come and pay for the keg soon.

And I would. I would find my resolve, and I would look him in the eye, and I would discharge my debts. I was going to be a good parent and set an example for my children. No relying on anyone, for anything.

Elias was staying at my place, but as his arrival time coincided directly with the kids' dinnertime, Jonah and Sadie had borrowed my car to pick him up from the airport. 'I can't *wait*,' Rosie enthused as I scooped ice cream into their bowls for dessert. 'It was so fun last time Uncle Elias was here.'

I forced the guilty memory of those weeks down. It had been January, only a few months after Matt had left, and I'd been holding on by a thread. The first time Elias had taken the kids out and I'd had the house to myself, I'd burst into tears with relief at the quiet.

'Remember, we have lots of time to have fun with Uncle Elias,' I said, trying and failing not to let the thought *Laura would never* enter my mind. 'You can stay up to say hello, and then it's bedtime, okay? He's going to be tired too, and—'

Headlights flashed briefly through the window. 'He's here!' Georgia shrieked, knocking her ice cream bowl off the table.

I sighed and bent down to pick it up as Rosie bolted too. I'd just mopped the floor that morning.

'Mum, I can do that.'

I looked up, surprised.

Lex gestured to the mess. 'Let me clean it up.'

'My goodness!' I heard Elias say in the front hallway as the girls squealed with excitement. 'What an elegant welcome sign!'

'That's all right, sweetheart,' I said to Lex, already halfway through imagining the condescending monologue Michelle would deliver if she saw them trying to parentify themselves like this. 'I've got it.'

Elias was good-naturedly deflecting the girls' pointed questions about whether he'd brought them any presents when I finally made my way into the living room. 'Hey, Fi,' he said warmly, pulling me into a hug.

'Hey, you.' My older brother smelled of sweat and faded cologne, his stubble scratchy as he kissed me on both cheeks. 'How are you? You must be exhausted.'

'I'm fine, actually. It's about ten am Munich time. I might have been flying for a whole day, but I'm wide awake.'

So too were the girls, high on adrenaline, and by the time I managed to get them to bed and Lex had retired to their room with a book Sadie had bought for them on a whim at the airport, Jonah had cracked open a bottle of Bibliophile riesling. 'We picked this up from our local down on the high street,' he explained to Elias, handing him a glass.

'The one with the absurdly generous somm, right?' Elias tilted his glass to the side, looking at the body. 'Bold move, little brother, pouring riesling to someone who's been in Germany for two years. I've got high standards.'

'It's a beautiful wine.'

I barely realised I'd spoken until Elias, Jonah and Sadie all looked at me. 'It's top-notch,' I said defensively. 'The winemaker's brilliant. He's won, like, eight thousand awards. Besides, Tasmania's got a great climate for riesling. It's cool but there's a lot of sunshine, so—'

'Okay, okay, Wikipedia.' Elias chuckled. 'I promise, Fi, I don't need a position paper to talk me into having a glass of wine.'

I knew he meant nothing by it, but it still stung. What might he – or any of them – say if I told them about the piece on Bibliophile I was halfway through editing for my new column? *Oh, nice, it's cute that you have a hobby. How did you find time to do it with the kids? Anyway . . .*

'Cheers, Fishers – and honorary Fishers,' Elias added to Sadie, who made a face. 'It's lovely to be in the same country again.'

We all clinked our glasses together. Jonah and Sadie looked each other in the eye, smiling knowingly. I dug the nails of my free hand hard into my palm.

'Oh, this *is* good wine,' Elias said. 'Sorry for the doubts.'

'I told you.' A little flash of pride cut through the tangle in my stomach. My brothers and I might have made leaps and bounds in our relationship over the past year, but it was still hard to get a Fisher to admit they were wrong.

'I hope you've got some more, Fi,' Jonah said, clapping Elias on the shoulder, 'because I don't think one bottle is going to do us.'

'Sorry.' The momentary flash vanished, and status quo was restored: Fiona Fisher, family disappointment. 'I'm out.'

'No drama.' Jonah pulled out his phone. 'I bet I know someone who'll deliver.'

It took me a second to realise what he meant. 'No! Tsundoku isn't that kind of—'

'But if there's one person they'd make an exception for . . .' He winked at me. 'Hi – Charlotte? This is Jonah Fisher. I'm at Fiona's place, and I was wondering . . .'

It turned into a three-way conversation as Elias started offering his opinion on which wines should go into the impromptu half-case Jonah was ordering. Sadie nudged me with her elbow. 'Are you all right?'

I nodded tightly.

She looked at me for a long moment before hooking her arm through mine and pulling me towards the front door. 'Come with me.'

'Fi, where are you taking my wife?' Jonah called, putting his hand over the mic on his phone.

'Wedding stuff!' Sadie replied. 'Mind your own business, Fisher.'

She sat me down at the table on the front porch, closing the door behind us. 'Okay, spill,' she said. 'What's wrong?'

'Nothing,' I said stiffly. 'I just don't like taking advantage of Tsundoku's generosity, that's all.'

'You're going to have to do better than that.' She gestured to her face. 'You've gone the same colour as when I caught you with Satoshi in the restaurant. White, with a hint of green. What is it?'

I hesitated.

'I know I've been teasing you about him.' Her tone was gentler now. 'If I've been poking at a sore spot—'

'No.' My voice was hoarse. 'It's fine.'

'You, however, are obviously not.' She reached across the table to me. 'What happened?'

I exhaled. The quickest way out of this conversation was probably going to be through.

Sadie listened impassively as I told her about our Thursday night arrangement, but her hands flew to her mouth when I recounted the story of Michelle catching us beside the bins. 'Oh *noooooo*.'

'It was mortifying,' I said. 'I wanted the ground to open up and swallow me – are you laughing?'

'I'm sorry!' Sadie wasn't just laughing, she was practically crying. 'I bet it was embarrassing – but come on, you have to admit that it's also—' she almost couldn't get the words out, she was laughing so hard '—*unbelievably* funny.'

I stared.

She clapped a hand to her heart in mock horror. 'Oh, *my stars*,' she said, in an affected imitation, presumably of Michelle. 'My delicate, innocent eyes! My mind simply cannot *process* the thought of someone actually getting some when my husband hasn't cared about anything but cricket and craft beer for ten years!'

It was, based on what I knew from the Fridays I used to spend volunteering with her, a pretty accurate read of the dynamic of Michelle's marriage, but I bristled anyway. 'You know people don't stop having sex just because they have kids, right?'

'Yes – yes – sorry.' Sadie wiped tears of laughter out of her eyes. 'That was mean. But come on. You must be, like, a cult hero now. "Woman gets over arsehole ex-husband by getting under hot younger guy who comes with bonus high-quality booze"? That's iconic.'

I didn't say anything.

Slowly, Sadie's laughter faded away. 'So . . . not funny, then.'

I shook my head. 'It was a wake-up call. That I – I'm being – I shouldn't be doing this.'

'Fiona, no.'

'I have to be realistic, Sadie. It's been wonderful, this past month, but it can't last.'

I took a long sip of my wine, trying to swallow down the lump in my throat. 'Satoshi's got this big glittering future ahead of him. He deserves a proper partner, someone who can really be there for him and support him and give him what he needs, not someone he has to put back together. And he's not just some stranger I can have a bit of fun with and then forget, either. He's in the kids' lives.'

I swallowed again, but the lump in my throat wasn't going away. 'I thought Thursdays could just be this secret little thing I did, just for me. But look what happened at the barbecue. If I let it keep going, the kids will find out. I'm lucky they haven't already. And if they do – then when it ends—' I swallowed again, once, twice, three times '—they'll lose someone else.'

'And so will you?'

'This isn't about me, Sadie.' I tipped my head back, looking at the stars. 'I can't let it be about me.'

She regarded me for a long moment. 'You really are a Fisher, aren't you?'

I blinked. 'What?'

'You clearly know how to construct an argument. Look at you, twelve logical leaps ahead.'

'Thank you?' I was strangely flattered.

'It makes total sense that you'd jump to the worst-case scenario, where everything turns to shit and you and the kids get hurt. It's already happened to you once, after all. But—' she leaned forward across the table '—you're still wrong.'

'Sadie—'

'Your logic is sound, but your premise is flawed. Everything you said relies on you not being able to have him – but I really think you can, Fiona. I think you can have it all.'

She nodded to the kerb, where Satoshi's car had just pulled up, the timing as perfect as if it had been scripted. 'That man,' she said, 'is not going anywhere. Hi!'

'Hi.' Satoshi closed his car door.

I couldn't help but watch as he took the half-case of wine out of the boot. He was in the more dressed-down version of the work ensemble I'd become accustomed to on our Thursdays together: tailored trousers paired with a white T-shirt, a tantalising triangle of smooth skin revealed by the V-neck. His glasses were forest green today, and his bleached hair was tousled less artfully than normal, like someone had run their fingers through it.

My heart started beating faster, a memory of being the someone to run their fingers through it rising unbidden to the surface of my mind. *You can pull it harder, if you want*, he'd whispered, as his lips traced a line down my throat, and—

'Come in,' Sadie said, opening the front door, making me realise that I'd just been standing there, staring. 'The boys will be happy to see you.'

I trailed after them, awkwardly hovering as Satoshi shook hands with first Jonah and then Elias, feeling like a ghost in my own house, unable to speak. 'Have a drink with us,' Jonah said, tapping his credit card against the portable reader Satoshi had brought. 'You can convince old mate here—' he elbowed Elias '—that Tasmanian wine is just as good as what he gets in Europe.'

Satoshi's gaze slid sideways to me. 'You don't need me to pitch you on Bibliophile when you've got Fiona. She can probably give you better tasting notes than I can.'

I wanted to shriek. How was he always so fucking *wonderful*?

'We insist.' Jonah gestured to Satoshi's outfit. 'Anyway, it's your night off, right?'

'Fiona,' Sadie interjected, 'how about you and Satoshi go and put the wine in the kitchen and find him a wineglass?'

I should have been grateful to her for forcing me into proximity with him, making me have the conversation I knew I had to have, but in that moment, I wanted to kill her.

'Sure,' I said instead. 'Um – this way.'

There was a silvery glow streaming into the kitchen from outside, so I didn't turn on the light. Better not to let myself really see him, or I'd never be able to stick to my resolve. 'Just put those on the table,' I said, going up on tiptoes to get him down a glass. 'Do you want to pick what we open next? We've been drinking riesling, so—'

'Fiona,' he said softly.

I couldn't bring myself to turn to face him. 'I'm sorry.'

There was a long, drawn-out pause.

'What for?' he asked.

'All of it,' I replied. 'Michelle. Running away. Asking you to come to the barbecue in the first place. For being such a terrible study buddy – fuck, you should be studying right now, shouldn't you? I'm sorry, I'm so sorry, every time I ask you come running and I shouldn't ask, it's not fair, and—'

'Mummy?'

If there was one word that could cut right through one of my spirals, it was that. 'Georgie-girl? What's wrong?'

'I had a bad dream.' Georgia sniffed, chin quivering, her elephant cuddled to her chest. 'I dreamed that I woke up and everyone was gone and I was all by myself.'

'Oh, honeybun.' I knelt down so I could put my arms around her. 'I'm right here, okay? I've got you.'

She sniffed again, nodding against my throat. 'Hi, Satoshi.'

'Hi, Miss Georgia,' he replied. 'That's a really elegant elephant.'

'Thank you. Mummy helped me make her a fancy ballgown.' Georgia pulled out of my embrace. 'What are you doing here?'

He hesitated.

'He brought some wine for the grown-ups,' I said. 'Come on. Let's get you back to bed.'

'Can I give Satoshi a hug first?'

It was my turn to hesitate. 'Only if he says it's okay. It's always best to ask first, remember?'

'You know what?' Satoshi crouched down. 'I'd love a hug.'

Georgia wrapped her arms around his neck. His hands came to rest on her shoulder blades as he hugged her back, eyes closing, and a light-headedness came over me, like my blood had suddenly turned very thin.

It took me a while to get Georgia back to bed, stroking her hair as she fell asleep. By the time I emerged, everyone else was most of the way through another bottle of riesling. 'I saved some for you,' Satoshi said, pouring the remainder of it into my glass.

Of course he had. 'Thank you,' was all I could reply before I turned away, so he didn't see how much that simple gesture made my heart ache.

He left soon afterwards. 'I really do have to get back,' he said, as my brothers – and Lex, who had emerged from their room when they realised he was here – urged him to stay for another glass. 'I've got a lot of study to do – and anyway, I'm driving.'

'Mum's going to bring me for hot chocolate soon,' Lex said. 'Aren't you, Mum?'

'Of course.' I dug my nails hard into my palm.

Satoshi bumped Lex's proffered knuckles. 'Looking forward to it, pal. See you soon.'

Then he turned to me. 'Thank you for welcoming me into your home, Fiona. It's beautiful.'

I dug my nails in harder and steeled myself. Time to be strong. 'You're welcome. I'll walk you out.'

Outside, crickets were singing in the summer night. It was warm, but I folded my arms around myself anyway, trying to find the right words. *Thank you so much for putting me back together, Satoshi, but I think it's better . . . I think it's best . . . For the sake of everyone, we should—*

'Can I ask you something?' Satoshi said abruptly.

My heart sped up, an uneven drum beat in my chest. 'Sure.'

'Was it really that embarrassing?'

I blinked.

'The other night.' He paused beside his car, running his hand through his hair. 'When you messaged me, you said it was mortifying, and I was just wondering . . . was it really so bad for you, getting caught with me?'

'Oh! Oh god, Satoshi, no!'

Something between horror and panic ran through me. He was always so careful with me, and the thought of him believing he'd hurt me made me want to throw up. 'You didn't do anything wrong,' I said. 'Not a single thing. You're perfect – and I'm fine, I promise.'

Even though I knew I shouldn't, that I was just making things harder for myself, I reached out and took his hand, kissing his knuckles then pressing my cheek to them. 'It's just – people talk, you know? And no one talks more than parents – you wouldn't *believe* how much they gossip – and then what they say gets filtered down to the kids. I can't tell you how many times the girls have come home from school with questions like "Mummy, what's a mistress?", "Mummy, what's a lovechild?". With Michelle – I could practically hear "Mummy, what's a toyboy?", and the thought of having to *explain* that . . .'

I let out a long breath. 'It's just . . . a lot. As usual, right?'

Satoshi didn't say anything.

'Besides,' I added, trying to sound as jokey as possible, even as my heart pounded even harder, 'I'm sure it wasn't on your bucket list to get caught kissing one of the mums at a school barbecue. Aren't you always telling me you have an image to maintain?'

'Fiona,' he said quietly, 'I'd kiss you in front of the entire world if you wanted me to.'

. . . oh.

I had to let this man go. I knew that. The longer I put it off – the more I let myself lean into him – the more difficult it would be. If I was sensible – if I was smart – I would do it right this second.

'Will you kiss me now?' I asked.

Satoshi blinked. 'Here?'

I glanced over at the house. I doubted anyone would be peering out the front window at us, but I didn't want to risk it. 'In here.' I opened the back door to his car, shepherding him in.

Inside, I draped myself over his lap, a knee on either side of his legs on the back seat. 'No one,' I said, kissing his lips, 'has ever been as lovely to me as you, Satoshi. You're so kind—' I kissed his cheek '—and so patient—' now the corner of his jaw '—and I'm so, so lucky to have you in my life.'

I kissed behind his ear, but either I hadn't found the right spot or it didn't feel to him the way it did to me, because he was stiff and still beneath me. 'Are you all right?' I asked. 'Did I do something wrong?'

'No.' He smoothed a hand over my hair. 'I just . . .'

He closed his eyes. 'I don't want to put any pressure on you,' he said at last. 'But if the thought that people might find out about us scares you so badly – is this really something you want to be doing?'

Here it was again. He was perfect, and so he'd provided me with a second perfect out, another opportunity to make a clean break, no harm, no—

'Yes,' I whispered. 'It is.'

I fisted my hands into his T-shirt and rested my forehead against his. 'But the second you don't want to anymore, just say, okay? I won't hold it against you. I might have to hit pause for a few weeks, anyway – Elias is staying with me and I don't know if I'll be able to sneak away on Thursdays – and I would completely understand if you were sick of me and all my messy bullshit, so— *mmph.*'

Satoshi's mouth crashed into mine, his fingers twisting hard into my hair, and by the time I managed to get out of the car, the windows were very, very foggy.

That wasn't what I thought about later, though, after another bottle of wine, when Sadie and Jonah had finally left and Elias had gone to bed. As I stacked the glasses in the dishwasher, I didn't think about the way Satoshi had kissed me, or the heat of his skin against my palms when I'd slid my hands under his shirt, or even the erection I'd felt against my thigh, literal hard evidence that he really did want me.

Instead, it was the way he'd gently thumbed a stray fleck of mascara off my cheek and helped me redo my ponytail so I looked presentable before I went back inside. The way he'd looked, crouching down on my kitchen floor, holding Georgia so carefully, so tenderly. The way he'd sounded, when he told me he'd kiss me in front of the whole world if that was what I wanted.

I knew better than to read into a statement like that. I'd let a man kiss me in front of the whole world once, and it hadn't meant anything in the end.

But even though it was careless – reckless – completely and utterly foolhardy – I couldn't stop Sadie's voice echoing through my mind. *I think you can have it all.*

Chapter Ten
Satoshi

Tasting today: ahead of vintage, pinot noir, Tasmania, Australia. Multiple vineyards are often blended to make quality Tassie pinots, but sometimes a single vineyard needs to stand alone.

'Try this,' Isamu said.

He used a glass wine thief to extract tiny amounts from two different barrels of pinot, dispensing them into the tasting glasses in my hands. 'These come from the two blocks I use to make the Noriko. I've always blended them before, but I'm considering releasing them as two separate single vineyard wines this time. What do you think?'

I looked at the wines against the white of my sleeve (both pale, one slightly more purple than the other), smelled them (fresh strawberry and raspberry in one; darker notes of cherry and baking spice in the other), then tasted them. 'Do you actually think they'll be better as single vineyard? Or do you just not want to make the Noriko anymore?'

'I'm genuinely wondering whether they'll be better as single vineyard.'

I tasted them individually again, then tipped one glass into the other and tasted them together, as we both pretended he hadn't already long since decided what he was going to do. 'You'll sacrifice some balance if you don't combine them, but as a blend, they're working at cross purposes – speaking over each other.'

'That's what I thought.'

Of course it was.

We spent ninety minutes walking around the winery, trying some of the wines Isamu had in progress. 'Thanks, Sato,' he said, as we emerged into the Sauternes-coloured sun of the late Monday afternoon. 'I appreciate getting your palate on these.'

'You're welcome,' I replied, like he hadn't been extremely obviously buttering me up.

I'd been bracing for a reckoning ever since I'd let the word *Onīsan* pass my lips, and I steeled myself for it now. *Okay, I've pretended I need your help, let's talk about how you clearly can't do anything without mine.*

As we trudged back up the hill, though, Isamu didn't say anything.

Okāsan was waiting for us in the doorway of the B&B. 'There you are!' she said in Japanese. 'Okaeri. I was wondering where you'd – oh, there she goes again.'

'There she goes,' Isamu echoed long-sufferingly. Yquem – who I'd dropped off before we headed to the winery – had launched herself at him and was wrapped around his neck like a scarf.

'It continues to be utterly mystifying to me,' I said, trying and failing to punch the pang of jealousy down, 'that even though I'm the one who looks after her every need, she likes you a thousand times better anyway.'

Isamu only grunted, blowing a tuft of Yquem's fur out of his face.

Okāsan had made chicken katsu. I took a brief look through Isamu's cellar and selected a bottle of Condrieu to pair with it. 'Itadakimasu,' Okāsan said, as we sat down to eat.

'Itadakimasu,' Isamu and I dutifully repeated.

Our mother was a great cook, and the wine was beautiful (it was from my brother's cellar, after all), but I was eating and drinking on autopilot, not really tasting anything. My head felt overfull, stuffed – not like it did when I tried to cram too much information from my theory binder into my head in too short a space of time, but like someone had cracked open my skull and rammed a whole heap of cotton balls in there with my brain.

No amount of my usual rituals had helped. I had drilled myself with flashcard after flashcard. I had done blind tasting after blind tasting, looking, smelling, tasting and spitting like an automaton, scratching black marks into deductive tasting grids. I had polished every glass in Tsundoku several times over. I had reorganised my already rigidly organised office ten times. In the dead of night, when I couldn't sleep, I'd gone downstairs to the bar and painstakingly re-genrefied and alphabetised all the books.

None of it worked, though. All I could think about was Fiona.

The things she'd said to me the other night made perfect sense. Of course she didn't want to be the subject of any more gossip, not when she'd already been the subject of so much.

What did that mean for me, though?

I might fantasise about a future where I stood beside her in her kitchen and presented the milk to her daughters, but Fiona only saw one where she stood alone and tried, scarlet-faced, to explain what *toyboy* meant. She'd jokingly said something about how kissing her at a school function couldn't be good for my image, but it wasn't hard to see that it was a polite inversion of what she actually meant: that kissing me wasn't good for hers.

I'd taken a chance. Even though I knew it was too far, too fast, too soon, I'd told her I'd kiss her in front of the whole world if she wanted – and she'd just ushered me into the back seat, where not a soul could see us.

She was everything to me. But to her, I would only ever be – could only ever be – someone she had to explain away. A shameful secret, someone she'd clandestinely make out with but not hold hands with in public. A guilty pleasure she knew she shouldn't indulge but couldn't quite make herself quit.

And I couldn't quit either. I'd kissed her back, because she'd started rambling about how *surely* I must be getting sick of her, and I'd panicked and pounced on her before she could follow that thought too much further. She'd already run once when she thought I'd kissed her purely for her benefit. I couldn't let her do it again.

But she was going to. Unless I could miraculously age myself up a decade or so, she was going to, and—

I startled as my mother touched my hand. 'You're quiet, Sato. Are you feeling all right?'

I nodded. 'I'm fine.'

She studied me. 'No, you're not.'

'I am, Okāsan, really.' I made myself smile. 'Tired, that's all.'

Isamu put his chopsticks down. 'And we need to talk about it.'

I resisted the urge to sigh. I'd walked right into that one.

'I appreciate you stepping in the other night when I had to run out.' I'd rehearsed this speech several times on the drive out to the vineyard. 'I was lucky you were there. But that was an isolated incident. I can—'

'It's not an isolated incident, though.' He gave me one of those looks, the ones that made me feel like a teenager again. 'We have to talk about Birdie.'

I set my chopsticks down too. 'We have talked about Birdie. Besides, she wasn't even rostered on the other night. That had nothing to do with her.'

'I talked to some of your staff.' His gaze was unwavering. 'It sounds like she's absent more than she's there.'

Of fucking *course* he'd snooped around.

'Sato,' he said, his tone gentler now, 'if you can't bring yourself to fire her, I'll do it for you.'

'I'm not going to fire her, Isamu!' I snapped. 'We've already had this conversation. You know my position.'

'Why not, though? I get that she's dealing with family stuff, but there has to be a limit. You can't have someone on staff who isn't doing their job. Particularly when it means you – *you*, who is insisting on studying for the hardest exam in the world – have to do it for her!'

I gritted my teeth.

'*Why*?' he demanded.

Because Fiona Fisher, more than a year ago, had sat across from me and said, *Speaking of Birdie, you're not going to fire her, are you?*

'It's none of your business,' I said.

'It'll be my business when you work yourself to death like Otōsan!'

'Isamu!' Okāsan said.

'You are just fucking like him.' Isamu jabbed a finger at me. 'So set in your ways you won't listen to anyone else. So convinced that only you can do things right that you won't accept help. So fucking obsessive that it's going to kill you!'

'Maybe,' I grated out from between clenched teeth, 'if you actually trusted that I can manage my own shit, I wouldn't have to work so hard to prove it to you.'

Isamu's nostrils flared. 'Sato—'

'Excuse me.' I stood, snatching up my glass of Condrieu. 'I need some air.'

It was nearly the summer solstice, so even though it was after nine pm, the sun had only just set, a few early stars speckling the sky. I sank onto the front steps, which were so low my knees almost ended up around my ears. I wanted to yell my frustrations out, to listen to them echo back to me off the vine-covered slopes, but that would only worry my mother, so I settled for a long, extended exhale instead, which did nothing to ease the snarl of feeling in my chest.

I had sat on these steps the night Otōsan died. He had collapsed in the vineyard, his heart giving out after decades of hard work and long days. Isamu – aged twenty-eight, but in everyone's eyes a man, not a boy – had stood stoically, arms folded across his chest, dealing with the paramedics, but after they'd taken the body away, he'd left, striding away through the vines. Noriko had gone after him, and Okāsan had retreated into the house, but I'd sat out here on the steps, and I'd looked up at the stars, and I'd cried.

I had cried tears of grief for my father, whom I had loved. But I had also cried tears of guilt and tears of relief, because this time he had gone somewhere he could not make us follow.

I wasn't like him. I *wasn't*. I would never do what he did: drag his family around the world in fanatical pursuit of glory, denying them any sense of stability. Hadn't I come back to do just the opposite? To build a home in Tsundoku, one that would make others feel at home too?

'Sato?'

I looked over my shoulder automatically, although I didn't need to. 'I'm sorry, Okāsan.'

My mother sat down, two stairs above me, knee just brushing my upper arm. 'You're having a tough time at the moment, aren't you?'

There was no point lying to her. 'Yes.'

'And your brother's not making it easier.'

I let out a long breath. 'He's trying to. I know that. But no, he's not.'

'Oh, my sons,' she said. 'My poor sons.'

She put her hand on my shoulder. I had to resist the urge to rest my head against her knee like a child.

'He's so lonely, you know,' she said, after a long moment. 'Out here by himself, with only me for company. Ever since she left.'

'That doesn't mean he needs to come and check up on me all the time.'

'Would you prefer he didn't?'

I didn't say anything.

My mother didn't say anything either. She'd always been good at that, at holding space open when it needed to be held.

'I don't want to be someone he checks up on,' I said. 'I want to be someone he visits. Someone he trusts. Someone who could even check up on him sometimes. I want to feel like his brother, not his son.'

That was at the heart of it, really. There were plenty of people who loved me. I had no illusions about that. But they never quite loved me the way I wanted. Isamu would never quite love me as an equal. My father had loved me, but not more than his work. Fiona . . . god, there was so much I could say about Fiona. Hell, even my cat didn't love me the way I wished she would.

I looked up at the stars. 'I don't want to be like this, Okāsan. I want to be taken seriously.'

'So that's it.'

I glanced over at her.

'The exam,' my mother said. 'That's why you're so desperate to do it.'

'No. Well – yes. The exam's part of it. But not all of it.'

I looked back up at the stars. 'There's . . . someone,' I admitted. 'Someone I like very much. And I started to hope that maybe I could have her. But it's complicated. She's older than me. She's got children. And . . .'

And I'll never be more than her dirty little secret, I could not bring myself to say.

‘That is complicated.’ Okāsan squeezed my shoulder. ‘Children make it especially complicated. No matter how much you love each other, children always make it complicated. Look at what happened with your brother and Noriko.’

A hollow ache built behind my ribcage. Isamu never talked about it, but it was no secret that he and Noriko had split up because she wanted kids and he didn’t.

‘Part of him will always love her,’ Okāsan said. ‘But in the end, he had to make a choice: between breaking his own heart once, very hard, or letting it be broken slowly, little by little, day by day.’

Tears pricked at the corner of my eyes.

‘Maybe that’s a choice you won’t have to make,’ she said. ‘Maybe this person will love you back the way you deserve – and you deserve to be loved, Sato. You deserve someone who will love you, who will respect you, and who will take you very, very seriously.’

I swallowed, hard.

‘But if you do have to make that choice,’ she said, smoothing her hand over my hair, ‘just know that it will hurt, but like your brother, you will survive it.’

Chapter Eleven
Fiona

Tasting today: 2L 'Fruity White' cask, South-Eastern Australia. Absolutely not worth drinking. Love yourself: pour it down the drain and find something better.

'No, Matt,' I said exhaustedly, standing in front of the meat section in the supermarket and trying to do the maths on cost-effectiveness versus quality. 'I told you.'

'I can't believe you're being like this *on Christmas*.' Matt's voice was whiny, irritatingly reminiscent of the girls when they were overtired. 'Is it really that much to ask? The divorce is final on the twenty-seventh anyway. I'm talking about you letting me see them two days early. Two days!'

'You heard their therapist.' I reached my hand towards a pack of pork loin steaks, then pulled it back. Elias was kicking extra money into my budget, but he also ate a lot more than me or the kids. 'No matter how keen you are to make things up to them, and no matter how well prepared they are, seeing you again will be traumatic, and I don't want to ruin their Christmas.'

'I'm their *father*.'

I put two packs of sausages that were on special into my trolley. 'If you want to set up a video call with them after the twenty-seventh, text me some times that will work. Before that, though, it's not happening.'

I hung up before he could make my head hurt worse than it already did. 'It's the countdown to Christmas!' the shop radio blared chirpily as I pushed my trolley towards the dairy section, at a volume loud enough I could feel it inside my skull. 'We've got holiday specials for you and your family!'

Countdown was right. It felt like there were several different ticking clocks hanging over me, each ticking slightly out of time, a ceaseless uneven rhythm that had me permanently on edge.

Some of them had clear endpoints – like 27 December, circled in ominous red in my mental calendar, the day after which I could no longer keep Matt from the kids, no matter how desperately I wanted to.

Some of them were less clear but still predictable. I was one hundred per cent sure that sometime in the next twenty-four hours, I would get yet another email from Laura to add to the five I hadn't answered, telling me that *of course* she understood why I was being like this but Matt missed the kids *so* much and Christmas was all about family so couldn't I please please please ~~stop being such a selfish bitch~~ be the bigger person and rise above it for the sake of the children?

And then there were the ones with no set endpoint, the ones that made my heart race and sweat break out on my brow even as my stomach felt like it was filled with cement. When I would be alone with Satoshi again? And would I be strong enough this time to do what I needed to?

I'd seen him a few times since the night he'd delivered the wine, but only in passing while I and some assortment of family members were in Tsundoku. His hand had brushed mine when I'd finally brought Lex in for the promised hot chocolate, and I'd nearly combusted on the spot. I'd thought about it later that night, buried under about seventeen layers of blankets despite the summer heat so that the kids or Elias wouldn't hear the vibrator through the wall, and for a few blissful moments, all the ticking clocks were silent. My mind jumped ahead a year, three years, five years . . .

But then, the next time I'd gone in, Elias and the kids in tow, Satoshi had been deep in conversation with Kieran. His eyes only flickered to me for an instant as we entered – a brief, polite smile passing over his face – before something Kieran said stole his attention back.

Lex had caught me watching as they kissed each other goodbye on both cheeks, Kieran's biceps rippling as he picked up the case of sparkling wine Satoshi had packed for him. 'Are you all right, Mum?'

'Fine!' I'd replied, as breezily possible. 'Just zoned out for a sec there.'

Lex nodded, seemingly mollified, and inwardly, I'd breathed a sigh of relief that at least one ticking clock seemed to have petered out. Michelle, to my great surprise, seemed to have stuck to her word and not told anyone about finding me and Satoshi beside the bins – or at least, had managed to keep it from circulating to the kids. *Fiona's children have been through enough,* she'd probably whispered to half the P&F Association. *They don't need to find out their mother is going through a second adolescence.*

The relief was short-lived, though. Elias had insisted on paying, and when we got home, I remembered that once again, I'd forgotten to pay for the keg. I wanted Satoshi so badly – more than I would allow myself to admit, even when I was buried under all those piles of blankets with my vibrator – but I couldn't even manage to repay this one simple debt. Even if Sadie was right – even if there was a world where I could have him – I would never, *ever* deserve him.

On Christmas morning, Sadie and Jonah arrived on my doorstep early, but the kids had been up since dawn. 'Uncle Jonah, Auntie Sadie, look!' Georgia yelled. 'Santa came!'

'I can see that!' Jonah was so weighed down with bags of groceries he was half hunched over. 'You must have been very good this year. Hi, Fi.'

He kissed me on the cheek. 'I'm going to go to the kitchen and get started. Lots to do.'

'Sure. Do you need any—

I was drowned out by a shriek from Rosie. 'Is that a puppy?'

'It sure is.' Sadie bent down so they could see the small, wriggling, black-and-tan dachshund puppy in her arms. 'This is Bunbury. He's mine and Uncle Jonah's Christmas present to each other.'

I was definitely going to hear, *Mummy, can we get a dog?* on a loop now, but for the moment, the presence of Bunbury was a blessing. The girls were so enthralled by him that they didn't notice that Santa's presents this year were, frankly, a bit shit due to her limited budget, and that Matt – despite all his pleading phone calls and all of Laura's emails – hadn't sent any at all.

Chess turned up not long after Sadie and Jonah, staggering under the weight of a case of Bibliophile, and we popped a bottle of blanc de blancs as we exchanged gifts. 'This one is for you, Mum,' Lex said, handing me an envelope. 'From me.'

I opened it. It was a twenty-dollar gift voucher to Tsundoku. 'Oh, sweetheart, you shouldn't have.'

'I wanted to. You deserve nice stuff too.'

'They insisted on paying with their own money.' Elias reached over to ruffle Lex's hair the way he'd used to when they were younger but caught himself at the last minute. 'I tried to bankroll them, but they weren't having it.'

'Because then the present would be from you.' Lex stuck their chin out stubbornly. 'It's from me.'

Jonah chuckled. 'You really are just like your mum, kiddo.'

I blinked, but he didn't elaborate. 'Anyone need a top-up?' he asked, gesturing with the bottle of sparkling.

When we'd finished that bottle, we opened riesling and chardonnay, drinking them outside in the sun with the beautiful seafood platter Jonah had prepared. As evening fell, Rosie and Georgia and Bunbury eventually exhausted each other and fell asleep in a pile on the couch; Lex, peopled out, retired to their room with all the books they'd received; and Sadie opened a bottle of the Noriko. 'Chessie's favourite,' she said, filling everyone's glasses.

Elias raised his glass. 'To family. Old and new.'

'Family,' I murmured along with everyone, and drank.

It had been more than a year since I'd tasted the Noriko. The last time had been right before Matt had left. Satoshi had poured him a glass to apologise for the fact that he'd borrowed his wife to be his waitress, and when Matt had stormed off, I'd downed half of it in a single swallow. Satoshi had watched me do it, an expression in his eyes I couldn't quite identify. No one had ever looked at me like that before – somewhere between amused and awestruck.

'We've all been through a lot of changes this year,' Elias said. 'Marriages—' he raised his glass to Sadie and Jonah '—and divorces—' he nodded at me '—and – I'm sorry, Chess, I don't know you very well, I don't know what to add to the list for you.'

'Just file me under "changes, miscellaneous",' Chess said. 'That'll cover it.'

'I doubt any of us are where we thought we'd be a few years ago,' Elias said, 'but I think we're all better off for it.'

The Noriko was a wine with a long finish. I could still taste it on my palate later, layers unfolding as I stacked the dishwasher. It was silky and red-fruited with a hint of gentle spice, an embrace to sink into, deeper and deeper.

And Elias's words, like the wine, lingered. Would I go back to who I was, the last time I had tasted this wine?

That Fiona was sure of so many things. She'd felt safe and secure and self-assured in a way that I hadn't for a single second since. I craved that feeling so badly it felt like a biological imperative, some deep, powerful, hardwired instinct I couldn't ignore.

But she'd also been wrong. She'd thought her husband loved her, but he didn't. She'd thought her brothers didn't, but they did.

And she hadn't felt like herself. Wasn't that what I'd told Satoshi that night, before I'd come home and Matt had blown up my life? How I'd disappeared into being a wife and a mother and I didn't know who *Fiona* was anymore?

'Fi, let me do that.'

I jumped. Jonah laughed. 'Sorry. Didn't mean to scare you.'

He filled the kettle with water and flicked it on. 'Seriously, let me do that. You go and relax.'

'It's okay. You cooked. The least I can do is clean.'

I slotted another plate into the dishwasher, pondering, before I spoke again. 'Jonah, can I ask you something?'

'Sure.' He lined up five mismatched mugs on the bench.

'What did you mean before? When you said Lex was just like me?'

'Hmmm? Oh. They're strong-willed.'

'What?' That was the last answer I'd expected. 'I'm not strong-willed.'

Jonah snorted. 'Come on, Fi. Yes, you are.'

He found the teabags. 'Elias and I rolled over for Dad so many times when we were younger. We let him shape us – mould us – but you never did. You were the only one who stood your ground.'

'Look where it got me, though.' I gestured futilely. 'You all tried to tell me marrying Matt was a terrible idea, and I didn't listen.'

'Sure, fine, maybe we were onto something that time, but even broken clocks are right twice a day.' The kettle boiled. 'No matter how it turned out – standing up to us took a spine of steel, Fi. And all three of the kids are just like you. Can you imagine someone trying to talk any of them out of something they wanted to do?'

My eyes filled with tears.

'Imagine trying to convince Lex to put their book down,' Jonah went on, pouring water into the mugs. 'Or Rosie and Georgia to – Are you all right?'

'Fine, fine.' I wiped my eyes with the back of my hand. 'That's just . . . really nice, Jonah. Thank you.'

He put his arm around me. 'They're the best kids in the world, Fi,' he said, squeezing me tight. 'And that all comes from you.'

The kids slept in the next day, but Elias was up early. 'You don't know how much I missed this,' he said, parking himself on the couch in front of the cricket. 'Christmastime in Europe has its perks, but this – this I missed.'

Jonah came around later with the puppy and the leftovers from the brunch he'd made for Sadie. 'We spent the morning together,' he explained, a dreamy look on his face making it pretty clear *how* they'd spent the morning together, 'but she and Chess are having a girls' afternoon, and I didn't want all this food to go to waste.' He got distracted by the beginning of the Sydney to Hobart yacht race, though, which Elias had switched over to in the lunch break, and plonked himself beside him on the couch.

My living room thus commandeered by my brothers, I ended up spending the afternoon outside, sitting in the shade and reading with Lex, the sound of the cricket a low hum through the open window as the girls played with Bunbury and the sun moved slowly across the cloudless sky. We were both reading our Christmas gifts from Sadie and Jonah: Lex was tearing through *Pet* by Akwaeke

Emezi, and I was making significantly less progress with *Part of Your World* by Abby Jimenez.

It wasn't the book's fault. It was perfectly good. But it was a romance novel about an older woman falling for a younger man – it might technically have been from both of them, but it didn't take a genius to see Sadie's fingerprints all over it – and it had sent my mind wandering, circling around the word *strong-willed* like water going down a drain.

My knee-jerk reaction had been that Jonah was wrong. He didn't have all the information, after all. Anyone who knew just how badly I was hesitating with Satoshi would never describe me as strong-willed.

But then there had been the way he'd put it: that no one could talk me or my kids out of doing something they wanted.

I wanted Satoshi. There was no denying that. And every time I tried to make myself give him up, I couldn't.

Was Jonah right? Was I actually so strong-willed that it had come all the way back around to stop me from doing what I knew I really should?

The kids and I had been in the backyard for about two and a half hours, during which time I'd managed to turn half the pages of my book while taking in approximately one per cent of the content, when the doorbell rang. 'I'll get it!' Jonah called from the living room. 'It'll be Sadie.'

'Okay!' I called back.

I picked up my phone, quickly googling a summary of the book. I was going to sit down and read it properly, but if Sadie asked me about it, I needed to have something to say.

'Fi, can you come here for a sec?' Jonah called.

I set my book and phone down on the table and shuffled inside, wondering what on earth he could possibly need my help with. He'd eventually won the battle over cleaning up last night, proving that even if he hadn't been when we were younger, Jonah was definitely now just as strong-willed as me, and—

'Hi, Fiona,' Matt said from the other side of the screen door.

I could barely see him behind the enormous pile of gifts he was carrying. I could barely see the gifts either, because dots had started swimming in front of my eyes.

Jonah put his hand on my lower back, steadying me. 'What are you doing here?' I managed to force out.

'Laura and I spent the holidays here,' Matt said, 'and – well, how could I resist bringing the kids their gifts in person?'

He shifted the weight of the stack in his arms. 'Can I come in and put these down? They're heavy.'

'No.'

'Come on, Fi.' I could feel his tone of voice in every fibre of my being, and it made me want to turn my whole body inside out. 'Don't be like this. I didn't come yesterday – I didn't want to tread on your toes—'

'How fucking dare you?' Jonah grated.

'Mate, stay out of it,' Matt said. 'This isn't about you. This is about me and her and the kids, and – come on, Fi, it's *one day*, the divorce is final tomorrow. Are you really going to send me away?'

I stared at him.

I was still married to this man. Until the clock struck twelve, I was still married to this loathsome sack of shit.

'I'm going to see the kids soon anyway.' His voice turned placating. 'Why don't we just rip the bandaid off now?'

Rip the bandaid off? *Rip the fucking bandaid off?*

'Laura's with Micah and Nikki in an AirBnB just around the corner. I could get them to come here. Or you could bring the kids to us, if that's more comfortable—'

'If you don't leave right now, I'm going to call the cops,' Jonah said.

Matt ignored him. 'It's Christmas, Fi. Are you really not going to let me give the kids their gifts?'

'So you could afford to buy all this,' I said hoarsely, gesturing at the pile in his arms, 'but not pay me one single cent of child support all year?'

'You'll get your money. I promise.'

Jonah had his phone out. 'I'm dialling.'

'I'm sorry I've been absent.' Matt's voice wobbled, and I wanted to scream like a banshee. 'I really am. But it's been so complicated – financially and emotionally, and now with the babies on the way . . . I've treated you terribly, Fi, I know, but I've been so overwhelmed, and – please, *please* let me see the kids. Let me try and make it right.'

'You think you can *buy us*?'

I turned. So did Jonah, his thumb hovering over the call button on his phone.

Lex had their fists clenched at their side, a red flush of anger slowly up rising their chest. 'Maybe the twins will fall for this,' they snarled, pointing at the gifts in Matt's arms, 'but you can't buy me, Dad.'

Matt's face went white. 'Lex, buddy, things have been complicated, okay? But if you'll let me, I can explain.'

'Fine! Explain!'

Matt opened his mouth, then closed it again.

'Now's your chance!' Lex exclaimed. 'I'm listening.'

'What's going on?' Elias asked, emerging from the living room. 'What's – oh no. Absolutely not.'

He pushed in front of me. 'You think you can just turn up here? How *dare* you?'

'Elias,' I said. 'I need you to stop yelling.'

'Fi—'

'It's not helpful.' My lips felt numb, like I'd been running an ice cube over them. 'If you want to help, please go and shut all the doors and windows. The girls are outside with the puppy, and I don't want them overhearing any more of this than they already have.'

Elias hesitated. 'Are you sure?'

'Yes. I'm sure.'

He went. I turned to Jonah. 'Will you please go out the back? Make sure the girls stay there?'

Jonah's gaze flickered back to Matt. 'I don't want to leave you alone.'

'I'll be fine.' I felt almost light-headed, like my anger was so strong that it might burn away gravity's hold on me. 'If I haven't come out in ten minutes, you can call the cops, all right?'

To his credit, Jonah didn't argue. He squeezed my shoulder as he left.

'Lex, please go with Uncle Jonah,' I said. 'Or you can go to your room if you want.'

'No.' Lex took Jonah's place beside me, crossing their arms across their chest. They were shaking, but their voice was firm. 'I asked Dad a question.'

'It's all – just so complicated, Lex,' Matt said. 'It's not that I don't love you and your sisters. I do. And I love your mother too.'

I managed to repress my snort, but Lex didn't. 'Oh, sure. You definitely loved your backup family so, so much.'

'Fi, didn't they work through this in therapy?'

That nearly sent me into space. 'Don't you *dare* suggest that there's anything wrong with them.'

'That's what he thinks, though!' Lex jabbed their finger at Matt. 'That there's something wrong with me!'

'Of course I don't,' Matt said. 'That didn't come out right. What I meant—'

But Lex was already barrelling onward. 'You were so ashamed when I told you who I was.' Their voice cracked. 'You said it was just a phase. That I'd grow out of it. You must have been so relieved that I wasn't one of your *real* kids!'

'Lex, no!' Matt and I exclaimed – for once, in perfect unison.

Tears started spilling down Lex's face. 'So you can fuck right off, Dad. I don't need anything from you! Ever!'

'Buddy, I'm so sorry.' Matt looked at me desperately. 'I know I said some misguided things when you came out. I'll never be able to make that up to you. But I'm going to do better, I swear, and—'

'No! I never want to see you again!'

'Matt,' I said, 'you need to go. Now.'

'But—'

'*Now.*'

He fled.

'Lex,' I said, 'sweetheart, can I—'

They threw their arms around my neck. 'I'm sorry, Mum,' they sobbed into my shoulder. 'I'm so sorry.'

I held them tight, one hand stroking their hair, the way I used to when they were little. I should be crying too – I cried at the drop of a hat these days – but the only thing left in me was fire. I was a creature made of flame now, a thing of nightmares that would torch anything that dared hurt her precious babies.

'You have nothing to apologise for.' I pressed my lips to their temple. 'You've done nothing wrong, all right? *Nothing.*'

'It's my fault.' They gulped down choked breaths of air. 'It's all my fault.'

'You listen to me, Lex.'

I pulled back, cupping their tear-streaked face in my hands so I could look them in the eyes. 'None of this is your fault. Your father has behaved horribly. I can't pretend to know or understand why he's done the things he has, but I know this: none of it is because of you.'

Their chin quivered as they tried to hold back a fresh wave of tears.

I stroked their cheekbones with my thumbs. 'Have you been carrying this all this time?'

'Dr Dell ss-ss-said it wasn't m-m-my fault.' Their teeth were chattering. 'B-b-b-but what else could it be? Nn-nn-nothing's wrong with you, or the t-t-twins, or—'

'Nothing's wrong with you either.' I kept my gaze as steady and my voice as firm as I could, even though a bushfire was roaring inside me. 'I promise you, your dad knows that. I know he said some very, *very* hurtful things when you first told us who you were, but he caught up eventually, remember?'

'Th-that's what I used to think. Th-th-that he was j-j-just old, and he didn't – didn't know m-m-much about b-b-being non-b-b-binary. But – but—'

But then he left. Then he *fucking abandoned his children*, and left my perfect, darling baby thinking they were to blame.

'He left because of *him*, sweetheart,' I said. 'He left because of a lie he'd been telling for a long time, since before you were even born. It had nothing – nothing! – to do with you.'

Lex's face crumpled. They started sobbing again, wailing in a way they hadn't since they were a baby. 'I love you, Mummy,' they bawled into my shirt, as I hugged them tight. 'I love you so much.'

'Not as much as I love you,' I said fiercely.

There was a flash of red in my periphery, the sunlight winking off Sadie's hair as she stood frozen at the front gate. With a calmness I couldn't believe I possessed, I gestured for her to sneak around the side. Those ten minutes I'd given Jonah must be nearly up, and the last thing the situation needed was a bunch of cops.

After Lex had cried themselves out and retired, exhausted, to their room, my brothers and Sadie and I had a conversation in hushed voices about what the situation actually did need. 'I don't want to disrupt things too badly, or make the girls think anything is wrong,' I said, still in the grip of that eerie composure, 'but I'd prefer they not stay here tonight, in case Matt comes back.'

'We'll take them,' Jonah said immediately.

'If they ask questions, we'll tell them we need help with the puppy,' Sadie said. 'Lex can come too.'

'I don't think Lex is up to that level of stimulation. Not tonight.' I turned to Elias. 'Mum sent me a hotel gift voucher. Can you take them?'

He blinked. 'But—'

'Please don't argue with me,' I said. 'There's something I need to do.'

🍷

Matt and Laura's AirBnB was two streets away. He was sitting at a table on the verandah, an open two-litre cask of wine with *Fruity White* emblazoned on the side and two glasses in front of him. 'Do you want one?' he asked me, gesturing at it as I walked up the path. 'I know it's not up to your usual standards, but I thought, when you texted . . .'

'No. I'm not staying.'

'But we have to talk.' He used his foot to nudge one of the chairs closer to me. 'We have to fix things with Lex.'

'*You* have to fix things with Lex. I'm not the problem.'

'Come on, don't be like that. We—'

'Don't get me wrong, we'll talk about it. You, me, their therapist. We're going to have a long discussion. But not tonight. That's not what I came here for.'

I wrapped my hands around the top of the chair. 'I have a question for you. And I need you to answer me honestly.'

Matt sighed. 'Okay,' he said, pouring himself a glass well over the standard size. 'Hit me.'

'Am I even a person to you?'

'Fi—'

'You don't have to spare my feelings. I don't think you could really hurt them anyway. The truth, Matt. Do you even think of me as a person? Have you ever? Or have I always been just some big joke to you?'

My knuckles went white as I clenched my fingers tighter. 'That's how you treated me today. Like the things I say don't matter. Like the agreement we made doesn't matter. I told you no, but you turned up anyway, because my no was just a fucking joke to you.'

'That's not what I intended. We were *here*. How could I be that close to the kids—'

'And you've sure as hell turned me into a joke.' I steamrolled right over him, the way he had tried to steamroll over me. 'An absolute laughing-stock. The woman whose husband had a whole second family she didn't have a clue about.'

'I didn't intend that either. I—'

'Then you left us high and dry, like we were *nothing*. If it weren't for my family, I don't know what I would have done. Thirteen years of marriage – three kids – and boom: you just say *clean break* and disappear. Was our whole life all just a joke to you?'

'Of course not.'

Matt stood up, his over-full glass of wine wobbling dangerously. 'I loved you. And I love the kids. But . . .' He nodded helplessly to the door. 'There's them. Micah. Nikki. Laura. And there came a point where I just couldn't do it anymore.'

I folded my arms. 'You were already with her when you met me. You were still with her when you married me. If you really did love me—'

'I'm *greedy*, Fiona!'

He ran his hand over his scalp. He'd cut his hair very short to cover the fact that he was balding, and his scalp was bright pink from sunburn. 'I always have been,' he said. 'That night we met – I'd intended it just to be a one-night thing. But you were just so young and gorgeous and vibrant, and I had to have you. And then before I knew it, I was proposing to you, and I was marrying you, and you told me you were pregnant, and I had every intention of spending the rest of my life with you. I loved you, I swear. Why do you think I haven't been able to look you or the kids in the eye?'

'What about the money? The child support you haven't been paying?'

He didn't say anything.

'Let me guess,' I said. 'You're greedy?'

'I'm just not very liquid. It's complicated. You wouldn't—'

'—understand? Because I'm too stupid to? Or because I'm a human being who can't understand how you could do that to your own children?'

'They're not my only children!'

He tugged at his non-existent hair again. 'When you told me you were pregnant with Lex, I decided to end it with Laura. But then she told me she was pregnant too, and I couldn't just *leave* her. I love her too. I always have.'

He hung his head. 'I thought I could keep it going forever. Because I was greedy, and I thought it could have it all. But – but – god, this sounds awful, you're going to hate me for this—'

'I already hate you, Matt. You can't make it worse.'

'Financially, it just wasn't working anymore.' He exhaled. 'And you have your parents, and I knew they'd look out for their grand-kids, and Laura doesn't have anyone, so—'

'Wait, wait, wait.' I held a finger up. 'Are you telling me that you picked her over me – your family with her, over me and the kids – because *my dad has more money*?'

'No! But . . .'

His voice trailed off. 'You know it wasn't the same between us, near the end,' he said eventually. 'You were . . . restless. I could feel you growing apart from me. Like I wasn't enough for you.'

'You do understand the irony of you, of all people, saying that, right?'

'Of course I do. And I know what I did was awful, but . . . isn't a part of you glad? That I let you go?'

I had a sudden, vivid flashback to what Elias had said the night before. *I doubt any of us are where we thought we'd be a few years ago, but I think we're all better off for it.*

The front door of the house opened and a tweenage boy came out. He was shorter than Lex, stockier, with more freckles, but the colour of his hair was exactly the same. 'Dad, my iPad's broken. Will you fix it for me?'

'Micah, honey, not now.' A hugely pregnant Laura followed him out. 'Leave your dad alone, okay?'

Her eyes met mine as she hustled Micah – oh my god, this was my kids' *brother* – back into the house. And as she lingered in the doorway, my mind spun a whole new scenario.

Me, coming home from Tsundoku that night. Matt, sitting me down and telling me about Laura. *But it's okay, baby,* this version of him said. *I ended it with her. It's all you, only you.*

What would I have done? Where I would be now, if I'd been the one he'd chosen?

Would I have shoved him away and told him no? Would I be exactly where I was now – still in survival mode, still just trying to get by, slowly putting my life back together, leaning so hard on everyone around me that it was amazing they hadn't collapsed beneath my weight?

Or would I have given in? Would I have eventually surrendered the way Laura had – for the sake of the kids, for the sake of stability, for the sake of having someone to rely on? Would I – fuck, would I be the one knocked up now, with more children of a man it surely made me sick to look at and even sicker to touch, sending emails to her in a desperate attempt to convince myself he really was a good person who'd just made some bad mistakes?

Who, of the two of us, was the punchline, really?

'It's all right,' I said, eyes still fixed on Laura's. 'I was just leaving.'

'Fi, wait,' Matt said. 'We still—'

'We'll talk in the new year. Once your first child support payment comes in. And it better, or I'm going to send my lawyers after you. You're going to follow the rules of our agreement to the letter, or so help me god, I will *never* let you see the kids again.'

I put my hand on the table. His untouched, overfull wine glass wobbled again, sending liquid splashing over the edge. 'From now on, you're going to respect me, Matt,' I said. 'Because I'm not a fucking joke.'

For the first time in a long time, my head was clear. All the knots I'd tied myself into – all the worry, the fear, the embarrassment – had burned away. I knew exactly where I was going, and exactly what I wanted.

Satoshi was behind the bar at Tsundoku. 'Fiona!' he said, visibly surprised, closing the binder of study notes he had open in front of him. 'I wasn't expecting you.'

I slid onto a stool. 'I wasn't expecting me either when I woke up this morning, but here I am.'

He studied me. 'Are you okay?'

'No,' I replied honestly. 'I'm not.'

'Can I get you a drink?'

'First,' I said, 'can I pay for the keg?'

He was still studying me. 'You don't have to.'

'Yes. I do.'

It was such a small thing, but I had to do it. I owed so many people so many things that I could never repay – owed *him* so much I could never repay – but this, at least, I would make good.

Satoshi offered me the EFTPOS reader. I tapped my credit card against it. 'Will you answer a question for me?'

His expression was unsure, but after a brief moment, he replied, 'Of course.'

I glanced around the bar. It wasn't full; apart from me, there were only two people, having a quiet drink near the crime shelves. 'Could you close early tonight?'

'Maybe? The kitchen's already closed and I doubt anyone else will come in. Boxing Day isn't normally a big trading day for us, it'll pick up in a couple of days when the Sydney to Hobart yachts start coming in. Why?'

'Because I'm only married until midnight,' I said, 'and I need to cheat on my husband.'

Chapter Twelve
Satoshi

Tasting today: 2017 Sauternes, Bordeaux, France.
Although rich and golden and sweet on the palate, many wines from this vintage do not live up to Sauternes' stellar reputation. If you pay attention, you can taste the sickness that plagued the grapes.

There is a moment, sometimes, when you try a truly transcendent glass of wine, where the world narrows to a single point.

Sometimes you know it's coming. You go through the ritual of tasting, and it builds, sign upon sign, a golden equation, all saying that what you have in your glass is special.

Sometimes, though, you don't, and it hits you like a runaway train – something ordinary which turns out to be extraordinary, bursting on your palate in a way which makes you want to burst into tears in turn.

Either way, though, a sommelier must be able to pull that wine apart, to analyse it, to break it down. So after that single, transcendent moment, you start to think, and the more you start to think, the more you start to question, until eventually, sometimes, you realise that what you have in your glass was not quite what you thought.

'I'm only married until midnight,' Fiona Fisher said, a spark in her eyes as she looked at me across the bar, 'and I need to cheat on my husband.'

The world narrowed to a single point.

Fiona, with me. Her body against mine, her hands fisted in my hair, her breath in my ear, my name on her lips. One sparkling image, for one sparkling second.

But then the second passed, and another, and another. The words she had said broke open in my brain – flavours bursting anew against my palate as I took another sip – and this time, they were not so pleasant.

She hadn't said, *Satoshi, I want you.*

She hadn't said, *Satoshi, I need you.*

She hadn't said, *Satoshi, I love you.*

She hadn't even said my name at all. Because this wasn't about me.

It was about him. She had come to me late at night, when the bar was empty and no one would see us together. For an ending, not a beginning; an exorcism, not an embrace.

'You don't have to say yes, obviously.' She tucked a stray strand of hair behind her ear. 'You don't owe me anything, Satoshi. But if . . . if you . . .'

My last two customers chose that moment to come up and pay. I had never had to dig deeper to find my customer service smile. 'How was everything?' I asked, keying in the wrong price on the EFTPOS machine twice before I got it right.

Fiona got up.

Panic shot through my heart, a sudden lightning bolt through the fog. If she left – if I let her go – she might never come back.

She reached over the bar, picked up a cloth, walked over to the table my customers had abandoned, and started wiping it down.

And there it was, that potent, golden, addictive elixir, pumping through my veins: relief.

'Have a good one, mate,' one of my customers said.

'I will,' I replied faintly, as they left. 'You too.'

Fiona couldn't give me what I wanted. I knew that. I'd known it for a long time, even if I couldn't admit it. The most I would ever be to her was a secret indulgence, kept carefully apart from the rest of her life. I would never be her home.

But that didn't change how much I loved her. She was the best person I had ever met, and I'd told her there was nothing she could ask of me that I didn't want to give.

I drained the last of a glass of disappointing Sauternes I'd been sipping, walked over to the front door, and snicked the lock.

Fiona straightened at the sound. Cloth dangling from her hand, she looked at me, and I looked back at her, heartbeat thundering in my ears.

'Put it down,' I said.

'This?' She held up the cloth.

'Yes. I'll clean before I open tomorrow.'

I had never once left the bar floor before cleaning down – the thought of it made my skin prickle uncomfortably – but I might never have this chance again.

Slowly, Fiona put the cloth down. 'Good,' I told her.

'It's your bar.' One corner of her mouth quirked upwards. 'You're the boss.'

I might never have this chance again, because she might be the death of me.

'I am,' I said, 'but you're in charge.'

I crossed the floor to her in five strides. I didn't touch her, but I held out my hand to her. Her breath was coming quickly as she placed hers in mine, and it caught as I kissed her knuckles.

'Tell me what you want,' I said. 'Are we back to first base? Second? Third?'

She always blushed when I asked her to clarify her boundaries, but this time, Fiona met my gaze. There was something glittering in her eyes – not mischief, but something close to it. A challenge, maybe, or a test.

'All of it, Satoshi,' she said. 'I want it all.'

Chapter Thirteen

Fiona

Tasting today: Junmai Daiginjo sake, Yamaguchi, Japan.
Few things taste as good as a drink shared with a lover.

The first time I had ever been up to Satoshi's apartment was the night Matt had left. I had cried myself hoarse in his office, barely enough voice left to rasp my agreement when he said, *Let me take you up to my place, okay?* He'd led me up the stairs, and even though my brain had been reduced to a primordial soup of terror and grief and humiliation, I'd noticed how his feet made almost no sound: how gently – how carefully – he stepped.

That was how he'd been with me almost every day since: gentle, careful, so tenderly restrained as he touched me. Satoshi Tsukamoto knew how to tread lightly, and it had been exactly what I needed.

But there was another Satoshi underneath. The Satoshi I'd once seen in an alley, shoving his lover up against a wall, and had, without being able to admit it to myself, been searching for glimpses of ever since. The Satoshi beneath the waistcoat and the glasses and the smile: the ravenous Satoshi, the voracious Satoshi, the Satoshi who *wanted*, burning with desire and zeal and passion.

He paused in front of the apartment door, key in one hand, the other in mine. He had not let go of it, this whole time. 'Are you sure? If you're not, I won't hold it against you.'

I squeezed his fingers. 'I would hold it against me.'

It was the truth. I was scared – petrified, even – but it was a dull murmur of a feeling compared to the strength of the one pulsing through me now. I wanted all of him – needed *all* of him – and I was sure, sure, sure.

I went up on my toes so I could brush my lips against his. 'If you're not, though,' I whispered, 'that's all right – oh!'

My back hit the door with a thud. 'I told you, Fiona,' Satoshi growled, 'you're not asking anything of me that I don't want to give.'

We almost fell into his apartment, stumbling backwards as he unlocked the door, his mouth hot and hungry against mine. He dropped the keys onto the floor and pressed me into the wall in the entranceway as we both toed our shoes off, a chaotic pile compared to the neat rows on his shoe rack, then he hoisted me into his arms and carried me across the room. Everything was fast and messy and hard, but the way he placed me down on the bed was delicate, like I was made of the finest porcelain. 'Wait here,' he said, thumbing some hair out of my eyes and kissing me quickly, 'I just need to – yes, I'm talking about you.' He caught Yquem as she leapt at us. 'This isn't for your innocent eyes, princess.'

No, it wasn't. It really, really wasn't.

There was a deep, cavernous hunger in me, the fire that had burned so hot and angry now darkly smouldering coals. I wanted to do filthy things to him. I wanted him to do filthy things to me.

I went up on my knees on the bed as Satoshi closed the bathroom door. 'Sorry about that,' he said, as Yquem yowled. 'She'll calm down in a second.'

'Satoshi,' I said, grabbing a fistful of his shirt and pulling him towards me, 'don't you dare apologise.'

The pins on his waistcoat clattered against the floorboards as I unbuttoned it and shoved it off his shoulders. I pressed my lips to his Adam's apple, the hollow of his throat, the line of his collarbone as I unbuttoned his shirt too. His skin beneath was smooth, the lightest smattering of hair over the lean, wiry muscles I'd felt but never seen before. 'Is this all from work?' I traced the line of one pec with a fingertip. 'Or do you have a secret gym routine?'

He made a sound deep in the back of his throat, somewhere between a growl and a gasp and a laugh. 'I promise, no secret gym routine. The thought of trying to fit that into my day might give me a panic attack.'

He unbuttoned his cuffs with two deft flicks of the wrist that made something in me turn molten. He let me slide my hands up his chest as we kissed again, long and deep, before he took them in his and pulled them away. 'Your turn.'

Self-consciousness penetrated the bubble of my surety, a bright, sharp shard of reality piercing through. 'I don't want you to get your hopes up,' I said, Kieran's perfect face and body blaring like a siren in my mind as Satoshi undid the sash of my wrap dress. 'I've had three babies.'

'I know.' He undid the inner tie as well.

'You might not know, though.' I grabbed at his biceps before he spread the dress open. 'What childbirth does to your body – it's not pretty. I might not look like—'

'Fiona,' he said, 'I have always, *always* thought you were beautiful. Nothing will change that. But if you don't want me to look yet – will you let me touch?'

I paused, swallowing, and nodded.

Satoshi leaned his forehead against mine, glasses pressed against my brows, eyes never leaving mine as he reached between the loosely hanging sides of my dress. His hands found my waist first, mapping the shape of it, thumbs stroking against the soft curves of my belly. 'I love the way you feel,' he said, the fingers of one hand sketching the line of my spine as the other curled hard around my hip.

My eyes drifted closed at the sensation.

'No.' He gripped my hip harder, fingertips digging in almost painfully. 'If you won't let me look at you, then you're going to look at me.'

With no fuss or fumbling, eyes fixed on mine, he flicked the clasp of my bra open. Swiftly, skilfully, with no wasted time or effort or motion, he slid his fingers under my right sleeve and tugged the strap out and over my wrist. He did the same with the left, before reaching between us, snagging the bra between the cups, pulling it away and throwing it across the room.

Oh my god. *Oh my god*. How had he made that – a manoeuvre I'd performed on myself countless times – so fucking sexy?

'You're going to have to let me look at you, Fiona.' His nose slid against mine as his hands smoothed up my sides to cup my breasts. 'Or else how will I be able to taste you here?'

His thumbs strummed across my nipples. I cried out. He did it again, brushing one nipple gently while pinching the other hard, and some dam inside me broke. 'Yes,' I gasped. 'It's okay. You can look.'

The fabric was a whisper against my skin as Satoshi pulled my dress off my shoulders, pooling behind me where I knelt on the bed. I was only in my underwear now – sensible black cotton – and it took all my willpower not to shy away as he stood there, studying me.

He didn't say anything. But he made a sound – a deep, dark, primal sound, something like a groan and a moan and a sigh all at once, before he shrugged his unbuttoned shirt off his shoulders and stepped in close, the long line of his beautiful body pressed against mine. 'I want to spread you out and have my way with you.' He nipped at my bottom lip, catching it between his teeth, one hand cupping the back of my head. 'Are you going to let me?'

My entire vocabulary had been reduced to a single word. 'Yes.'

In an instant, Satoshi had me on my back – hard, forceful, but careful, one hand still cradling the back of my head. 'Thank you,' he said.

It was such a small phrase – two such simple, everyday words – but they made tears spring to my eyes anyway.

He kissed his way slowly down my body, pausing to lave one of my nipples and then the other with his tongue. 'What are you going to let me do to you, I wonder?'

He kept going, nuzzling the stretch marks on my belly. 'Are you going to let me touch you here again?' He stroked my clit lightly through my underwear, and I almost screamed. 'Yes?'

'Yes.' I was practically sobbing. 'Yes.'

'You're going to let me take these off?' He curled his fingers into the waistband of my underwear.

'Yes, Satoshi, please – oh!'

He tore them, the worn elastic digging briefly into my skin then ripping, and knelt on the floor beside the bed, slinging my thighs over his shoulders. 'And you're going to let me taste you?'

I was so hot, so wet for him, but his breath was hotter still against me as he teased me apart with his thumbs. 'Yes,' I gasped. 'Please.'

The first long, stroke of his tongue against me made me jump violently, expected and yet so entirely unexpected, familiar but so new, and so, so good. 'Oh no you don't,' he growled, banding his left forearm across my hips. 'You're not running away from me, Fiona. Not this time.'

'Sorry,' I tried to say, but it came out as a scream as he bent his head to me again.

The first orgasm hit me quick and hard – had anyone ever been as good at this as him? – but he ignored it, slowing only slightly to let me catch my breath before he kept going. Two fingers teased at my entrance as he sucked at my clit, a question that didn't need words, and when I moaned my assent, he slid them inside me.

'Is this—' an open-mouthed kiss against me, tongue licking at me in the same rhythm as his fingers '—what you wanted?'

I clutched at his arm, still banded hard against my hips. 'Yes.'

'Is this what you've been thinking about?' He sucked at my clit again, then rubbed circles around it with his thumb. 'When you touch yourself? When you use that vibrator you told me about?'

My whole body was taut as a bowstring. It was too much, the way he was touching me, too good, too intense, but if he stopped, I might die. 'Yes.'

'Who do you think about, Fiona?' He pushed down harder with his forearm, and his eyes met mine.

'You,' I panted. 'Always you.'

The word came out of him in almost a snarl. 'Good.'

Then his mouth was back on my clit, his fingers stroking hard and fast inside me, and if he hadn't been holding me down, I would have completely come apart. The first orgasm had run me over, but this one split me open, a beam of white light shattering apart into a rainbow as I bucked against him and screamed his name.

I couldn't say how long he let me lie there, trembling, slowly reassembling myself into something that resembled Fiona Fisher. His lips were delicate pinpricks of feeling as he brushed kisses against my inner thighs, the iron band of his forearm against my belly loosening, his thumb caressing my hipbone. The fingers of his other hand were still inside me, but they were still, like he knew if he moved them even a millimetre I would fall apart again, and this time, I might not be able to put myself back together.

'Satoshi,' I breathed.

He paused, looking up at me. 'Hello.'

He smiled at me, eyes creasing just slightly at the corners behind his glasses, and – god, he looked so much like *himself*.

Out of nowhere, there was a lump in my throat. My next breath came out as a sob, and his smile shifted immediately into concern. 'What's wrong? Did I – was it . . .?'

'No, no, no.' Tears were beading at the corner of my eyes, but I blinked them away, smiling back at him. 'Nothing's even a little bit wrong. I'm just – it's just – will you come here?'

He let me tug him up to me so I could kiss him, fingers slipping out of me as I cupped his face between my hands. 'Thank you,' I whispered. 'For making me feel like this again.'

'Like what?' He braced himself on his right forearm, stroking the hair sticking to my forehead out of my eyes with his pinky.

'Beautiful.' I slid my nose against his, more tears springing to the corner of my eyes. 'Desired. Wanted.'

His response was immediate. 'You are.'

He kissed me – hard, this time, demanding – before he licked the fingers that had been inside me clean. 'You have no fucking idea how badly I want you, Fiona.'

I should have been wrung dry, burnt out, but the sight of his fingers in his mouth did something to me, a spark catching anew. 'I don't know.' I hitched a thigh around his hip so I could feel his cock, reassuringly hard between us. 'I might have some idea.'

I caught his wrist, tugging his fingers out his mouth so I could take them into my own. He made a guttural sound as I ran my tongue along the length of them, the faint taste of me mingled with the taste of him, and then another as I fastened my lips around them and sucked.

I released them after a few moments. 'Will you stand up?'

He did. My whole body still felt like liquid, quicksilver in the vague shape of a woman, but I managed to push myself to a sitting position. My eyes were level with his nipples, and I leaned up to kiss one of them as I unbuttoned his pants and tugged them down his hips, taking his underwear with them.

'Oh,' I breathed. 'Oh, Satoshi.'

I pressed my lips to his chest, then rested my forehead against it as I traced the length of his cock with the tip of my finger. He groaned again, his hand coming up reflexively to cup my head, then went very still as I wrapped my fist around him and stroked.

'Fiona,' he said.

I kissed his chest again, just over his heart, then slid off the bed, onto my knees. His cock curved very slightly to the left, I realised, as I licked along the length of it. He was reasonably well-endowed, but not so big that it would be painful; generous, rather than intimidating.

I flicked my tongue against the groove on the underside of the head. The sound he made was so sudden and so surprised that it made me laugh, humming against him as I took him into my mouth.

'No.' His hand tangled in my hair and tugged sharply. 'Stop.'

I drew back immediately. 'Did I do something wrong?'

'No, no.' His chest was heaving. 'It's just – this is about you. Not me.'

'I want to.'

'*No.*' He tugged at my hair again, pulling me to my feet. 'How do you want it?'

The subtext suddenly became clear. If I used my mouth on him, he wouldn't last.

The sting of rejection eased, turning into something akin to satisfaction. He really *did* want me.

'Hard,' I said. 'Fast. Fuck me, Satoshi. Please.'

It was my turn to make a noise of sudden surprise as he flung me back onto the bed, flipping me onto my front and pulling me up onto my hands and knees. There was a mirror on the door of his wardrobe, and I could see him moving behind me, opening a drawer, taking out a foil packet, and rolling a condom on.

My mouth went dry at the sight of him, the long, lean lines of his body as he stood there naked, wearing nothing but the condom and his moss-green-framed glasses. *You're so beautiful,* I wanted to say, but the words got stuck in my throat.

He knelt on the bed, positioning himself behind me, nudging my knees further apart so he could fit between them. The head of his cock brushed against me, and I braced myself.

But then, instead of pushing inside, he reached down and pulled me up to him. My back was pressed to his front, his left arm banded strong against me, his hand splayed open over my heart.

With his right hand, he guided himself to my entrance, and met my eyes in the mirror. Every inch of my body was displayed in it – my slightly uneven breasts, sagging more than they once had; the softness of my belly with all its silvery stretch marks; every one of my insecurities laid bare – but when he looked at me like this, the strain of wanting and restraint on his face, it was hard to feel like anything but a goddess.

'Are you ready?' His breath was hot behind my ear.

I turned my head so I could kiss him. 'Yes.'

The pressure of his hand against my breastbone increased. 'Watch.'

It hurt a little as he slid slowly inside me – not much, not truly painful, just the pleasurable, aching stretch of unused muscles. I moaned with the sensation, head falling back against his shoulder, and he stopped. 'No,' he growled. 'Watch, Fiona.'

'You're—' I gasped, as another inch of him disappeared inside me in the mirror '—you're the boss.'

His right hand traced the line of my thigh before coming to rest on my belly, fingers just brushing my clit as I took all of him. 'That's right. So let me give you what you need.'

He bit my earlobe, hips grinding against mine. This position didn't come with a great range of motion, but it didn't matter – I could feel him everywhere.

'You're in *my* bed, Fiona.' He circled my clit with his fingers, as he pulled out then thrust sharply back in, so hard it made me cry out. 'These are *my* hands on you. *I'm* inside you.'

'Yes,' I managed to say, as he thrust again.

'Say it.' The heel of his hand was pressed so hard now against my heart it might leave a bruise, holding me in place as he drove up into me. 'Who's fucking you?'

'You are, Satoshi.' I wrapped my hands around his left forearm, using it as leverage so I could catch his rhythm. 'Just you. Only you.'

'That's – fucking – right.' He bit the words out, short, staccato, punctuated with thrusts. 'Tonight, you're mine.'

'Yes.' I drove myself down onto him, taking him as deep as I could, ignoring the bitter protests of my knees and hip flexors. 'Yours.'

It was fast and hard and urgent and sweaty, the kind of sex I would feel for days afterwards. His fingers were insistent against my clit as he pounded into me, our skin slipping together as I tried to match him, the sound of it visceral, carnal, the sight of it in the mirror almost too much to bear. 'I'm going to come,' I panted, my legs shaking violently with the force of it. 'Satoshi, I'm so close.'

He kissed the spot behind my ear – a featherlight gesture, small, chaste – and it tipped me over the edge. The sound that came out of me was animal as I clenched tight around him, the white heat of the sensation going on and on as he bit my shoulder hard and groaned my name, driving as deep as he could and holding me there as he followed.

In this position, I had nothing to cling to but him. I snaked my right arm behind me, hooking it around his neck in a way that would have been awkward and uncomfortable if my whole body hadn't been drained of any semblance of resistance. His left hand was still pressed hard against my heart, and I covered it with mine, twining my fingers through his.

He buried his face into my throat, heedless of his glasses. I could feel his breathing against my skin as he gulped down air, swift and shaky and uneven.

'That was . . .' I tried to find the right words to describe it, rubbing my cheek against his hair. 'That was more cardio than I've had in a long time.'

His snort of surprised laughter was muffled against my neck. 'Is that why your heart's racing?'

I slid my fingers deeper into the gaps between his and pulled his hand up to my mouth. 'Yes.' I kissed the veins in his wrist, then the base of his thumb. 'But it's not the only reason.'

Satoshi looked up. His eyes met mine in the mirror.

And there wasn't a single word I could find for what I wanted to say. None that could possibly encompass how it felt to be held by him, surrounded by him, enveloped by him like this; the flood of emotion it sent rushing through me.

All I could do was press his hand to my heart again, and hope he understood what I did not know how to express: that this meant everything to me.

When I woke later, it was dark, and I was alone.

I blinked, scrabbling automatically for my phone on the nightstand. It was just after two in the morning.

I didn't know when I'd fallen asleep. I'd checked my phone at about half past ten when Satoshi got up to get rid of the condom, in case Elias or Jonah had messaged me about the kids. There had been nothing, though, and I'd grinned as Satoshi emerged from the bathroom, an aggrieved Yquem in his arms. This was, I thought, as he cooed to her, holding her close to his bare chest and stroking her head until she calmed down, a very specific – and effective – type of pornography.

Then he'd come back to bed, and we'd lain down together, him spooning me. *This is nice*, I'd whispered, running my fingers up and down his forearm.

Mmmm, he'd replied, the vibration of his voice a low hum against the back of my neck. *Yes.*

He'd kissed a gentle line across my shoulder. *Do you want to talk about it? What happened today?*

I'd sighed. *Not really.*

But I'd spilled the whole story anyway: Matt turning up on my doorstep, Lex's outburst, the way I'd sent the kids off with my brothers so I could finally have it out with him. *I've never been so angry in my whole life. The fact that he thought he could just show up like that – like I'd roll over for him . . .*

No wonder you wanted to cheat on him, he'd murmured.

I'd taken his hand and pressed it to my lips. *I don't want to think about him anymore, Satoshi.*

We'd had sex again, long and slow and languid this time, and then I must have fallen asleep. My last memory was of Satoshi at my back, our fingers tangled together, one of his thighs between mine, his breath warm in my hair.

But now he was gone.

I sat up and used the torch on my phone to look around his apartment. Yquem was draped along one of the arms of the sofa, but Satoshi wasn't anywhere.

I paused for a moment, then set my phone down and flicked on his bedside lamp.

My ruined underwear was nowhere to be found, but he'd folded my dress, my bra sitting neatly on top of it on the coffee table. My shoes were no longer in the messy pile with his that they'd been in when we kicked them off – rather, they were sitting on the top row of his shoe rack, aligned precisely perpendicular to the wall.

I retied the sash on my dress, the thought of him taking the time to get up and tidy making my heart ache. I rubbed at it with the heel of my hand, the skin still tender from how tight he'd held me to him, a memory that made it ache even more.

I found Satoshi downstairs in the bar. He was only in his underwear – his boxer briefs were royal blue, I noted, unable to stop myself smiling at the fact that they matched his glasses, a different pair than the green ones he'd been wearing before – as he wiped down tables, mop and bucket propped against the wall.

He turned, a couple of glasses in one hand, and saw me. 'Oh. Hi.'

'Hi,' I replied.

'I – um . . .' I'd never seen him at quite so much a loss for words before. 'I couldn't sleep. Sorry. Nothing to do with you, I just . . .'

'It makes you antsy when the bar's not clean?'

He tugged at his hair, his expression sheepish. 'That obvious?'

My heart, which had been aching, melted. This man. This beautiful, *beautiful* man.

'Do you want to finish wiping down tables,' I asked him, 'or do you want to mop?'

'What?'

'I'll mop,' I decided. 'You finish the tables.'

'Fiona – I – no, you don't—'

'Don't worry, boss.' I wrinkled my nose fondly at him. 'You can check my work after.'

We worked in silence for a while – not an uncomfortable silence, but a companionable one, the swish of the mop against the floor and the clatter of glasses as he stacked them in racks and carried them out to the kitchen the only sounds. He relinquished his cloth to me so I could wipe down the bar as he carried the mop bucket out to empty it. It was impossible not to admire the long lines of him as he walked away, the tendons in his left arm standing out from the bucket's weight.

I'd just had sex with this man. I'd just had sex with Satoshi Tsukamoto, and it had been the best sex of my entire life.

I pressed my tongue to the roof of my mouth, trying to swallow the laugh rising up inside me, but I couldn't. It bubbled out of me, rushing, fizzing, like a bottle of champagne that had been shaken up.

'What's wrong?' There was a worried look on Satoshi's face as he re-emerged from the back.

'Nothing!' I managed to gasp. 'I'm just – will you come here?'

He did. I wrapped my arms around him as tight as I could, hiding my face in the curve where his neck met his shoulder, and laughed.

One of his hands came to rest between my shoulder blades, the other stroking the back of my head. 'I thought you were crying.'

'No.' I kissed the hollow at the base of his throat. 'Not this time.'

He drew back. 'You're all right?'

'Satoshi,' I went up on tiptoes so I could kiss his lips, 'I'm *great*.'

He smoothed his hand down my shoulder. 'Do you need to go? Or can I pour you a drink?'

I would need to go at some point. The sun would come up, and the world would be waiting for me, and I would have to meet it.

But right now, there was just this. Right now, there was just him. Outside, there might be storms aplenty, but here, in this place – this one special, safe place – everything was quiet and calm.

'I would love a drink.'

I slid onto my regular barstool, ogling Satoshi shamelessly as he bent down to get something from the lowest tier of one of his wine fridges. 'I like your new uniform. Very fashion-forward.'

He chuckled. 'Do you think it'll draw in more customers?'

'Without a doubt.'

He turned the bottle in his hand slowly upside down before righting it and removing the cap. 'What's this?' I asked.

'Sake.'

Rather than taking glasses from the overhead rack, he bent down again, emerging with two small pottery cups and a carafe. They were dark green, with a delicate white floral design on the side.

'This is Junmai Daiginjo sake from Yamaguchi.' He decanted some of it from the bottle into the carafe. 'Where my mother's from.' He handed me one of the cups. 'Hold it for me. Like this.'

I did what he said, cradling it between my palms. 'Two hands,' I noted as he poured, right hand around the neck of the carafe while he supported the base with his left. 'The girls would approve.'

'The formal serving rituals for sake are different from wine. With sake, you use two hands. That's how you show the person you're pouring for care and respect.'

He filled his own cup, then put the carafe in the fridge. 'That's why the cups are so small. Sake is social. It's meant for drinking with other people. The more you refill the cups of the people around you, the more you show that you care for them.'

The ache in my chest was back. 'That's lovely, Satoshi,' I said softly. 'Thank you for pouring this for me.'

He smiled at me – smiled the way he'd smiled a million times at me, only this time, it made me want to burst into tears. 'You're very welcome.' He held his cup up. 'Kanpai.'

I clinked my cup against his. 'Cheers.'

We looked each other in the eye as we drank. 'So, turns out this really pays dividends,' I commented.

'Mmmm?'

I pointed at my eyes with two fingers, then at his. 'Seems like it's pretty effective. If we hadn't been so diligent about warding off seven years of bad sex, who knows how tonight would have gone?'

'Who knows,' he echoed.

Then, he didn't say anything, and a sudden shard of uncertainty pierced my heart. 'It was good for you too, right? You put in so much work to make sure it was good for me, but—'

'Fiona,' he said, 'it was fucking incredible.'

'Really?'

Satoshi reached over the bar, taking my hand and squeezing reassuringly. 'Really.'

I squeezed back as I took another sip of the sake, crisp and slightly sweet as it slid down my throat.

'I'm going to remember tonight for the rest of my life.' His thumb traced circles over the base of mine. 'Forever. Always.'

'Me too.'

I drew his hand to my mouth so I could kiss his knuckles. 'Although next time you have to let me go down on you.' I bit gently at one of them. 'You might be the boss, but I insist.'

'Next time?'

I froze.

'Do you not want to?' I forced out eventually. 'If you don't, that's fine, obviously that's fine, but—'

'Of course I want to! But do you?'

Satoshi sighed, disentangling his hand from mine so he could run it through his hair, black roots almost as long as the bleached ends in the dim light. 'I know how complicated your life is, Fiona. I know how many things you have to worry about, and I know I'm not even close to the top of the list. And that's completely fine. That's the way it should be.'

'Oh,' I said, a little stung.

'I don't want to make things harder for you.' His Adam's apple bobbed. 'So if tonight was all you needed, that's fine. Nothing has to change. If you want to go back to what we were doing, that's fine. If – if you've got it out of your system now, that's fine too. I'll be here for you anyway, same as always. Tsundoku will be here too, and—'

'Will you pass me the sake?'

Satoshi looked at me.

'Please?'

He took it out of the fridge and handed it to me.

'Pick up your cup,' I told him.

He did. With his long, strong fingers wrapped around it, it looked almost comically small, but he held it in two hands anyway.

Trying not to let my hands shake, doing my best to mimic the way he'd held the carafe, I refilled it.

'You're not wrong,' I said. 'My life is complicated. There are a lot of things I have to worry about. But when I'm here – with you – I don't have to worry at all.'

Satoshi didn't say anything. His chest rose and fell as he took in a long breath.

'Not just because you make me come so hard I forget everything,' I added. 'Although that helps, obviously.'

That drew a surprised, stunned laugh.

'I'm kind of obsessed with you,' I said. 'I always have been, I think. You're so . . . I've spent my life surrounded by passionate, dedicated people, but them – their world – has always felt so closed to me. Like it wasn't *for* me. But from the very first time I met you, it was like – like you were standing in front of an open door. Like you were saying, *Welcome to my world, come on in, make yourself at home, there's room for you here.*'

'That's hospitality, Fiona,' he said softly. 'That's my job.'

I shook my head. 'No. I – I see you, Satoshi, all of you, and this *is* you. It would be so easy for you to be so single-minded – most brilliant people are – but you . . . you use your powers for good. You're so passionate – and you've got this laser focus – but you're also so kind and generous and patient. The attention you pay to what people need – the way you carve out space for them – the way you turn that laser focus on *them* – I don't know if you understand what a rare, special quality that is. How rare and special you are. And how – how – how . . .'

'How what?' he asked, when the moment had stretched out a little too long.

'How privileged I feel, to be seen by you.'

I took a deep breath, trying to steady myself. 'You've always seen *me*,' I said. 'Not just the kids' mum, or the idiot who didn't realise her husband had a whole other life, or a disappointment of a daughter, or a sister who might never measure up to her brothers. Whenever you look at me, I feel like – *Fiona*.'

I closed my eyes for a second, before opening them again. If I was going to do this – if I was going to attempt this absurd leap – if I was going to get this carried away – I needed to look at him.

'I know I don't have much to offer,' I said. 'I'm a mess. My life is a mess. But if I try and wait until it's not a mess anymore, I'll be waiting forever, and I'm so sick of being frozen in place.'

'Fiona,' Satoshi said, 'what are you saying?'

'That I want to explore this . . . thing we have. Properly. For real.'

For a long moment, there was silence. I looked at him, and he looked at me, and I could hear my own heartbeat, racing in my ears.

'I'm not suggesting that I be – like, your girlfriend or anything.' The word *girlfriend* felt uncomfortable the second it came out of my mouth, a too-small dress which clung in all the wrong places. 'I mean, fuck, I've been divorced for – what, three hours? But I – I want more than what we've been doing. More than friends with benefits. Not . . . casual.'

There was a long pause before he spoke again. 'The way I feel about you, Fiona,' he said at last, voice low, 'has never been casual.'

'We would still have to go slow.' I pressed my tongue to the roof of my mouth, trying not to get too far ahead of myself. 'Not that – I don't want to go back to only kissing, but – in terms of a . . . relationship, we would need to go slow. It's not that I'm not over Matt – I am, trust me – but it's still so soon.'

'Of course.'

'So I totally understand that I might be asking too much. I'm not the only one with needs, and your needs matter too, Satoshi.

I *know* you have them, and it would make me sick to think you were denying yourself because of me. So if this isn't what you want, that's obviously completely fine, and—'

'Come here.'

I slid off my barstool and went behind the bar.

Satoshi grabbed me by the waist and set me on top of it, stepping between my parted knees. 'There is nothing you can ask of me,' he said fiercely, holding my face tight between both his hands, 'that I don't want to give you, Fiona.'

It was different between us this time. It started hurried and frantic, mouths hot and hard and hungry against each other, even his deft fingers slipping as he untied the sash of my dress again. I wrapped my legs tight around his hips and clawed at him, trying to get closer, but after I knocked a bowl of citrus off the counter with a flailing hand, sending lemons and limes bouncing to the ground and making us both laugh, it slowed down. Our foreheads stayed pressed together as we touched each other, breathy gasps and sighs co-mingling.

'Are you sure?' he asked, when I told him to get a condom. 'We went so hard before. I don't want to hurt you.'

I kissed him. 'You won't.'

He probably would. It was easy to make promises, and harder to keep them. He was beautiful and brilliant and one day he was going to wake up and want more than me. It was foolish of me, to put myself in a position where I could get hurt again.

But maybe, I thought, clutching at his hair and pressing my lips to his pulse point as he moved inside me, it would be worth it. Because even if he did hurt me in the end, I would have these memories of him, precious and perfect – something I did just for myself.

'Can I ask one more thing?' I asked afterwards, as we held each other close, trying to catch our breath.

'Of course.' Satoshi reached over and snagged the sake carafe and our cups, handing me mine. 'Anything.'

'Do you mind if we keep this to ourselves?'

He had been about to refill my cup, but he stilled. 'You want it to be a secret?'

'Not a secret, exactly. But for a while, can this just be . . . ours?'

I stroked the side of his face. 'Everything's so simple, when it's just you and me,' I whispered. 'And I have the kids to think about. They've already been through so much upheaval, and they're about to go through more, seeing Matt again. I . . .'

'You have to be careful.'

I nodded, grateful that he didn't make me spell it out. 'So can it just be us for a bit? Before we throw the world at it?'

Satoshi took a long breath and let it out slowly before he answered.

'Of course, Fiona,' he said. 'Whatever you want. Whatever you need. Whatever you can offer – I want it.'

JANUARY

Chapter Fourteen

Satoshi

Tasting today: seventeen-year-old single-malt whisky, Yamanashi prefecture, Japan.
A classic whisky made in the Scottish style: everything in balance, flavours restrained, completely and utterly in control.
Perfect at the end of a long (long) day.

FIONA

Happy New Year, Satoshi xxx

Hope the party at the bar went well!!

SATOSHI

It did 😊

Although it would have been much better if you'd been here to kiss at midnight xx

FIONA

I wish I could have been, but Elias flew back to Germany yesterday, and asking Jonah and Sadie to babysit on NYE might have been a bit much

I ended up babysitting for them instead

Fiona sent a photo.
[Photo: Rosie and Georgia, playing with Bunbury.]

SATOSHI

I ended up babysitting *them*

Satoshi sent a photo.
[Photo: Jonah and Sadie, kissing at midnight.]

I only just managed to herd them out the door

FIONA

Oh god, I'm sorry

It's so late, you must be exhausted xx

SATOSHI

Speaking of – why are you still up?

Was there a rager at the Fisher family house I wasn't invited to?

FIONA

The girls insisted they were going to stay up until midnight, but they were already drooping by the 9 pm fireworks, and everyone was well and truly in bed by 10 pm

Including me, but . . .

SATOSHI

Can't sleep?

FIONA

No

Matt's first child support payment is supposed to come through today and I can't stop obsessively refreshing my bank account

Because if he *doesn't* pay (very on brand for him),
I have a whole new mess to deal with

Anyway. You don't need to hear about this.

SATOSHI

I *want* to hear about this

You can tell me anything x

FIONA

I know x

Let me rephrase: I don't want to talk about it

I want to think about it *less*

Ideally, I never want to have to think about it at all

SATOSHI

Can I try and take your mind off it?

FIONA

What were you thinking?

SATOSHI

Tell me what you're wearing

FIONA

It won't be the mental picture you're hoping for

An extremely ancient T-shirt

So old it probably predates the dinosaurs

SATOSHI

I would love to see you in an extremely ancient T-shirt that predates the dinosaurs, but that isn't what you're wearing right now

FIONA

I promise you, it is

Fiona sent a photo.
[Photo: Selfie of Fiona in bed, wearing a very old T-shirt.]

SATOSHI

No it isn't

Take it off

FIONA

I might not be brave enough to send you a picture of that

It's been a while since I took a nude

SATOSHI

That's fine x

My imagination is very powerful 😉

But have you taken it off?

FIONA

Yes

There's a chance I may have skipped ahead and taken off my underwear too . . . ?

SATOSHI

That *is* skipping ahead

Because we're going to go slow

Here's what you're going to do

You're going to touch yourself

Gently

Slowly

You're going to trace your fingers down your throat

Along your collarbone

Down the lines of your arms and along your belly

You're going to cup your tits in your hands, and you're going to rub your nipples, and you're going to tell me all about what feels best

You are going to check your vibrator is charged

But you are not – I repeat, *not* – going to turn it on yet, and you are not going to touch your pussy

FIONA

That might be hard

SATOSHI

Don't talk to me about hard

Satoshi sent a photo.
[Photo: Satoshi's tented grey trousers.]

You are going to do what I said while I clean down the bar, and you're going to think about what you've done to me while you do it

Then I'm going to go upstairs, pour myself a whisky, and call you, and then – only then! – will you be allowed to come

🍷

FIONA

Thank you so much for last night, Satoshi

It was both the hottest thing that's ever happened to me and genuinely helpful – I managed to stop spiralling and get some sleep

BTW – Matt paid

SATOSHI

1) That's great news. What a relief!
2) You don't need to thank me. I got just as much out of it as you did 😉

FIONA

1) You have no idea what a relief it is!! I nearly burst into tears when I looked at my bank account and the money was there
2) That simply cannot be true. The depths of orgasm debt I'm sinking into are enormous. I'm on track for orgasm bankruptcy

SATOSHI

1) I'm so glad xxx
2) 'orgasm debt' is not real. That is not a thing.

FIONA

1) Thank you x
I'm expecting Matt to turn up on my doorstep and demand to see the kids *immediately* now he's paid for the privilege, so it's not all sunshine and roses, but at least it's something

2) I agree in principle, but one of us has been doing the heavy lifting, and it hasn't been me

Are you free this morning? The girls are obsessed with Jonah and Sadie's puppy, so they offered to take them for the day, and Lex went too

So I have some time in which to, ahem, start making repayments 😉

SATOSHI

I can't do today, sadly – cellar consult

FIONA

On New Year's Day?!

SATOSHI

It's for a rich old (and badly organised) Frenchman who's flying to Paris tomorrow. This is the only time he had

But if J&S want to take the kids overnight: all I'm doing after close is studying, and I know something I'd much rather be doing

Sorry, *someone* I'd much rather be doing

FIONA

The kids are back with me this evening

Besides, I know you need to study. Hardest exam in the world and all that x

But what if I came with you to your consult? I could be your assistant 😉

SATOSHI

Are you sure? This guy's kept zero track of what wine he has, so I'm fairly sure today will just be me clambering around in a basement full of spiders trying to figure out what he's stored down there

And he only speaks French

FIONA

I'm sure

I'm not scared of spiders

I love watching you work

And I'd *love* to hear you speak French

Besides, it'll be fun watching you get dirty 😉

SATOSHI

I haven't been dirty enough for you?!?!

I need to up my game

FIONA

You are precisely the right level of dirty xx

But you're always so clean-cut and perfectly pressed. Who knows what seeing you get a little grimy will do to me . . .

FIONA

Well, now you know what seeing you get a little grimy will do to me 😉

SATOSHI

And I may never recover

Seriously, I have to stand behind the bar all evening and my legs are still shaking

FIONA

I told you I wanted to 😇

Although maybe doing it *in* the spider cellar wasn't the best idea I've ever had. When I picked up the kids, I had to think fast when Rosie asked me why my knees were all dirty.

SATOSHI

What did you tell her?

FIONA

That I dropped one of my earrings in the garden and I'd been kneeling down looking for it

And then Georgia said, 'But Mummy, you aren't wearing earrings', and . . . 🙈

SATOSHI

You could have told them the truth, you know

Not the whole truth, obviously – but that you were helping me out in a dirty cellar

FIONA

Is that what the kids are calling it these days? 🤣

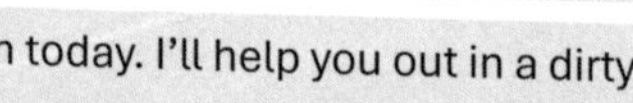

Seriously, though, I had fun today. I'll help you out in a dirty cellar whenever you like x

It gave me an idea for my next column, actually – how many people have all this incredibly valuable wine just randomly stashed under the house???

SATOSHI

Oh, I can tell you some STORIES

And connect you to some people who can tell you some stories, so I'm not your only source

FIONA

You really are very useful to have around x

Just sent off the very final edits for my Bibliophile piece, btw – it'll be published at the end of the month

SATOSHI

Congratulations!!

I'm going to frame a copy for the bar and get you to sign it x

FIONA

Maybe wait for me to get my nerve up to tell Jonah and Sadie about my little career pivot first

It's intimidating, showing your writing to two English PhDs . . .

SATOSHI

I'll hold your hand, if that'll help

FIONA

That might be a giveaway for something else as well

From: birdie.philips@mail.com.au
To: hello@tsundokubar.com.au
Subject: Resignation

Hi Satoshi

I'm so sorry, but I have to resign my position at Tsundoku, effective immediately. My mother's condition has got worse and I have to go to Melbourne to care for her.

I know I'm letting you down, and that I haven't been the best employee anyway. I really appreciate your endless patience with me, and I hope you can forgive me.

Sorry again

Birdie

From: hello@tsundokubar.com.au
To: birdie.philips@mail.com.au
Subject: Re: Resignation

Dear Birdie,

I'm so sorry to hear this. Love to you and your mother from all of us.

And please don't feel like you need to apologise. Of course, family has to come first!

If you find yourself back in Hobart, you'll always have a job here.

Best wishes,

Satoshi

SATOSHI

Heads up – I'm about to place an ad for a new junior somm

You will be delighted to hear Birdie quit

ISAMU

I'm sorry – but this sounds like the best thing in the long run

In the interim, when do you need me to work?

SATOSHI

Isamu.

Vintage starts soon

Do your own job

ISAMU

I can do days in the vineyard and a few nights in the bar

I'm not the one studying for the MS

A few weeks won't kill me

SATOSHI

A few weeks won't kill me either

~~I'm not Otōsan~~

🍷

MS TRAUMA BOND SUPPORT CIRCLE

SATOSHI

Do either of you know any out-of-work somms?

Or someone willing to moonlight for a few weeks?

Lost my junior, and now my roster has a *lot* of holes

CARLTON

No, sorry – we just lost one here too

Took us ages last time we hired – classic Tasmania and its population of three people and some quolls

MAXI

Same here ☹

SATOSHI

No problems – thanks anyway!

SATOSHI

Fiona, I'm so sorry, but I have to work this Thursday

Birdie quit

FIONA

Oh no! Is she ok?

SATOSHI

Her mum's sick, unfortunately

Which means I'm running every shift until I can hire someone new

FIONA

Poor Birdie ☹

Can I help?

I do have some experience working at Tsundoku, after all . . .

SATOSHI

I'll figure it out, don't worry! It'll just be a bumpy few weeks until I find someone

FIONA

What about Charlotte?

SATOSHI

I need someone who's done Certified, not just Intro, and they're not running that qual again here until April

But please don't let the inconvenient fact that I have to work keep you away x

FIONA

I'll be there, don't worry

I'll sit at the bar while you work

Then afterwards, you can sit and I'll do all the work 😉

SATOSHI

What happened to 'you're the boss'?

FIONA

Doesn't being the boss mean you get to put your feet up while your minions do everything for you?

SATOSHI

Compelling point 🤣

Please note that the boss is going to call his minion after he closes tonight, and she is going to do *exactly* what he tells her

🍷

From: no_reply@aussommoftheyear.com.au
To: hello@tsundokubar.com.au
Subject: Nomination: Young Australian Sommelier of the Year
Attached: ASY_Invitation.pdf

Dear Mr Tsukamoto,

We are pleased to inform you that you have been nominated to compete for the title of Young Australian Sommelier of the Year, honouring the country's best sommeliers under the age of 30.

This year's competition will consist of a **service examination** and a **blind tasting**, with an awards dinner in the evening. It will be held in Naarm/Melbourne on 28 February. You can find full details in the attached invitation. Please RSVP by 14 February.

Sincere congratulations on your achievement.

In vino veritas,
Chandler Michaels, MS
Convenor
Australian Sommelier of the Year Awards

@tsundokubar shared a new photo to Instagram.

[Photo: Satoshi standing behind the bar at Tsundoku, sipping from a glass of champagne.]

[Caption: @tsundokubar Here's our co-owner Satoshi celebrating his nomination for Young Australian Sommelier of the Year! Come into Tsundoku and browse through our lovingly curated wine list, or tell Satoshi what you like and let him choose for you – he's here every day!]

🍷

ISAMU

Congratulations on your nomination, Sato

Well deserved

SATOSHI

Thank you

ISAMU

If you don't have a junior ready to run the floor by then, I'll cover so you can go to the awards ceremony

Dates are in my diary

How's the search going?

SATOSHI

• • •

• • •

Getting there.

🍷

MS TRAUMA BOND SUPPORT CIRCLE

MAXI

Congrats on the nom, Satoshi! You deserve it.

CARLTON

What Maxi said – huge congrats, mate!

SATOSHI

Thank you 😊

It was a lovely surprise

MAXI

I'll bring something special for us to blind next study group 😊

I was going to suggest we meet more often anyway – we'll never be ready to sit this bastard exam in August if we don't knuckle down – but now we definitely should so we can get you ready to take the Young Aus Somm title home!

I'll ask my boss if you can stage if you want to practise service

SATOSHI

That'd be great, although Mondays are my only night off atm

Speaking of – you're both welcome to stage at Tsundoku whenever you want. I could use the cover

🍷

FIONA

Satoshi!!!!!

Fiona sent a photo.
[Photo: Screenshot of @tsundokubar's most recent Instagram post]

CONGRATULATIONS!!

SATOSHI

Thank you 😊

It doesn't mean much outside the industry, but in my world it's a pretty big deal

Well, a reasonably sized deal

To a limited group of people

FIONA

Translation: it's an *enormous* deal

I'm so thrilled for you!

And so proud of you

And I plan on demonstrating that at great length next time I get you alone 😉

SATOSHI

Can't wait x

Literally, I can't wait – any chance you could come in before Thursday?

FIONA

You will definitely see me before Thursday, but not for the reasons you're hoping

I promised Lex I'd bring them by tomorrow afternoon

Matt's first formal visitation is in the morning, and Lex is Not Thrilled

SATOSHI

Matt's coming to Hobart?

FIONA

Just a video call

But he's requested that I bring the kids to Melbourne next month so they can meet their siblings in person

Including the new siblings – Laura will have given birth by then

Spoiler: I'll be asking you to take my mind off it a lot. Like, A LOT.

SATOSHI

Spoiler: delighted to x

But question – when in Feb will you be in Melbourne?

FIONA

End of the month

We're on a monthly visitation schedule, but Matt asked that the Feb one be as late as possible in case Laura goes past her due date

Which she won't. Twins are almost always early.

Which he should remember from when the girls were born, but . . . 🙄

SATOSHI

Will you be there on the 28th?

FIONA

Yes. Why?

SATOSHI

That's the Aus Somm awards dinner, and I have a +1

You could meet some people in the wine world – make some connections for your column

FIONA

Can I think about it?

SATOSHI

Of course

FIONA

It's not that I don't want to, but I'll have the kids with me

And I don't exactly want to leave them with Matt, Laura, and their half-siblings they've only just met

Including two newborns

SATOSHI

• • •

• • •

• • •

Of course I understand if you can't make it work, but if you can, I'd love to take you

How many people get to have the Australian wine scene's hottest new columnist on their arm?

FIONA

You really are perfect, aren't you?

FIONA

Thanks for spending so long chatting with Lex today

I know how busy you are x

SATOSHI

Lex and I are pals 😊 I always have time to chat with them

They didn't say anything about Matt, in case you were wondering – we mostly just talked about books

In that they talked, I listened

FIONA

That's how most discussions about books with Lex go 

But thanks for listening – it means a lot to them, feeling like they're being heard. Particularly on a day like today.

SATOSHI

How did it go?

If you want to talk about it, that is?

FIONA

TL;DR: about as well as could be expected

Lex stared at the screen and refused to say anything, and Matt got the girls so amped up about meeting their new siblings that they're not going to talk about anything else for a week

Was so glad you and I managed to sneak some time today, even if it was just a couple of minutes making out in your office x

The way being with you lets me escape my life for a while always makes me feel so much better

SATOSHI

~~I don't want to just help you escape your life, though~~

What if I came around to your place tonight after close?

I could sneak in after the kids are in bed, sneak out again in the early morning

Not angling for sex here, btw – just to literally sleep with you.

FIONA

I would love that, but it's probably not a good idea

That's just *asking* for Rosie or Georgia to wander in in the middle of the night and scream, 'Mummy, why is Satoshi sleeping in your bed???'

Which would turn into them announcing it to every single person they've ever met

SATOSHI

• • •

• • •

Offer's open if you change your mind x

From: jonah.fisher@lyons.edu.au
To: hello@tsundokubar.com.au; info@bibliophilewine.com.au
CC: sadie.shaw@lyons.edu.au
Subject: Wedding
Attached: guest list.docx; run sheet.docx

Hi Satoshi and Isamu

This is just a quick email to touch base with you about our wedding at the winery on 2 Feb.

I've attached the finalised guest list and a draft run sheet. It's not very big (only twenty people), so hopefully this will be a pretty easy event. The only complicated bit is that we'd like to Zoom in my brother Elias briefly during the reception to give a toast – he won't be able to make it. Is that okay?

Also: we know you're our hosts, but Sadie and I hope you'll consider yourselves our guests too. You've been so generous to us – we'd love you to be part of our celebration.

When you're putting together the final cost of the event, please include yourselves* as part of the headcount – we'd be delighted to subsidise you to eat your own food and drink your own wine.

Best,

JF

*and a +1, if you'd like!

From: info@bibliophilewine.com.au
To: jonah.fisher@lyons.edu.au; hello@tsundokubar.com.au
CC: sadie.shaw@lyons.edu.au
Subject: Re: Wedding
Attached: fishershaw_menu_final.docx

Dear Jonah

Thank you for this information.

Twenty people will be very manageable. As previously discussed, we can accommodate the ceremony outside; but in the case of wet weather, we can hold both ceremony and reception in the cellar door. The Zoom element is no problem.

I have attached the menu for your sign-off, which includes the price per head. It also includes our in-house suggested matched wines.

Thank you also for your kind invitation. I will not require a +1, but would be delighted to raise a glass with you.

Regards,
Isamu

From: hello@tsundokubar.com.au
To: jonah.fisher@lyons.edu.au; info@bibliophilewine.com.au
CC: sadie.shaw@lyons.edu.au
Subject: Re: Wedding

Hi Jonah and Sadie,

The standard matched wines list Isamu has sent you is great, but I'd be happy to assist you with some bespoke pairings – that is, of course, my area of expertise. Perhaps you might like to come by the bar for a tasting?

And I'd also be very happy to toast to your happiness (no +1 required).

Cheers,
Satoshi

From: sadie.shaw@lyons.edu.au
To: hello@tsundokubar.com.au; info@bibliophilewine.com.au
CC: jonah.fisher@lyons.edu.au
Subject: Re: Wedding

Hi Satoshi,

Who are we to turn down a wine tasting with an expert (congrats on your award nom, by the way)!

I'll get Jonah to babysit sometime this week and bring Fiona along so she can help me pick some good ones – she knows more about wine than either of us.

Also: how would you feel about me having my hens' night at Tsundoku on 31 Jan? I know you have a no hens' nights policy, so no hard feelings if the answer is no, but I can solemnly promise this won't be a rowdy night of drunken debauchery where we trash the place. It'll only be four people (me, Chess, Fiona and my friend Julia), and it'll be nice calm adults eating cheese vibes, not penis cake vibes.

Thanks,
Sadie

From: hello@tsundokubar.com.au
To: sadie.shaw@lyons.edu.au
CC: jonah.fisher@lyons.edu.au; info@bibliophilewine.com.au
Subject: Re: Wedding

Hi Sadie,

For you, I can relax the no hens' night policy. I've made a booking for you on 31 January.

Looking forward to seeing you and Fiona for a tasting soon.

Cheers,
Satoshi

🍷

FIONA

OMG Satoshi I am so sorry about today

SATOSHI

Why?

I got to see you

I didn't get to touch you, and I suspect many courts of law would consider that a crime, but I would much rather see you than not see you x

FIONA

You are so sweet that sometimes I think I made you up x

I meant about Sadie!

Who knew one person could fit so many pointed looks and innuendos into an hour and a half?!

I'm sorry if it made you uncomfortable

SATOSHI

Well, we are doing all the things she was hinting at 😉

FIONA

I know, but . . .

SATOSHI

• • •

• • •

• • •

This is a genuine question and not an attempt to pressure you into anything: why don't you tell her the truth?

She already knows part of it – if she knew all of it, she might lay off the suggestive comments

Which might be more comfortable for you than the speculation

FIONA

See, that makes perfect sense

Because she would definitely be supportive

But I can't – not yet

If you and I were just sleeping together, maybe I'd feel differently

And if Sadie weren't married to my brother, then I'd definitely feel differently

But she is, and asking her to keep secrets from him feels very unfair

SATOSHI

• • •

• • •

• • •

FIONA

I assume what you're trying to ask is, 'Why don't you just tell Jonah, there's an obvious solution right in front of your face?'

SATOSHI

That is not the phrasing I was planning to use

FIONA

I know x

The answer is: childhood trauma

Well, early twenties trauma, which is basically childhood

SATOSHI

Do you want me to call you?
Talk this through on the phone?

I'm working, but I could get Charlotte to watch things for a few minutes

FIONA

Text might be better, tbh

It's easier for me sometimes to write things down – you know how my mouth can get ahead of my brain x

Basically: when I announced I was getting married, my family all told me I was making a massive mistake

My mum called me stupid and short-sighted

My dad said me marrying Matt would make me worse than a failure

Elias told me not to be an idiot

And Jonah looked me in the eye and said, 'Can you explain why this ISN'T the worst choice anyone has ever made in the history of the world?'

Which really stung, because we were close back then and I'd been counting on him supporting me. Not very fair of me to put that on an 18yo, but still . . .

Anyway: I'm not comparing you + me to Matt + me. Two totally different situations, two totally different people x

And you are the single loveliest person in the world – this is, I promise, really not about you at all xx

But on paper . . . just like 'naïve 22yo drops out of uni and marries rich older dickhead who immediately knocks her up and moves her to an island', 'middle-aged single mother starts dating hot younger man fifteen minutes after getting divorced' isn't a story people expect to end well

So even though Jonah *knows* you, and he's an adult now, and he'd probably just be like, 'Good for you, Fi' and mayyyybe – at most – raise an eyebrow at how quickly I've jumped into another relationship, I've still got the memory of that night in my bones

And he and I have only really just come back from that. The thought of hearing something like that from him again . . .

SATOSHI

I see.

FIONA

None of this is fair to you. I'm sorry.

SATOSHI

You don't need to apologise

I'm never going to push you to do something you're not comfortable with x

FIONA

I will tell him eventually x

But we're still so new, Satoshi

What if I told him tomorrow and then you got sick of me next week? Then Jonah would feel morally obliged to stop coming into Tsundoku, and I cannot in good conscience cost you business like that.

SATOSHI

Fiona.

FIONA

Plus, if I'm being *really* honest: I'm not sure how to say 'Hey, I'm getting railed by the nice boy in the bar' to my baby brother without the ground opening and swallowing me whole

SATOSHI

Speaking of you getting railed: see you Thursday?

I have to work, but I can promise you wine, orgasms and breakfast the next morning

FIONA

You're on. I'll come in as soon as I've dropped the kids off x

I'll bring my laptop – I have some reading I want to do for my spider cellar piece

And then I'll help you clean up after close (in order to get to the railing with the greatest possible efficiency) 😉

SATOSHI

How can I refuse such an offer?

Feel free to pencil 'reading and railing' in your diary for every Thursday night for the foreseeable future 😉

FIONA

Ah yes, the true meaning of R&R 🤣

SATOSHI

~~Just wondering – any further thoughts about being my date to the Aus Somm of the Year dinner? I know it's complicated with childcare, but I would really love for us to be a couple somewhere that isn't my bar or my bed.~~

MAXI

Hey Satoshi, just checking to see if you're doing ok!

You weren't your normal cheery self at study group

SATOSHI

I'm fine, don't worry!

Just a tad overworked atm

MAXI

NO idea how you do it, honestly

If I was running a business on top of studying for this bastard exam, I'd die. I'm drowning when all I do is work in someone else's.

ISAMU

Any progress on finding a new junior somm?

SATOSHI

A few applications, but no one with the right skills or experience yet

I'm going to run another ad

In the meantime, I've been giving Charlotte extra training

I'd prefer not to have her run the floor before she passes Certified, but in a pinch, she could probably do it

🍷

FIONA

R&R, after R&R

Fiona sent a photo.
[Photo: Satoshi, fast asleep in bed, rays of morning sun spilling across his skin.]

xxx

SATOSHI

You should have woken me up!

FIONA

I did, remember? With breakfast.

SATOSHI

Which I promised to make you!

FIONA

Could you stand to wake this boy?

Besides, you work so hard

And then I made you work so hard 😉

SATOSHI

You think that was hard work? You just wait till next time I see you, Fiona Fisher. Someone is going to get worked. Hard.

FIONA

I'll make sure I stretch beforehand 

Seriously, though, you were out like a light last night.

Everything ok?

SATOSHI

Bit chaotic without Birdie, but it's all under control x

FIONA

If ever you need me to work on Thursdays instead of sitting at the bar like a princess, just say the word x

From: hello@tsundokubar.com.au
To: contact@bpscateringequipment.com.au
Subject: URGENT – commercial dishwasher repair

Hi,

I've called several times today, but to follow up in writing: I'm requesting an urgent repair service for my commercial glasswasher.

It started leaking late yesterday and now no longer functions. My business is a wine bar, so it is imperative this be fixed ASAP. At present, we are washing our stemware by hand.

Best wishes,
Satoshi Tsukamoto

From: contact@bpscateringequipment.com.au
To: hello@tsundokubar.com.au
Subject: Re: URGENT – commercial dishwasher repair
Attached: BPS_callout_fee_schedule.pdf

Dear Tsukamoto,

We have received your request. One of our technicians will be despatched to your location in 5–7 working days.

Please find attached a list of our callout fees.

Kind regards,
Customer Service
BPS Catering Equipment

🍷

MS TRAUMA BOND SUPPORT CIRCLE

CARLTON

Thanks for hosting study group today, Satoshi!

That Beechworth chardonnay you got us to blind was *insane*

SATOSHI

My pleasure

Sorry I had to keep jumping up to serve people

I offered my bar staff extra shifts to help out with our glasswasher situation, but not many have taken me up on it

MAXI

No worries – we know what hospo is like!

Thanks for hosting anyway – fuck knows I would have cancelled if I was working with a broken glasswasher

SATOSHI

No choice, if I want to be ready for the Aus Somm comp next month (not to mention the MS)

Btw – standing offer to stage at Tsundoku whenever you like, but I really need cover on Sat 2 Feb. Are either of you free?

MAXI

I'm afraid not – daughter's birthday

CARLTON

Me neither – I'm rostered on, and we're stretched so thin rn that switching shifts is basically impossible

SATOSHI

Thanks anyway!

🍷

From: tom.carmichael@lyons.edu.au
To: hello@tsundokubar.com.au
Subject: Complaint

To whom it may concern,

I am writing to complain about the appalling service I received at your bar on Tuesday night. Not only did the food my colleague and

I ordered take almost an hour to reach the table, but it took nearly fifteen minutes to receive a simple glass of wine!

I should also note that your much-vaunted bookshelves contain an astonishing amount of trash – not at all what I had been led to expect by your reputation.

Regards,
Professor Tom Carmichael

From: hello@tsundokubar.com.au
To: tom.carmichael@lyons.edu.au
Subject: Re: Complaint

Dear Professor Carmichael

My sincere apologies for the poor service you received.

Tsundoku is currently experiencing some staffing issues, as well as the breakdown of our commercial glasswasher, which is why we were unable to serve you as speedily as we would customarily. Please rest assured that this was an exception to our high service standards, not the norm.

We would be happy to issue you a full refund if you come into the bar with your receipt, as well as a bottle of wine as an apology.

Best wishes,
Satoshi

🍷

@tsundokubar shared a new photo to Instagram.

[Photo: The Tsundoku bar logo with the phrase 'CLOSED 2 FEBRUARY' underneath.]

[Caption: Please note that we will be closed this Saturday 2 February for a wedding. We will reopen as normal on 3 February.]

🍷

SATOSHI

Before you ask: I've decided to close this Saturday because Charlotte isn't ready to run the floor yet

I let her do a trial the other night and it didn't go very well

I'm going to keep working with her, as well as running another ad

This is only a short-term hiccup

It's under control

ISAMU

Noted

But if you need help, ask

🍷

SATOSHI

Will you do me a favour?

FIONA

Of course

SATOSHI

You know that green dress of yours? The one you wore to Abode that makes your tits look incredible?

Will you wear that tonight?

I just had to pay a king's ransom to get our glasswasher fixed, and the fact that Sadie rudely scheduled her hens' night on R&R Thursday has put me in a bad mood

Seeing you in that dress, though, might cheer me up . . .

FIONA

You mean this dress?

Fiona sent a photo.
[Photo: Fiona half-wearing a green dress, breasts exposed.]

SATOSHI

. . . sorry, I think I passed out for a moment

I didn't remember it making your tits look quite THAT incredible

FIONA

Give me your honest opinion: how do you rate this?

Because I haven't taken a nude in . . . a decade, probably?

I have no idea how to get the right angles or lighting or anything

Plus, I'm working with some obvious limitations

SATOSHI

My professional appraisal: this is an exceptional vintage, with outstanding body and legs. Extremely pleasing to the eye, but this pales in comparison to the taste.

FIONA

My professional appraisal, as a writer: your ability to be so sweet and so filthy at the same time indicates a rare talent x

SATOSHI

I'm feeling better already

Though I'm reconsidering asking you to wear the dress tonight, because seeing you in it and not being able to take it off you might end me

FIONA

xxx

Also: It's out!

Fiona sent a link.
[Web link: 'Brothers, Books and Booze: The Bibliophile Story' from casksofamontillado.com.au]

SATOSHI

Fiona!!

I hope everyone is as proud of you as I am xx

FIONA

I hope so too

If I ever get my nerve up to tell them, anyway

SATOSHI

Offer to hold your hand is always on the table x

FIONA

Typing this under the table and I'm a bit tipsy so sorry if there are any weird autocorrects

Watching you in your element is the hottest thing in the world

I'm doing my best to pay attention to Sadie and Chess and Julia but my god Satoshi

The way you move around the bar

No wasted motion

Your hands

The way you manage to be in like 7 places at once

The way you do so many things at the same time and make it look effortless

You're standing at our table right now pouring us chablis and telling us about it and I haven't taken in a word you're saying because I'm so busy listening to you

I have to keep texting you because if I look at you then everyone in this bar is going to know how badly I want to tear your clothes off

SATOSHI

Say you're going to the bathroom

FIONA

I can't

Sadie will know IMMEDIATELY if we both disappear at the same time

SATOSHI

Please

Two minutes

I won't even mess up your lipstick

~~I could really use a hug~~

FEBRUARY

Chapter Fifteen
Fiona

Tasting today: NV 15yr sercial madeira.
Brace yourself. This is a lot.

My parents descended on me the day before Sadie and Jonah's wedding, turning up on my doorstep unforgivably early. 'What are you doing here?' I asked, rubbing my eyes, head woolly with the hint of a hangover. 'I thought you were staying in a hotel.'

'Of course we are,' my dad boomed, at a volume that made me wince. 'But your mother wanted to see the grandkids.'

'They're not here.' My parents were lucky I was, to be honest. If there had been a way for me to linger at Tsundoku so I could spend the night with Satoshi that wouldn't have made Sadie, Chess and Julia very suspicious, I would have done it in a heartbeat. 'They spent the night with Jonah. He'll drop them off later.'

Dad ignored me. 'And I wanted to see what I've been paying for.'

I let out a long breath, feeling exhaustedly ancient and like a teenager again all at once. My brothers might sometimes accidentally make me feel like Fiona Fisher, Family Fuckup, but that was nothing compared to my dad, who did it on purpose and all the time.

'Hi, honey.' Mum leaned over to kiss my cheek as Dad pushed past me into the house. 'How are you?'

'Good. How are you?'

'You look tired.'

'I was up late. Sadie's hens' party was last night.'

'Still.' She made a tutting sound. 'I worry about you. That you're not looking after yourself.'

'I'm actually doing a lot better.' I shepherded her towards the kitchen, where the coffee was. 'I didn't realise what a big milestone being formally divorced would be. Financially, of course – the child support has made a huge difference.' The first thing I'd done that morning was check my bank account to make sure Matt's February child support payment had landed. 'But emotionally too. I feel . . . lighter.'

There was no chance in hell I was going to tell her why, but it was true. My problems hadn't disappeared, but it was amazing how much easier they were to bear.

Because for the last month, Satoshi had been perfect. There was no other word for it. He had been absolutely *perfect*.

He'd walked me home after that first, mostly sleepless night we'd spent together, fingers laced through mine. The sun was just coming up, the sky pink and silver and pale gold, catching in the ashy blond ends of his hair. He'd looked like some otherworldly creature, an elfin fantasy of a man who might dissolve into a sunbeam at any moment.

When he'd kissed me goodbye, long and lingering, and left me alone in my empty house, part of me wondered if I had imagined it. If it hadn't been for the ache between my thighs, I might have believed I had. Surely this was too good to be true.

But it had been over a month now, and instead Satoshi was just . . . there. Always.

And while the adult part of my brain was trying to take it slow, the part of me that could never help getting carried away felt like she was deep into a bottle of wine, unable to resist pouring another glass, and another, and another.

'Well, I'm glad *you're* feeling lighter,' my dad grumbled, dragging me back to reality. He'd made himself at home, putting two pieces of bread in the toaster and leaving a trail of crumbs on the counter. 'Because my wallet certainly has been.'

'I'm so grateful for your help, Dad.' I grabbed a cloth so I could clean up after him. 'I'll never be able to thank you enough.'

He had his head in the fridge. 'Do you have any marmalade?'

'No. There's honey, though. Or jam.'

He made a noise of disapproval, which I chose to ignore. 'I'm going to do my best to repay you,' I said. 'It'll take me a while – a long while, probably – but I'm going to.'

'With what?' Another noise of disapproval. 'The child support that chump is finally paying you? Or those silly little copywriting jobs you do?'

'Christian,' my mother said, in a tone which could be read as admonishing if you squinted.

I pressed my tongue to the roof of my mouth. The first payment for my wine column had also arrived in my bank account that morning, and even though it wasn't much, I'd carefully quarantined a portion of it in my new PAY BACK DAD fund. 'I'll figure it out.'

Dad snorted. 'Don't make promises you can't keep, Fiona.'

'We don't expect anything like that from you,' Mum said, patting my hand.

Ironically, even though her tone was gentler, it hurt more. My pompous professor father being dismissive of my abilities was to be expected. My fellow university dropout mother, though . . . that one stung.

'How about I make you both a coffee,' I suggested, 'and you can tell me what's going on with you?'

Somewhat ironically, given all the baggage my upbringing had left me with, my dad was one of the most reliable people in my life.

I could always count on him for money, to make me feel shit about myself, and to carry a conversation. He was midway through a rant about some new lecturer named Rory they'd hired at his university who wasn't measuring up when Jonah dropped the kids home.

'Grandma!' the girls shrieked, throwing themselves at my mother.

'Hello, my darlings!' Mum peppered their faces with kisses. 'It's so lovely to see you.'

'Hi, Grandma,' Lex said. 'Hi, Grandpa.'

They held out their knuckles for my dad to bump. He patted them. 'Hello, Lex.'

'Mum, Dad, I didn't realise you'd be here.' Jonah ran his hand through his hair. Belatedly, I realised I should have texted him to warn him. 'Nice to see you.'

'Nice to see you too, Jonah.' My mother – still entangled in the girls, who were excitedly telling her about their flower girl dresses – blew him a kiss.

'Is that wife of yours with you?' Dad peered disapprovingly around him, as if Jonah had Sadie concealed behind his back.

'No. She's still asleep.' Jonah glanced at me. 'She said you had fun last night.'

I turned around to pour him a coffee, in case my face flushed incriminatingly. 'Yeah, we did.'

Between the kids and the bar, Satoshi and I hadn't been able to get our schedules to line up for a week, so even though we'd talked and texted a lot, last night had been the first time I'd actually seen him since the previous Thursday. Perhaps because of that – or perhaps because I was simply so pathetically addicted to him – it had taken everything in me not to physically launch myself at him.

He had clearly noticed, because he'd convinced me to pretend to go to the bathroom, following me out there about thirty seconds later and bundling me into his office. Before I could get a single word out, he'd picked me up, set me on the desk, and buried his face in my throat, arms so tight around me that I almost couldn't breathe. *Fiona,* he groaned into my skin.

I'd grinned, looping my arms around his neck. *Hi.*

He'd looked sheepish when he finally drew back. *Sorry. I just really . . . needed you.*

The thought that I could put that look on his face made something in me burn, and I'd curled my fingers into his waistcoat. *I need you too. So badly.*

Do you now? His hand snaked under my dress. *How badly?*

When I went back out to the table a few minutes later, my legs were wobbly and I wasn't wearing any underwear.

'Sadie's friend Julia seems nice.' I handed Jonah his coffee, forcibly pulling myself out of the memory. 'I've never met her before, but I liked her.'

Jonah hesitated. 'You know that she's . . .'

'That she's what?'

'Nothing. I'll tell you later.' He downed his coffee in two gulps. 'I'd better be going. Tonight'll be the first night I've spent apart from Sadie since we got married, so I want to spend the day with her before Chess whisks her away.'

Mum made an *aww* sound. Dad scoffed. 'Will she be wearing her wedding dress next time you see her?' Georgia asked.

'She sure will.'

'We saw her try it on,' Rosie said earnestly. 'She looked so pretty, Uncle Jonah. Like a princess.'

'She always looks pretty.' Jonah's eyes turned dreamy. 'Anyway, I'd better get back to her. Bye, everyone.'

'Mummy,' Georgia asked, when Jonah had left, 'will Daddy have a wedding with the other lady, do you think?'

'I don't know, Georgie-girl,' I replied. 'I suppose he might, one day.'

It was incredible how little it hurt to say. Every second I spent with Satoshi made me more grateful I wasn't the married pregnant chosen one.

'Would we be the flower girls?' Rosie asked.

I opened my mouth to respond, but Lex got in first. 'Of course not,' they almost spat. 'It'd be *Nikki*.'

'Oh.' Rosie's voice was small.

'Hey, hey, let's not worry about something that hasn't even happened,' I said. 'How about we think about what we should do this afternoon instead? We could go to the park, or—'

'Actually,' my mother said, 'I thought you—' she kissed Rosie on the head '—and you—' now Georgia '—and you—' she held her knuckles out to Lex '—could spend this afternoon with me and Grandpa, so Mummy can have a break.'

'What?'

She took an envelope out of her handbag. 'A little treat.'

I opened it. It was a massage gift certificate for the day spa on the Bellerive high street, with an appointment time that afternoon on it.

'This is lovely, but it's really not necessary.' Kieran worked at that spa, and much as I was starting to trust that Satoshi actually liked my body and wasn't just saying he did, I wasn't anywhere near comfortable enough to be that close to his so-beautiful-it-was-like-staring-into-the-sun ex. 'How about you go instead of me? I'm sure you could use a massage after the plane ride.'

'Nonsense.' Mum waved her hand at me. 'We're going to have a lovely time while you get pampered. Aren't we, my darlings?'

To my surprise, Lex was the one who responded. 'You should go to Tsundoku after, Mum.'

I blinked. They gestured at the voucher. 'That's across the road from Tsundoku, right? You should go there after.'

'Don't you want to wait until you can come with me?' I started to say, but Dad talked right over me.

'What's this you're talking about?'

'It's this cool place Mum and I like,' Lex replied. 'You might like it too, Grandpa. They have *heaps* of books. That's what tsundoku means – it's Japanese for collecting lots of books and letting them pile up because you haven't read them yet.'

'You should always read the books you own,' Dad said severely.

'I do,' Lex said stubbornly. 'But don't you think it's exciting? The idea that you have so many books there's always something left to read?'

'Hmph,' my dad replied.

By his standards, that was conceding the argument, and my heart swelled painfully with pride for my brilliant, perfect child.

'All right,' I said. 'Maybe I will.'

I'd walked past the day spa plenty of times, but I'd never actually been in. It was on the second floor, up a narrow set of stairs, and I had a stern conversation with myself as I went up them. *You're about to have a perfectly lovely afternoon. Lots of people work here. Don't catastrophise about something that probably won't happen.*

But, of course, it did. 'Welcome!' Kieran said, smiling brightly at me from behind the reception desk. 'You must be—' he checked his screen '—Fiona, right?'

I made myself smile back. 'That's me.'

'I'm Kieran. I'll be your therapist today.' He looked at me closely. 'Have we met before? You look familiar.'

'I – not formally, I don't think. But—'

He snapped his fingers. 'You're one of Satoshi's regulars.'

I could only hope my expression didn't look too pained as I nodded.

'Well, then, you're a woman of great taste.' He waggled his eyebrows at me. 'He is my very favourite ex. And you'll appreciate our post-treatment glass of bubbles – he's our supplier. Come with me and we'll get you set up.'

Kieran left me in a treatment room with instructions to take off everything except my underwear – truly, *truly* not something anyone should ever have to hear from their hot young lover's hot young ex. 'Where are you feeling the most tension?' he asked when he came back in, straightening the towel I'd clumsily laid over my back with a few quick, deft movements. 'I'm guessing neck and shoulders, right? You seem like a woman who works hard.'

My brain translated that into so many negative comments about how aged and withered and haggard I was that it was impossible to draw out just one. 'Um, yes. I sit at a desk a lot, when I'm not chasing around after my kids.'

'A mum! Wow. That's the hardest job of all.' Kieran folded the towel down, exposing the length of my back – and then, in a way that would have been fine if it had been any other masseuse but was mortifying because it was him, tugged my underwear down slightly to expose the tops of my butt-cheeks. 'I hope your husband doesn't make you do *all* the work.'

'No – ah! – husband. Just me.'

Kieran had dug his thumbs hard into the small of my back. 'Just what I suspected. You might not feel it day-to-day, but you're carrying a *lot* of tension in your lower back. I'm not surprised, if you're raising a family all alone.'

I winced as he did it again. 'Not all alone. I've got – ah! – help. My – oh god, that hurts – family—'

'I'll back off a bit.' The pressure of his thumbs eased, and I let out a long breath. 'We're not here to torture you today – even if it would make you feel better afterwards.'

I had a sudden flashback to one of my Thursday nights with Satoshi. It had felt like torture – he'd brought me to the brink of orgasm probably ten times before he'd let me come (*Trust me,* he'd whispered, pinning my wrists above my head as I almost sobbed with how close I was, *it'll be worth it, I've got you*). When he finally had, I'd absolutely detonated, and afterwards, it had felt like I'd ascended to some higher plane.

'But we'll still pay some attention to it, okay? The body keeps the score, and we carry more emotion in the hips than we realise.' Kieran's hands smoothed up the length of my spine, forcing me to remember that they had once been on Satoshi too. 'Any pain here?' He pressed two fingers into the side of my jaw, just in front of my ear.

'Some.' Dealing with my dad always made me grit my teeth.

'I can tell. You've got some swelling in your jaw.'

Your face is swollen and misshapen, my brain immediately translated.

'It's totally normal, don't worry.' Kieran returned to my back, running his hands rhythmically across the top of my left shoulder. 'Lots of people clench their jaws. We'll give it some love when we flip you onto your front and see if we can relieve some of that tension.'

Part of me almost didn't want it to work, but it did. As I sat in the spa's relaxation room afterwards, wrapped in a fluffy bathrobe, sipping a glass of what I recognised as Bibliophile non-vintage sparkling, the ever-present ache in my jaw and neck and temples had dissipated. Kieran had magic hands.

. . . if only I could stop imagining him using them on Satoshi.

'How are we going here?' Kieran stuck his head around the doorframe, interrupting my self-torture session. 'Can I offer you a top-up?' He winked at me conspiratorially, holding up the bottle of sparkling. 'I don't do this normally, but a friend of Tosh is a friend of mine.'

The pet name stuck in my teeth. It wasn't something I'd ever heard anyone call him before – *Sato,* sometimes, but never *Tosh.* 'No. Thank you, though.'

He shook his head. 'Fiona.'

'What?' What horrifying tidbit was he going to reveal next?

'You're clenching your jaw again! You're going to undo all our hard work before you even leave the building.'

Kieran pulled up a chair and sat in front of me, knees brushing mine, a position which made it impossible not to notice how devastatingly good-looking he was. 'Let me show you some exercises. Practise these when your jaw starts to hurt, okay? And I'd love you to come and see me again. We did a relaxation massage for you today, but I think you'd really benefit from some remedial treatment.'

There was no polite way to refuse booking another appointment. 'You're making a great call,' Kieran told me. 'We can really get into those hips next time. It might hurt, but—' he flashed me a cheeky grin '—who's more of a warrior than a single mum?'

I managed a faint laugh, trying to calculate how soon I could call to cancel.

He held up the bottle of sparkling again. 'Sure you don't want a top-up? Your homework today is to relax, and it might help.'

'That's all right. I might – um – run across the road and get one from the source.'

'Great plan.' He patted my hand. 'Give him my love, okay?'

It was an idiom – I *knew* it was an idiom – but my brain immediately conjured up a detailed narrative about Kieran confessing his undying love to Satoshi, and what Satoshi would say to me when he broke things off between us. 'Sure. So you're . . . still friends?'

'Of course. I could never give up my Tosh.'

Oh god.

'But I did have to set him free.' Kieran leaned back, folding his hands behind his head, biceps rippling. 'He's too soft-hearted, that one. He was still talking marriage and kids when it was clear things had run their course—'

My mind, which had been racing, came screeching to a halt. 'Kids?'

'He'd be such a good dad, don't you think? Can't you just imagine him with a baby in his arms?'

I nodded weakly.

'Anyway, I had to let him go,' Kieran said. 'We were never going to work out, but he would have flung himself into a brick wall trying to make it work forever if I'd let him.'

🍷

It had been a while since I'd hesitated before going into Tsundoku, but I lingered for more than a moment before I pushed open the door. 'Hi. Hope I'm not – oh my goodness, your hair!'

'Hello to you too.' Satoshi was serving some customers, but he took a moment to smile over at me. His glasses frames today were dark burgundy, only a slight contrast from his black – black! – hair. 'Let me finish making these, and I'll be right with you.'

Usually, I would watch his hands as he made cocktails – they moved so fast it was like magic – but not this time. 'What are you thinking?' he asked, when he finally managed to make his way over to me.

'You look so different!'

'I meant about what you wanted to drink.' He wrinkled his nose at me. 'But we can start with my hair, if you like.'

'You look very handsome. But why the change?'

'Because I kept running out of time to get my roots done. You saw what my regrowth was like.'

I had. He'd fallen fast asleep on my shoulder the last time I'd stayed the night, and I'd spent half an hour peacefully combing my fingers through his hair. It had been intimate in a way that even sex wasn't, and I hadn't felt that close or connected to someone since—

Since my kids. Since those late nights when they were babies, sitting up with them, skin to skin, exhausted and terrified all at once because my heart existed outside my body now, outside my control.

I swallowed. *Can't you just imagine him with a baby in his arms?*

'So when I finally got five minutes to go to the hairdresser, I thought I might as well revert to something easier to maintain.' Charlotte handed Satoshi an order slip, and he glanced at it before pulling a bottle of chardonnay out of the fridge. 'Plus, I'm going to a wedding tomorrow, and I was hoping the prettiest lady there might save a dance for me if I scrubbed up nicely.'

'I'm sure Sadie would love to dance with you.'

'Ha, ha.' He set a glass on the bar for Charlotte to collect. 'Drink? What's the vibe?'

'Um . . .'

Kids, my heart was pounding. *Kids, kids, kids.*

'The vibe is that my parents are here,' I said, 'and I need to fortify myself.'

'How about we do an actual fortified, then? Something to cleanse your palate before you go home to face them?'

'Sounds great.' Dare I hope a palate cleanser could wash away what Kieran had told me?

Satoshi poured me a glass of madeira, but he'd only just started to explain why he'd chosen it when his attention was pulled elsewhere. I sipped at it – rich and golden but not too sweet, molasses cut through with citrus and sea-spray – as I watched him work, trying to slow my rapid heartbeat.

Something was off with the flow of the bar. It wasn't wrong, exactly, but it seemed rushed, disjointed. 'Everything all right?' I asked, when there was finally a lull.

'The glasswasher broke again.' Satoshi was making spicy margaritas, hands moving even faster than normal. 'It started leaking at the start of service.'

'Oh no.'

'Oh no is right. I couldn't get anyone to work an extra shift today, so we're understaffed, and the technician can't come back until Monday.' He set the margaritas on the bar. 'How much longer can you stay?'

I checked the time on my phone. 'Probably half an hour or so.'

'Give me a second to finish up these last few orders and then sneak out the back with me? I can probably manage a fifteen-minute break before the dinner rush.'

It took several seconds before Satoshi could make a thin excuse to Charlotte about how he had some books for me out the back, and several more seconds before he could convince her that yes, she'd be all right watching the floor on her own for a bit, he'd be just down the hall if she needed him, but eventually, we made our way to his office. 'Is Charlotte okay?' I asked, as he closed the door behind us. 'She seems a bit on edge.'

'I let her try running the floor by herself on Tuesday. It's normally quiet, but we had some horrible customers in and they monstered her.' Satoshi sank into his office chair and pulled me onto his lap. 'I'm so happy to see you. I wasn't expecting to until tomorrow.'

Most of the time, when we managed to snatch moments like this, he'd have me pressed up against something or bent over something by now, but instead, he just wrapped his arms around me and rested his head against my shoulder. The new, shorter texture of his hair tickled against my skin, and I carded my fingers through it. 'I'm happy to see you too.'

'Mmmm.' His eyes were closed. 'That feels good.'

The word *kids* was burning in my throat, but this was clearly not the time to talk about it, not when he was obviously so tired, not when I was so deeply afraid of what he would say. I scratched at his scalp instead. 'Like this?'

'Mmm-hmmm.'

I traced circles around his temples. 'How about this?'

'So good.' His voice was muffled in my shirt. 'You can go harder.'

'Like this?'

'Mmmm. Yes.'

I let my fingers move to the back of his neck, caressing and then kneading. 'I'm sorry you're having such a shitty day.'

'Not your fault – oh, yeah, there.'

'My parents are going to be around for a week or so.' I dug my knuckles in, trying my best to approximate what Kieran had done to me. 'How about I get them to babysit on Sunday, and I'll be your dish pig?'

He lifted his head. 'You'd do that?'

'Of course.' I kissed the tip of his nose.

'What would you tell them?'

'The truth.'

He stilled. 'Really?'

'I would say, "Family, we owe Satoshi a favour."' I kissed one of his dimples. 'Because even though Jonah and Sadie are paying for their wedding, there's no way he's breaking even on this.' I kissed the other one. 'I saw you're closing the bar tomorrow.'

He buried his face in my neck again. 'It's only one day of trade. It'd be a huge pain with a broken glasswasher anyway. Plus, I'd be anxious leaving someone who didn't know the venue in charge, even if it was Maxi or Carlton.'

'That's still a significant chunk of money.' I went back to combing my fingers through his hair, shoving the feelings it sent bubbling to the surface down as hard as I could. 'So, I would say, "Family, the least I can do for this lovely man is wash some glasses."'

'You don't need to, though. Dish pig work is the worst job in hospo. It's messy, and sweaty, and—'

'Satoshi—' I tugged his face up to mine and kissed him '—just let me do this for you, okay?'

I slipped off his lap and on the floor. 'Fiona, no,' he protested weakly, as I unzipped his trousers. 'You don't—'

'I want to.' I pressed my lips to his thigh as I drew him out of his underwear. 'You've had a bad day. Let me take care of you.'

He'd said something similar the first time I'd ever gone down on him. *Fiona, no,* he'd said, as I went to my knees in front of him in an old Frenchman's grimy wine cellar. *You don't have to.*

But he'd been hard within seconds, hand fisting in my hair. *Oh god,* he'd moaned, *oh Fiona, how are you so good at this, oh fuck,* and I'd hummed with laughter around him in sheer delight at the thought I could give him so much pleasure.

This time, though, was different. 'Stop,' Satoshi said, tugging gently at my hair as it became clear his cock wasn't going to cooperate. 'It's okay.'

I stood awkwardly while he tucked himself away and rezipped his pants. 'Sorry,' he said, pulling me back onto his lap. 'It's not your fault. Just . . . you know, long day.'

'It's okay. *I'm* sorry.'

'Hey.' He caught my chin in his fingers and kissed me. 'Don't apologise. Everything's all right.'

It wasn't, though. Some little cog in the machinery which had been running so smoothly had come loose, and even though nothing had technically gone wrong, something wasn't quite right, either.

Chapter Sixteen
Satoshi

Tasting today: Fernet-Branca, Milan, Italy.
A shot of Fernet is typically called a bartender's handshake, because it's supposed to shock you awake in the middle of a long shift. Sometimes, though, it just feels like stepping on a rake.

'My initial conclusion is that this is a warm climate wine, from a hot, dry vintage.' I took another sip, let the wine sit on my palate for several seconds, then reached for the spittoon. 'I'm almost certain it's grenache. It could be from Lirac or Châteauneuf-du-Pape, but I feel strongly that it's new world, so my final conclusion is that this is grenache from McLaren Vale, vintage 2020.'

'No, but you're on the right track.' Maxi took the sleeve off the bottle and showed it to me. 'It's zinfandel from Sonoma.'

I exhaled. 'That's not on the right track at all.'

'Oh, come off it, you perfectionist.' Carlton shoved me in the shoulder. 'Most of your working was right – and warm climate grenache and zin are easy to mix up. If you make a call that close in the Young Somm comp, you'll be in with a solid shot.'

The high street was starting to bustle as we wrapped up, joggers weaving between people grabbing coffee and lining up at the bakery. 'Thanks for agreeing to have study group at the crack of dawn,' I said. 'This is the only window I have this week and I desperately need the practise.'

'No worries,' Carlton said. 'I wish I could cover for you today. Losing a Saturday's trade is rough.'

'Yeah, I'm so sorry about that,' Maxi agreed. 'But you're still on to stage at Filigree on Monday night, right?'

The last thing I wanted to do on my one precious night off was work a demanding shift in a fine-dining restaurant, but I nodded. 'Thanks for getting your boss to let me.'

Once they'd left, I carried our tasting glasses out into the kitchen. I hadn't swallowed any of the wines we'd blinded, but I could still feel them heavy on my palate, the tannins sucking all the moisture out of my mouth.

I chugged an enormous glass of water and then made myself an even more enormous cup of coffee, but it didn't shift any of the fog clouding my brain. I dropped a glass while washing it, and it shattered all over the floor.

I sighed as I went to get the dustpan and brush. This fucking glasswasher was going to be the end of me.

When I was finished, I took a second, equally gigantic cup of coffee upstairs. My bed looked very inviting, but if I allowed myself even fifteen minutes to lie down, there was a chance I might not be able to get up again – or, worse, that I'd just lie there the way I had last night, repeatedly reliving the horrifying moment I hadn't been able to get it up for Fiona.

She understands, I told myself, glaring at my reflection in the mirror as I combed product through my too-short hair. She'd been married for years. There must have been times when Matt couldn't perform.

Although maybe he'd been some kind of sexual machine. After all, he'd managed to keep two women satisfied enough to be clueless about each other for more than a decade.

And there was no skill shortage on Fiona's end. The woman was a fucking master at fellatio. I'd never, ever say it to her, but I'd wondered, after the first time she'd nearly blown the top off my skull, whether part of the reason Matt had strung her along for so long was because he couldn't bear to give up head that good.

I hadn't been craving anything carnal yesterday, though. All I'd wanted was to hold her close and snuggle into her. Like a *child*.

I splashed water onto my face. 'Shut up, Sato,' I muttered.

I flicked through the suits in my wardrobe harder than I needed to, passing over my dove grey work suits and a few brightly coloured ones to reach for the charcoal one, pairing it with a dark green tie and glasses. In the mirror, with my newly black hair and no pins on my lapel, I looked like a banker.

I wrestled Yquem into her carrier, brushed cat hair off me – rookie mistake, not corralling her before putting my suit on – and poured my third cup of coffee into the largest keep cup I owned. Given her entire family would be present, I doubted Fiona would want to sneak away with me today, but if she did, I couldn't let my tiredness get the better of me.

When I arrived at the vineyard, I dropped Yquem off with Okāsan and then went up to the cellar door. 'Okaeri,' Isamu started to say, and then stopped.

'What?' I simply didn't have it in me to negotiate one of his lectures today.

He gestured to my hair.

'You noticed.'

'I might not have your finely honed aesthetic skills, but I know the difference between blond and black.' He paused. 'It makes you look . . .'

'What? Older?'

It took him a moment before he answered. 'Like Otōsan.'

Just the thought of opening up that can of worms made me feel even more exhausted. 'How's set up going?'

'Everything's on track.' Of course it was. 'The bride and bridesmaid arrived last night. I took them both a glass of sparkling about half an hour ago.'

'Which one?'

'The 2022 blanc de blancs, like you told me. Okāsan has prepared the adjoining room for the rest of the bridal party when they get here – that's the flower girls and the mother of the groom, correct?'

'Correct.' As Fiona was the best man, her mother was on Rosie-and-Georgia duty.

'The groom's party will get ready in the library.' Isamu nodded in the direction of the lounge next to the bar. 'I thought it'd be best if you looked after them, and I'll look after the bridal party.'

'That sounds sensible.' I resisted the urge to take my glasses off and rub at my scratchy eyes.

'Otherwise, we're good to go. The cellar door is ready for the reception. The tech is sorted for the brother to Zoom in. We just need to set up for the ceremony – I'll pull a couple of the waitstaff to help with that – and I thought you'd want to prep the bar.'

It was unusually sensitive of him to allow me that level of control; and yet, if he had prepped the bar himself, I might not have complained *too* much.

'You thought correctly.' I took down a bottle of Fernet-Branca. 'Bartender's handshake?'

Isamu raised his eyebrows.

'It's going to be a big day,' I said.

He looked at me, and for a moment, I thought he could see right through me, but, 'All right,' he said.

I poured us each a shot, and we clinked our glasses together before knocking them back. I winced at the taste – like bitter mouthwash – but Isamu didn't. 'I'm just going to check with Chef that everything is on track in the kitchen,' he said, taking out his phone.

Then, of all things, he smiled.

I blinked. The Fernet had clearly not done its job. It was supposed to be a shock to the system, a way to jump-start your brain – there was a reason shotting it was a sadistic hospo ritual – but if Isamu was smiling, there was a strong chance I was hallucinating. 'What is it? Is Chef done?'

'No, no, sorry.' He put his phone back into his pocket. 'Something else. Can you grab me a bottle of sparkling? I'll go and top up the bridal party.'

I passed him the last bottle of the 2022 blanc de blancs from the fridge, as well as one of a lightly flavoured sparkling mineral water from the beverage carry-case I'd brought with me. 'For the B&B fridge. The flower girls will want to be included.'

I stood there for a long time after Isamu left, hands braced on the bar, letting it take my weight. Maybe it was just my haze of tiredness, but I couldn't remember the last time I'd seen my brother smile like that.

Gravel crunched under tires outside. I considered doing another shot of Fernet but decided against it. The last thing I wanted to do was get tipsy on top of tired and make a bad first impression on Fiona's parents.

Fiona and a pale-looking Jonah were unloading her car when I went outside to meet them. 'Satoshi!' Georgia squealed.

'Hello, Miss Georgia.' I submitted to her hug. 'I've heard a rumour that you and your sister are going to be the two most elegant young ladies at the wedding today.'

'We are!' Her eyes were alight, her resemblance to Fiona so clear. 'Grandma's going to help us get ready! My dress is green and Rosie's dress is pink and—'

'Georgia, leave the nice man alone,' an older woman who must be Fiona's mother said. Rosie was clinging to her wrist.

'He's not just a man, Grandma.' Georgia rolled her eyes. 'He's *Satoshi*.'

'Satoshi Tsukamoto.' I pasted my customer service smile to my face as I offered her my hand to shake. 'Welcome to Bibliophile.'

'So *you're* the one responsible for the bookshop my grandchild won't stop talking about.'

The man who was surely Fiona's father took my outstretched hand before his wife could, nearly crushing my fingers in his sweaty palm. 'You and I need to have a chat about the books Lex is acquiring from you.'

'I told you, Grandpa,' Lex said. 'I like the books I get there.'

'They're not going to push you, though – not like the classics will. You're about to start high school. You need to think about your future development. Improving your mind.'

'Lex's mind is perfect just the way it is,' Fiona said. 'Hi, Satoshi.'

She was laden down with garment bags, and my head was full of fog, but when her eyes crinkled at the corners, I had a moment of blessed relief. 'Hi, Fiona. Let me take some of those for you.'

She surrendered some of the bags to me, and I led the family into the cellar door. 'The groom's party will get ready here,' I said, opening the concertina doors to the library. 'If you want to make yourself at home—'

'Can I get a red wine?' Fiona's father plonked himself down in one of the leather armchairs.

'Of course. What would you like?'

'Barossa shiraz. Three ice cubes.'

It was hard to imagine a more ridiculous order than South Australian shiraz in a Tasmanian winery renowned for its pinot – like ordering a Big Mac at a French restaurant – but I nodded. 'Jonah, let me get you a drink too. You look like you need it.'

Jonah nodded, half-sitting, half-slumping into a corner of the sofa. 'Um – silly question – Sadie *is* here, right?'

'Yes. She and Chess are getting ready in the B&B.'

'Okay.' He swallowed. 'Good.'

'I don't want to sound unsympathetic, Jonah, but she did already marry you once.' Fiona patted Jonah's shoulder. 'I'm going to take Mum and the girls down to the B&B. Back in a bit.'

'Give me two seconds to get these drinks, and I'll walk you down.' If I walked them down, then Fiona and I could walk back alone, and maybe five minutes with her would make everything all right. 'What can I get you, Lex?'

'Hmmm?' They were already absorbed in the bookshelves.

Once I had her father, Jonah and Lex set up, I led Fiona, her mother, and her daughters down the path from the cellar door to the B&B. 'This is where my mum lives,' I explained to the twins. 'She's going to help you and your aunts and your grandma out today.'

'You need to be on your best behaviour, all right, girly-pops?' Fiona said as I rapped on the open door to let Okāsan know we'd arrived. 'I know it's very exciting, but don't get so excited that—'

'—we're all tired out by the wedding,' Georgia replied long-sufferingly. 'We *know*, Mummy.'

Okāsan appeared in the hallway. 'Okaeri, Sato.' She patted my arm before turning to everyone else. 'And welcome.'

'This is the rest of the bridal party,' I said. 'These are the flower girls, Rosie and Georgia. And this is—'

'—Angela,' Mrs Fisher said. 'Mother of the groom. Thank you for hosting us.'

'My sons did all the work.' Okāsan patted my arm again. 'And this is . . .?'

'I'm Fiona.' Fiona extended her hand for Okāsan to shake. 'Thank you for so much for all your help, Mrs Tsukamoto. If the girls get too rowdy, please don't hesitate to call me. My mother has my number.'

'I also raised three children, honey,' her mother said. 'The girls and I are going to be fine.'

'Let me show you to your room,' Okāsan said. 'It was nice to meet you, Fiona.'

Her hand was still on my arm, and as she squeezed slightly, it was obvious that she'd put two and two together. My mother knew *exactly* who Fiona was.

'You too,' Fiona replied, thankfully not reading the subtext.

Mrs Fisher followed Okāsan down the hall, Georgia behind her, but Rosie lingered on the doorstep. 'Mummy?'

'Yes?' Fiona asked. 'What's wrong?'

'Nothing. It's just . . .'

Rosie's chin was quivering when she finally got the words out, an explosion of a sentence that happened all at once. 'Would Daddy really ask Nikki to be his flower girl?'

'Oh, Rosie-girl.' Fiona knelt down swiftly. 'That's not something you need to worry about, okay? Daddy isn't even planning to *have* a wedding, not right now.'

'But what if he did? He already lives with the other lady and the other kids. And today – and today—' Rosie gulped. 'Today is the most important day of my life. And Daddy's not here.'

For a moment, a shadow of the betrayal Fiona must have felt penetrated the fog in my brain. How could anyone ever walk away from this little girl?

Fiona smoothed Rosie's hair away from her face. 'I know you miss him, honeybun. But we'll take so many pictures and videos for him, okay? He won't miss a thing.'

'I'll tell you what.' I crouched beside Fiona. 'How about I take charge of filming? I'll get there early, and I'll push everyone out of the way, like this—' I mimed shoving people aside '—and I'll find the best seat in the wedding, so I can take the greatest flower girl video ever.'

Rosie looked at me for a long moment. My heart thumped in my chest, so loudly she and Fiona could probably hear it.

But then her face crumpled. 'It's not the *same!*'

Fiona put her arms around her. 'Go,' she mouthed, nodding with her head back up towards the main building, as Rosie sobbed into her shoulder.

It was the mildest possible dismissal, and it felt like getting kicked in the stomach.

My feet were heavy every step back up to the cellar door, but even once I'd arrived, I made myself keep moving. If I stopped, the fog would crowd in even heavier, and I might drown.

I'd hauled six cases up from the cellar and started re-organising the fridges for service when Fiona finally reappeared. 'Hi,' she said wearily, leaning her elbows against the bar.

'Hi. Is everything . . .?'

She nodded. 'I got her calmed down.'

'Sorry for interfering. I was just trying to help.'

'It's not your fault, don't worry. There are no magic words you can say to a child to make them feel better in a situation like this.' Fiona exhaled. 'It's the hardest thing I've ever had to learn, as a parent. Sometimes you can't make things better. Sometimes all you can do is be there.'

Go, I heard her saying, all over again.

There was a stone in my stomach as I said the only thing I could think of. 'Can I pour you a drink?'

'Please.' She offered me a smile, although it was awkward rather than luminous. 'Just one, though. I'm going to need my wits about me to keep Jonah together until he gets to the altar. I've never seen him like this.'

I took one of the bottles of sparkling I'd just brought up from the cellar out of the fridge. 'He did look pale,' I commented, trying to keep my voice light. If I could make things sound like they were all right, then maybe I could make them all right. 'I hope he's not coming down with – shit, shit, sorry!'

I'd clearly agitated the sparkling too much when I'd carried it up, and my hand must have slipped when I was uncorking it, because instead of the usual noiseless hiss, the bottle opened with an enormous bang, spraying wine over us both. 'Oh my god, Fiona, I'm so sorry!' Blood burned in my cheeks as I passed her a napkin.

'It's fine, don't worry.' Fiona mopped at the damp patch on her shirt. 'I'm about to change out of these clothes anyway. Besides, it happens to all the guys.'

'Not to me! Do you know how many bottles of sparkling I've opened in my career? God, if I fuck up like this in—'

'It was a joke, Satoshi!'

She held up her hands. 'It was a joke,' she repeated. 'Not a very good joke, granted, given our problem seems to be the opposite – oh god, Fiona, shut up shut up shut up.'

She closed her eyes. 'Sorry. I shouldn't have even brought it up. I just – I thought – maybe if we made a joke of it, then—'

Something in me sagged. 'Come here?'

Fiona opened one of her eyes, peeking at me. I held out a hand to her. 'Please?'

She paused for a moment, during which I died a thousand different deaths, but then she came around the bar. 'Sorry.' Her voice was muffled in my shoulder as she wrapped her arms around my waist. 'I'm the worst.'

'Yesterday wasn't your fault.' I pressed my lips to her temple, resisting the urge to do what I actually wanted, which was crush her to me, sink to the floor, and not let go for several hours. 'Please tell me you know that.'

She nodded, her hair silky against my cheek. 'You were tired. I know. I just . . .'

'You just what?' I kissed her temple again.

She drew back, so she could look me in the eye. 'If you, um . . . ever decide you . . . that this isn't working for you – that it isn't what you want – you'll tell me, right?'

I blinked. 'What?'

'It's all right.' Her fingers slid up my chest to curl into my lapels. 'I'm tough. I can handle it. I know I – I come with a lot of baggage, and there might be . . . things you want that I can't give you.'

'Fiona, all I want is you.'

Her throat moved as she swallowed.

'Yesterday wasn't about me not wanting you.' I framed her face between my hands. 'It was just one of those days.'

'I know. But . . .'

'But?' I prompted her, when the silence stretched on too long.

'Will you promise me anyway?'

Her fingers curled tighter into my lapels. 'You're so young, Satoshi. You've got so much ahead of you – and I don't want to limit you. I don't want to tie you down.'

Another kick, directly to the stomach. *You're too young. You're clearly not ready to be a stepfather.*

'I want to tie you down.'

I'd meant it sincerely, but the expression on her face made me swiftly walk it back. 'You enjoyed it last time.' I brushed my lips against hers, a rock in my throat. 'Remember?'

She made a sound, somewhere between amusement and exasperation. 'I'm being serious, though.'

A third kick to the stomach, even harder this time. *How am I ever meant to take you seriously?*

'I have some . . . sensitivities,' she said. 'About being with someone who wants something else, while I have no idea. So please – promise me? That if you want to end this – that if you decide you want someone else – something else – you'll tell me?'

There was only one thing I could say.

'Yes,' I told her, even though the words felt like the most astringent, heavy tannins in my mouth. 'I promise.'

Chapter Seventeen
Fiona

Tasting today: 2019 shiraz, Barossa Valley, Australia.
If you want a wine so obvious it'll slap you in the face, this is the one.

When I made it back to the lounge, Jonah had progressed from pale to sweaty. 'Oh, thank god,' he said, half-snatching one of the glasses of sparkling from the fresh tray of drinks that Satoshi had brought and swallowing half of it in a single gulp.

'I don't know what you're so worried about, Jonah,' Dad commented. 'You're already yoked to the woman. It's too late for you to have cold feet.' He picked up the glass of shiraz Satoshi had set down next to him, eyeing it critically. 'Ice cubes?'

'Of course,' Satoshi replied with perfect poise and politeness, despite Dad's excruciating rudeness. 'Sorry about that. I'll just get some for you.'

He put a lemonade beside Lex, handed me the other glass of sparkling, then disappeared. Dad harrumphed. 'You'd think a bartender would be better at remembering orders.'

'He's not a bartender,' I said. 'He's a sommelier. An outstanding one. He's studying for the Master Sommelier exam – the hardest exam in the world.'

'The hardest exam in pouring drinks, you mean.'

'No. I mean the hardest exam in the world. You've probably supervised more PhDs than there are Master Sommeliers. There's less than three hundred, total.'

Dad raised his eyebrows. 'I know you've never been the brightest spark, Fiona, but if you're trying to convince me that an exam in pouring drinks is more difficult than making an original contribution to human knowledge, then things are worse than I thought.'

'Dad!' Jonah and I both said.

Satoshi chose that moment to reappear, ice bucket and tongs in hand. 'My apologies for the error.'

'So I hear you're studying for an exam, young man.' Dad eyeballed him.

'Yes, I am.' Satoshi carefully doled out three cubes into his glass.

'What about pouring wine qualifies you to recommend all these trashy books to my grandchild?'

'Dad!' Jonah and I said again, with Lex adding in, 'Grandpa!'

'Well?' Dad demanded.

'Satoshi, you don't need to answer that,' I said firmly. 'You can go.'

There was a strange look in his eye as he said, 'All right,' and left, and it made me sick to my stomach. This beautiful man deserved so much better than being barked at by my dickhead of a dad.

He left. Dad shook his head. 'Can't even remember how I take my wine and yet you trust him with Lex's reading.'

'First of all, I'm the one constantly passing him lists of books for Lex,' I said hotly. 'So if you want to yell at someone because your queer grandkid is reading books about other queer kids instead of, I don't know, *Martin Chuzzlewit*, you can yell at me. And secondly, you know why he forgot? Because that's an idiotic way to drink red wine!' I gestured at his glass. 'Ice cubes? Really? Why not just ask for a drop of wine with your water? And why the hell are you ordering massive slap-you-in-the-face red in *Tasmania*? The best pinot noir in the country comes from here, and—'

'Since when were you such an expert, Fiona?'

I pressed my tongue to the roof of my mouth. If Dad turned up his nose at the MS, then my pathetic little Intro certificate was going to mean nothing to him. I could just imagine what he'd say if he ever found out about my column. *So, this is all you've amounted to, Fiona. Babbling on about drinks.*

And if I ever told him about Satoshi and me, what would he say to that? *I suppose it tracks,* he'd comment loftily, waving some abomination of a glass of wine at the dinner table, *that the best my daughter can do is a bartender.*

. . . and even though it was obvious to anyone with eyes that I was punching so, *so* far above my weight, Satoshi would just sit there and smile politely and take it.

'Jonah, let's go for a walk,' I said tightly. 'You need some fresh air. Lex, do you want to come?'

They shook their head, a glint in their eye. 'Grandpa and I need to talk about books.'

My heart swelled painfully with pride and love. Lex was going to run circles around my dad, the way I never could.

Satoshi loved Lex too. I knew that. He was so good with all my children, and he would love them all so much, if I'd let him all the way in.

But would they be enough?

I swallowed. He'd promised me. I hadn't been able to get the words *kids* out, too afraid of the answer, but he'd promised me if I wasn't giving him what he wanted, he'd tell me. He'd *promised.*

The sun was bright as Jonah and I went outside, the gentle summer breeze riffling through our hair. Jonah tipped his face up to it, closing his eyes for a moment. 'That's better,' he murmured.

'Sorry about before.' I shoved the feelings in my belly down, hard. 'It's your big day. I shouldn't pick fights with Dad.'

'Hmm? Don't worry about it. I wasn't paying that much attention, to be honest.'

Instead of taking the path that led to the B&B, we went the other way, towards the sculpture garden. 'What's got you so in your head anyway?' I asked. 'Far be it for me to be Team Dad, but he's right about one thing – it's too late for you to have cold feet.'

'It's not cold feet.' Jonah sighed. 'The opposite, really. Today just . . . means so much.'

We entered the garden, tangles of flowers interspersed at regular intervals with weatherproof sculptures. 'I love Sadie so much,' he said. 'And it just hit me last night, spending the night by myself. It would wreck me if I lost her. There is no me without her, not anymore.'

He half-sat, half-collapsed onto a bench. 'This is incredibly insensitive of me, but – Fi, I don't know how you did it. I don't know how you kept going. Because I keep having all these visions of what it would be like if Sadie left me, and I honestly don't think I would survive it.'

I should have thought about Matt.

Instead, my mind went straight to Satoshi. How long did I have left before I was in Jonah's position, unable to go on without him?

'Sadie's not going to leave you,' I said, pushing that thought away too. 'She's here, drinking sparkling with Chess, getting ready to marry you. Again.'

'I know. It's not even like we had a fight or anything – everything's fine – but . . .' Jonah held his hand out in front of him. It was shaking.

'Do you want me to call her for you?' I reached for the soothing tone I usually used when the kids were sick in bed with a cold.

'Seeing her before the ceremony is a no-no, but maybe it would help to have a quick chat.'

He thought for a moment, then nodded.

Sadie picked up on the second ring. 'What's wrong? Did Jonah forget his shoes? I *told* him he would if he didn't put them in the same bag as his suit. Or has he changed his mind about the cake again? Or—'

'Everything's fine, don't worry,' I said. 'I'm going to put you on speaker. Someone's freaking out a bit and needs to hear your voice.'

'Hi, darling,' Jonah said sheepishly.

Sadie laughed, and I could feel, as well as see, my brother sag in relief. 'Have you gone soft on me, Fisher?'

'I've always been soft on you, Shaw,' he replied. 'You know that.'

Sadie's laugh was a hum this time. 'I love you. And I can't wait to marry you. For real this time.'

I blinked.

'I'll see you at the altar, all right?' she said. 'I promise.'

'I'll be there.'

Sadie hung up. Jonah tilted his head back to the sky, exhaling. 'Thanks, Fi. That was exactly what I needed.'

'You're welcome. But – what did she mean?'

'Hmmm?'

'That she was going to marry you for real this time.'

I gestured to Jonah's hand. He'd taken his wedding ring off in preparation for the ceremony, but the tan line from it was plainly evident. 'It's always looked pretty real from where I'm sitting.'

'It is. It's just . . .' He exhaled again. 'I suppose I was going to have to tell you this eventually, so it might as well be now.'

'Tell me what?'

He paused. 'When Sadie and I got married the first time,' he said eventually, 'it wasn't exactly for romantic purposes.'

'I know. You had to, for work. So even though you hadn't been together that long, you—'

'We weren't.' Jonah folded his fingers together in his lap. 'Together, I mean.'

I stared.

'I don't understand,' I managed to choke out at last. 'It was *fake*?'

'Not exactly. It's never been fake, not for me. I've loved Sadie since the first time I met her. But we weren't . . . a couple, when we got married. Not yet.'

The puzzle pieces rearranged themselves in my mind.

Jonah telling me that he'd been shortlisted for a job in Hobart, and me – freshly abandoned, physically and emotionally exhausted, and with no pride left to lose – weeping at the thought of having someone close by I could rely on.

Him calling a few weeks later and apologising profusely for not getting the job, as I wept again.

Then another call, another few weeks later. His arm around Sadie's shoulders on the Zoom screen, telling me all about the wonderfully convenient coincidence that was his girlfriend getting the job and how they were getting married so she could bring him with her on a partner hire . . .

'You got married for me,' I said numbly.

'No!' Jonah said. 'I got married for *me*.'

'That's why you're having a second wedding.' I was having an out-of-body experience. 'Because the first one was fake.'

'No, it wasn't! We are very much married. We had to be, for the university to agree to partner hire.'

'Legally, sure. But it wasn't some grand romantic gesture, some realisation that you were both so in love you couldn't bear to be apart, was it?'

'Fi—'

'You did it for me. You – you put your entire future on the line *for me.*'

I couldn't seem to get enough air into my lungs. 'What if it hadn't worked out, Jonah?! What if you'd taken this huge step and it'd been a disaster? What if—'

'Shhh, shhh, Fi. Listen to me.'

Jonah wrapped me up in his arms, one hand cupping the back of my head, the same way I hugged the twins when they were melting down. 'That didn't happen, okay?' he said fiercely. 'It all turned out all right. Because Sadie and I love each other. You *know* how much we love each other.'

I did know. Jonah and Sadie loved each other so much and so obviously and so passionately that it sometimes made me sick with jealousy. That they loved each other was something I'd been sure of ever since the first time I'd seen them together – but it had been a lie.

And there was a version of the future where it didn't turn out all right. Where Jonah and Sadie, yoked together, ended up hating each other. Where Jonah ended up hating me too, simmering in quiet resentment at what his desire to bail me out had forced him into – and where I, clearly so bad at recognising what love looked like, had no idea that I'd ruined my brother's life.

'It's all right, Fi,' Jonah murmured, stroking my hair.

But my mind had already skipped tracks.

I don't want to tie you down, I'd said to Satoshi – but I did. Every day it got stronger, this inexorable temptation to tie him to me forever.

I wanted him to be there in the morning when I woke up. To be there at school drop-off – always with me at first, but eventually by himself sometimes, hugging the girls goodbye and bumping knuckles with Lex. For him to come home to me after the bar closed, to slide into bed with me after he'd eaten the dinner I'd left in the fridge for him, to wrap his arms tight around me.

I wanted my home to be his home. I wanted him to be there next Christmas, him and Isamu and his mother too, piled into my place with all the Fishers and Shaws. I wanted him to be there for all the milestones – his and mine and the kids'. I wanted him to see my hair turn grey and tell me I was beautiful anyway.

When he said, *Fiona, all I want is you,* I wanted so badly to believe that it would always be true.

Eventually, though – when the sparkle had worn off, when our illicit Thursdays turned into mundane routine, when my dad had been horribly rude to him too many times, when he was ready for a child of his own but I was too old and too tired to give him one, when I'd finally taken more than he was prepared to give – would he regret it? Would he think back to that day in his office when he'd told me I deserved pleasure and that he'd love to give it to me, and wish those words had never come out of his mouth? What would the loveliest man in the world tell himself on his wedding day, this beautiful soft-hearted man, this man who was far, far too good to be true? *We've come too far for me to back out now. She's been humiliated so badly once before, and she relies on me – I can't let her be left again.*

He'd made me a promise. But if Matt could lie, and Jonah could lie, then so could Satoshi – and once again, I would probably have no idea.

'I'm sorry.' Jonah squeezed me tighter, and I realised I was crying. 'We weren't trying to keep secrets from you. It's just – there didn't seem to be any point telling you. You already had so much to worry about – and then it was real, and serious, and there was nothing *to* tell.'

'It's okay,' I forced out. 'I understand.'

I pulled back and got to my feet, managing not to stumble despite the roaring in my ears. 'Come on. Sadie will never forgive me if I don't get you to the altar on time. Especially if it actually counts this time.'

Jonah stood, studying me. 'Are you sure you're okay, Fi?'

I pasted on a smile. 'I'm fine.'

Chapter Eighteen

Satoshi

Tasting today: nothing.
Sometimes you can't taste anything.

Some of the best vineyards in the world were misty. In the mornings, before the sun had reached its zenith, it felt like you were walking through a cloud.

One of my earliest memories was of my father waking me very early and taking me out into a misty vineyard in Alsace when I was a toddler. He'd got distracted – typical of him, hyperfocusing on his work at the expense of everything else – and I'd wandered off into the fog. Isamu had eventually found me sitting underneath one of the vines, sobbing.

Oh, Sato, he'd said, impossibly large in my memory, although he wouldn't have been more than fifteen. *Did you get lost?*

My only response had been incoherent wailing. *Onīchan – Onīchan—*

It's okay. I've got you. He let me wind my arms around his neck and cry snottily into his shoulder. *But you've got to be careful in the vineyard, all right? Stay where someone can see you – or botrytis will grow all over you.*

He'd showed me some grapes, covered in grey mould. *You don't want to be covered in this, do you?*

Botrytised grapes produced beautiful dessert wines. The rot made little holes in the skins, evaporating the water and concentrating the sugars and flavours, and the resulting wines were so lovely I'd named Yquem after one.

But I'd never forgotten it: the terror of being lost in a cloud, and then the visceral repulsion I'd felt looking at those grapes and imagining being lost forever, grey mould creeping up my skin.

That was how I felt now, sitting in the third row of Sadie and Jonah's wedding ceremony. The sun was high in the sky, the mood lively and bright, bride and groom both weeping with joy as they professed their love to each other – but I was deep in the mist, unable to find my way out, being slowly enveloped by rot that was going to pierce my skin and drain me dry.

Standing beside Jonah, Fiona looked flawless. Her hair was swept back from her face, her neck a long line disappearing into the sweetheart neckline of her rose-pink dress, her makeup pristine and even, concealing that tiny constellation of five freckles beside her nose I loved so much. But even as she smiled at her brother and his bride, there was a furrow cutting a line between her brows, and her fingers were twisted tightly together, knuckles white.

I had seen her fall apart enough times to know that she was only just holding it together, and it made me feel like the marrow was being sucked out of my bones. I wanted to go to her – to put my arms around her and hold her tight and not let go – but what would I even say to stop her slipping away from me? *I can give you what you want. I can be what you need. I'll never want anyone but you, so please let me keep trying to make you happy.*

People around me started clapping. The groom was kissing the bride, and even as I started clapping too, sunshine beating down on the back of my neck, everything around me was cold and grey and murky.

I escaped to the cellar door as quickly as I could, grateful to have the excuse of the bar, something tangible I knew how to manage. I had to reach down deep to dredge up my customer service smile, but I found it, and I plastered it across my face like the rictus grin of a skull. 'It was a beautiful ceremony, wasn't it?' I said, over and over again, pouring glasses of sparkling wine and taking ten seconds longer than I needed to open each new bottle. 'Jonah and Sadie are a beautiful couple.'

There was no amount of busy I could be, however, that would keep me from noticing when Fiona entered. She and Chess were walking together behind Jonah and Sadie, the respective pink and green of their dresses matching the flower girls, who had run in ahead. Sadie murmured something to Jonah then leaned up to kiss him before she and Chess peeled off in the direction of their table, leaving Jonah and Fiona there alone.

Jonah put his hand on Fiona's elbow. They stood there for a long moment as he said something to her. Fiona nodded, and they hugged. Jonah was incandescently happy – there was no trace left of the drawn, white-faced man from earlier – but even though Fiona was facing away from me, I could see the long lines of tension in her body.

I wanted to go to her. *I've got you,* I would say, and maybe she would believe me. *I swear, I promise, whatever you need, I've got you. It's only you, forever.*

But instead, I just watched her. Jonah let her go, and she walked away, over towards the table where Sadie and Chess and the kids were, and Jonah came up to the bar.

There was a buzzing in my ears, like static from an old television. 'Congratulations, Jonah,' I said. 'Can I get you a drink?'

'Please. For the table, if that's okay.'

I uncorked another bottle of sparkling – no spray, but a pop loud enough it would have earned me a lecture from every head somm I'd ever worked under – and nodded to one of the waitstaff to help me.

'Satoshi, tell me you're going to sit down at some point!' Sadie said, as the waitress set out wineglasses and I followed her with the bottle. 'You're supposed to be one of our guests.'

I made myself laugh. 'What kind of friend would I be if I didn't make sure you had the ultimate beverage experience on your wedding day? And now for the most important people—'

I presented a bottle of sparkling apple juice to the kids. I'd brought it with me in my carry-case, the best child-appropriate colour-match I could find to the blanc de blancs. 'Does this meet your approval?'

Georgia clapped her hands. 'Yes please!'

I poured, careful to use two hands. *Please, Fiona, I can be what you need, I can be what your kids need, I can be enough.* 'Satoshi,' Rosie asked, 'did you film us being flower girls? Like you said?'

'I sure did.' I finished pouring Lex's glass, then knelt between the twins, taking my phone out. 'Let me show you.'

Rosie's face was serious as she watched the video I'd taken. 'It's a bit shaky.'

'I know. I'm sorry.' My hands had not been properly steady all day. 'But you know how sometimes you get so excited you can't stay still? I couldn't wait to see the two best flower girls in the world do their thing.'

'And if the video's not great, then don't worry.' Jonah draped his arm around Sadie's shoulders. 'We had a professional photographer taking photos and videos too. There'll be lots to choose from.'

In that moment, despite the fact it was his wedding day, I could have gleefully murdered him.

'Will you send it to Mummy anyway?' Rosie asked.

'Of course. I'll do it right now.'

I texted Fiona the video. I didn't know what to say – my brain was moving too slowly to think of anything even vaguely appropriate – so I just sent her a string of kisses with it, *xxxxx*, each one more desperate than the last.

'Mummy, did you get it?' Rosie said.

Fiona took her phone out of her clutch. I saw her see the line of kisses, saw her throat move as she swallowed. 'Yes, I got it. I'll send it to Daddy tomorrow, okay?'

Rosie nodded. 'Thank you, Satoshi,' she said seriously. 'For trying your best.'

Tears pricked at the corner of my eyes. I really had, and it still wasn't going to be enough. 'You're very welcome, Miss Rosie. Now, if you'll excuse me, I should get back to work.'

This, at least, I knew how to do. Six twists to loosen the wire cage, thumb over the cork, bottle at a forty-five-degree angle as I rotated it to open it. A splash to wet the glass before I poured it, glass tilted to minimise the foam, never more than two-thirds full so it wouldn't sit too long and go flat.

But then I looked over at Fiona and the wine fizzed over, so badly there was barely any left in the glass. 'So sorry about that!' I apologised for what felt like the millionth time, fingers slippery no matter how many times I dried them. 'This batch of sparkling is being very temperamental.'

'Sato, you can take a break,' Isamu said to me quietly, as another cork popped out of a bottle too loudly. 'Sit down for ten minutes.'

'Later.' If I sat down, the mist would close around me, mould creeping up my arms and up my neck and down my throat. 'It's time for the toasts. I need to refresh everyone's glasses.'

'The waitstaff can—'

I didn't stay to hear the end of the sentence.

The face of Fiona's brother Elias appeared on the screen as I strode around the room, clenching and unclenching my fist before each glass I poured in the hopes it would help me regain the fine motor control that was slowly deserting me. 'My brother Jonah is not only one of the cleverest people I know, but the luckiest,' Elias said. 'Plenty of academics have rivals. It's only the very luckiest who also find in them the love of their life.'

'Oh, fuck off,' the woman whose glass I was topping up murmured.

'My apologies,' I said quietly.

'Not you!' She looked up at me, sheepish, and I recognised Sadie's friend Julia. 'Just – never mind.'

'I'm sorry I can't be there today, little brother,' Elias said. 'But I do have a surprise, one that I hope you'll consider a wedding present. I've decided to leave academia—'

'What?!' Fiona's dad bellowed.

'—and move to Hobart.' On the screen, Elias held up a sheaf of paper. 'I've just accepted a job as an art historian at the Museum of Old and New Art. I start in March.'

'Oh, *fuck off*,' Julia breathed.

'I'll give you all the details later,' Elias said. 'But I can't wait to raise a glass in Hobart with you all – to be a proper part of the family again.'

I chanced a glance at Fiona as I moved onto the next guest. Her face was pale as milk.

According to the run sheet, Chess was supposed to give a speech next, but Fiona's father grabbed the mic. 'I have a few things to say,' he announced.

'Dad—' Jonah said, half-rising.

'I was unimpressed when you told me you were getting married, Jonah,' he said, steamrolling right over him. 'I thought you were putting your emotions before your intellect; humbling yourself at the altar of your basest desires. But I have to say, I've been pleasantly surprised. Because marriage has made a man out of you.'

He gestured expansively. 'Look at your life. You're flourishing professionally – unlike your brother, it seems – despite all the obstacles that have stood in your way. And then there's the way you've supported your sister. Lesser men would have let her lie in the bed she made for herself, but not you. This isn't something I say very often, because it's something that has to be earned, not simply given—'

Fiona got to her feet. She leaned down, whispered something to her mother, then slipped out of the room.

'—but I'm proud of you, son. And if you want to give us some more grandchildren, then . . .'

Both Jonah and Chess tried to wrestle the microphone away from him, but I wouldn't have heard the rest of what he was saying anyway. Without signalling to Isamu to cover the bar – without even making a conscious decision to do so, like I was a migratory bird, unable to fight the instinct to fly south – I went after Fiona.

I found her in the darkened library, standing at the window, looking out over the vineyard, shoulders rising and falling as she quietly wept. 'Fiona?'

'Go back to the wedding, Satoshi.' She sniffed, once, twice, her voice catching in her throat. 'I'll be okay in a second. I just need to pull myself together.'

I hesitated for a moment, and then crossed the room to her, putting my arms around her. Maybe I could make this all okay – make this awful grey feeling stealing through me go away – if I could just be what she needed. 'Your dad's a fucking idiot.'

Her laughter was choked. 'No, he's not. He's an arsehole, but he's not an idiot.'

'Yes, he is.' I held her tighter. 'You're the one who pulled your life back together. *You*, not Jonah.'

She made a noise, somewhere between a sob and a hiccup.

'I know how much it's meant to you, to have him here.' I pressed my lips to her hair. 'I know he and Sadie have helped you a lot. But you're the one who's held it together. Who's made sure your kids are safe and happy and loved. You're the strongest person I've ever met, Fiona.'

'I need you to stop, Satoshi.' She sniffed again.

'I need you to know this. I need you to know how remarkable you are.'

More tears slipped down her face. 'Please,' she choked. 'Stop.'

I cupped her face in one of my hands, brushing her tears away on one side with my thumb while I kissed them away on the other. 'I've never met someone I'm so in awe of.'

There was desperation in my voice, but I didn't care. I felt like we were standing on the top of a very tall building, so tall we were among the clouds, and if I could just make her see herself the way I did, then maybe she would see me the way I wanted her to, and I could pull us both back from the edge, collapsing backwards into a pile together, limbs and lives intertwined. 'There's no one in the whole world I admire more. You're astonishing, Fiona.'

'I need you to *stop*!'

She tore herself away from me. 'Stop!' she said, hands holding her own elbows, arms crossed over her torso. 'Please, please stop.'

'I'm sorry.' My knees felt like jelly, and I wanted to fall to them in front of her, to rest my forehead on her feet and beg. 'What do you need? Just tell me what you need and I'll do it.'

'I know you will! That's the problem!'

She sank down into one of the leather armchairs, her head in her hands. 'You are the loveliest man in the world, Satoshi.'

My legs would no longer hold me, so I surrendered, letting them fold beneath me, melting to my knees before her. 'I don't understand what's wrong, Fiona,' I whispered, curling my fingers around her wrists. 'I don't know how to fix it.'

She was weeping, breath coming in hitches and hiccups. 'The loveliest, kindest man in the world. Which is saying a lot, considering what my brothers have done for me.'

'What?' The fog was rolling in thicker, the words not cohering into meaning.

'Every time I need you, you're there. Everything I ask, you do. No questions asked. No complaints, not once.'

'Because I—' The tannins were back in my mouth, my tongue thick and heavy. 'I adore you, Fiona.'

'I'll never be able to repay you for what you've done for me.' She caressed my cheek, and I leaned into her hand, the way Yquem always did for Isamu. 'You put me back together. You made me feel like myself again.'

No one had ever had as much power over another person as Fiona Fisher did over me in that moment. I pressed my forehead against her knees, begging, worshipping, unable to find a single word that wasn't *please*.

She was crying in earnest now. 'I adore you too, Satoshi,' she said. 'Why is why I – I can't be selfish anymore.'

'No,' was all I could say. 'Fiona, no.'

'You are the best person I've ever met.' Her hands were in my hair, her forehead resting against the back of my head as she curled over me. 'But the longer we let this go, the harder it's going to be.'

'No.' There was only one word left now, in the fog, grey rot beneath my skin, sucking the life out of me. '*No.*'

'It's for the best, I promise.' Her breath was coming in gulps and hiccups. 'For us both. The longer it goes, the harder it will be for me when it ends. And the longer it goes, the harder it's going to be for you to leave.'

'No.' It took a gargantuan effort to lift my head, to look at her.

'You're too kind, Satoshi. Too soft-hearted. You're going to – you're going to – the more this goes on, you're going to feel obligated.'

She kissed me, the salt of her tears on her lips. 'And I think – I think I've known it all along,' she whispered. 'That's why it had to be a secret – because when people find out, you'll be trapped. You're not like Matt. You're too kind to ever walk away from me.'

'But I promised,' I managed to force out. 'Before – I *promised*.'

'I know.' She kissed me again. 'But I know you, Satoshi. You won't be able to bring yourself to do it to me. To do it to the kids. You'll stay, even if you don't want to, because we'll – I'll – have come to rely on you. And you – you're too good to make me look like a joke again.'

'No.' I was three years old, incoherently wailing in a cloudy vineyard in Alsace. 'No, Fiona.'

'You deserve the world.' She was choking on the words. 'And I – I can't give it to you. So I'd – I'd rather end it now, and have it hurt like hell, than for me to ruin your life and for you to end up hating me.'

'*No*.' I framed her face in my hands, made her look at me. 'Fiona, I love you.'

I'd imagined a thousand different versions of her reaction to those words, from her fleeing in horror to flinging herself into my arms, but instead, she just shook her head, tears streaming down her face.

'I *love* you,' I said again.

I took her hands in mine, clasping her fingers tight. If she pulled away, I was going to fall from the top of this building, into the cold cloud of the fog.

'I know I'm not who you envisioned spending your life with.' Sheer desperation forced the words past the thick grey mould coating my throat. 'I know I'm younger than you, and you don't think I'm ready, and I know – I know you might not be ready either, to take me as seriously as I take you.'

'Satoshi—'

'But I can be what you need, Fiona, if you'll just let me.' The world was a blur around me now, and I was so tired, every bone in my body heavy, pulling me down into the earth, but I made myself look her in the eye. 'Please, please, don't push me away.'

She didn't say anything.

'I love you,' I said.

Another moment's silence, then, 'I can't let you,' she said softly.

This time, in the quiet and the still, I could hear my heart, which had been breaking little by little, shatter all at once.

'This time with you has been perfect. But it's been a fantasy, Satoshi. A honeymoon. And it can't last forever.'

Please let me try, I tried to say, but the words would not come out. There was a roaring in my ears, and no breath left in my lungs.

Fiona let go of my hands, cupping my face in hers so she could kiss me. 'I never should have taken advantage of your generosity,' she whispered. 'I never should have asked the things of you that I've asked. I'm so sorry I've made you feel like this – that I've made you hurt like this – but I promise, it's for the – Satoshi?'

I could barely hear her through the fog.

'Satoshi?' The ground had risen up to meet me, and something was warm beneath my cheek. Her hand? Her lap? 'Oh my god, Satoshi, please—'

A rattle from the concertina doors. 'Fiona, it's time for your – Sato!'

Strong arms lifting me up, my head lolling against a hard shoulder. 'What happened?' Isamu demanded.

'I don't know!' Fiona said. 'We were talking, and he just fainted!'

'Onīsan,' I managed to groan.

'It's okay, Sato, I've got you.' I could feel the vibrations through my brother's chest as he spoke Japanese to me, his arm an iron band beneath my upper back, two fingers searching urgently for my pulse, relaxing when they found it. 'You're having a panic attack, I think. Try and breathe. What did you say to him?'

Fiona's voice sounded like it was coming from underwater. 'I – I—'

'Spit it out. He hasn't had a panic attack in years. What did you do to him?'

'I – I – I—'

A growl, coming from somewhere deep in him. 'You broke his heart, didn't you?'

Her intake of breath was sharp and sudden. 'How did you—'

'Everyone in the fucking world knows he's in love with you, Fiona! Now—'

The rest of the sentence faded away as the fog swallowed me up.

Chapter Nineteen
Fiona

Tasting today: water.
Eventually, the party is over, and you need to be sensible again.

I ran.

I ran the way I had the night Matt told me about Laura, not thinking, only feeling, my racing heart the only thing faster than my feet. I ran from the library, from the crumpled form of the beautiful man on the floor, from his brother looking me in the eye and snarling, *Everyone in the fucking world knows he's love with you, Fiona, now get out.*

I ran from the way he'd gone sheet-white, the way he'd pressed his face into my knees, clutched so tight at my fingers it felt like they might break. I ran from the awful, horrible moment his eyes had glassed over and he'd slumped sideways, and I ran from the words he'd said before it happened.

I love you.

The heavy front door thumped closed behind me, shutting the merry chatter of the reception away. It was quiet in the carpark, and I bent down, putting my hands on my knees and trying to get some air into my lungs.

Some animal instinct was telling me to get into my car and drive. To not stop until I got to Tsundoku, that one constant, that one safe, stable place. To rap on the door until Satoshi answered, until he put his arms around me and held me close and whispered into my hair that it was all right, that he had me.

But he wouldn't be there. Because he was inside, on the floor, and – oh god oh god oh god.

I squeezed my eyes tight shut. 'You did the right thing,' I whispered to myself.

The way he'd *looked* at me.

'You did the right thing.'

The way Isamu had looked at me, like I'd driven a knife right through his brother's heart.

'You did the *right thing*.'

The stabbing pain in my own heart, the breath that would not come no matter how hard I tried.

'Fiona?'

I straightened, digging my fingernails into the palm of my hand. 'Just getting some air, Mum,' I forced out. 'I'll be back in in a minute.'

'You missed your best man speech.'

Fuck. 'I – uh—'

'Have been crying?' My mother laid a hand on my back. 'I'm so sorry for what your father said, honey.'

I barely remembered it now. There'd been Elias's announcement – I vaguely recalled a sickening realisation that he'd almost certainly given up academia so he could help out with the kids, another brother making a huge sacrifice on my behalf – and then my dad, unable to resist pitting his children against each other, had taken some potshot at me in his toast, one that had tipped me over the edge and sent me fleeing, but it had all blended together, a background blur of guilt and humiliation.

Satoshi, though, was in sharp focus.

I love you. He'd sounded so desperate. *I* love *you.*

'I'm sorry that I didn't stand up to him.' Mum rubbed her hand comfortingly between my shoulder blades. 'I should have, but – well, I've never been very good at that.'

She nudged me. 'Not like you.'

I pressed my tongue to the roof of my mouth.

'I hope you know how proud I am of you, honey.'

'Thanks, Mum,' I said hollowly.

'I mean it.' She hesitated. 'I know what it's like, to be married to a – a big man. Someone who takes up a lot of space, who makes you feel like you have to shrink yourself, to mould yourself around him, to fit only in the gaps he leaves you. And even though that's not always pleasant, I . . . well, I can only imagine what it feels like not to have it anymore.'

I did the right thing. *I did the right thing.* I could not do to Satoshi what Matt had done to me. I would not force him into a box that was too small for him, when he deserved everything he wanted.

It would have only hurt more the longer I left it – but, oh god, it hurt, it hurt, it hurt.

Mum put her arm around me. 'It must have taken incredible strength, Fiona,' she said quietly. 'I'm so, so proud of you.'

I nodded. If I tried to say anything, I was going to scream, or cry, or throw up, or all three, all at the same time.

We stood there in silence for a long moment, the chorus of the crickets and the muffled merriment from inside the only sounds. When Mum spoke again, her tone was conversational. 'I thought your article about this place was brilliant, by the way.'

I startled. 'What – how did you . . .?'

'Imagine my surprise when I googled the place my son was getting married and the second result was an article by my daughter.' Mum nudged me again. '*Fiona Fisher, New Viniferous Voices winner.* I wish you'd told me. I would have put it on my

Facebook. And I will, when I get home. Every new piece you put out, I'm going to make sure everyone I know reads it.'

'That's okay. You don't—'

'*Everyone*. Including your father. And if he doesn't tell you he's proud of you, then he can start sleeping in his office. Because it's a beautiful piece, Fiona. There's so much love in it and – oh, honey, don't cry.'

'I'm sorry.' I wiped my face with the back of my hand. 'I – um – it's just – that's really nice, Mum, and – sorry.'

'Sit down.' Mum pushed me gently in the direction of a large rock near the front door. 'I'll go and get you some water.'

She disappeared back inside. I tilted my head back and looked up at the stars, heart pounding painfully.

I loved him too. There was no denying that. Somewhere along the way, I'd fallen in love with Satoshi Tsukamoto.

I loved him, so I couldn't keep him. He would never be the one to break it off, so I had to be the strong one.

But the look on his face – the desperation in his voice – the way he'd gone so terrifyingly limp when he fainted . . .

I pulled out my phone, took a long, shaking breath, and called him.

Unsurprisingly, he didn't answer, so I dug through my emails until I found Isamu's number. 'It's Fiona – don't hang up,' I blurted out, when he answered. 'I just want to know if he's all right.'

There was a short pause before Isamu spoke. 'He'll be fine,' he said, voice clipped. 'We're at the hospital. The doctor's with him now, but it looks like it was a panic attack, coupled with exhaustion. He's been working too hard.'

Mum reappeared beside me, glass of water in hand and a quizzical look on her face, but I held up a finger, telling her to wait. 'Is there anything I can do?'

'No,' Isamu said. 'You've done enough.'

Chapter Twenty
Satoshi

Tasting today: sencha green tea.
Familiar, homely, comfortable – a hug that might make you feel better, even if it won't fix a broken heart.

When I woke, I was in Isamu's bed. Sun was streaming through a gap in the curtains, and Yquem was basking in it. She was draped across Isamu's lap in the armchair, and they were both fast asleep.

The last thing I remembered was the hospital. How had I got from there to here? Had Isamu carried me, like a child?

And had he stayed here with me, the whole time?

I eased myself up to a sitting position, trying not to wake him. My arms trembled, my body ached, and my thoughts were coming too slowly – although it was more groggy than foggy now, the kind of exhaustion that came from sleeping too much rather than too little. How long had I been out?

I reached for my phone, which someone – Isamu? Okāsan? – had placed on the nightstand. It was half-past one in the afternoon, my battery was nearly dead, and I had a missed call from Fiona.

Fiona.

It came flooding back all at once, the pop of a cork from the bottle. I flung the covers back and got out of bed. I had to go to her – I had to fix it – I had to—

'Sit down.'

Isamu's voice was like the crack of a whip. I tried to resist, but my body wouldn't obey me, and I was powerless to do anything as he shoved me back into bed. When had he woken up?

'You're not going anywhere.' He rearranged the covers over my knees. I was wearing pyjama pants that were too broad in the waist and too short in the legs, clearly a pair of his. 'Or doing *anything*.'

'But—'

'The bar is closed.' He showed me an Instagram post on his phone, which read, *Due to a family emergency, Tsundoku is closed on Sunday 3 February.* 'You have nothing to do and nowhere to be. And you are going to stay in that bed, Sato, so help me God.'

'But—'

'Don't move.' He plonked Yquem on my lap. 'I'll get you some tea.'

I exhaled, scratching her behind the ears. 'That is the ugliest social media graphic I've ever seen, princess,' I muttered.

Isamu was back quickly, carrying a tray with a pot of green tea, looking visibly relieved that I hadn't tried to mount some kind of daring escape. 'Here,' he said, pouring me a cup.

My fingers shook as I accepted it, and he paused. 'Have you got it? I can help—'

'I've got it!'

The line of his jaw tightened.

'Sorry,' I said. 'I – um – thank you.'

He poured his own cup, turned away, and didn't say anything.

'For last night, I mean,' I said. 'I'm sorry.'

'Do you know how scared I was?'

He hadn't turned back around. I could only see him in profile, the severe lines of him silhouetted by the window. 'I thought you'd had a heart attack. I thought I was going to have to watch you die.'

'I'm fine, though.'

'No, you're not.'

He was right. I might not have had a heart attack, but it felt like I had gone through open heart surgery anyway; like Fiona had cut me open and ripped something essential out of me.

'We have to talk, Sato. And you have to listen this time. Because I can't – I can't—'

'Isamu,' I said softly, as a tear tracked down my iron brother's cheek.

'Don't make me watch.' He looked at me at last. 'I can't do it again. Okāsan can't do it again. We already lost Otōsan. We can't lose you too.'

I sighed. It wasn't exasperation this time, but resignation, surrender. 'What do you want me to do?'

'Nothing.' He thumbed the tear away. 'I want you to do nothing. Just rest.'

'What about the bar?'

'I'll worry about the bar.' He sat back down in the armchair, cradling his teacup between his palms. Yquem mewed, looking at him longingly, but – perhaps recognising how badly I needed her – stayed where she was. 'At least for the next little while.'

'But you've got your own job to do. And vintage'll start any minute now.'

'I'll bring in help if I need it.' He exhaled. 'I called Noriko. She's agreed to cover shifts at Tsundoku if I'm stuck in the winery.'

I blinked. 'Isamu—'

'We won't have to see each other.' The way he looked at me was almost apologetic. 'But she said to tell you that she's happy to help cover until you find a new junior somm.'

He sipped his tea. 'Speaking of,' he went on, his tone more businesslike, 'I'm going to take over your search.'

'No.'

'Yes.'

'*No.* They'll be working for me, not you. Besides, that's the one bit of my job I can do from here.' I tapped my hand against the bedspread.

It took him a long moment before he gave in. 'Fine. But if this one is anywhere near as unreliable as Birdie, you're going to fire them – or I *will* do it for you.'

'Isamu, you know this is the shit I hate, right?'

'What?'

'You steamrolling over the top of me. Like you don't trust me.' I sighed again. 'I know I don't have a leg to stand on when I'm in this bed, but I know how to do my job. I'm really fucking good at it, actually. But whenever you do shit like this – whenever you sail into the bar because you've got some "meeting"—' I put scare quotes around it with my fingers '—you make me feel like a child who needs constant supervision. And then I have to try even harder to prove myself to you, and—'

'The meetings are real, Sato!'

I rolled my eyes.

'They are,' he said. 'They're . . . it doesn't matter what they are. But they're real. I'm not checking up on you.'

I scoffed.

'Well, not as much as you think, anyway. The Birdie thing . . . you have to admit you were much too accommodating. You always are when your feelings get involved.'

'It's not like I was in love with her,' I muttered, toying with a loose thread on the bedspread.

'I know. You're in love with Fiona.'

I didn't say anything.

'Which is why you're going to hate the next thing I have to say.' Isamu finished his tea, setting the cup down. 'I want you to choose. Between her and the MS.'

I opened my mouth automatically, but all the words in every language I knew had deserted me.

'I know how badly you want to be a Master Sommelier,' he said. 'But you don't need to prove how good you are. Not to anyone, but especially not to me. I know I've been . . . suffocating you a bit, but it's not because I think you can't do your job. The opposite, really. You're too good at it. You got our father's ambition and his obsession along with his talent, and – I know where that can lead.'

He put his hand over his heart. 'This, though, is different. The way you love, Sato – Otōsan never had that. And that's what scares me the most, because all he was obsessed with was being the best, and it still killed him. You're obsessed with being the best *and* you're obsessed with Fiona. I know you'd do anything for her, that you'd throw yourself headfirst into being a stepfather for her kids if she'd let you, but you can't do all of it, you physically can't, and *this cannot happen again.*'

He dropped his head almost to his knees. 'I can't force you to choose,' he said, a crack in his voice, 'but please, Sato. Please don't make me watch this happen again.'

I wanted to go to him – to hug my brother – but even if my legs would hold me he'd probably tackle me back into bed, so instead, I just drained my teacup. 'It's all right, Onīsan.'

He looked at me.

I set the cup on my nightstand, my fingers still shaking, my heart aching in my chest. 'It's all right,' I repeated. 'There's no choice anyway. Fiona made it for me.'

Chapter Twenty-One

Fiona

Tasting today: 2010 Moscato d'Asti, Piedmont, Italy.
Low alcohol, high sugar, gentle acid: the perfect wine for beginners just trying to find their feet.

On Monday, I sat at my desk, staring into space.

I really needed to take advantage of the quiet. Lex was at their first day of high school; my parents had taken the girls, who didn't go back to school until tomorrow, to MONA (*Let's check out this ridiculous gimmick of a museum your uncle has thrown his career away for*, Dad had grumbled); and I had several copywriting jobs I needed to knock over so I could focus on my next wine column.

It was useless, though. The ache of longing and wanting and grief hadn't abated, no matter how many times I chanted *you did the right thing* to myself.

Worse, though, was the guilt. *You've done enough,* I couldn't stop hearing Isamu snarl.

Because he was right. I *had* done this to Satoshi. Helped to, anyway. I wasn't the only factor – there was the bar and Birdie quitting and his studies and all the extra hours he'd been putting in to get ready for the Young Somm competition – but I was a major one. He – like half my family, it turned out, reorganising their entire lives around my needs – had run himself ragged trying to make me happy.

I buried my face in my hands. I *had* done the right thing – but it had taken me so long to do it, and Satoshi was the one who'd paid the price.

I probably could have sat there for hours – days, even, weeks – torturing myself with all the ways I'd hurt him, all the signs he was struggling I hadn't seen, but eventually, I had to pull myself together and go and pick up Lex from school. 'How was your first day, sweetheart?' I asked, when they emerged from the gates.

They didn't reply, their flag pins crooked on their collar as they walked straight past me to the car, and something inside me clenched with worry. 'Lex—'

'Fiona!'

Fucking hell, not now. 'Hi, Michelle,' I said wearily.

'Long time no see!' Michelle put her hands on my shoulders and kissed the air six inches away from both my cheeks in quick succession. 'I've been thinking about you all holidays. How *are* you?'

'I'm a mess. Is that what you want to hear?'

'Oh, Fiona, hon, I'm so sorry to hear that.' Her face was a mask of earnestness. 'Is there anything I can—'

'No.' I walked away.

Lex was silent the whole car ride home, and quiet all through dinner as well, speaking only in monosyllables when my parents asked about their day. '*Good* isn't an answer,' Dad boomed, jabbing his finger into the dinner table. 'Is that what you're going to write in your essays? They'll ask you to give an informed critique of a text, and you'll just write *good*?'

'No.' Lex stabbed morosely at a pea.

'Dad, leave them be, okay?' I topped up Lex's water glass. 'They had a big day. Give them time to process.'

'This is *important,* Fiona. You might not understand—'

'Christian,' Mum said sharply, 'listen to your daughter.'

Dad looked at her, startled.

'Mummy,' Rosie said, 'did Daddy write back anything about the flower girl video?'

'Yes, he did,' I replied. 'He said you both looked gorgeous, and you did a great job.'

'Is that all?' Georgia asked.

'I'm sure he'll have more to say when you see him.' I would text Matt back and make sure he knew he better.

My dad and Lex made identical scoffing sounds in the back of their throats.

After dinner, once I'd got the girls to bed and my parents had gone back to their hotel, I tapped on Lex's door. 'Sweetheart? Can I come in?'

They grunted in response, which I chose to interpret as assent. 'I just wanted to check in and see how you were doing,' I said, perching on the end of their bed.

'I'm fine.' They hadn't emerged from behind their book.

I hesitated for a few moments. 'Starting high school is a big leap. And maybe there are some kids who don't know you yet, who haven't quite got their heads around your pronouns, or—'

'School's fine. I met another non-binary kid within, like, the first five minutes. It's heaps better than primary school.'

'Oh, that's great!'

I held out my knuckles to them, but they didn't move.

'Lex, sweetheart, please tell me what's wrong.' I paused. 'Is it Dad?'

'It's *you*, Mum!'

I blinked. 'What?'

Lex put their book down. 'You broke up with Satoshi, didn't you?'

I stared.

'You both disappeared at the wedding,' they said. 'Then when you finally came back, it was obvious you'd been crying, and he didn't come back at all.'

'He – um—' My mind, normally so far ahead, was struggling to catch up. 'Lex – how did you . . .?'

'I've known for ages. Henry's mum saw you kissing at the graduation barbecue last year. He told me the next day.'

I closed my eyes. Goddamn *fucking* Michelle.

'And I was really happy,' Lex said. 'But now you've ruined it.'

It took me a few moments to get my thoughts together enough to speak. 'Yes, Satoshi and I were . . . seeing each other. But it's complicated, sweetheart. He's – well, he's in a different place in his life to me. Sometimes the kindest thing you can do is set someone free.'

'It's not complicated. He loves you. You love him.'

'Lex—'

'And it's not like he doesn't know you. Do you really think he started dating you not knowing what he was getting into? He *knows* we're a package deal.'

'Yes, but—'

'If you're worried about me and the twins, don't be.' Lex's jaw jutted out stubbornly. 'It'd suck if you went out for a long time and then broke up, but do you think anything could be worse than when Dad left? And we got through that. It wasn't fun, but you know what we found out? We don't even really *need* him.'

I had to press my tongue to the roof of my mouth, hard, against the tears that were threatening to fall.

'You're all we need, Mum,' Lex said. 'We could lose everyone else in the world, and as long as we have you, we'll be all right.'

I sniffed. 'Sweetheart—'

'And you deserve to be happy. Like Satoshi makes you. Whenever you see him, your eyes light up. They sparkle. So do his, when he sees you.'

A tear escaped. I wiped it away roughly with my wrist.

'Maybe you're right, and it won't work out,' Lex went on. 'It'd be sad, but we'd be okay. We'd all be okay, because you have us and we have you.'

More tears now, inexorable, unstoppable.

'But maybe it will work out,' Lex said. 'Because Satoshi loves you. He *really* loves you. And if you don't at least try, then – then I think that's pretty stupid, actually.'

🍷

Unsurprisingly, the next couple of days were a blur. By day, in the few moments where no one needed me, all I could do was stare into space. By night, alone in bed, all I could do was stare at the ceiling, and think.

On one level, Lex was right. Satoshi loved me. I loved Satoshi. It should be simple.

But I still didn't think I'd been wrong. He might love me now – love me so much that he tore himself apart for me – but I knew better than anyone that love didn't always last.

And Isamu was right too. We'd only been together for a little while – barely together, at that – and I'd already hurt him so badly.

On Thursday, as I sat at my desk staring into space again while the kids were at school and my parents were out sightseeing, I got a text from Matt. *Babies born,* was all it said, with a picture of two tiny red-faced infants in fluffy blue blankets attached. *Know our agreement is once a month but would like to call kids to introduce them.*

I looked at the picture, and – for the first time in the last few days – felt almost nothing. *Ok*, I texted back.

We did the call when the kids got home from school. 'This is Stephen,' Matt said, voice tinny through my laptop speakers, 'and this is Blair, your new little brothers.'

Lex didn't say anything, and Rosie was gnawing at her bottom lip, but Georgia leaned forward, peering. 'Is their last name Sinclair too?'

'It sure is. You'll get to hold them when you and Mummy come to Melbourne in a few weeks. Are you excited—'

'Blair is a stupid name.'

'Georgia!' Matt and I exclaimed in unison.

'Well, it is!' Georgia looked to me for validation. 'Blair Sinclair. It rhymes.'

Lex turned away from the camera. I could sense, rather than see, them laughing.

After we hung up, Georgia's expression was still thoughtful. 'Mummy,' she asked, 'is it silly that we have Daddy's last name instead of yours?'

'Well, it's your last name as much as his,' I replied. 'You have as much right to it as he does.'

'But it's not *your* last name. It's not even part of it anymore. If you had another baby, their last name wouldn't be Sinclair, would it?'

'I'm really not planning to have another baby, Georgie-girl.'

The words tasted sour as soon as they came out of my mouth, Kieran's voice echoing through my mind. *Can't you just see him with a baby in his arms?*

'Georgia's right,' Lex said. 'We should be Fishers. Not Sinclairs.'

Their eyes met mine. *Satoshi loves you,* I heard them say again. *He* really *loves you. And if you don't at least try, then – then I think that's pretty stupid, actually.*

'I think so too,' Rosie said. 'Because you're *here,* Mummy. And Daddy isn't.'

'Changing your names is a big decision.' I swallowed down the inevitable lump rising up in my throat. 'But we can talk about it, all right?'

. . . which was what I hadn't done with Satoshi. In my effort not to be selfish – to minimise the hurt for us both – I'd—

Oh shit. I'd tried to do exactly what Matt had. I'd tried to make a clean break.

I had to resist the urge to bury my face in my hands and groan. Why hadn't I stopped? Why hadn't I *thought*? Why had I let myself get carried away at the wedding and do to him what had been done to me?

I owed Satoshi far, far better than that. Even if I'd hurt him too badly for us ever to come back from it – even if I couldn't give him what he really wanted – I owed him a conversation.

Sadie and Jonah were on their honeymoon, so the kids weren't going to their place that night, but my parents were coming around again, and after dinner, I pulled my mother aside. 'If I go out for a bit,' I asked her quietly, 'can you put the kids to bed?'

'Of course,' she replied. 'Where are you going?'

'I, uh . . .' I swallowed again. 'I need to do something for myself.'

'Good.' Mum smiled at me, caressing my arm affectionately. 'I'm proud of you, Fiona.'

Isamu was behind the bar when I pushed open the door to Tsundoku. 'What do you want, Fiona?'

Satoshi had complained to me before about his brother's penetrating stare, but I'd never been on the receiving end of it before. It took every ounce of willpower I had not to turn on my heel and flee.

But I wasn't going to run and hide, not this time. 'Can I please see him?'

'He's upstairs resting.'

'I'm not here to disturb him. I just want to talk.'

Isamu folded his muscular arms across his chest and said nothing.

It was like standing in the face of an oncoming blizzard. 'Please?'

His nostrils flared, and several long moments passed before he spoke. 'All right.' He jerked his head towards the corridor. 'But if you upset him, Fiona, I will ban you from this bar for life, no matter what he says.'

I nodded. 'I won't. I promise.'

I took the steps up to Satoshi's studio two at a time, half-desperate to see him, half-convinced Isamu was going to change his mind and haul me back downstairs. At the top, though, I paused, pressing a hand to my beating heart. *You'll be all right, Fiona,* I told myself. *No matter what happens, you'll be all right.*

I exhaled slowly and knocked.

'Dōzo!' Satoshi called.

I wasn't entirely sure what that meant, but I steeled myself and pushed the door open anyway. 'Hi,' I said hesitantly. 'Can I – you can say no, obviously, I totally understand that you might not want to see me, but . . . can I come in?'

I didn't quite know what to do with the way he was looking at me – startled, scared, like he'd seen a ghost, but there was something else in the cocktail too, like it was a ghost he was at least a little bit happy to see. 'Of course.'

I toed off my shoes, setting them on the spot that had become mine on his shoe rack. 'Thank you.'

Satoshi was sitting on his bed, on top of the covers. He was wearing black satin pyjama pants with a white T-shirt, Yquem sprawled over his knees. There was only a water glass on his bedside table, no wineglasses, but one of his theory binders was open beside him. His hair was messier than usual – no product in it – and he ran his hand through it. 'Hi,' he said. 'Can I get you anything?'

'Absolutely not.' I couldn't figure out where to sit – the couch seemed too far away, the bed too familiar, so I settled for hovering awkwardly somewhere between. 'If I let you move a muscle, Isamu will throw me into the river.'

He chuckled, brief, mostly humourless. 'I take it he read you the riot act.'

'Yes.'

'If it's any comfort, it's not really about you.' He ran his hand through his hair again. 'He was with our father when his heart gave out. Seeing me pass out was a bit triggering for him, and – oh, Fiona.'

'I'm sorry.' I wiped furiously at the tears beading in my eyes. 'I'm so sorry, Satoshi.'

'Come here?' He held out his arms to me.

I hesitated. 'You really want me to?'

He nodded. 'Please just let me hold you.'

There was no version of me, no matter how iron-willed, that ever would have been able to say no. I went to him, burrowing into the safety of his embrace.

We sat together for a long moment in silence. Usually, when we were cuddled together like this, we were always moving, always touching – his fingers tracing circles on my bare skin, mine combing through his hair – but this time, we were still. The only motion was our shared breathing, the only sound a heartbeat, although I wasn't sure if it was his or mine.

'I'm too scared to say anything,' Satoshi admitted at last. 'I'm worried if I do, it'll be the wrong thing, and you'll leave again.'

'You should want me to.'

'Fiona—'

'You *should*. I've been awful to you.' I turned my face into his shoulder. 'Why didn't you tell me how bad things were getting?'

He sighed.

'I knew you were having a rough few weeks. I knew you were tired. But I didn't know you were so exhausted that . . .' I bit the inside of my cheek. 'You don't know how scary it was when you just went down like that.'

'I'm sorry.' He stroked my hair. 'I didn't mean to frighten you. It was . . . you know I've got a history of panic attacks. And I've been – I've just been a bit . . . overwhelmed.'

'And I've been making it worse.'

'Fiona, no.'

'Yes. I have.'

I made myself sit up straight. If I let myself fall into him, I wouldn't have the strength to walk away, and if that was what was best for him – even if it wasn't what either of us wanted – that was what I was going to have to do.

'Before you fainted,' I said, 'you said something to me. That you could be whatever I needed.'

Satoshi's Adam's apple bobbed as he swallowed.

'But – and I need you to be honest, not just tell me what you think I want to hear – what do *you* need? Because if you're so exhausted you're fainting and so stressed you're having panic attacks and I don't even know about it – if I'm part of the problem, and not the solution – you're not getting it.'

I took one of his hands in mine. 'I love you too, Satoshi,' I said softly. 'But – oh.'

'I'm sorry.' He took off his glasses and wiped his eyes with his wrist. 'I just . . . I've loved you for so long, Fiona, and I never thought you'd ever say that to me.'

'I do.' I pressed my lips to his knuckles. 'I love you. So much that it really, really frightens me, because I can't be with you, not if it's going to hurt you.'

'You won't.'

I gestured to him. 'Look at what I did to you.'

'You didn't. This is—'

I put my finger to his lips. 'I didn't help,' I said. 'So – please, tell me what you need.'

He was silent for a while before he spoke. 'I need to feel like I'm enough for you.'

I bit back my first response, which was to fling myself at him and tell him that of course he was, he was more than I could ever, ever deserve. 'Will you tell me what that means? What that looks like?'

'I need to be able to hold your hand in public,' he said. 'I need to be able to kiss you where people can see. I – I don't want to be in the closet with you, Fiona. I need you to be able to introduce me to people and say *this is my partner*, not *I can explain*.'

Oh shit. That was what I'd said to Michelle the night she'd caught us beside the bins, wasn't it?

'I know I'm younger than you,' he went on. 'And I know how I look, with the glasses and the hair and the pins – like I'm not . . . not a serious person. But I am serious, Fiona. I'm so serious about you, and I don't want you to – I need you not to hide me away.'

I closed my eyes. 'Oh, Satoshi,' I said. 'Satoshi, I'm so sorry.'

He let out a long breath. 'No, I'm sorry,' he said quietly. 'I understand why you need to – that it's complicated, with the kids, and—'

'No, no, that's not what I mean.' I opened them again. 'I'm so sorry I made you feel that way. Like I was . . . ashamed of you.'

I kissed his knuckles again. 'Because I'm not,' I said. 'Yes, I've been worried about what people would say, but not because of you. Because of me. *Look at Fiona, hooking up with someone way out of her league. She's just going to get her heart broken again, because there's no way someone like her can be what someone like him needs.* And . . .'

I wanted to close my eyes while I said what I had to say next, but I made myself keep them open. I owed him that much. 'And they might not be wrong. I might not have been wrong either, the other night. Even if we tell the whole world about us, I don't know if I can give you what you need.'

'What I need is *you*, Fiona.' It was Satoshi's turn to kiss my hand. 'Just you.'

'But can I really make you happy?'

I pulled my hand away and crossed my legs under me so we weren't touching. If he touched me, I might melt, and I needed to be strong. This was not the kind of thing that could be fixed with a conversation, a few words that could paper over a misunderstanding and make it all right. He had put his heart in my hands, and I had a responsibility to treat it with care and respect.

'You deserve the very best, Satoshi,' I said. 'You deserve someone who can make you their whole world, who can meet you on your level, and I just – can't. The boundaries of my world were set a long time ago. And I . . . I know you want kids, and I – I really don't know if I can do that again.'

He opened his mouth to respond, but I held up a finger. 'I know what you're going to say. It doesn't matter, that you want me anyway, but—'

'No, actually.'

I blinked.

'I was going to say,' he said, 'that this is why I fell in love with you.'

He carded his fingers through Yquem's golden hair. 'Your first instinct, always, is kindness. To put the needs of everyone around you before your own. I should have anticipated this, really – that you'd try and break up with me for my own good.'

Yquem mewed, nuzzling her head into his hand. He scratched behind her ear. 'If you won't be selfish, then I will. I want you, Fiona. I love you. And we are going to be together, because I'm going to be miserable if we're not, which will probably mean me working myself to death – and you wouldn't want that, would you?'

My laugh was short, sharp, surprised.

'This is where you say, "It's your bar, Satoshi",' he said, winking. '"You're the boss."'

'It's not that simple, though.' I let out a long breath. 'The kids thing. That's not just going to go away.'

'Where has this come from?' He nudged me gently with his knee. 'We've never talked about kids.'

'Kieran. I went to him for a massage – long story – and he told me.' I bit my lip. 'I've been too scared to ask you about it. I love being with you so much, and I was terrified of your answer.'

'I get it.' His voice was soft. 'I've been terrified to tell you how I really feel about you. How much I love you. I've been so frightened that if I let it slip before you were ready to hear it, I'd scare you away.'

'I love you too.' I bit my lip again, tasting blood. 'But I can't promise I'll ever be ready for another baby. And if you really want kids, Satoshi . . . I can't take that away from you.'

'What I really want is *you*.' He nudged me again, more emphatically this time. 'You want a relationship non-negotiable? That's it, Fiona. It has to be you. Nothing else matters.'

Yquem sprang off Satoshi's lap as he reached out to me. 'I do want kids,' he said, taking my hand again. 'But the idea of them being biologically *mine* – that wasn't important when I thought I'd have them with Kieran, and it's not important now either. I adore your kids. I'd do anything for them. And if there was a future where you'd let me be some kind of parent to them, I would love them just as much as if I'd been there the day they were born.'

My eyes filled with tears.

'I'm not asking to marry you and become their stepdad tomorrow.' He squeezed my fingers. 'We can go as slow as you want. But I don't want to be an escape from your real life. I want to be part of it.'

He kissed my knuckles. 'Please say that's okay, because I'm not above begging.'

I pressed my tongue to the roof of my mouth. I wanted it – wanted him – so, so badly.

‘On one condition,’ I said at last.

‘Anything.’

‘You have to promise to tell me what you need. Always.’

I surrendered to my urge to go up on my knees so I could stroke the side of his face with my knuckles. ‘You’ve been the perfect partner to me, Satoshi, but I’ve been a terrible one to you. You’ve made me feel like a queen, but I’ve made you feel like shit, and I had no idea I was doing it.’

‘No.’

‘Yes,’ I insisted. ‘If you can’t promise me, then I can’t do this. I can’t be with another man who isn’t honest with me. I can’t worry that I’m a burden on you, an obligation, someone who’s keeping you from being happy instead of making you happy. There are two people in a relationship, and I need to carry my share of the weight.’

I took a long breath before I kept going. ‘If this is going to work, I need the real you. All of you, even the parts you hide away. You’re so strong, Satoshi, and so steady, and I love that about you, but I love that there’s this . . . hungry, needy person underneath it all too. I love getting to see that side of you. I love feeling like I’m satisfying those needs, but I don’t just want to do it in bed. I want to do it always. Because I *love* you.’

I pressed the back of his hand to my cheek. ‘I need you to tell me what you need. To ask things of me – to rely on me – instead of just putting my needs first. To tell me the truth, even if it’s going to upset me – and even if turns out that truth is that I’m not what you need anymore. I need you to promise, and I need you to mean it.’

Satoshi let out a long breath. ‘Right now,’ he said, ‘I need you to come here.’

I did, snuggling into him, my head on his shoulder, his arms around me. ‘I promise,’ he whispered, pressing his lips to my hair. ‘It’ll always be you, Fiona, but I promise.’

'We'll see.' I turned my face into his throat so I could kiss his pulse point. 'Let's see how you feel after your first Fisher family dinner.'

He stilled. 'You want me to come to dinner?'

'It feels like a good place to start, if we're going to ease the kids into *Mummy and Satoshi are dating.* Although – actually, maybe I should have mentioned this earlier – Lex already figured it out.' I looked up at him. 'And they gave me a very stern talking to about breaking up with you.'

Satoshi smiled, dipping his head to kiss me. 'They're a genius.'

'I think so.' I wrinkled my nose fondly at him. 'Is it asking too much to invite you tomorrow night? My parents will still be here, so that'd really be throwing you into the Fisher family deep end, and I know you're still recovering.'

'Definitely not too much to ask. Although I might need to sneak out of here like a teenager. Isamu will have some opinions about me overexerting myself.'

'Fiona also has some opinions about you over-exerting yourself, so really, if you're not up to it—'

'I'm *fine.*' He cupped my face in one of his hands, brushing his thumb over the lip I'd bitten. 'Yes, I've been overdoing it, but a few days' rest has done me a world of good. And . . .' he leaned his forehead against mine, 'as much as I hate it, I'm going to suck it up and let my brother help me.'

'As someone whose love language is also acts of service,' I said, touching a fingertip to the dimple in his left cheek, 'I have some experience in having to let people help you while you feel like you're giving nothing in return, if you need someone to complain to.'

'That is definitely something I need.' Satoshi kissed me, quick, chaste, but tender. 'Because Isamu taking control over my bar like this? I *hate it.*' He paused. 'Even if he did get the glasswasher fixed in about five seconds. I eavesdropped on him talking to the technician. He nearly made him cry.'

I kissed him back. 'How about I rewrite the copy on your ad for Birdie's replacement? See if we can get some more hits?'

'That would be—' more kisses, one, two, three, in quick succession '—incredibly helpful.'

I brushed his hair back from his forehead, kissing him again. 'Is there anything else I can do?'

Satoshi thought for a moment. 'Yes.'

He gestured towards the little wine fridge in the corner. 'Pick something, my love. Let's have a drink together.'

I chose a bottle of moscato. It was sweeter than either of us typically preferred, but it had low alcohol, and given he was on bed rest, that felt like a good idea. 'You might regret this,' I said, pouring us both a glass.

'If I do, I'll tell you.' He took the glass I handed him, inhaled the aroma and grinned. 'But I don't think I will. Cheers.'

I looked him in the eye, no bar between us now, a promise of far more than seven years this time. 'Cheers.'

Chapter Twenty-Two
Satoshi

Tasting today: MV grande cuvée champagne, Champagne, France. Traditionally served at the reception where new Master Sommeliers are announced, it's often said this cuvée tastes like failure, due to the exam's low pass rate. However, those who pass are usually doing so after several previous failed attempts. This wine tastes like trying again.

'We'd like you to design and serve a flight for us,' the Young Somm examiner told me, 'to pair with the following three-course menu.'

I looked at the menu they'd handed me: scallop ceviche, coffee-crusted loin of venison, chocolate and black truffle pannacotta. 'Of course. It would be my pleasure.'

There was a message from Fiona on my phone when I got out of the service exam. *Just checking in to see how things are going! xx*

Quietly confident, I texted back. I'd thought of a better pairing for the venison as I was double-decanting the Priorat garnacha I'd chosen – it would work well, but gran reserva Rioja would have been even better. Otherwise, though, it had gone perfectly. I'd opened the sparkling Vouvray I'd selected for the first course so silently that the examiners hadn't even noticed me do it, one of them blinking in surprise as I started to fill their glass. *Fingers crossed for tasting this afternoon. How are things going with you? xx*

About as well as they could be, Fiona replied. *The girls took a while to warm up to Nikki, but they're getting there. And I was positive Lex wasn't going to say a single thing, but – to my surprise – they're really making an effort.*

I was less surprised. Lex and I had had a conversation in the airport yesterday, when we'd done a drinks run while waiting for our flight to Melbourne. *Satoshi,* they'd asked, *if I try and get along with Dad's other kids, am I being disloyal to Mum?*

I'm not an expert, I'd answered, selecting a couple of juices for the girls, *but I don't think so. It's not their fault your dad did what he did.*

Dr Dell said that too. But it just feels . . . wrong. Like if I get to know them, then I'm forgiving him somehow.

Have you talked to your mum about this?

Lex shook their head. *I don't want her to worry.*

She's going to worry anyway, pal, so you might as well tell her what's on your mind. We'd shuffled another step closer to the front of the queue. *She's a strong woman. She can handle it.*

'Satoshi Tsukamoto?' the exam administrator asked. 'They're ready for you in the tasting room.'

Got to go, I sent to Fiona, *but tell me all about it later, ok?*

She sent back a row of kisses. *Can't wait.*

The Young Somm comp had put me up in the hotel where the awards ceremony was being held, and I went back to my room after the tasting exam had wrapped up to get ready. Fiona and I had decided that it was better if I stayed there while she and the kids – and Elias, who'd arrived back in Australia the week prior and decided to come along as moral support – stayed in the AirBnB Matt had rented for them. *Lex wouldn't care,* Fiona had murmured to me, fingers sketching patterns on my chest as we sat curled together on her couch, *but we need to take it slower for the girls.*

We've only just made the leap to 'Mummy and Satoshi are going on dates'. There's a while to go before we can get to 'Satoshi is sleeping in Mummy's bed'.

I'd brushed her hair out of her eyes and kissed her forehead. *We can move as slow as you need,* I'd told her tenderly, *as long as we're moving.*

The knock on my door came as I was finger-combing product through my recently re-bleached hair in the mirror. 'Coming!'

I took a moment to straighten my tie – a conservative black, although my suit was light pink, the colour of a pinot rosé – then opened the hotel room door. 'Hi,' I said. 'Sorry that – oh, wow.'

Fiona smiled shyly. 'It's not too much?'

I shook my head. I had forgotten every word of the English language, and most of Japanese and French as well.

She looked stunning. She was wearing a simple little black dress, the hem hitting just above the knee, her legs made longer by her strappy silver heels. The sleeves sat off the shoulder, her décolletage unadorned, her cleavage looking fucking *delicious*. 'Are you sure it's not too much?' she asked again, cheeks flushing as I unabashedly looked her up and down. 'Sadie helped me pick it out, and she really put the hard sell on me.'

'I owe Sadie a drink.'

'I still need to do my makeup, though.' She entered the hotel room, and I closed the door behind her. 'I've tried about fifty times to get this winged eyeliner right, and I just can't get it even. Plus, it was too hard to concentrate while the girls were all hyped up after meeting Matt's kids.'

'Do you want me to do it for you?'

She blinked. 'My eyeliner?'

I shrugged. 'I've got a steady hand. And I was pretty good at eyeliner, once upon a time.'

Fiona grinned and went up on tiptoes to kiss me. 'Show me what you've got, Satoshi.'

We watched a YouTube tutorial together before she surrendered her makeup bag to me. 'So, tell me more about how today went.' I cupped the nape of her neck, careful not to disrupt her hair as I tipped her head back gently to catch the light in the bathroom. 'The kids got on okay?'

'Mmm-hmm.' She was trying not to move her face, so the words came out between her teeth. 'Lex really tried, bless them. They sent Elias out on a quest at the crack of dawn this morning to buy books for Micah and Nikki. I don't think Micah is much of a reader, but it seemed like he appreciated the gesture. God knows how Lex'll react if he tries to reciprocate and turns up next time with a football or something, though.'

'Open your eyes and look up for me?'

She did. 'Nikki was clinging to Matt at first. Like, physically clinging. And the girls were . . . I don't know if *offended* is quite the right word, but they didn't like it. Rosie in particular is so sensitive about the idea of Matt loving his other kids more than them, and it all nearly ended in tears.'

'Close your eyes again?'

The skin of her eyelid was delicate beneath my thumb as I carefully filled in her lash-line. 'But then one of the babies started crying, and Matt had to pick him up because Laura was feeding the other one, and Georgia twigged that Nikki was upset because she was no longer the centre of attention. So she started firing questions at her about what it was like to have babies in the house, and Rosie joined in. Nikki seemed to find it pretty cathartic to complain, so it all worked out in the end.'

I kissed her cheek. 'Happy?'

'I mean, it was uncomfortable. But it could have gone so much worse.'

I tapped her on the end of the nose. 'I meant with your eyeliner.'

Fiona laughed, opening her eyes. 'Sorry,' she said, turning to look at herself in the mirror. 'And – oh wow, Satoshi. Is there anything you're not good at?'

With a little practise, I knew I could get it perfect. Some of the lines weren't as clean as I wanted them to be. But Fiona was happy, and that was good enough for me.

I put my arms around her from behind, stooping slightly to rest my chin against her shoulder. 'I'm glad it went well.'

'The real test will be how they react to it over time.' Her hands drifted up to cover mine. 'That's what their therapist told me, anyway. The excitement will wear off, and they'll start thinking. And I really am worried about Rosie. She's starting to grasp the implications of what Matt did in a way that Georgia hasn't quite yet, and . . .'

She let out a long breath. I kissed the corner of her jaw.

Then Fiona smiled at me in the mirror. 'But there's nothing I can do about it tonight,' she said, a spark igniting in her eyes. 'Tonight I get to be the date of the sexiest young somm in the world.'

I did not win Young Somm of the Year. 'I'm sorry, Sato,' Isamu said, when I called to let him know, ducking outside the hotel ballroom, fingers in one ear so I could hear him. 'I know you wanted it.'

'It's all right.' I meant it, too. A year ago, not winning might have crushed me, but even though I was disappointed, I was proud of how I'd performed. 'It would have been nice to win, but just getting nominated is great. And it was good practise for the MS exam.'

'You're still going to do what we agreed, though? Just focus on theory for now?'

I rolled my eyes, but it was with fondness rather than irritation. 'Yes, Isamu. Don't worry.'

We'd had this conversation after Fiona and I got back together. *I'm not giving her up,* I told him. *I love her. And I'm not giving up on being an MS either – but I want to be sensible about it.*

And so, we'd arrived at a compromise. Except in emergencies, I would never work more than four shifts a week at Tsundoku so I could take the time I needed to study; and instead of aiming to pass the tasting, service and theory portions of the MS exam all at the same time, I'd focus on them one at a time over a space of a couple of years. I could tell Isamu didn't believe me when I promised to take things slowly with Fiona too – his response to that had been to snort derisively and say, *I assume we'll be hosting your wedding in, what, three months?* – but I'd promised anyway.

'How's Theo going?' I asked, switching the phone to my other ear. People were starting to stream out of the ballroom and they were rowdy, carrying bottles of wine filched from the tables as they headed back up to their rooms.

'He's solid,' Isamu replied. 'I've got him running the floor right now – while I supervise, don't panic. His knowledge of the list needs some work, but that'll come with time. He's got the service skills down. You chose well, Sato – he looks like he's shaping up to be a great junior somm.'

'Thanks.' I paused. 'And thanks for covering for me. I know I've been an insufferable diva about it, but – thank you.'

He grunted. 'Thank Noriko. I've got a vested interest in the bar succeeding. She did it for standard hospo wages, two cases of Bibliophile, and gratitude.'

'Has it—' I paused again. 'Have you . . . been okay?'

Isamu didn't say anything.

'I know what it must have cost you, reaching out to her,' I said. 'That the wound is still raw. So – are you okay?'

He was silent for a long moment before he replied. 'I'm okay. I'm – I'm actually seeing someone new.'

I blinked. 'What? Who? Since when?'

'Don't ask me any questions, because I won't answer them.' Isamu's tone made it clear that his word was final. 'It's no one's business but hers and mine.'

Fiona emerged from the ballroom, chatting brightly to some of the people who'd been sitting at our table. She waved at me, eyes creasing at the corners as she smiled. 'If that's what you want, then fine,' I told my brother. 'But when you're ready to talk about it, I'm here. Always.'

'Who do you think it is?' Fiona asked, as we took the lift back up to my hotel room. She had her shoes in one hand, the other in mine.

'No idea.' I set the bottle of champagne I'd swiped on the ground so I could open the door without letting go of her hand. 'I have no idea where Isamu would even meet someone, to be honest. But I suppose this explains what some of those meetings he kept having were.'

I picked the champagne up again and closed the door behind us. 'Drink?'

Fiona set her shoes down. 'Please.'

The cork came out silently – the faintest hiss, pressure released, relief – and I took down the two wineglasses from the minibar. 'I don't know why he won't just tell me who she is. What does he think I'm going to do? Make fun of him?'

Fiona accepted a glass from me. 'Maybe he can't bear to tell you because it's very, very precious.'

I looked at her.

'I felt like that about us.' I'd taken my jacket off, and she caressed my shirtsleeve between two of her fingers. 'There were a lot of reasons I wanted to keep it to myself – good ones, real ones – but there was also this feeling that if I said it out loud, then it got to be . . . the world's, somehow. Instead of ours.' She glanced up at me. 'Does that make sense?'

'Not really.' I tucked a stray wisp of hair behind her ear. 'But I think I understand anyway.'

She smiled. 'Cheers?'

'Cheers.'

We held each other's gazes while we drank. 'How long can you stay?' I murmured, tracing her neckline with my finger.

Her laugh was a hum. 'Elias basically shoved me out the door and told me he'd be furious if I got home before dawn.' She went up on tiptoes to kiss my pulse point. 'It's very disconcerting, being shooed out of the house by your big brother and told you'll be in *huge* trouble if you don't go and spend the night with a boy.'

I let my lips drift over the sensitive spot behind her ear. 'Well, I wouldn't want you to get in trouble.'

Fiona's hands slid up my chest to loop behind my neck. 'It's not going to be sexy, getting this dress off, though,' she warned. 'And fuck knows how we're going to get it back on again. There's Hollywood tape and one of those stick-on bras and a whole infrastructure under here. It's very complicated.'

I undid her zipper. 'That's all right,' I told her. 'I can deal with complicated.'

AUGUST

Epilogue
Fiona

Tasting today: 2020 rosé, Bandol, France.
Rosé is renowned for being simple and easy, but this wine is all the more compelling and captivating for being complex.

'Mummy, Satoshi, are you going to bring us home any presents?' Georgia demanded. She and Rosie were sitting on either side of Lex, squished in tight to fit in frame on the laptop screen.

'There might be one or two things in my suitcase for you.' I wrinkled my nose at her. Satoshi had been neck-deep in study for the first few days we'd been in Paris, preparing for his MS theory exam, but I'd made him take an afternoon off to go strolling around Montmartre, and we'd picked up several little gifts for the kids. 'But tell me what you've been doing. Have you been having fun with Uncle Jonah and Auntie Sadie?'

The girls nodded. The kids had spent the first week of mine and Satoshi's two-week trip to France with Elias, who'd been living with us for nearly six months now, but he'd had to go on a business trip this week, so Jonah and Sadie had taken over. 'We made crepes for dinner!' Rosie said. 'Uncle Jonah said you and Satoshi were probably eating lots of them, so he helped us make them so we could be French too.'

'Uncle Jonah's very smart,' Satoshi said. Even though the European summer had made it a little too warm in our un-air-conditioned hotel room, he had his arm draped over my shoulder, fingers brushing my sleeve. 'That's exactly what we're going to do today.'

'Madison's mum said she was so jealous of you, Mummy,' Rosie remarked. 'When we were at soccer training, she said she wished she had a boyfriend who would take her to Paris.'

It was impossible to resist the urge to lean into Satoshi, so I didn't. 'I'm very, very lucky,' I said, as he turned his head so he could kiss my temple.

'How did your exam go, Satoshi?' Lex asked. 'It was yesterday, right? Did you pass?'

Satoshi grinned. 'I sure did, pal. All that study you and your mum helped me with really paid off.'

We'd spent many nights studying together: at his place if it was a Thursday, at mine if it wasn't. Lex and I had both been drilling flashcards with him, from which Lex had retained a frightening amount of information – *they'll be able to pass the MS before they ever take their first sip of wine at this rate,* Satoshi had murmured, late on one of the first nights he'd stayed over, *god, they're smart, my love* – and it had paid off. He'd emerged from his one-hour oral examination yesterday with a huge smile on his face.

'And how about you, Mum?' Lex asked.

'I passed too.' I picked up my shiny new Certified Sommelier pin from the bedside table and showed it to them. 'And I got to interview some really cool French winemakers for my next article.'

My column had proved to be a hit. *I had no idea you could write like this, Fi,* Jonah had told me, after I'd finally got up the nerve to put my Bibliophile piece in our siblings group chat. *You've got a real talent.*

I might have believed he was humouring me – Fisher family trauma ran deep – but the numbers didn't lie. I was now officially on staff for the website, and I'd been approached by some other wine magazines to write for them too. While they didn't pay much, my trip to France had been partially subsidised by one of them: Satoshi and I were heading off to Jura tomorrow so I could profile some emerging cult vineyards.

My new qualification – the next step up from the introductory course I'd done last year – hadn't been subsidised, but when I'd decided to do it, Mum had helped me out, paying for half of it. *Having you around to answer all my questions is great, and I've learnt so much from helping you study, but I need to improve my baseline knowledge if I'm* really *going to be a wine writer,* I'd told Satoshi. *Plus, it'll mean I can help you out in the bar sometimes.*

That was what we were going to do when we got home. Satoshi had a very capable junior somm in Theo – and Charlotte, after some hesitation, had decided to study for her Certified exam too – but he was going to start training me as well so he had extra cover if he needed it in a pinch. *You can't give me any special treatment,* I'd warned him, as we lay together in bed. *If I do things wrong, you have to tell me.*

I'll tell you, don't worry. He nuzzled my hair, fingers snaking up my inner thigh. *I'll save the special treatment for right . . . here.*

Once we'd finished talking to the kids and they'd run off to play with the puppy, Jonah and Sadie sat down in front of the laptop. 'So,' Jonah said, 'we have something we need to tell you.'

A hundred different awful scenarios unspooled immediately in my mind. 'Is everyone okay? Is it Elias, or Mum, or—'

'Nothing like that!' Jonah held up his hands. 'The opposite, actually.'

He and Sadie looked at each other, and, like it always did when his attention was focused solely on his wife, something in my brother softened. 'We're having a baby.'

'Oh my god, Jonah!' I wanted to leap to my feet, to hug them both, but given we were on the other side of the world, all I could do was press my hands to my heart. 'Congratulations!'

'It's early days,' Sadie said. 'I only just hit twelve weeks. You're actually the first people we've told.'

'Congratulations,' Satoshi said. 'I'll revise all the non-alco options we have at Tsundoku the second I get back – make sure we've got the very best for you while you can't drink.'

'Thanks, Satoshi,' Sadie replied. 'And – Fiona, do you mind if you and I have a quick chat on our own? I have a few questions about . . . you know, mum stuff.'

'Sure.'

Jonah kissed Sadie's cheek, waved goodbye, then disappeared off screen. 'I'll go sit in the cafe downstairs,' Satoshi told me. 'Meet me there when you're finished?'

I nodded. 'See you soon.'

When the door had snicked shut behind him, I turned back to the laptop. 'Okay, hit me,' I said. 'What do you need to know?'

'Fiona, I'm terrified,' Sadie said. '*Terrified.* Jonah and I have talked about having kids, but, like, at some point in the future, not now. But then this just *happened*, and . . . I'm happy, of course I'm happy, but I'm so unbelievably shit-scared.'

She let out a long, shaking breath. 'I have no idea how to be a mother. Mine died when I was a teenager, and it wasn't like she was doing much parenting before that. And sure, Jonah and I look after your kids a lot, but they're – you know, people. I've never been around babies. What the fuck do I know about looking after one?'

'Sadie, it's going to be okay. I promise.'

I shifted position on the bed, crossing my legs underneath me. 'I know it's scary. I remember when I got pregnant with Lex – I felt exactly the same. But it's going to be okay. Jonah will be there with you every step of the way.'

'I know he will. But . . . I can talk to him about being scared, and he'll do his best, but he can't really *understand* it. Like, the visceral reality of it. There's this – thing – growing inside me, and most of me is excited about it, but – what's it going to do to me? What if it rips my body apart and I never really heal properly? And what am I going to do to it? What if I do the wrong thing or eat the wrong thing and I fuck it up before it's even born? Not to mention all the ways I could fuck it up after it's born – god, there are so many of those.'

'The fear's natural. I'm afraid for my kids every single second. It's terrifying, having your heart live outside of you like that. I'm not going to tell you not to be scared.'

Sadie's throat bobbed on the screen as she swallowed, eyes closing.

'But you're not alone,' I said. 'You've got Jonah, and you've got Chess, and you've got a whole family around you that are going to love this baby so much and give you more help than you could ever possibly want. And – look at me.'

She obeyed, her face pale.

'Whenever you're freaking out,' I told her, 'whenever you need advice from someone who's been through it before – whenever you need the kind of help that only another parent can provide – you always, *always* have me, okay? I've got you.'

Satoshi had a glass of Bandol rosé in front of him when I made my way down to the cafe, the bottle in an ice bucket. 'How's Sadie?' he asked, pouring a glass for me.

'Panicking.' I slid into the chair beside him. 'But she'll be okay. Cheers.'

'Cheers. To your new nibling.'

I clinked my glass against his, looking him in the eye, unable, as usual, to not smile at him. We'd been together for nearly nine months now and I didn't know if I ever would stop smiling. 'To *our* new nibling,' I said, 'Uncle Sato.'

He grinned. 'I like the sound of that.'

We both drank, the wine fresh and crisp and surprisingly complex, raspberries and cherries and roses on the palate. 'Will the kids be excited to have a cousin?' Satoshi asked.

'So excited. Georgia especially. She's enthralled by Matt's boys, so having a baby around that she actually gets to see and hold more than once a month will be thrilling.'

'That tracks.' He sipped his rosé. 'She's been making some very pointed suggestions lately.'

I looked at him.

'"Satoshi, I've had a great idea," he said, pitching his voice a little higher. '"What if Mummy had another baby and *you* could be their daddy?"'

I closed my eyes, but there was no way to stop the blood rushing to my face. 'Sorry.'

'Don't apologise.' He kissed the tip of my nose. 'And I was very diplomatic, don't worry. No promises were made.'

'I would think about it,' I blurted out.

He looked at me for a few moments. 'Fiona,' he said at last, 'what are you trying to say?'

'I would think about it,' I repeated. 'Having a baby. With you.'

I took another sip of my wine to gather my thoughts. 'After the twins, I never thought I'd want to have another baby. I still don't exactly *want* to – my writing career's just beginning to take off, and it's finally starting to feel like things are stable again, and throwing another child into that would be a lot. But it's not just about me, and . . . if you wanted to, Satoshi, I would think about it. I would really, really think about it. Whether my body would be capable of it is another matter – I'm not getting any younger – but it wouldn't be an automatic no. Not with you.'

Satoshi stroked some hair behind my ear. 'I love you, Fiona.'

'I love you too.'

'I'd love to have a baby with you someday.' He leaned over and kissed me. 'And if we did, it wouldn't all be on you. We'd work out how to manage it with both our careers. But if we don't, it's not going to break my heart.'

I hesitated. 'Are you sure?'

'Yes.' He laced his fingers through mine. 'If we made Georgia's wildest dreams come true and gave the kids a baby sibling, that would be wonderful, but if we don't, it doesn't matter. If I get to have you, and I get to have them, then I have everything I need.'

'Do you want to move in?'

He blinked.

'I want that too,' I said. 'A life with you: you, and me, and the kids – and Yquem, of course, and probably Elias too, given he's shown no desire to move out of my spare room.' I squeezed his fingers. 'So how about we take the next step?'

Satoshi kissed my knuckles.

Then he topped up our glasses and looked me in the eye as he held his up. 'My love,' he said, 'I'll drink to that.'

Acknowledgements

Anyone who has ever been to a party I've hosted is in for both a wonderful and terrible beverage experience. I'll pour you something delightful that I've done my very best to match to your palate. (My close friends can attest to the detailed mental spreadsheet I keep of their preferences: this particular act of service is one of the ways I express my love.) However, you *will* have to listen to me tell you about what I've just poured you in much more detail than you ever wanted.

I often get asked, 'So, did you do any research?' about my books – a question which makes a lot of sense, given that my other career is in academia and research is very literally my profession. Up until this book, the answer has mostly been *no*: my Marry Me, Juliet trilogy is rooted in the many years of research I'd already done on reality dating shows when I started writing it, while *An Academic Affair* . . . well, I probably don't need to explain why that book didn't require much research.

For *A Study in Sparkling,* though, the answer was yes: I *did* do research, and quite a lot of it. I wanted to set a book in the world of wine for the very simple reason that I love it, and making sure Satoshi sounded like a credible Master Sommelier candidate gave me a wonderful (and tax-deductible) reason to move beyond being a very enthusiastic wine dilettante to someone who, like, actually knows some stuff.

What I didn't anticipate, though, was the way that writing *A Study in Sparkling* really helped me rediscover my genuine love of research – something that, as readers of *An Academic Affair* will know, working in a university can often blunt. This wasn't just because I got to drink some very nice wines along the way (although let's be real, it didn't hurt) – it was because it allowed me to use parts of my brain I rarely get a chance to. Alongside all the book-learning, learning properly about wine involves learning how to see, how to smell, how to taste. These are sensory experiences that I simply don't get in the many, many hours I spend per day sitting at my desk in my dual author/scholar careers – and letting other parts of my brain shoulder the load for a while has been, frankly, a blessed relief.

Therefore, I want to begin my thank yous for this book with everyone who has been a part of the research process. I have to start with Aaron Crothers and Chris Parker of Our Terroir, as well as James Er, who have answered frankly incredible amounts of questions for me (and who, perhaps most crucially, helped me find just the right name for Satoshi's cat). Similarly, the formal wine learning I've done with Andy McIntyre and Maddy Horrigan at Melbourne Wine School has been invaluable for fleshing out the world that the Tsukamoto brothers work in. Anything the characters get wrong about wine is all on me.

Fiona and Satoshi agree that wine should be about pleasure, and that talking about it together is one of the things that gives them that pleasure. I've been lucky enough to find (as an adult, no less!) a group of friends who'll talk about wine with me. Joe, Tu, Dave, and both Sarahs – meeting you all in this past couple of years has been an absolute delight, and here's to many more blind wine and/or trivia victories in our future.

Enormous thanks also go to the friends who have been with me for years and have patiently listened to my many wine monologues. Kate, Adele, Katie, Anna, Meg, Claire: I cannot overstate how thrilling it was when you got that wine bus named after me (thanks also go to Jon and Sara of HopIt for that!), and I adore you all. The same is true of the friends I don't get to see so often: Steph, Rashmi, Mel, Sonya, Mabel, Hannah, Monique, Amy – I hope we can raise a glass together sometime soon. And I can't forget my mum and my sister, who have let me drag them around to approximately infinity wineries in the name of research – thank you (although I don't think you were exactly suffering).

Then there's everyone in my professional life who stood by me while I stubbornly insisted that *no*, I didn't want to write another book about academics, it was time for a book about wine. No one has ever had my back like my literary agent Alex Adsett, without whom I simply would not have a career. Anthea Bariamis, Lizzie Levot and Shannon Grey have been wonderful shepherds for Fiona and Satoshi at Atria Australia, along with Cassandra di Bello in the early stages; as have Ifeoma Anyoku, Kaitlin Olson, Camila Araujo and Aleaha Reneé at Atria in the US. A special mention also goes to Andrew Deck, whose sensitivity read of the manuscript was incredibly valuable for finding the right nuance in some critical places. My name might be on the cover of this book, but it wouldn't be even close to being out in the world without all these people (and many more) backing both it and me – thank you, thank you, thank you, and I owe you all a glass of something nice.

And finally, there's you, the reader, the most important person in this equation. Fiona and Satoshi's story means a lot to me, and I hope it resonates with you too. Enjoy it with a beverage of your choosing, and sit, sip and savour.

About the Author

Jodi McAlister, PhD, is an author and academic from Kiama, Australia. She is the author of *An Academic Affair* and the Marry Me, Juliet trilogy. She is currently a Senior Lecturer in Writing, Literature and Culture at Deakin University in Melbourne, and the President of the International Association for the Study of Popular Romance. For more, visit JodiMcAlister.com.au or find her on Instagram @jodimcalister.